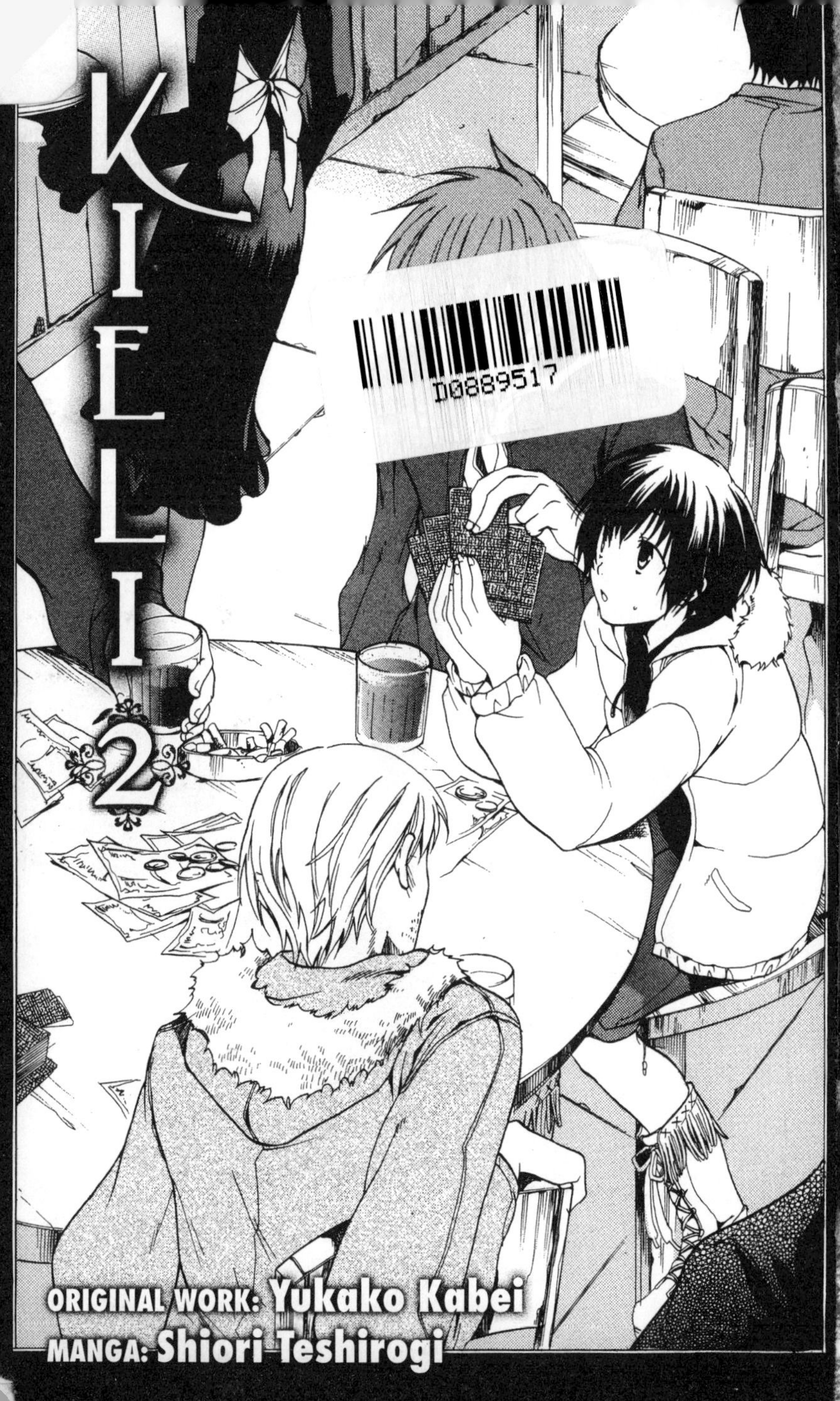
KIELI
2
ORIGINAL WORK: Yukako Kabei
MANGA: Shiori Teshirogi
D0889517

CONTENTS

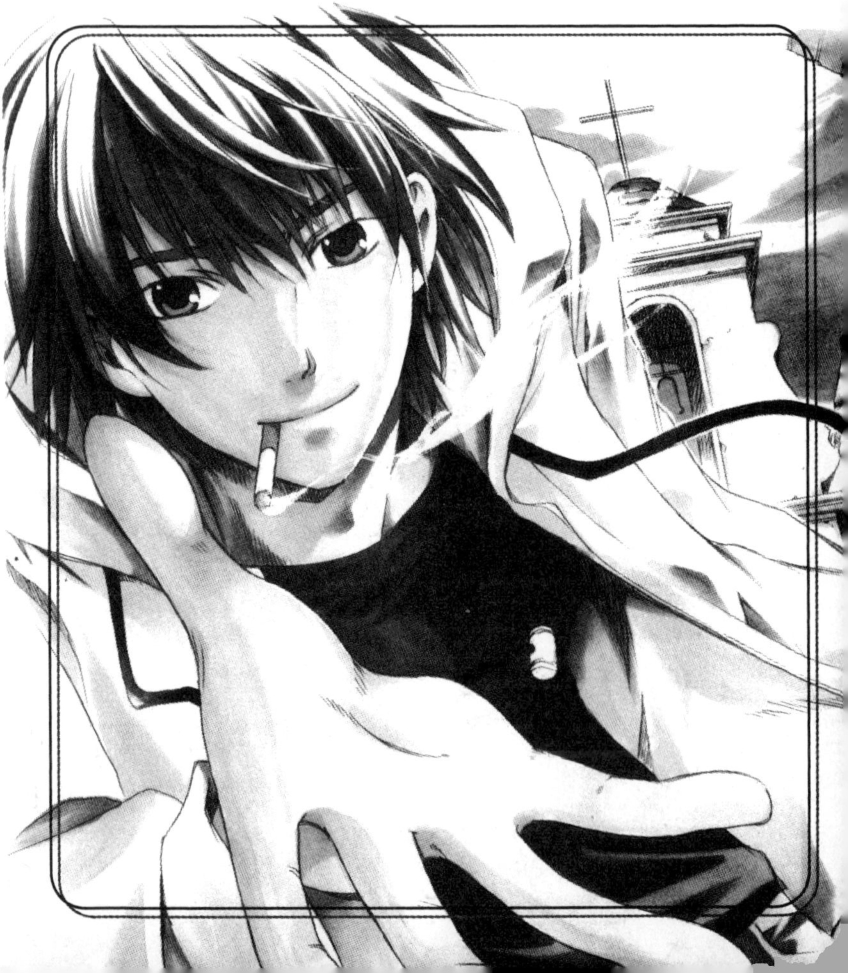

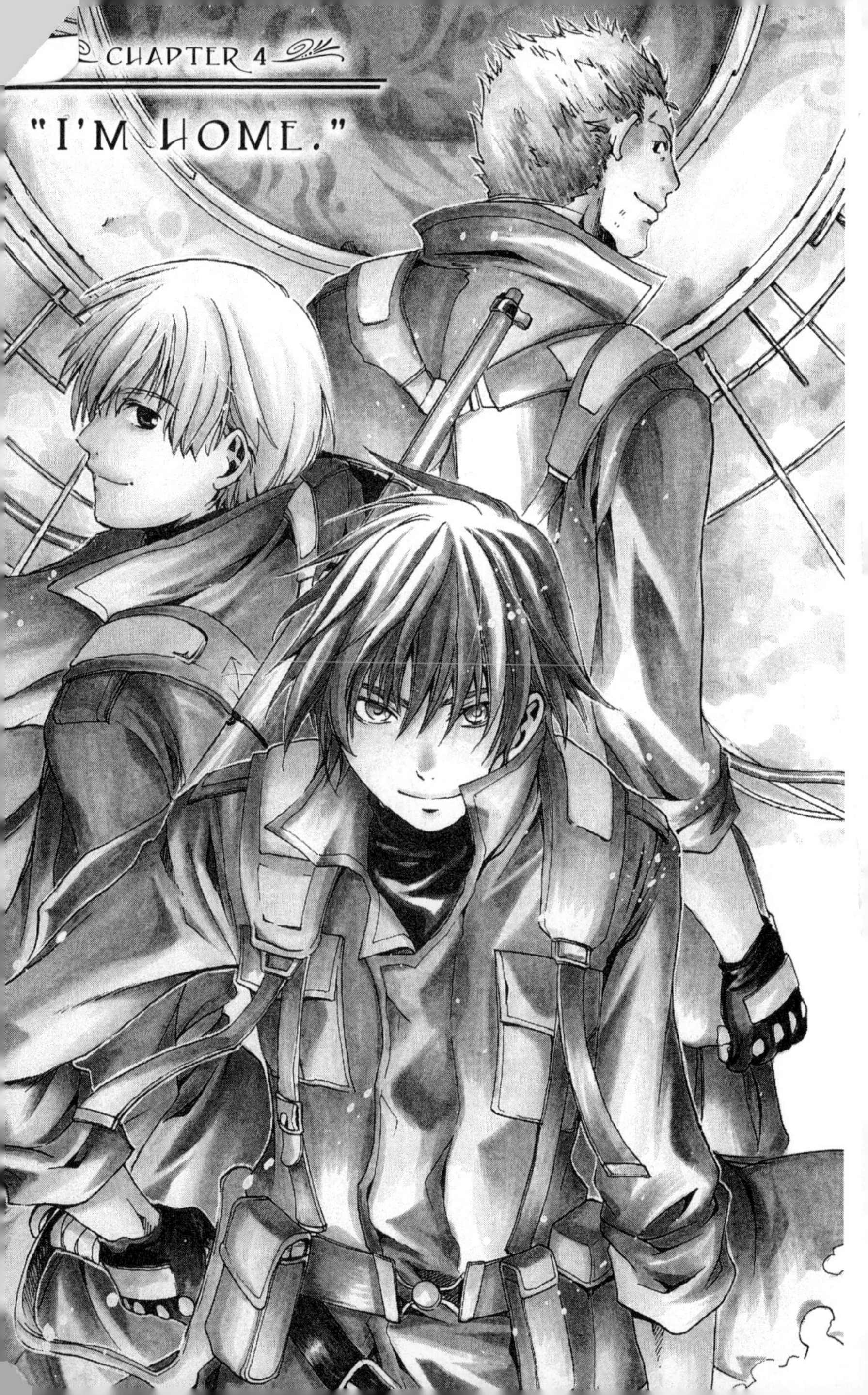
CHAPTER 4
"I'M HOME."

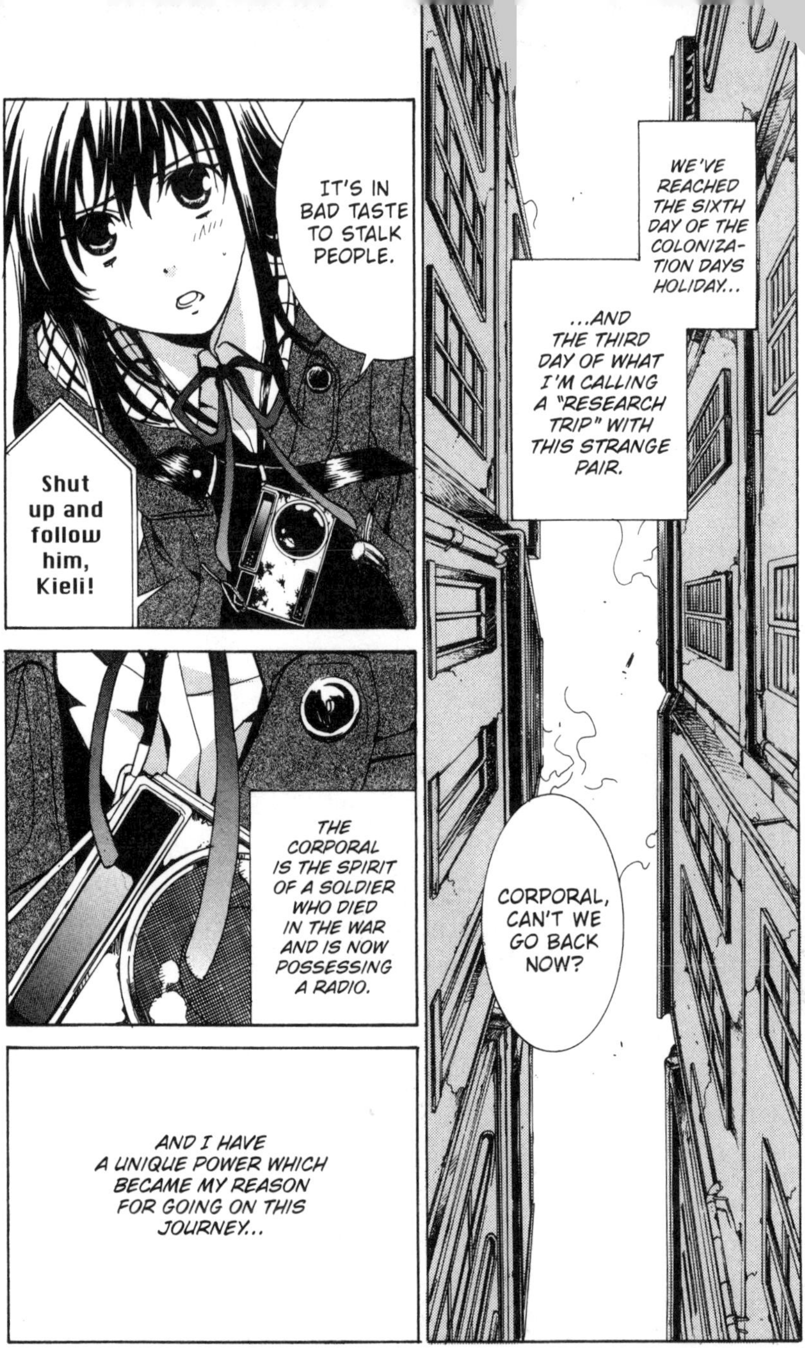
WE'VE REACHED THE SIXTH DAY OF THE COLONIZATION DAYS HOLIDAY...
...AND THE THIRD DAY OF WHAT I'M CALLING A "RESEARCH TRIP" WITH THIS STRANGE PAIR.
CORPORAL, CAN'T WE GO BACK NOW?
IT'S IN BAD TASTE TO STALK PEOPLE.
Shut up and follow him, Kieli!
THE CORPORAL IS THE SPIRIT OF A SOLDIER WHO DIED IN THE WAR AND IS NOW POSSESSING A RADIO.
AND I HAVE A UNIQUE POWER WHICH BECAME MY REASON FOR GOING ON THIS JOURNEY...

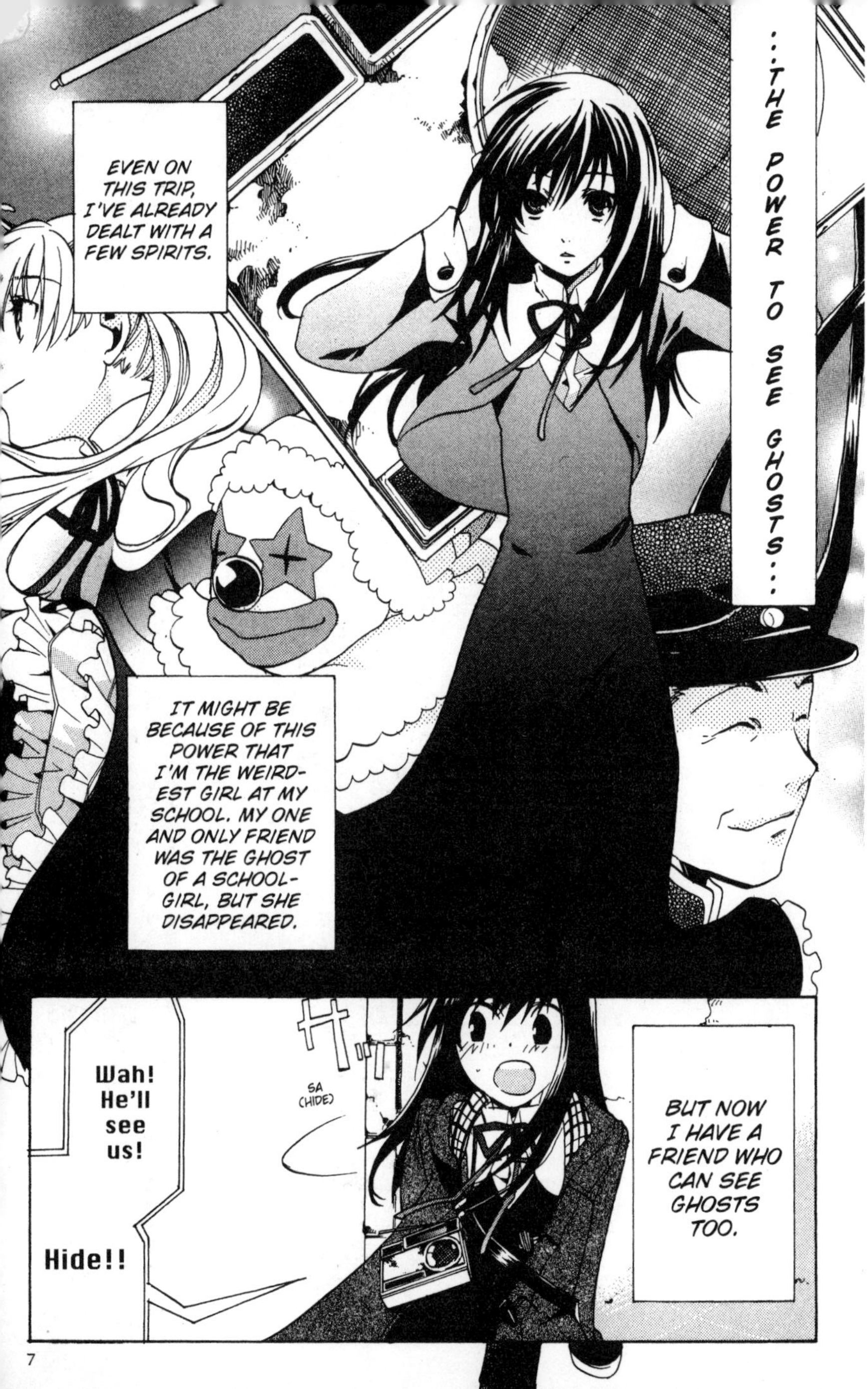
...THE POWER TO SEE GHOSTS...
EVEN ON THIS TRIP, I'VE ALREADY DEALT WITH A FEW SPIRITS.
IT MIGHT BE BECAUSE OF THIS POWER THAT I'M THE WEIRDEST GIRL AT MY SCHOOL. MY ONE AND ONLY FRIEND WAS THE GHOST OF A SCHOOLGIRL, BUT SHE DISAPPEARED.
BUT NOW I HAVE A FRIEND WHO CAN SEE GHOSTS TOO.
SA (HIDE)
Wah! He'll see us!
Hide!!

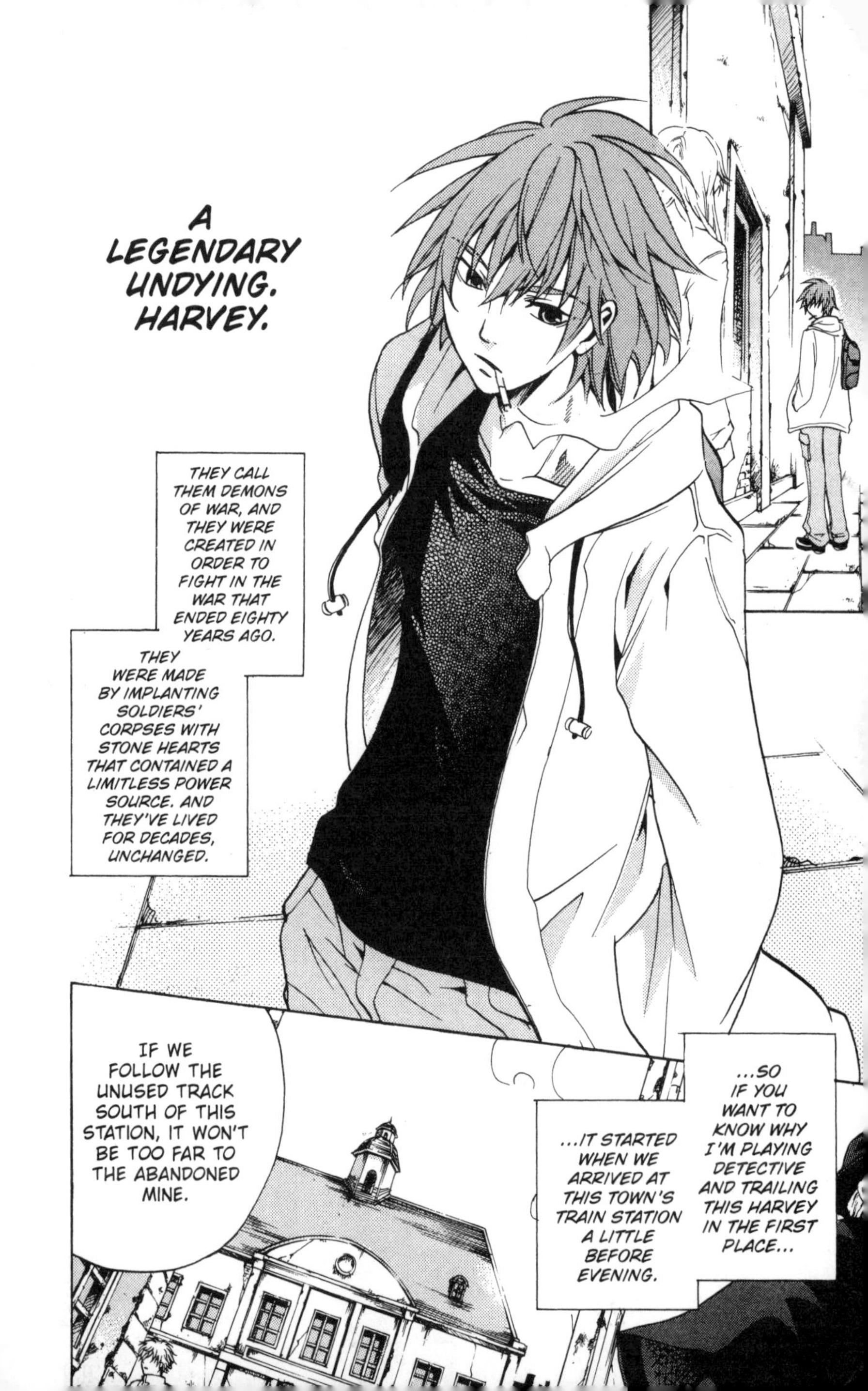
A LEGENDARY UNDYING. HARVEY.
THEY CALL THEM DEMONS OF WAR, AND THEY WERE CREATED IN ORDER TO FIGHT IN THE WAR THAT ENDED EIGHTY YEARS AGO.
THEY WERE MADE BY IMPLANTING SOLDIERS' CORPSES WITH STONE HEARTS THAT CONTAINED A LIMITLESS POWER SOURCE. AND THEY'VE LIVED FOR DECADES, UNCHANGED.
...SO IF YOU WANT TO KNOW WHY I'M PLAYING DETECTIVE AND TRAILING THIS HARVEY IN THE FIRST PLACE...
...IT STARTED WHEN WE ARRIVED AT THIS TOWN'S TRAIN STATION A LITTLE BEFORE EVENING.
IF WE FOLLOW THE UNUSED TRACK SOUTH OF THIS STATION, IT WON'T BE TOO FAR TO THE ABANDONED MINE.

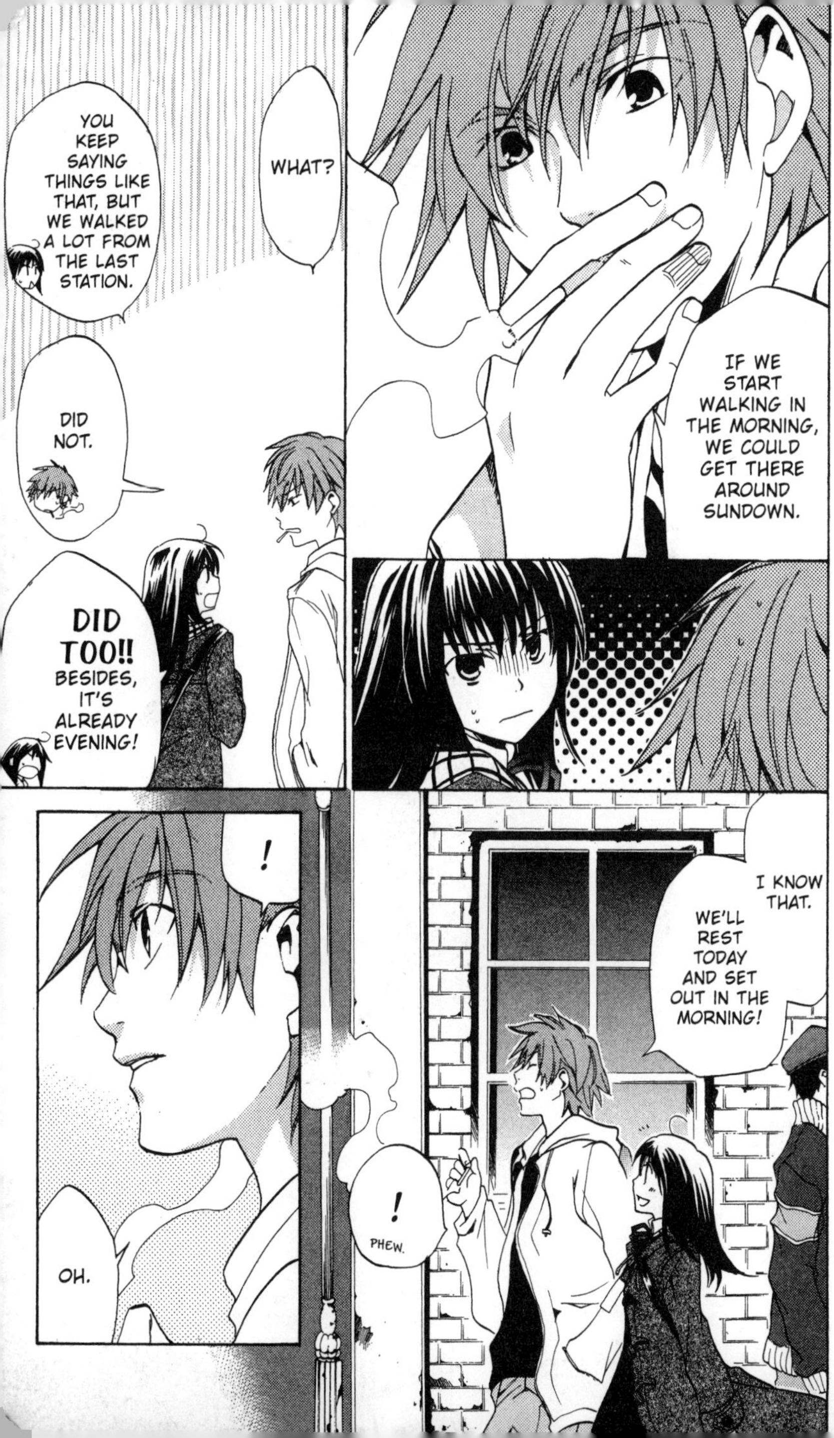
IF WE START WALKING IN THE MORNING, WE COULD GET THERE AROUND SUNDOWN.
WHAT?
YOU KEEP SAYING THINGS LIKE THAT, BUT WE WALKED A LOT FROM THE LAST STATION.
DID NOT.
DID TOO!! BESIDES, IT'S ALREADY EVENING!
I KNOW THAT. WE'LL REST TODAY AND SET OUT IN THE MORNING!
!
PHEW.
!
OH.

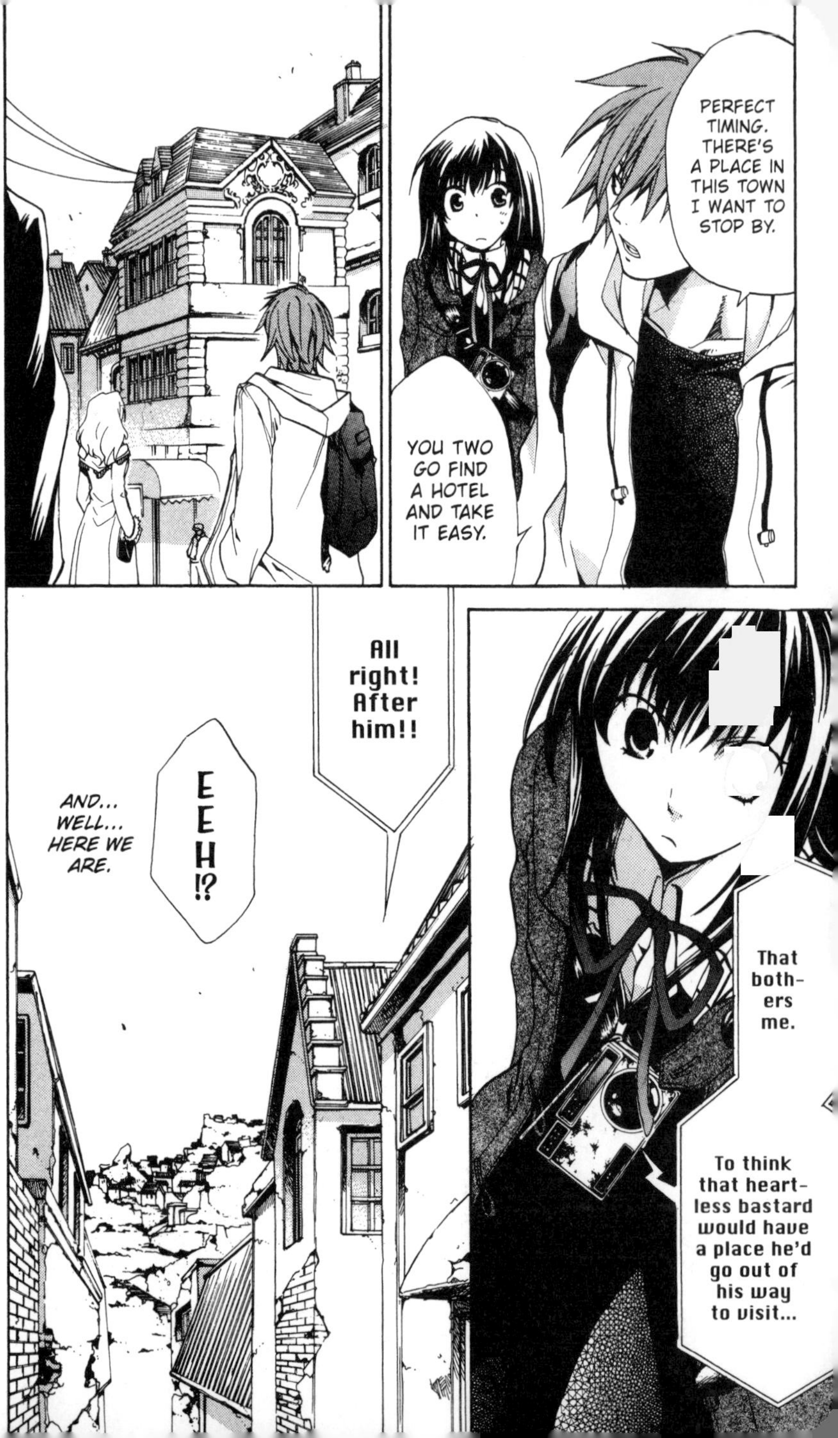
PERFECT TIMING. THERE'S A PLACE IN THIS TOWN I WANT TO STOP BY.
YOU TWO GO FIND A HOTEL AND TAKE IT EASY.
That bothers me.
To think that heartless bastard would have a place he'd go out of his way to visit...
All right! After him!!
EEH!?
AND... WELL... HERE WE ARE.

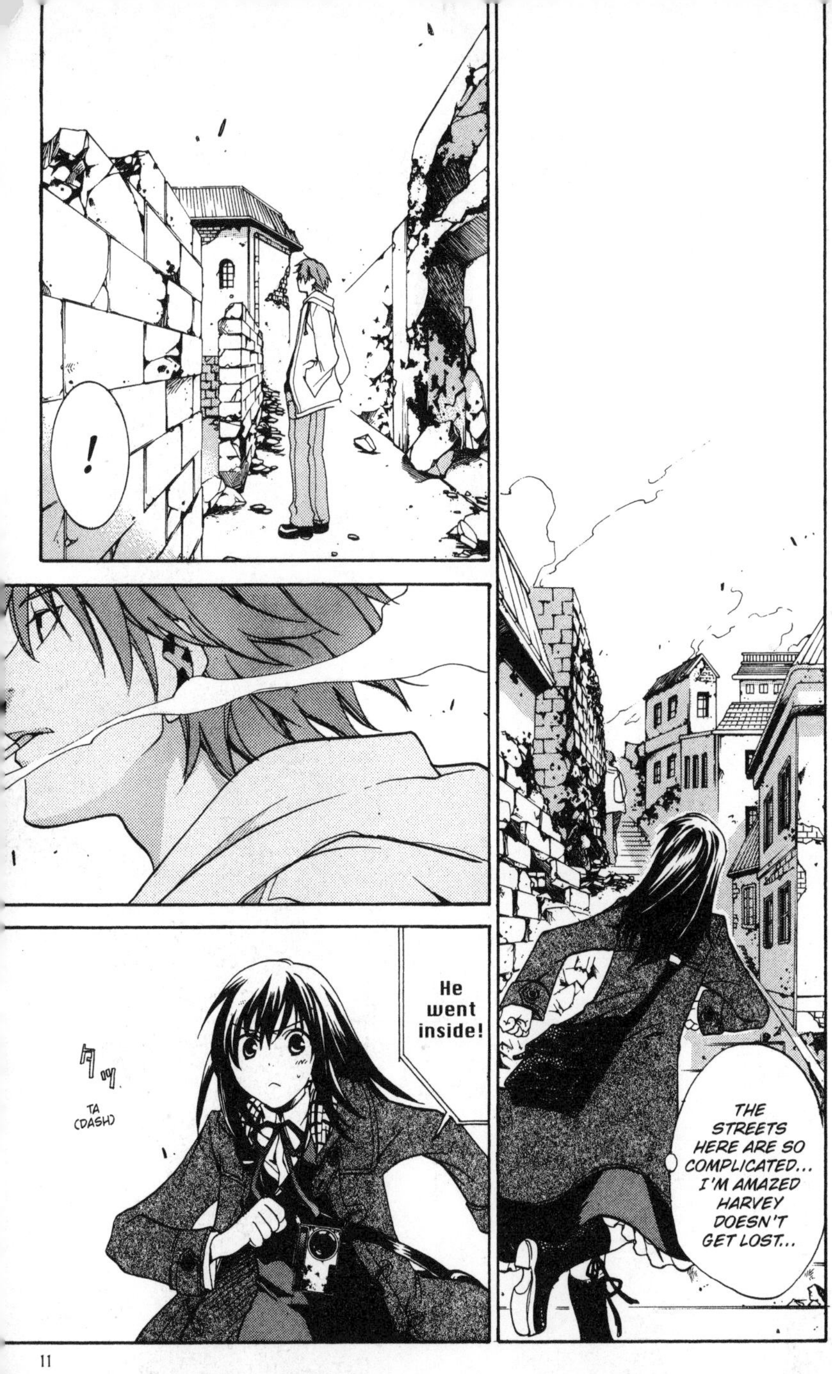
THE STREETS HERE ARE SO COMPLICATED... I'M AMAZED HARVEY DOESN'T GET LOST...
!
He went inside!
タッ
TA (DASH)

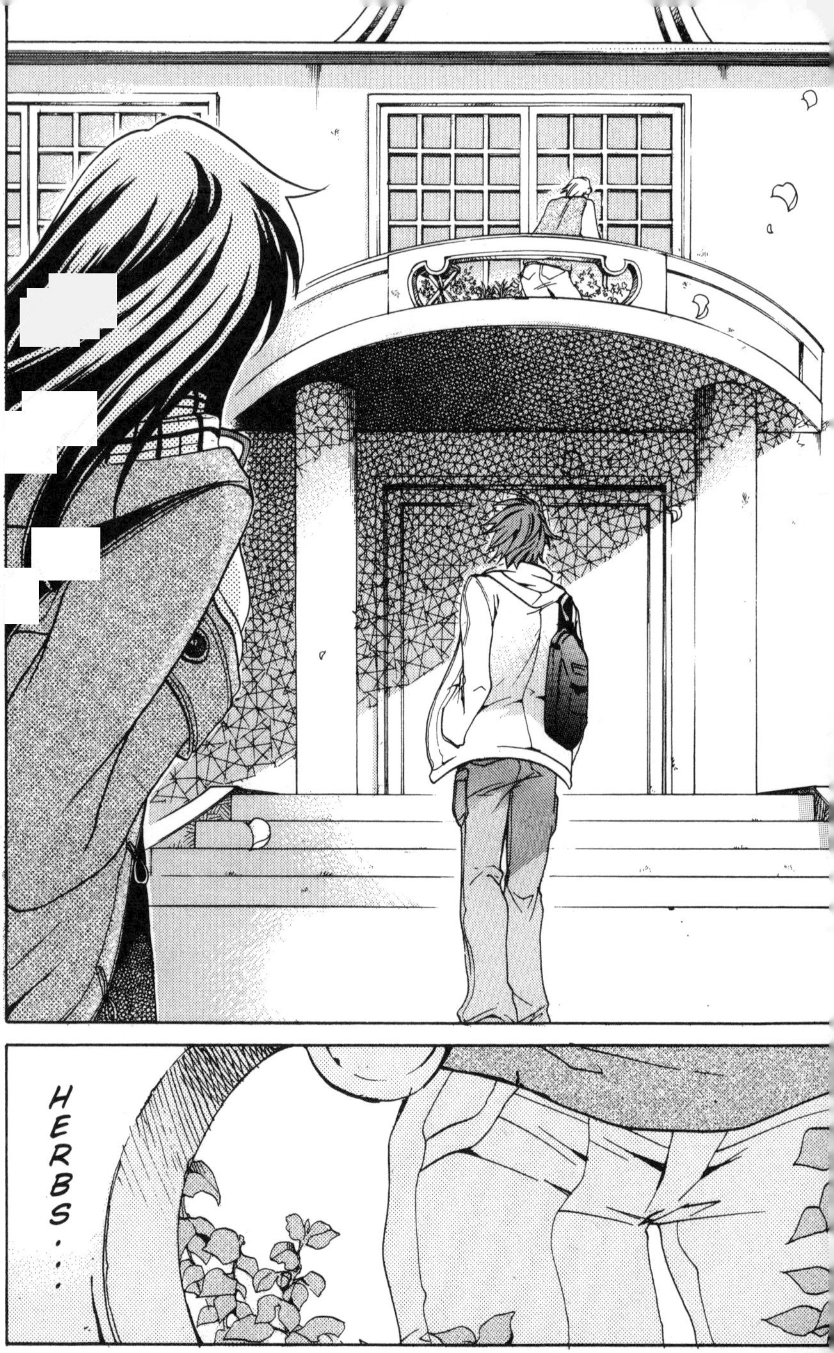
HERBS...

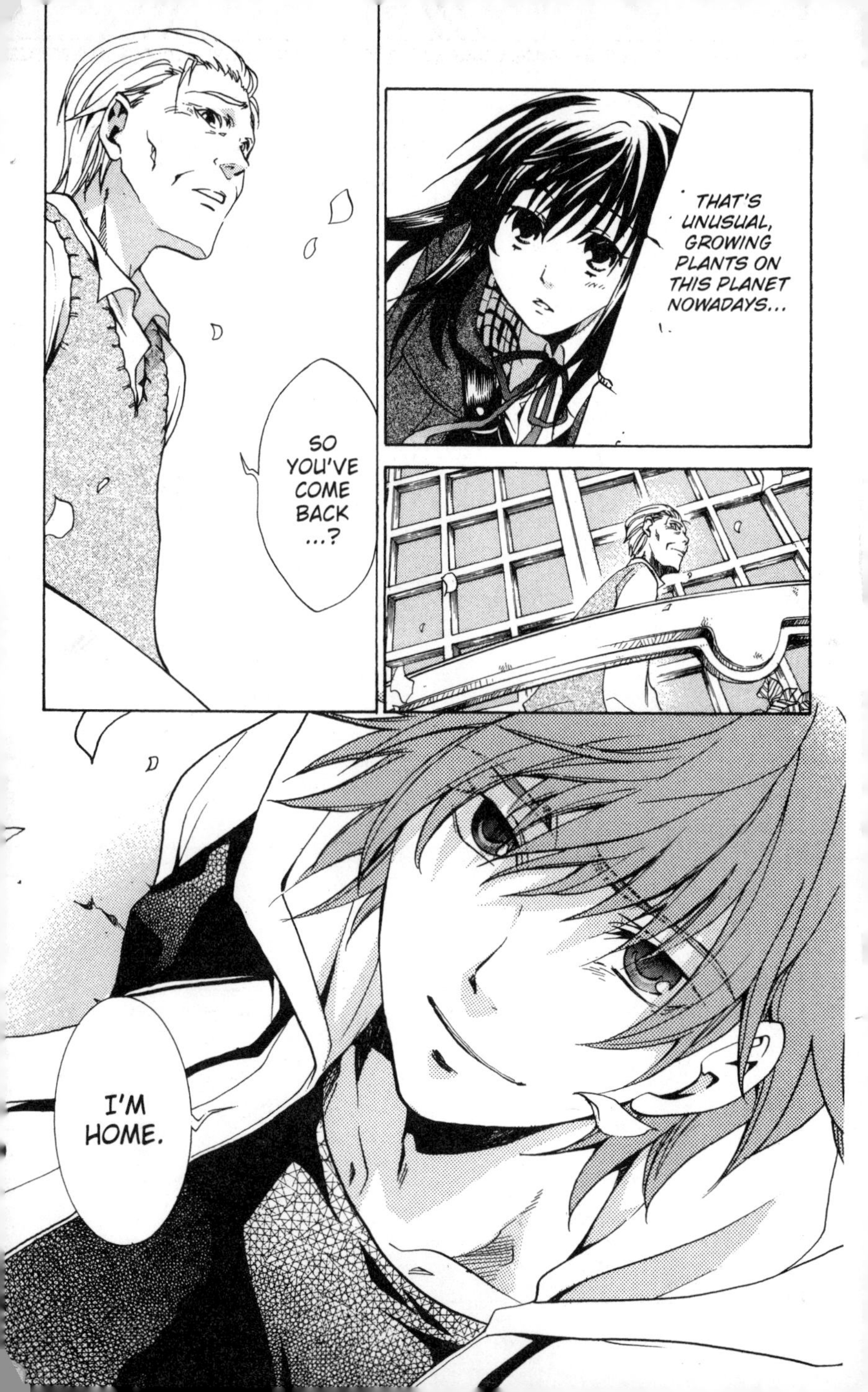
THAT'S UNUSUAL, GROWING PLANTS ON THIS PLANET NOWADAYS...
SO YOU'VE COME BACK ...?
I'M HOME.

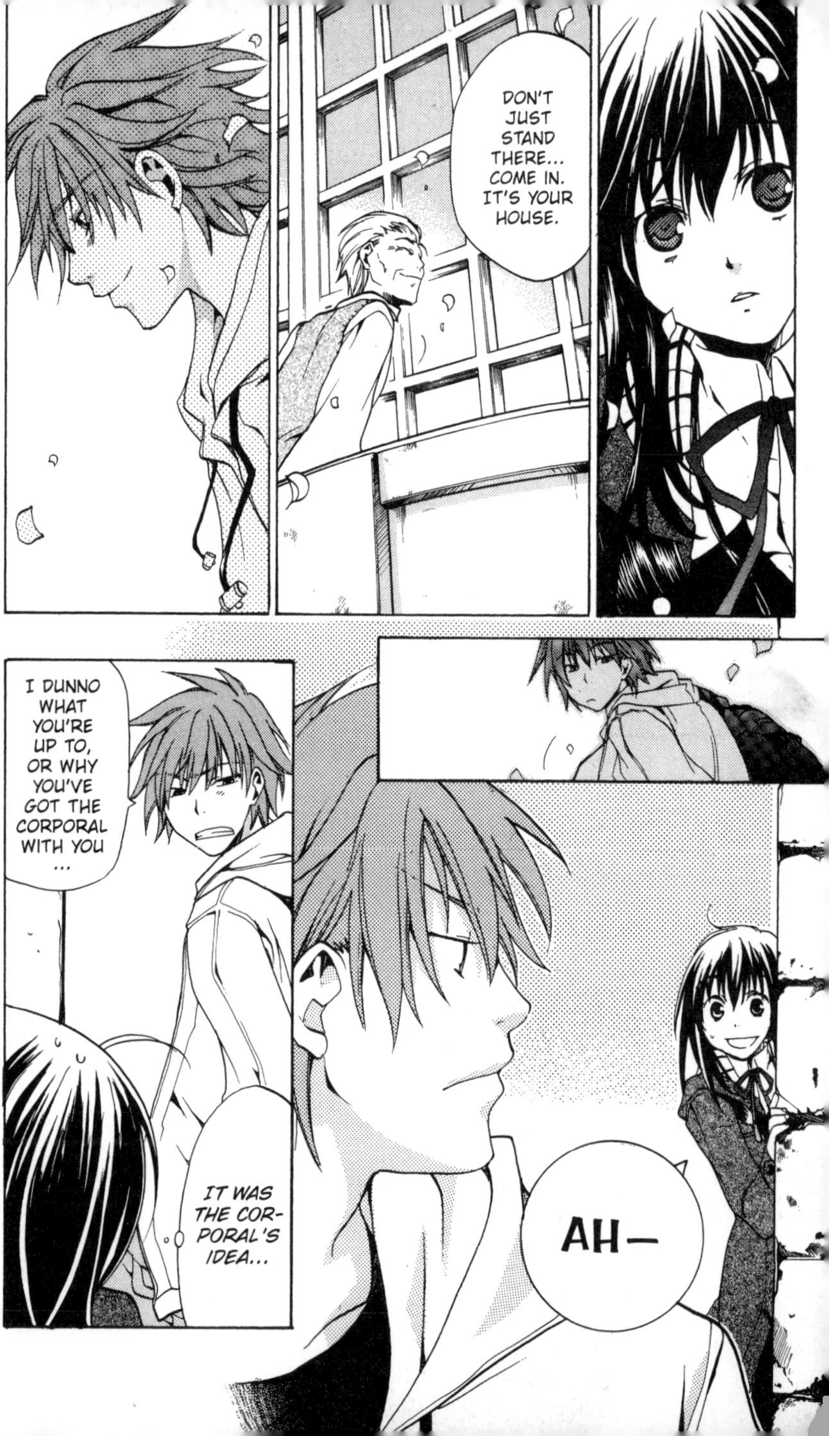
DON'T JUST STAND THERE... COME IN. IT'S YOUR HOUSE.
I DUNNO WHAT YOU'RE UP TO, OR WHY YOU'VE GOT THE CORPORAL WITH YOU ...
AH—
IT WAS THE COR-PORAL'S IDEA...

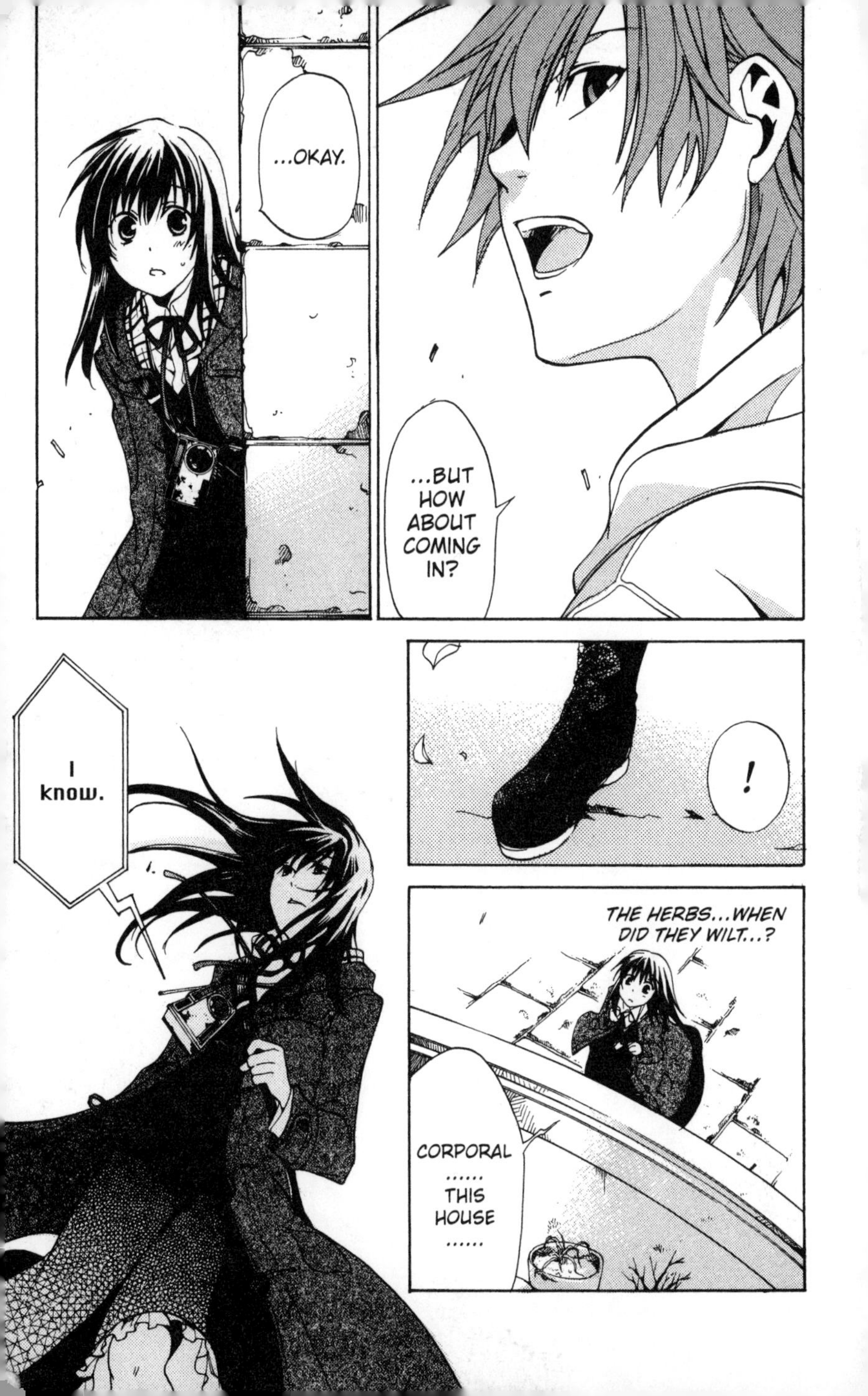
...BUT HOW ABOUT COMING IN?
...OKAY.
!
THE HERBS...WHEN DID THEY WILT...?
CORPORAL ...... THIS HOUSE ......
I know.

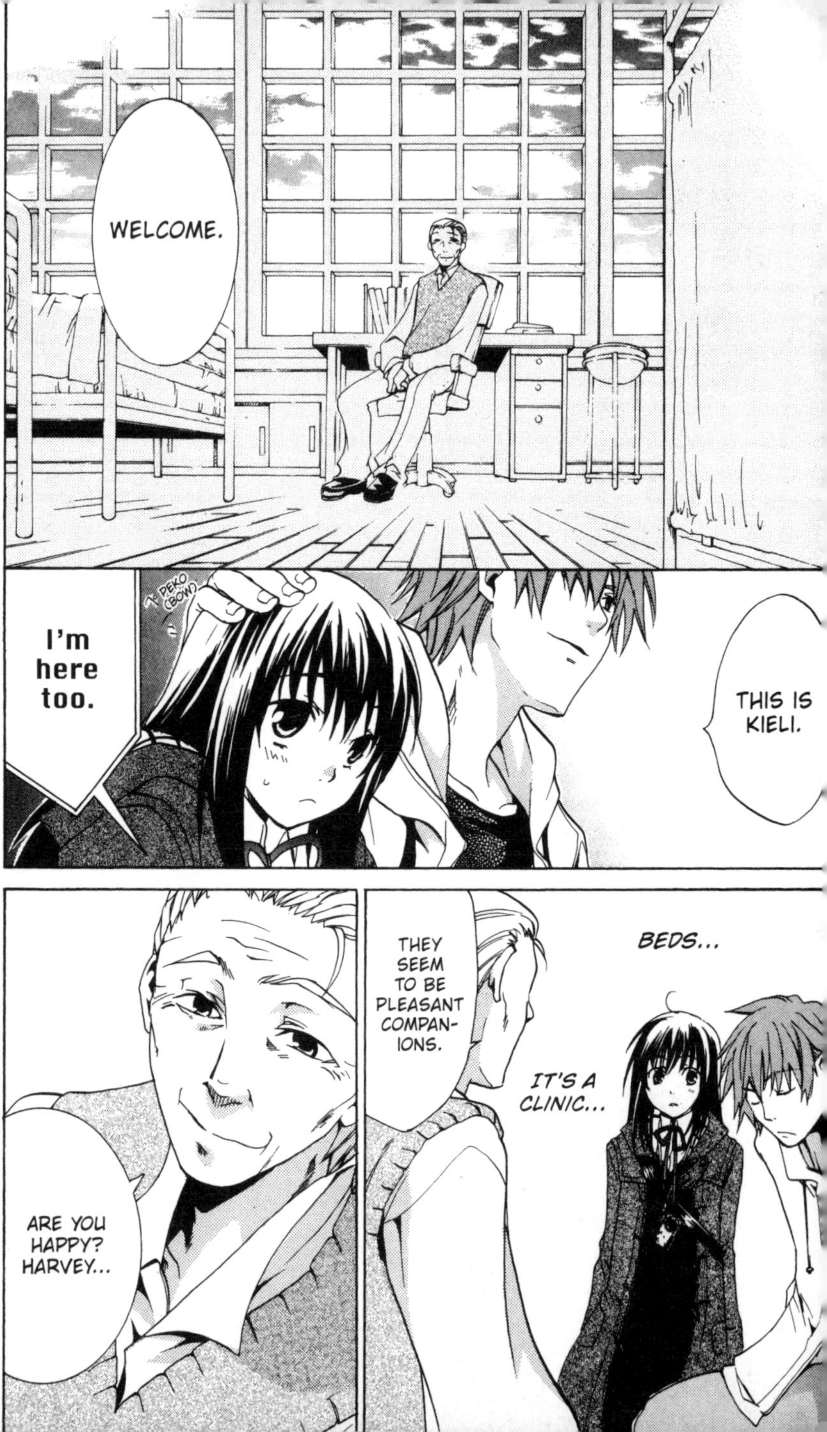

WELCOME.
THIS IS KIELI.
PEKO (BOW)
I'm here too.
BEDS...
THEY SEEM TO BE PLEASANT COMPAN-IONS.
IT'S A CLINIC...
ARE YOU HAPPY? HARVEY...

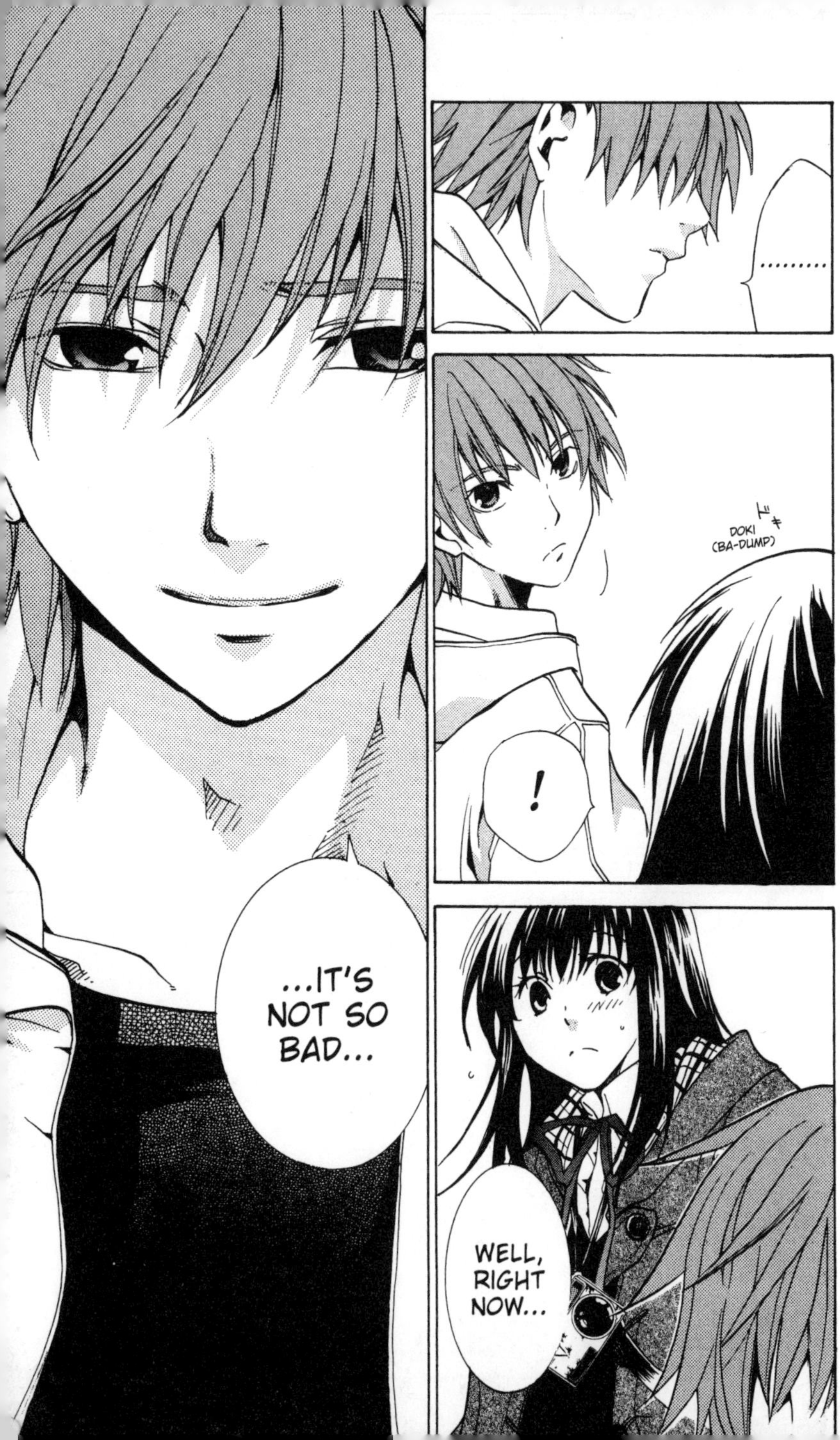
....
ドキ
DOKI
(BA-DUMP)
!
WELL, RIGHT NOW...
...IT'S NOT SO BAD...

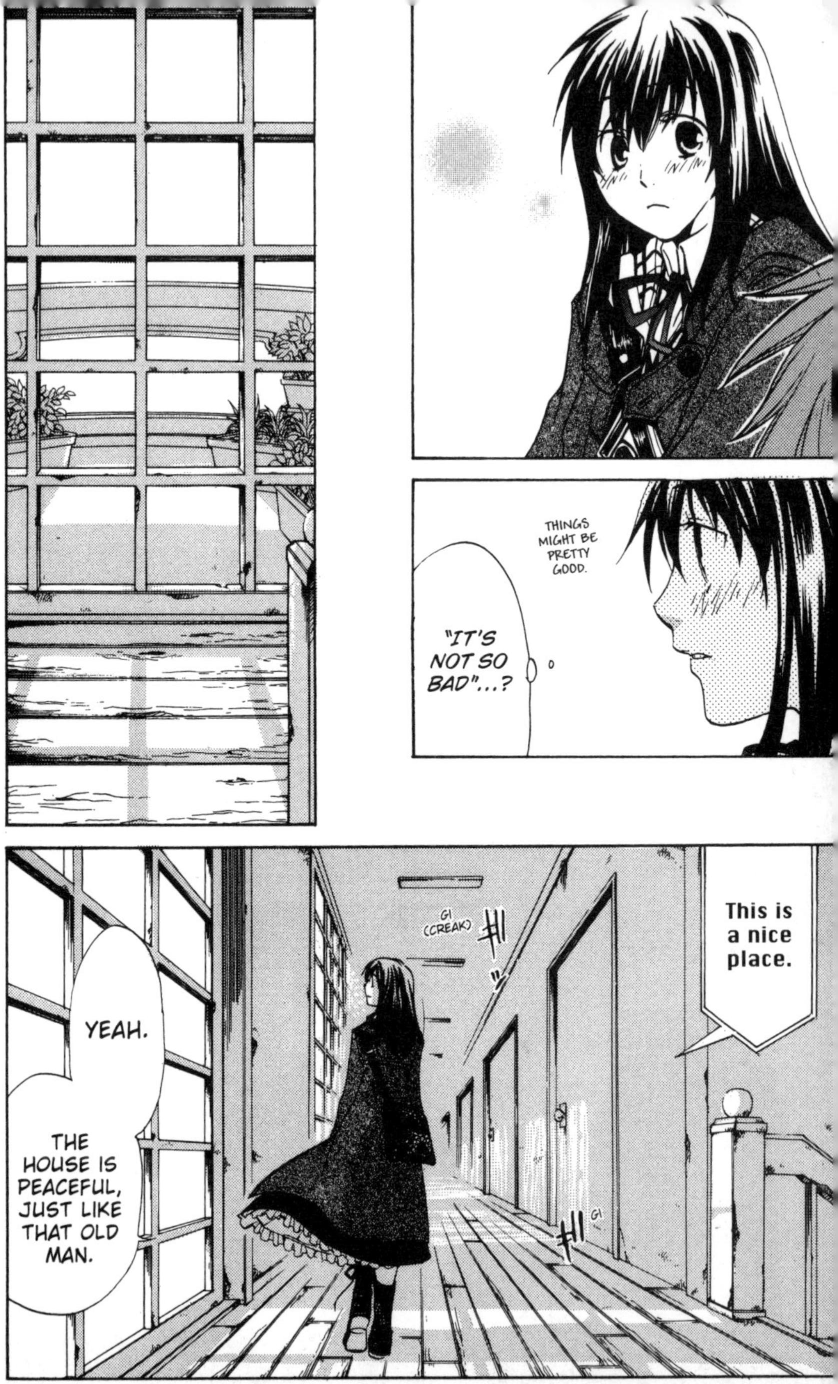
THINGS MIGHT BE PRETTY GOOD.
"IT'S NOT SO BAD"...?
This is a nice place.
GI (CREAK)
YEAH.
THE HOUSE IS PEACEFUL, JUST LIKE THAT OLD MAN.
GI

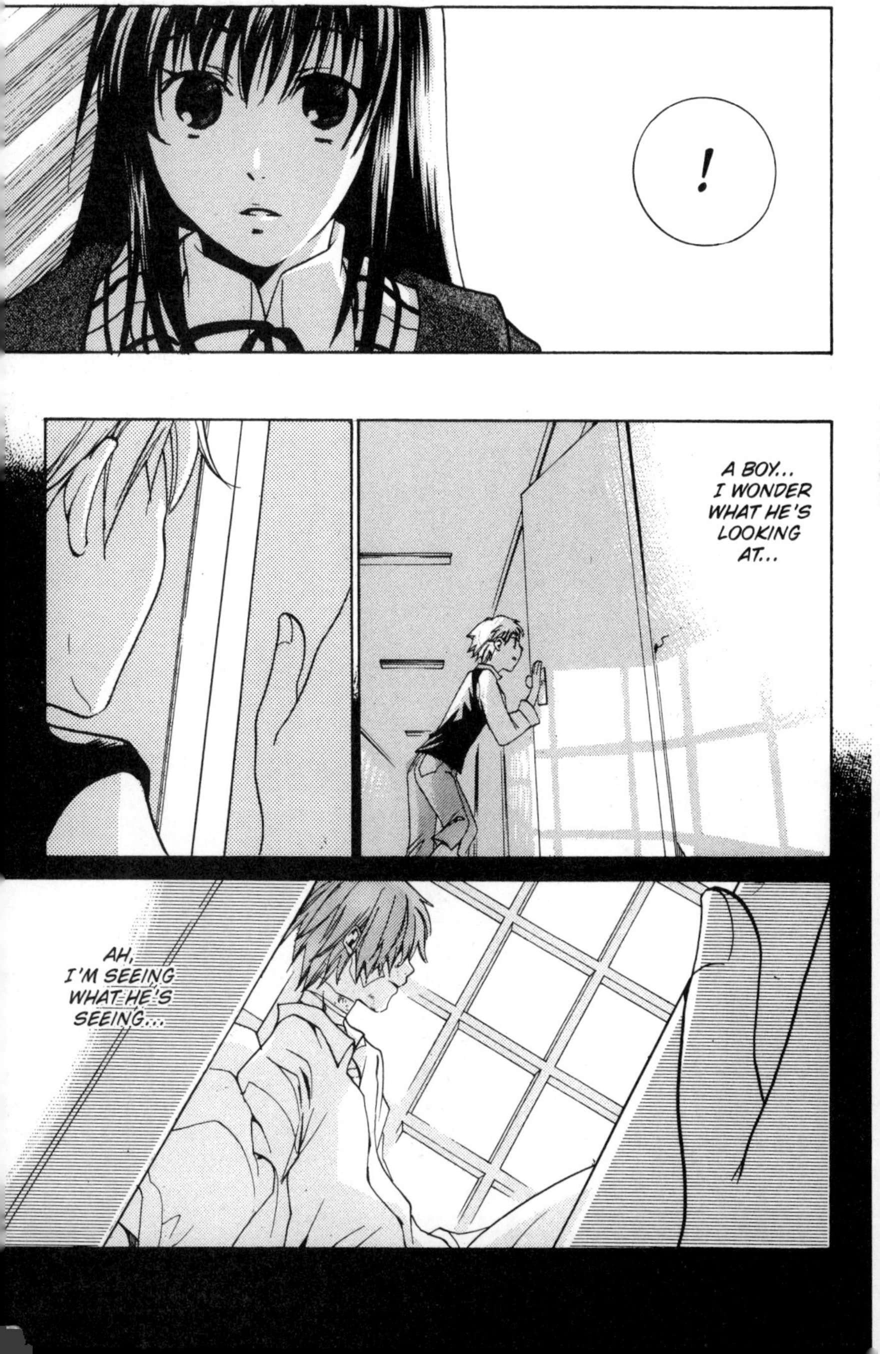
!
A BOY... I WONDER WHAT HE'S LOOKING AT...
AH, I'M SEEING WHAT HE'S SEEING...

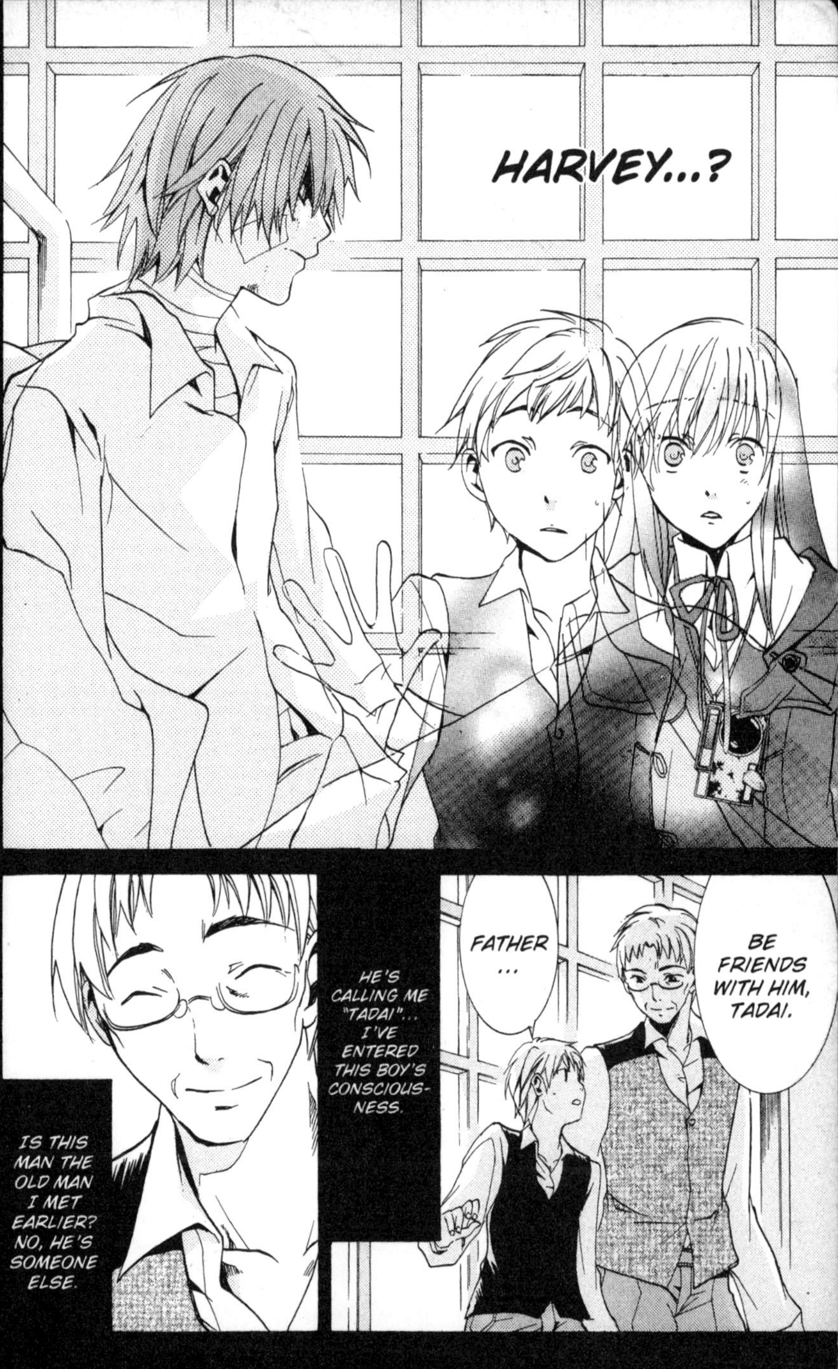
HARVEY...?
BE FRIENDS WITH HIM, TADAI.
FATHER ...
HE'S CALLING ME "TADAI"... I'VE ENTERED THIS BOY'S CONSCIOUSNESS.
IS THIS MAN THE OLD MAN I MET EARLIER? NO, HE'S SOMEONE ELSE.

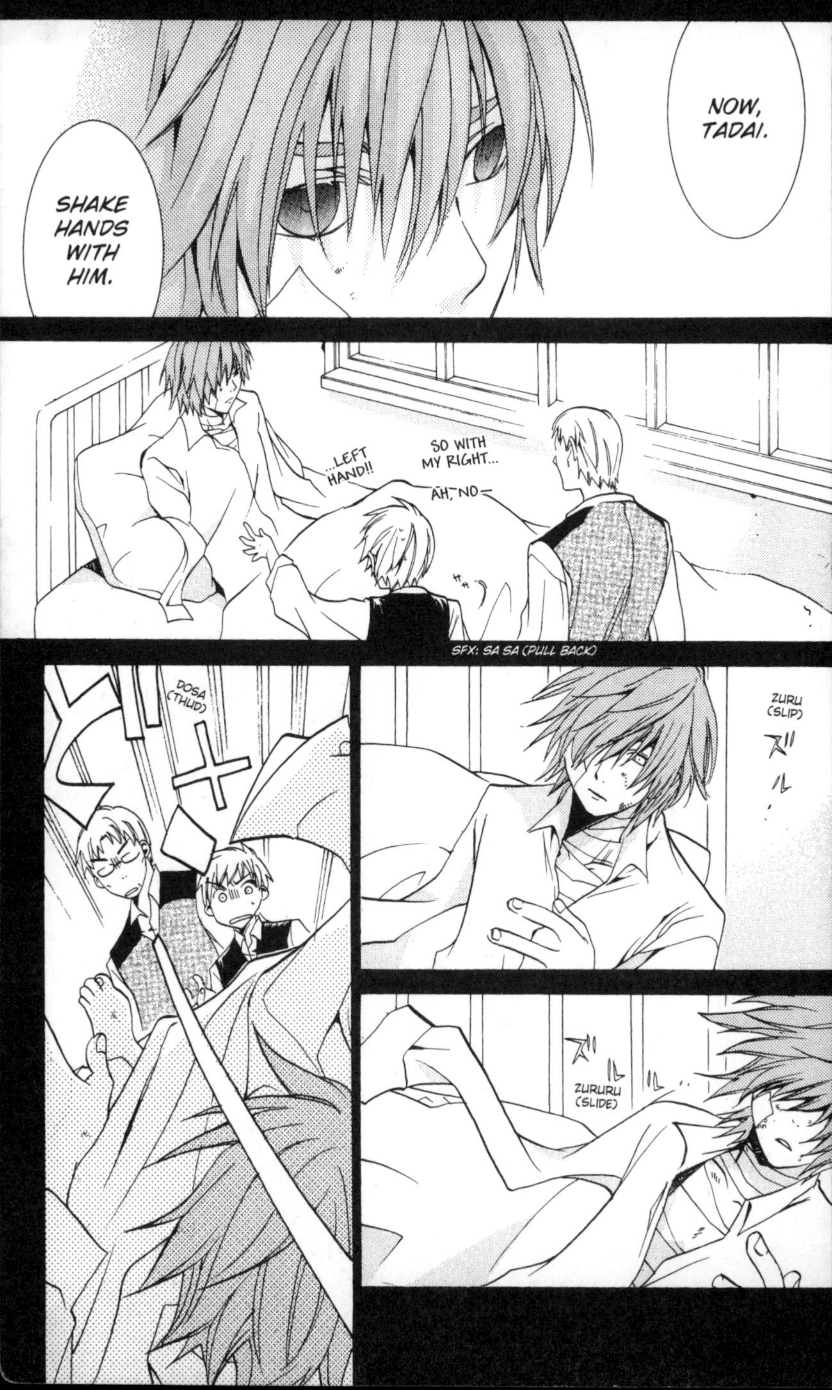
NOW, TADAI.
SHAKE HANDS WITH HIM.
SO WITH MY RIGHT...
AH, NO—
...LEFT HAND!!
SFX: SA SA (PULL BACK)
ZURU (SLIP)
ZURURU (SLIDE)
DOSA (THUD)

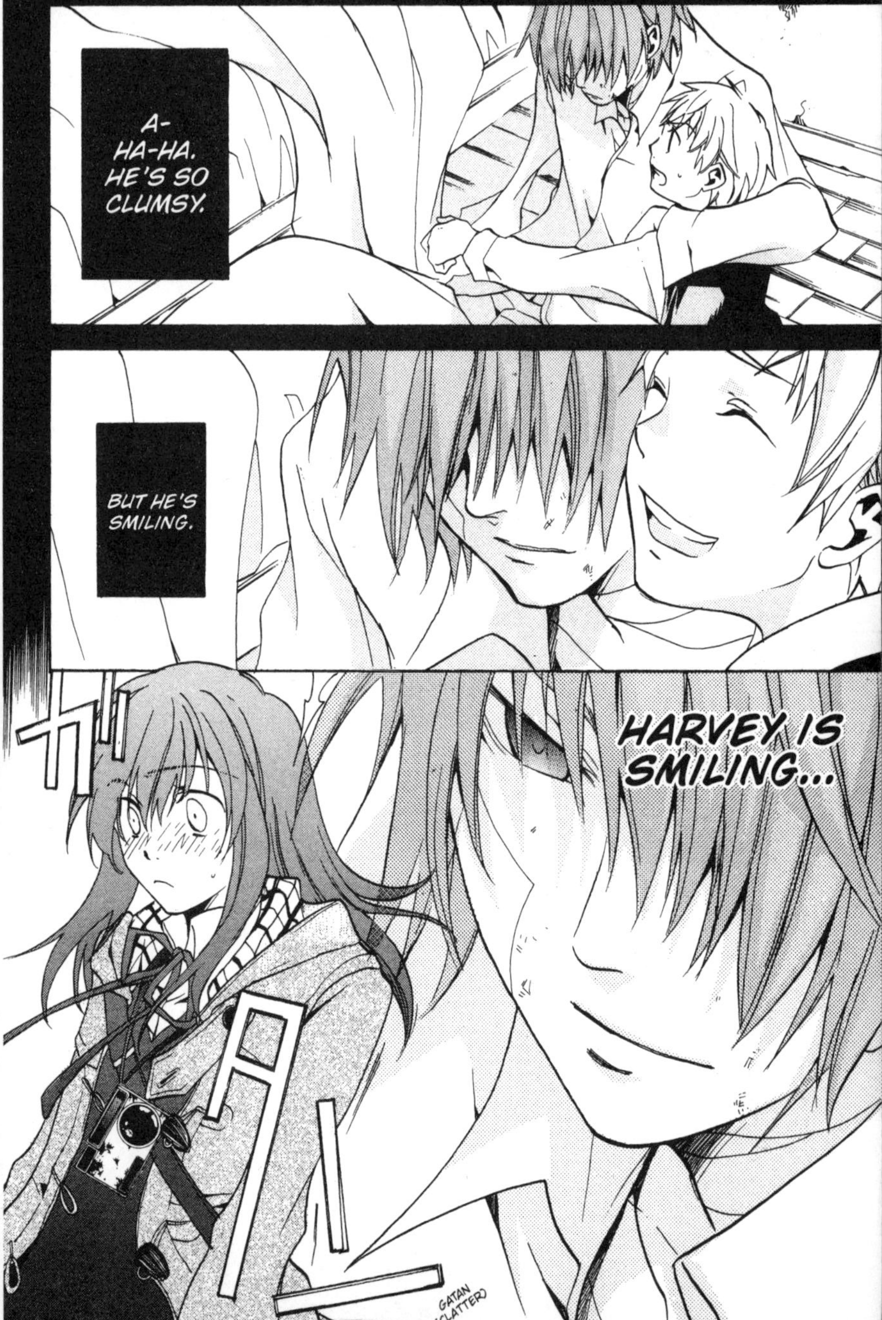
A-
HA-HA.
HE'S SO
CLUMSY.
BUT HE'S
SMILING.
HARVEY IS
SMILING...
GATAN
(CLATTER)

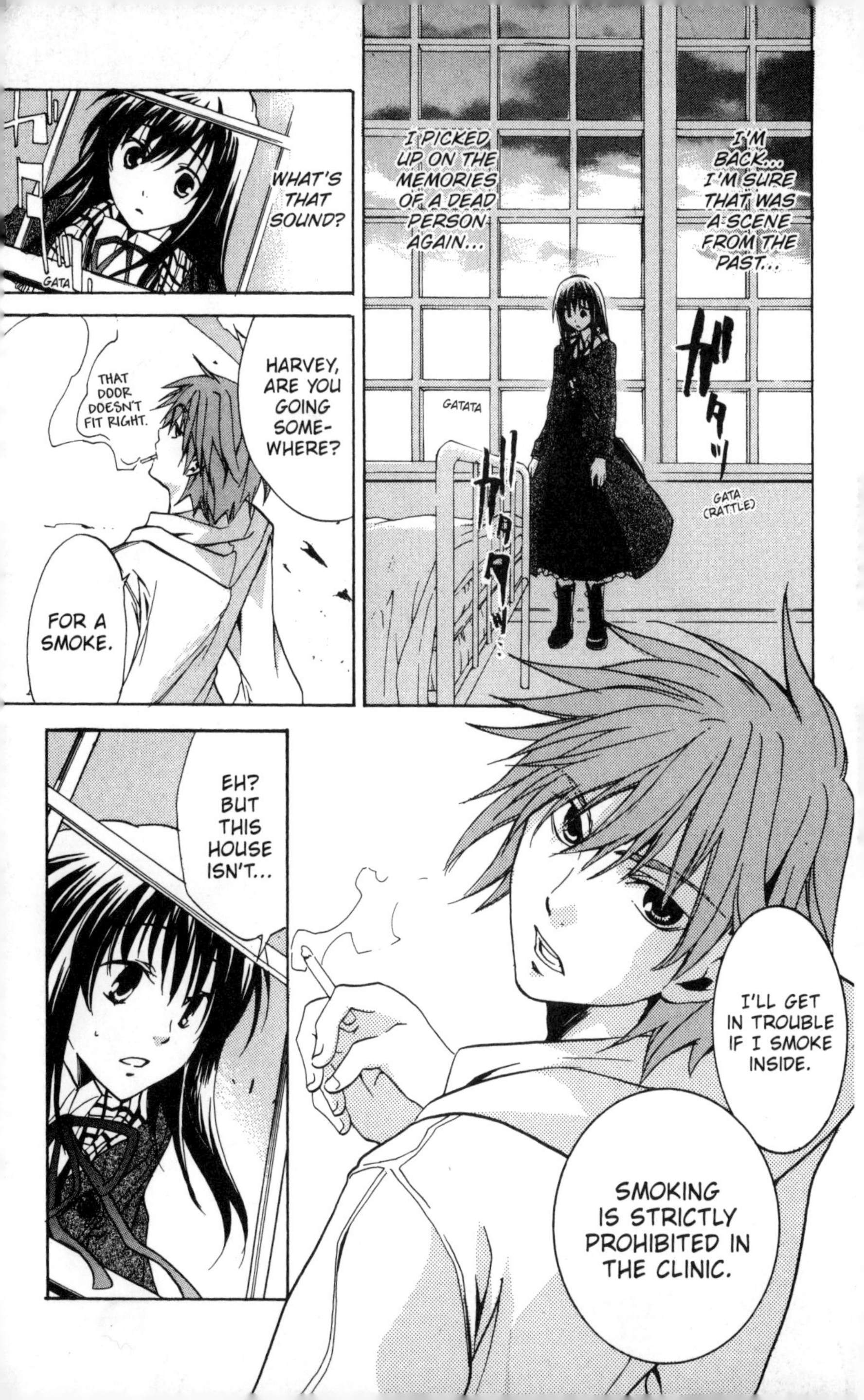
I'M BACK... I'M SURE THAT WAS A SCENE FROM THE PAST...
I PICKED UP ON THE MEMORIES OF A DEAD PERSON AGAIN...
GATA (RATTLE)
GATATA
GATA
WHAT'S THAT SOUND?
HARVEY, ARE YOU GOING SOME-WHERE?
THAT DOOR DOESN'T FIT RIGHT.
FOR A SMOKE.
I'LL GET IN TROUBLE IF I SMOKE INSIDE.
SMOKING IS STRICTLY PROHIBITED IN THE CLINIC.
EH? BUT THIS HOUSE ISN'T...

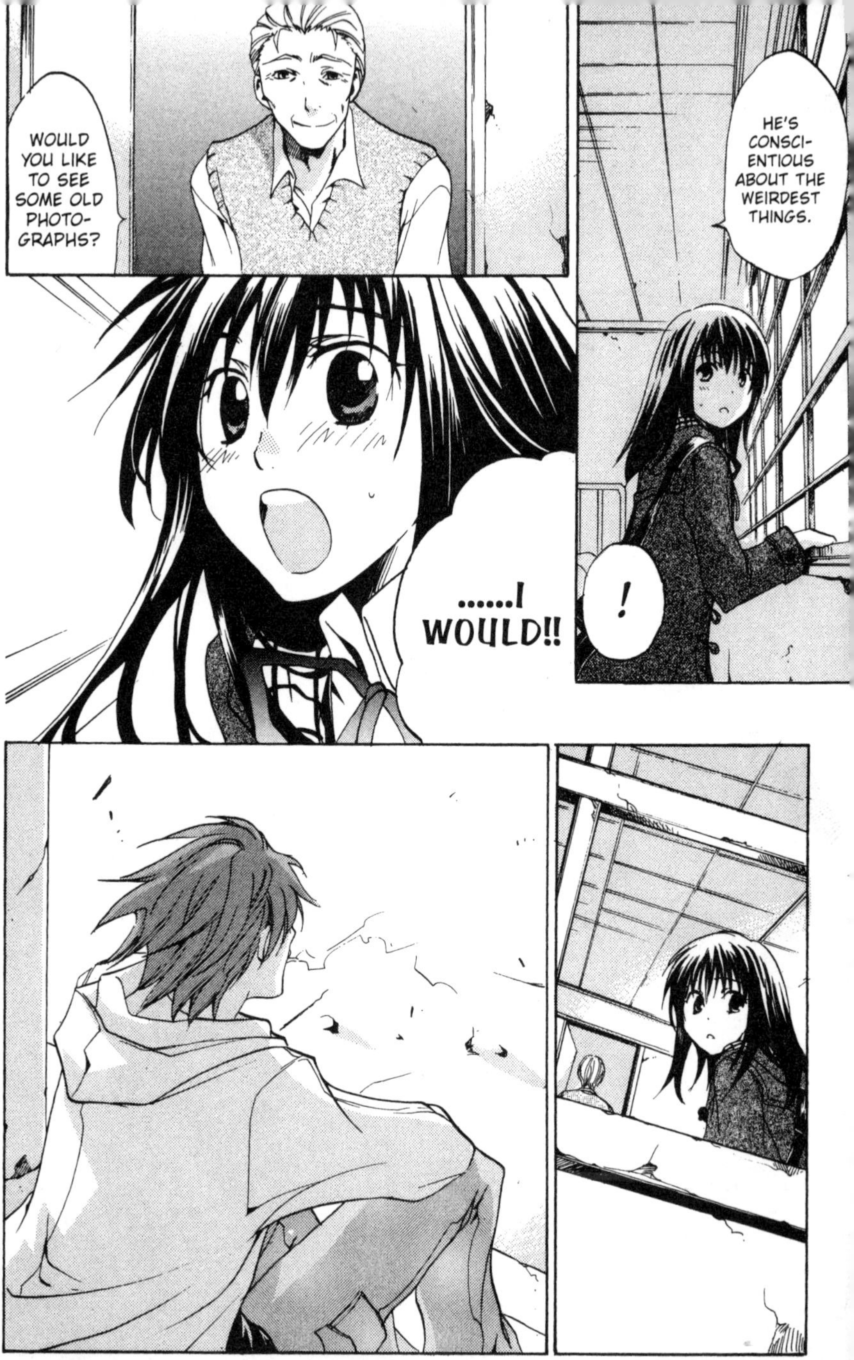

HE'S CONSCIENTIOUS ABOUT THE WEIRDEST THINGS.
!
WOULD YOU LIKE TO SEE SOME OLD PHOTOGRAPHS?
......I WOULD!!

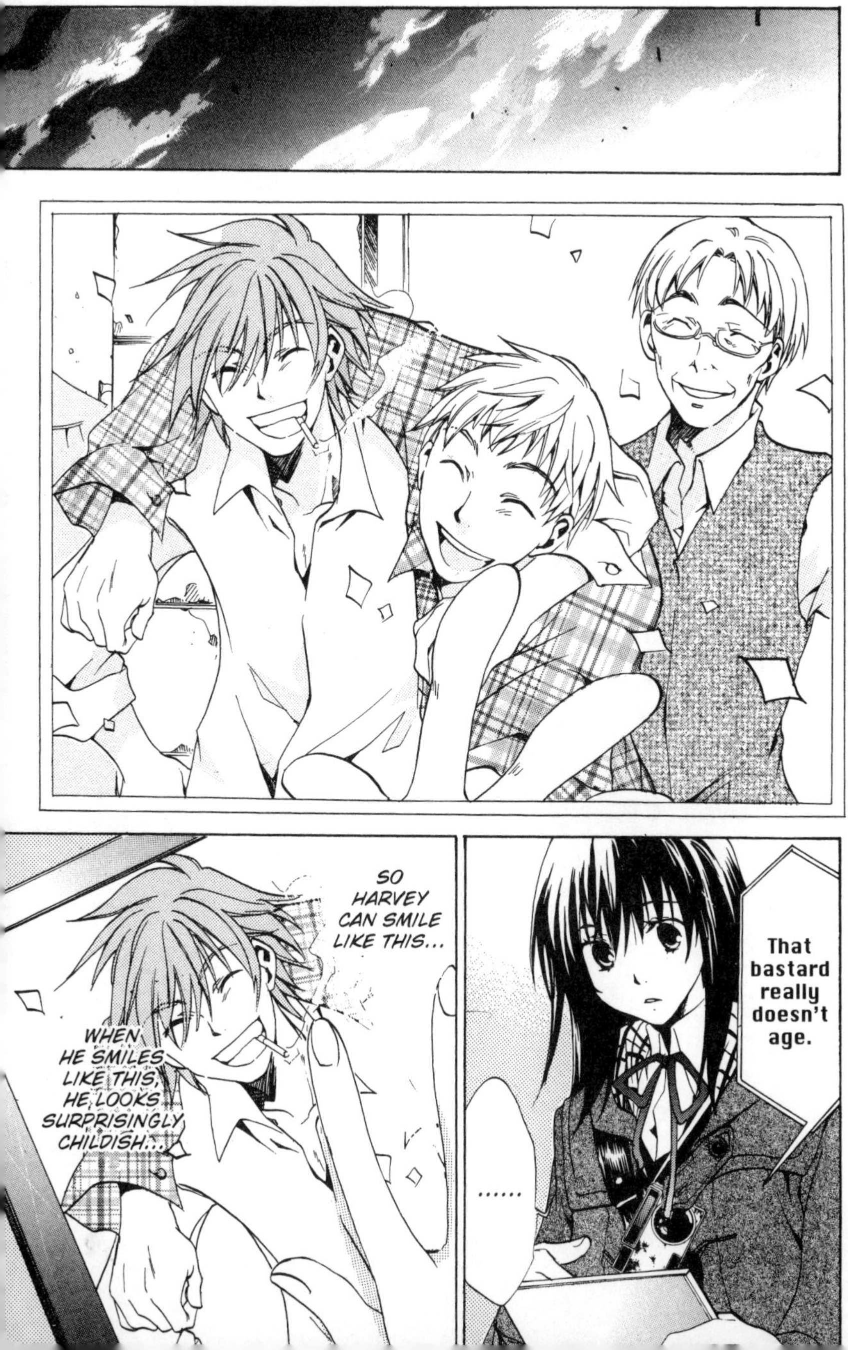
That bastard really doesn't age.
......
SO HARVEY CAN SMILE LIKE THIS...
WHEN HE SMILES LIKE THIS, HE LOOKS SURPRISINGLY CHILDISH...

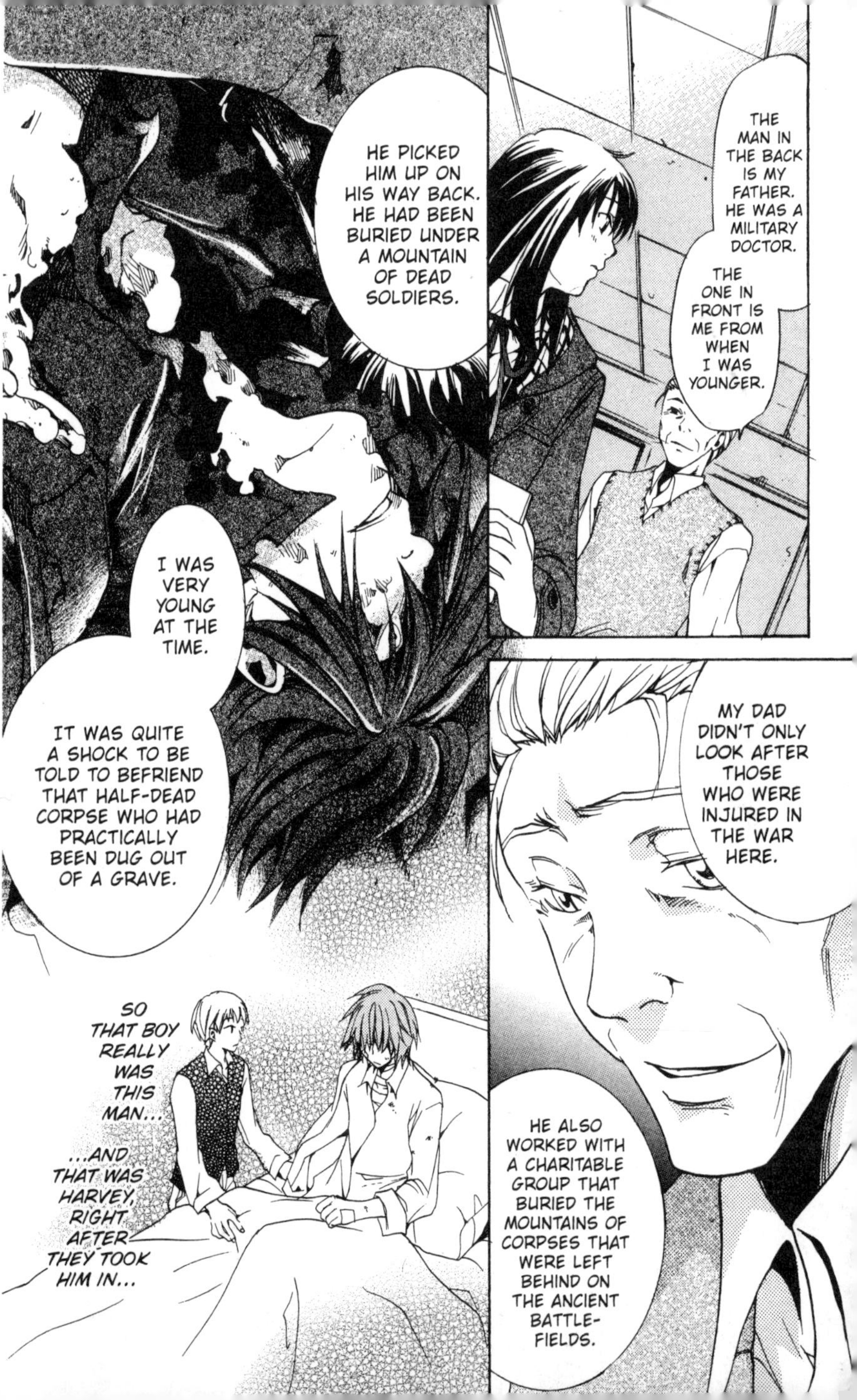
THE MAN IN THE BACK IS MY FATHER. HE WAS A MILITARY DOCTOR.
THE ONE IN FRONT IS ME FROM WHEN I WAS YOUNGER.
MY DAD DIDN'T ONLY LOOK AFTER THOSE WHO WERE INJURED IN THE WAR HERE.
HE ALSO WORKED WITH A CHARITABLE GROUP THAT BURIED THE MOUNTAINS OF CORPSES THAT WERE LEFT BEHIND ON THE ANCIENT BATTLE-FIELDS.
HE PICKED HIM UP ON HIS WAY BACK. HE HAD BEEN BURIED UNDER A MOUNTAIN OF DEAD SOLDIERS.
I WAS VERY YOUNG AT THE TIME.
IT WAS QUITE A SHOCK TO BE TOLD TO BEFRIEND THAT HALF-DEAD CORPSE WHO HAD PRACTICALLY BEEN DUG OUT OF A GRAVE.
SO THAT BOY REALLY WAS THIS MAN...
...AND THAT WAS HARVEY, RIGHT AFTER THEY TOOK HIM IN...

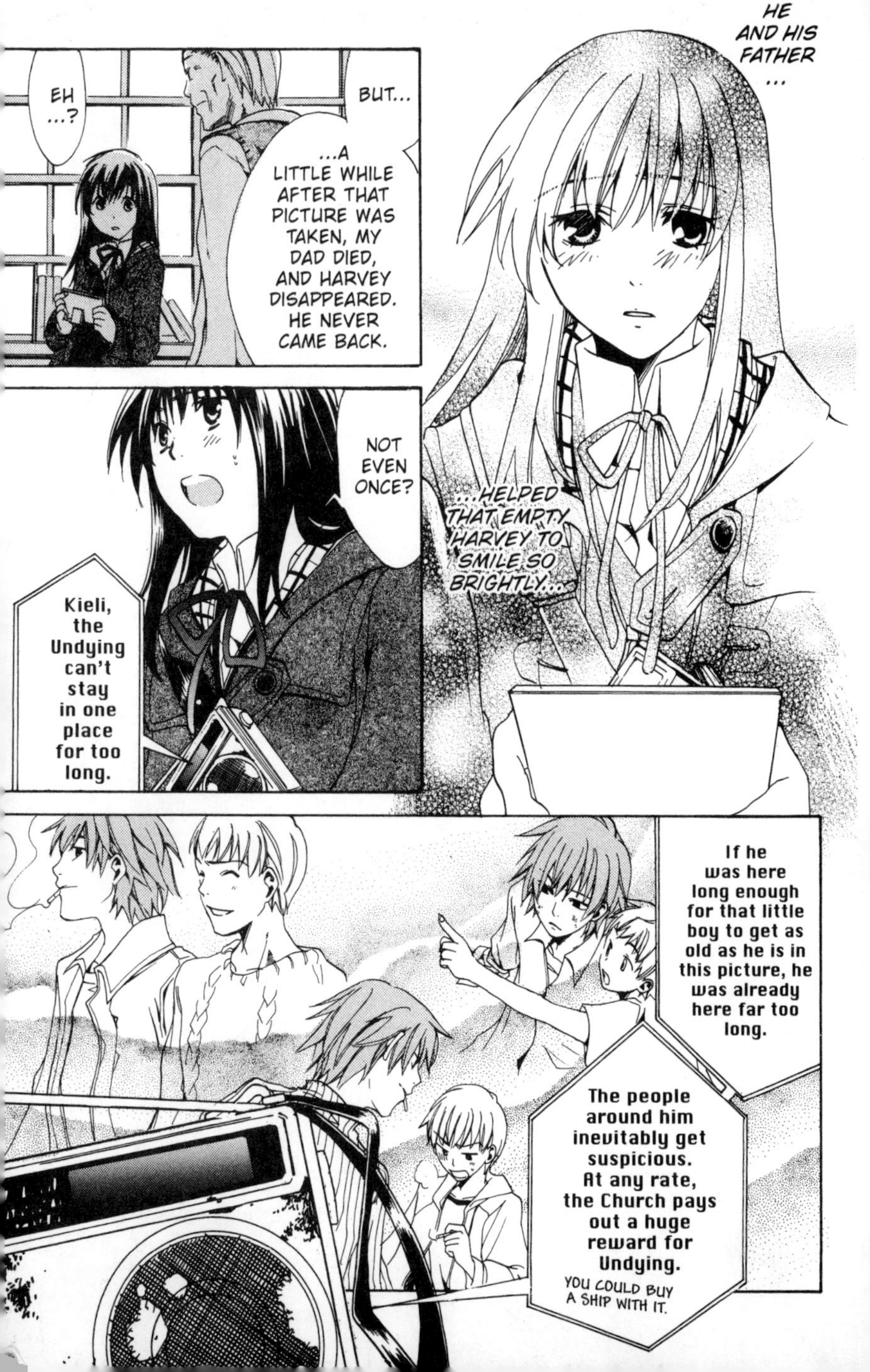

HE AND HIS FATHER ...
...HELPED THAT EMPTY HARVEY TO SMILE SO BRIGHTLY...
BUT...
...A LITTLE WHILE AFTER THAT PICTURE WAS TAKEN, MY DAD DIED, AND HARVEY DISAPPEARED. HE NEVER CAME BACK.
EH ...?
NOT EVEN ONCE?
Kieli, the Undying can't stay in one place for too long.
If he was here long enough for that little boy to get as old as he is in this picture, he was already here far too long.
The people around him inevitably get suspicious. At any rate, the Church pays out a huge reward for Undying.
YOU COULD BUY A SHIP WITH IT.

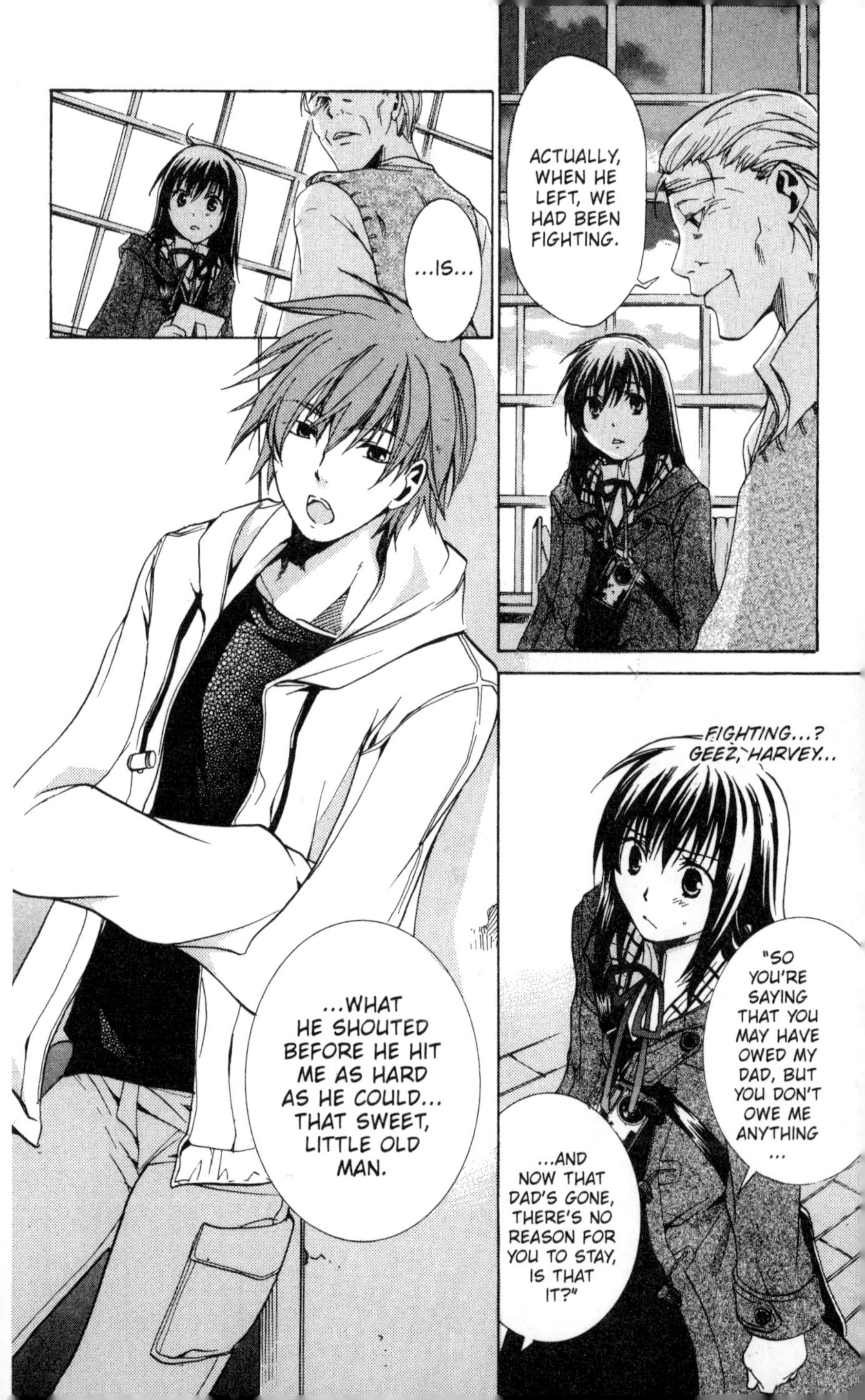
ACTUALLY, WHEN HE LEFT, WE HAD BEEN FIGHTING.
FIGHTING...? GEEZ, HARVEY...
"SO YOU'RE SAYING THAT YOU MAY HAVE OWED MY DAD, BUT YOU DON'T OWE ME ANYTHING ...
...AND NOW THAT DAD'S GONE, THERE'S NO REASON FOR YOU TO STAY, IS THAT IT?"
...IS...
...WHAT HE SHOUTED BEFORE HE HIT ME AS HARD AS HE COULD... THAT SWEET, LITTLE OLD MAN.

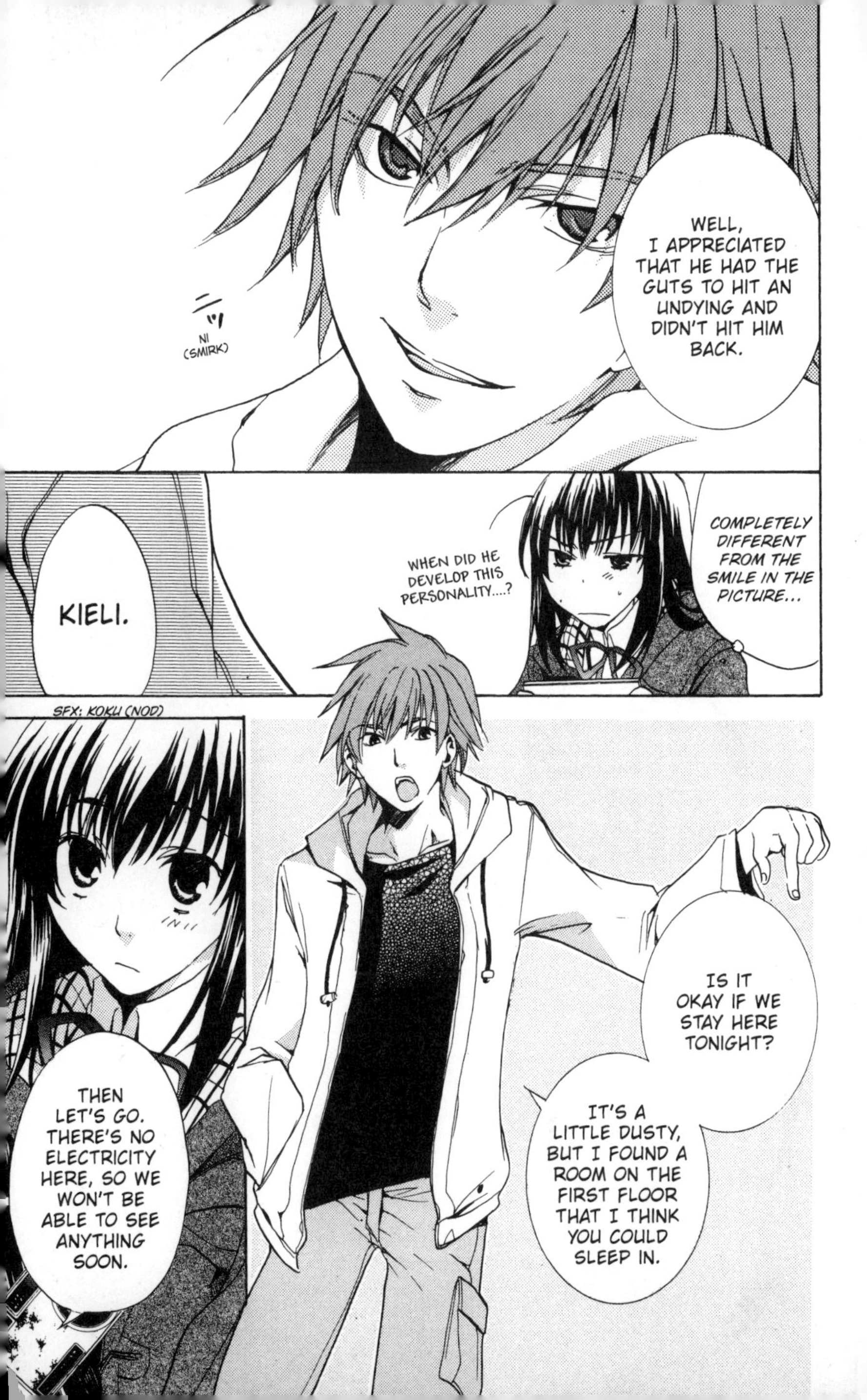
ニッ
NI (SMIRK)
WELL, I APPRECIATED THAT HE HAD THE GUTS TO HIT AN UNDYING AND DIDN'T HIT HIM BACK.
COMPLETELY DIFFERENT FROM THE SMILE IN THE PICTURE...
WHEN DID HE DEVELOP THIS PERSONALITY....?
KIELI.
IS IT OKAY IF WE STAY HERE TONIGHT?
IT'S A LITTLE DUSTY, BUT I FOUND A ROOM ON THE FIRST FLOOR THAT I THINK YOU COULD SLEEP IN.
SFX: KOKU (NOD)
THEN LET'S GO. THERE'S NO ELECTRICITY HERE, SO WE WON'T BE ABLE TO SEE ANYTHING SOON.

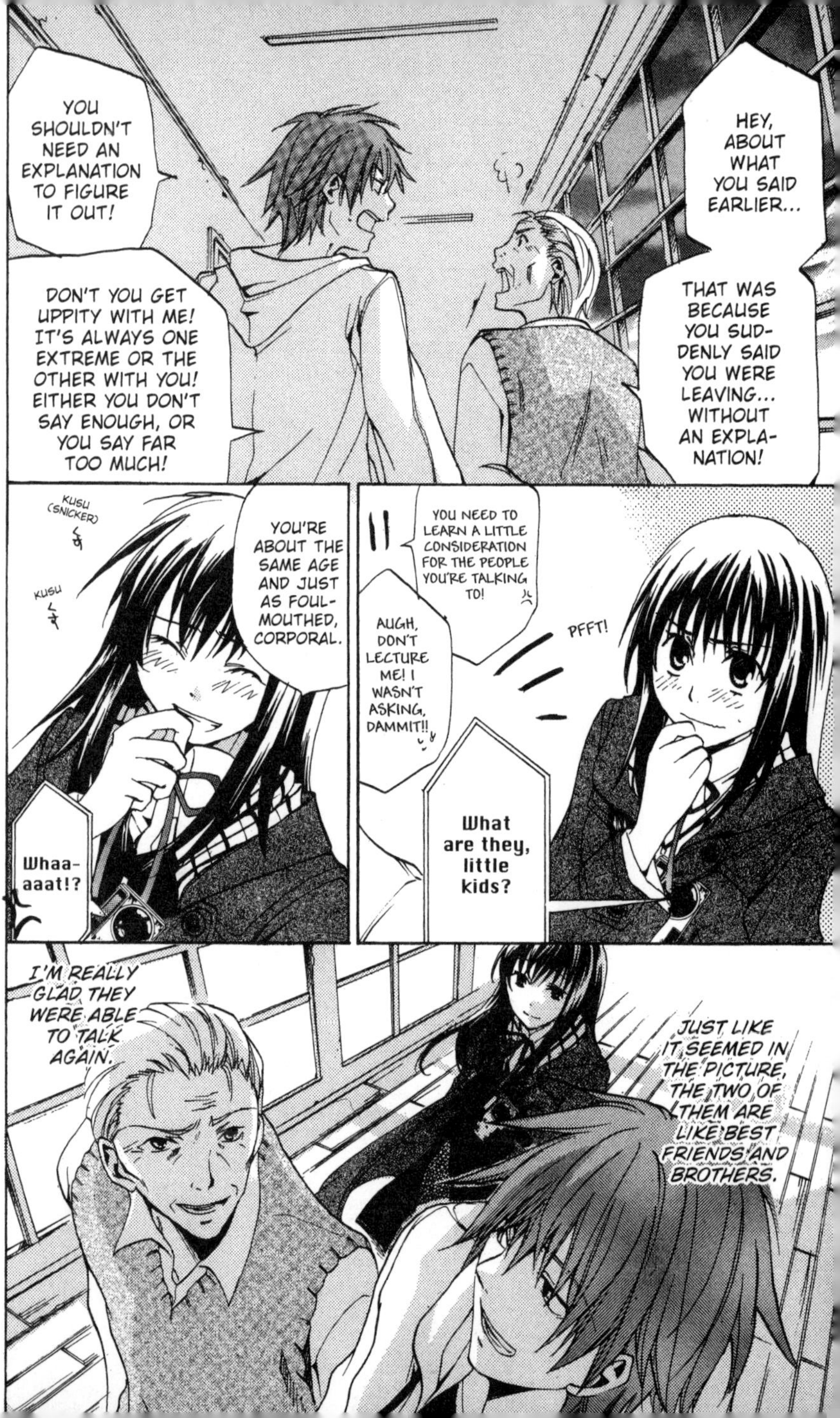
HEY, ABOUT WHAT YOU SAID EARLIER...
YOU SHOULDN'T NEED AN EXPLANATION TO FIGURE IT OUT!
THAT WAS BECAUSE YOU SUDDENLY SAID YOU WERE LEAVING... WITHOUT AN EXPLANATION!
DON'T YOU GET UPPITY WITH ME! IT'S ALWAYS ONE EXTREME OR THE OTHER WITH YOU! EITHER YOU DON'T SAY ENOUGH, OR YOU SAY FAR TOO MUCH!
YOU NEED TO LEARN A LITTLE CONSIDERATION FOR THE PEOPLE YOU'RE TALKING TO!
AUGH, DON'T LECTURE ME! I WASN'T ASKING, DAMMIT!!
PFFT!
What are they, little kids?
YOU'RE ABOUT THE SAME AGE AND JUST AS FOUL-MOUTHED, CORPORAL.
KUSU (SNICKER)
KUSU
Whaa-aaat!?
JUST LIKE IT SEEMED IN THE PICTURE, THE TWO OF THEM ARE LIKE BEST FRIENDS AND BROTHERS.
I'M REALLY GLAD THEY WERE ABLE TO TALK AGAIN.

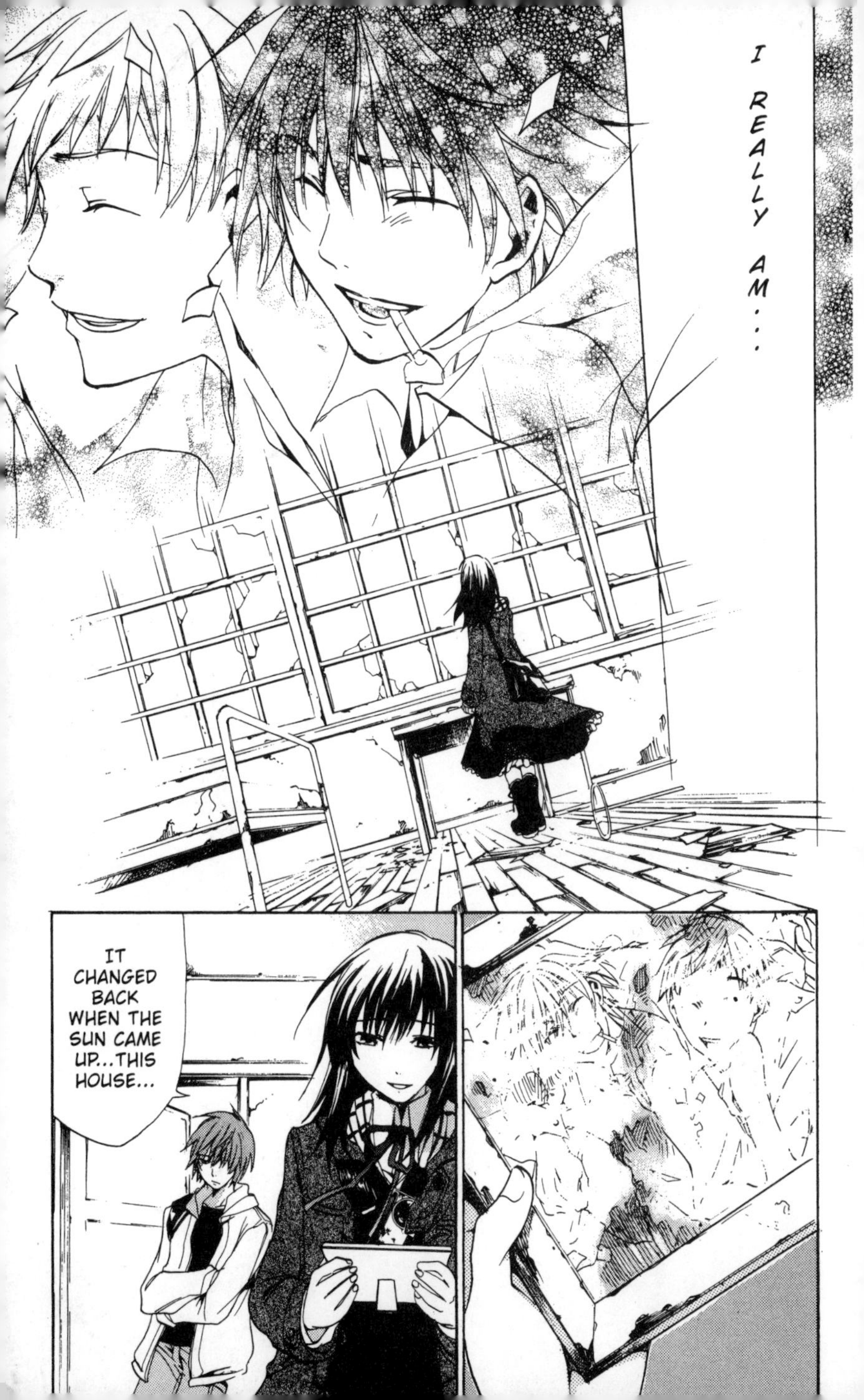
I REALLY AM...
IT CHANGED BACK WHEN THE SUN CAME UP...THIS HOUSE...

I'M SORRY ABOUT DRAGGING YOU ALONG YESTERDAY.

OH, DON'T BE.

I'M GOING TO VISIT HIS GRAVE. WILL YOU COME?

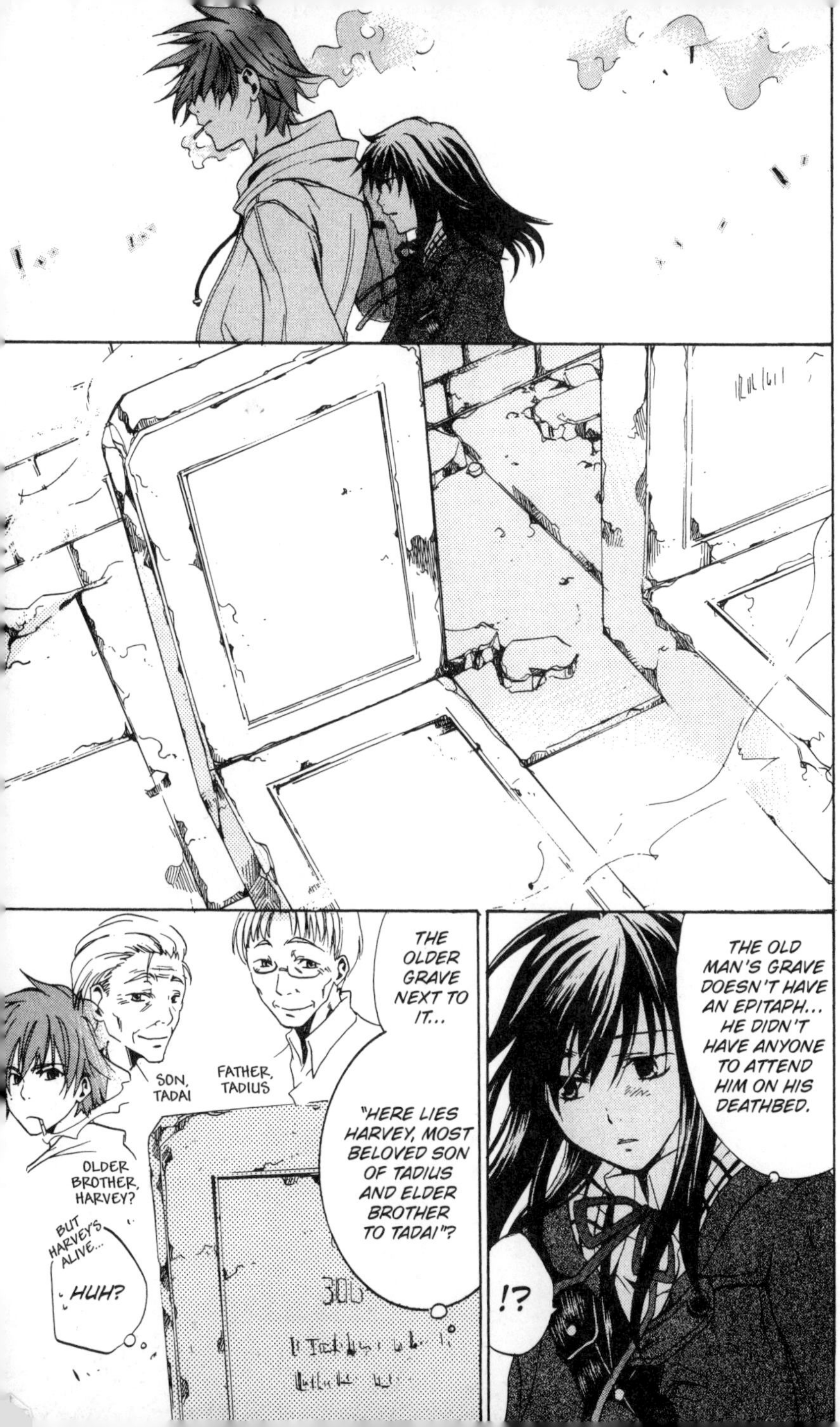
THE OLD MAN'S GRAVE DOESN'T HAVE AN EPITAPH... HE DIDN'T HAVE ANYONE TO ATTEND HIM ON HIS DEATHBED.
!?
THE OLDER GRAVE NEXT TO IT...
"HERE LIES HARVEY, MOST BELOVED SON OF TADIUS AND ELDER BROTHER TO TADAI"?
FATHER, TADIUS
SON, TADAI
OLDER BROTHER, HARVEY?
BUT HARVEY'S ALIVE...
HUH?

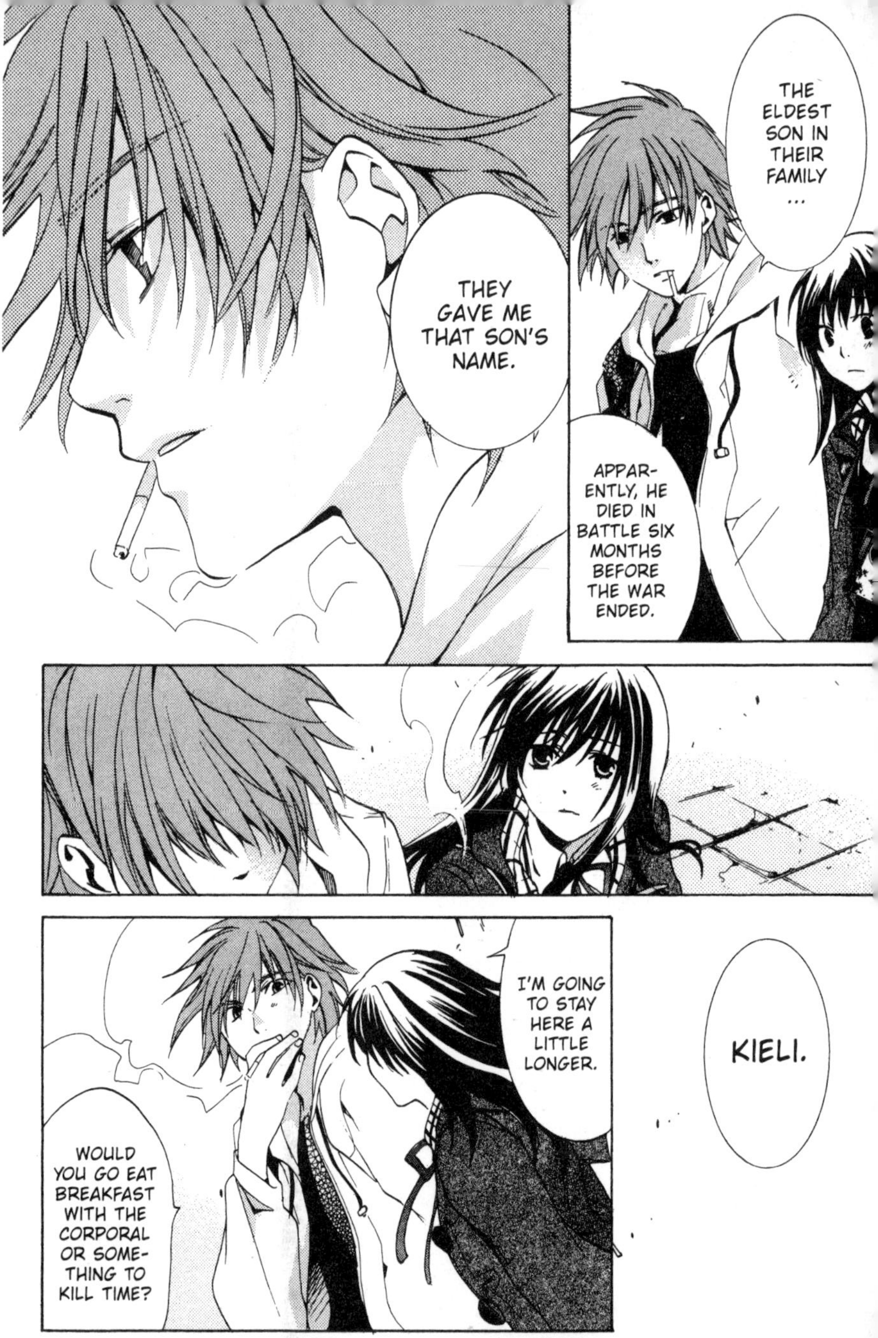
THE ELDEST SON IN THEIR FAMILY ...
APPAR-ENTLY, HE DIED IN BATTLE SIX MONTHS BEFORE THE WAR ENDED.
THEY GAVE ME THAT SON'S NAME.
KIELI.
I'M GOING TO STAY HERE A LITTLE LONGER.
WOULD YOU GO EAT BREAKFAST WITH THE CORPORAL OR SOME-THING TO KILL TIME?

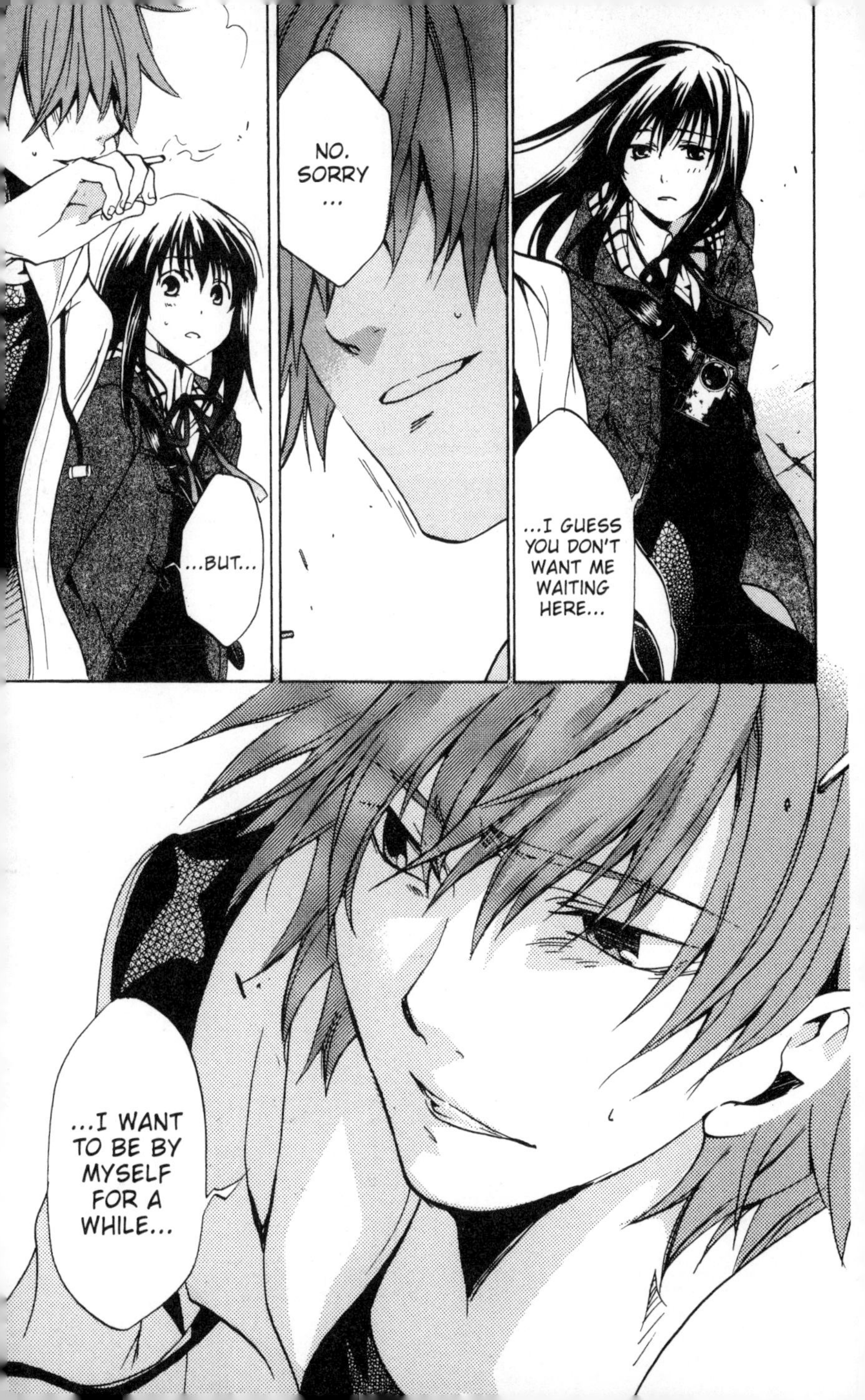
...I GUESS YOU DON'T WANT ME WAITING HERE...
NO. SORRY ...
...BUT...
...I WANT TO BE BY MYSELF FOR A WHILE...

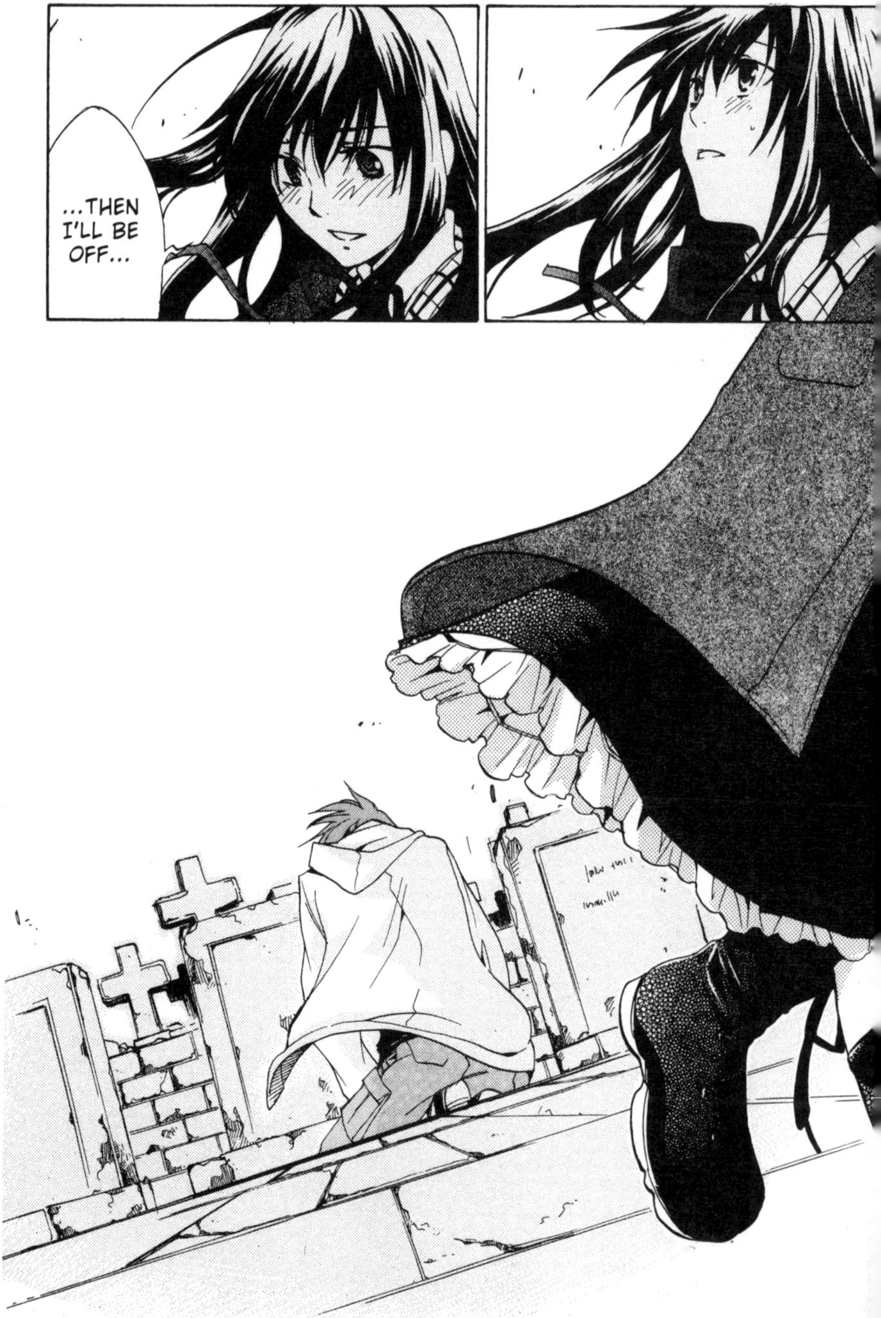
...THEN I'LL BE OFF...

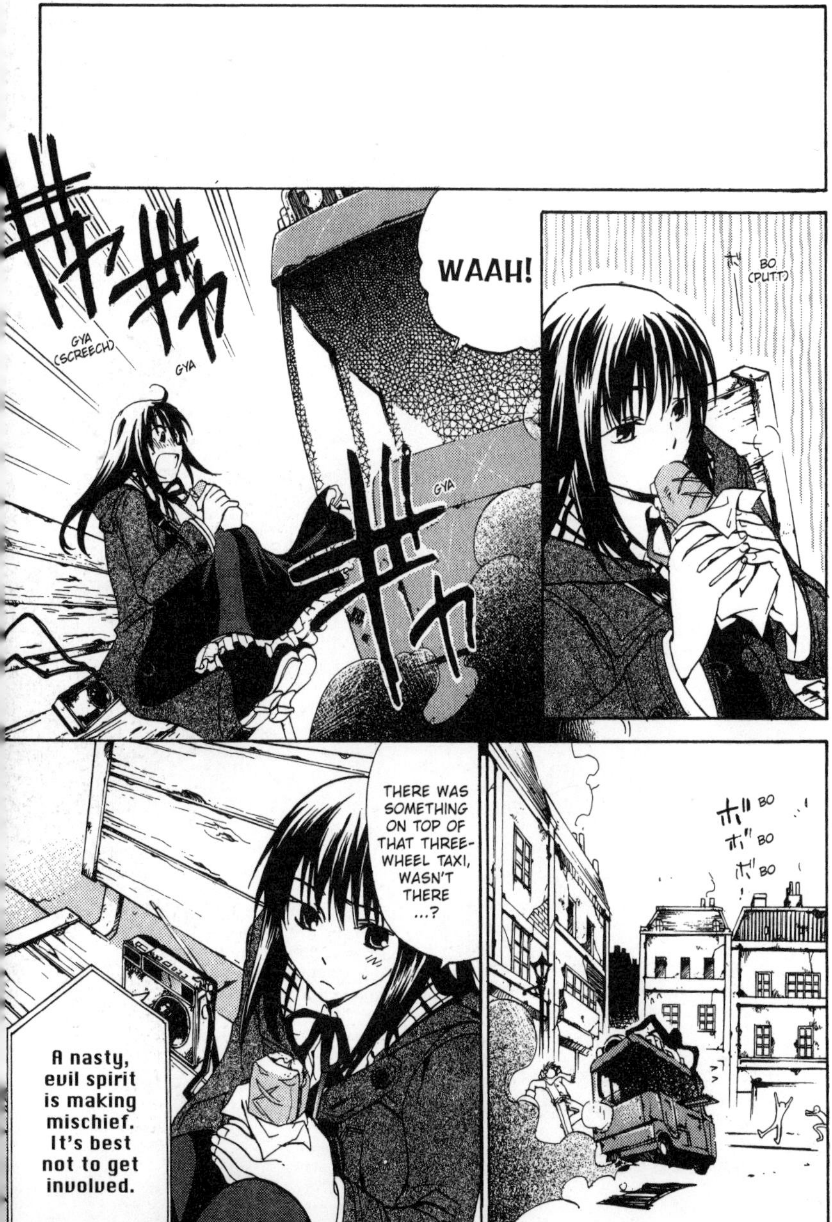
BO (PUTT)
WAAH!
GYA (SCREECH)
GYA
GYA
BO
BO
BO
THERE WAS SOMETHING ON TOP OF THAT THREE-WHEEL TAXI, WASN'T THERE ...?
A nasty, evil spirit is making mischief. It's best not to get involved.

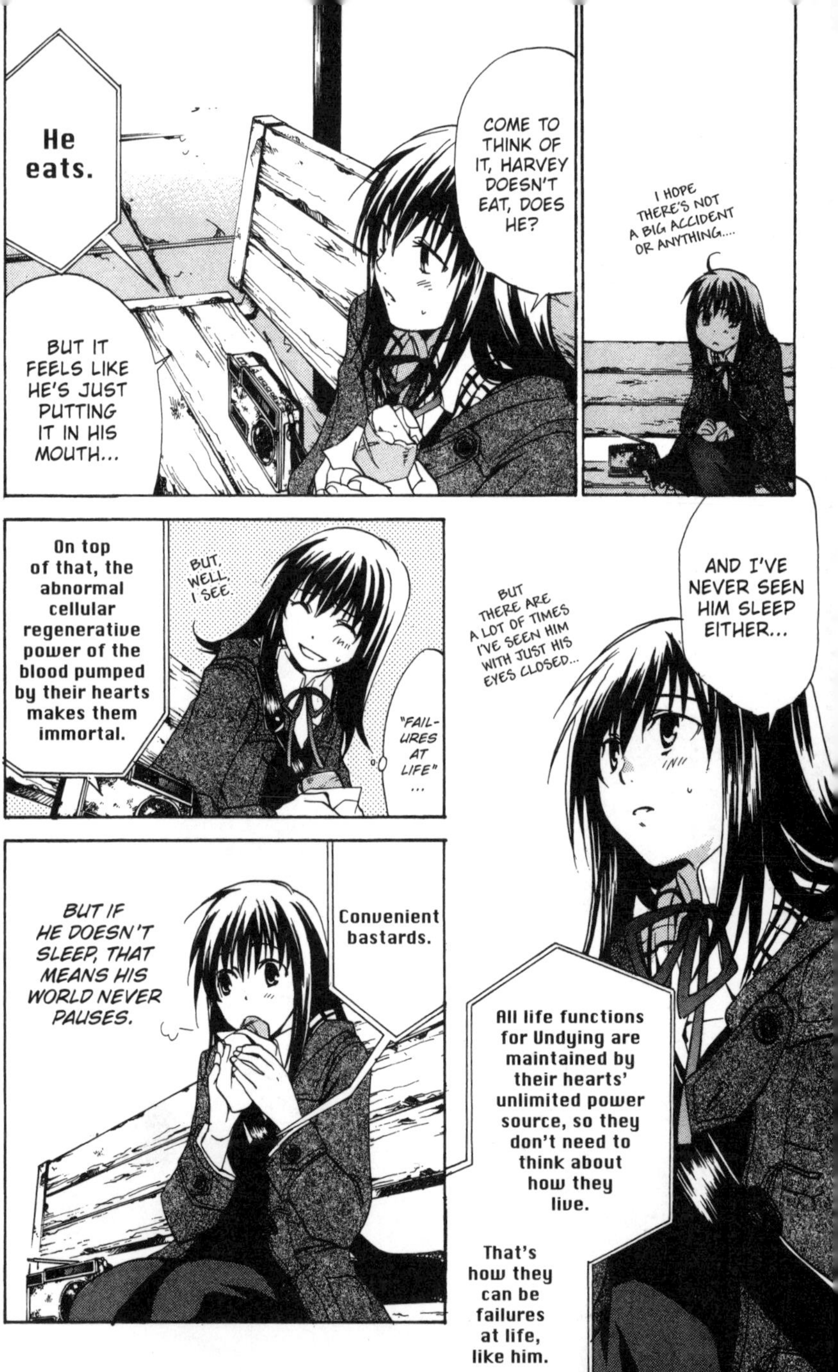

I HOPE THERE'S NOT A BIG ACCIDENT OR ANYTHING....
COME TO THINK OF IT, HARVEY DOESN'T EAT, DOES HE?
He eats.
BUT IT FEELS LIKE HE'S JUST PUTTING IT IN HIS MOUTH...
AND I'VE NEVER SEEN HIM SLEEP EITHER...
BUT THERE ARE A LOT OF TIMES I'VE SEEN HIM WITH JUST HIS EYES CLOSED...
"FAILURES AT LIFE" ...
BUT, WELL, I SEE.
On top of that, the abnormal cellular regenerative power of the blood pumped by their hearts makes them immortal.
BUT IF HE DOESN'T SLEEP, THAT MEANS HIS WORLD NEVER PAUSES.
Convenient bastards.
All life functions for Undying are maintained by their hearts' unlimited power source, so they don't need to think about how they live.
That's how they can be failures at life, like him.

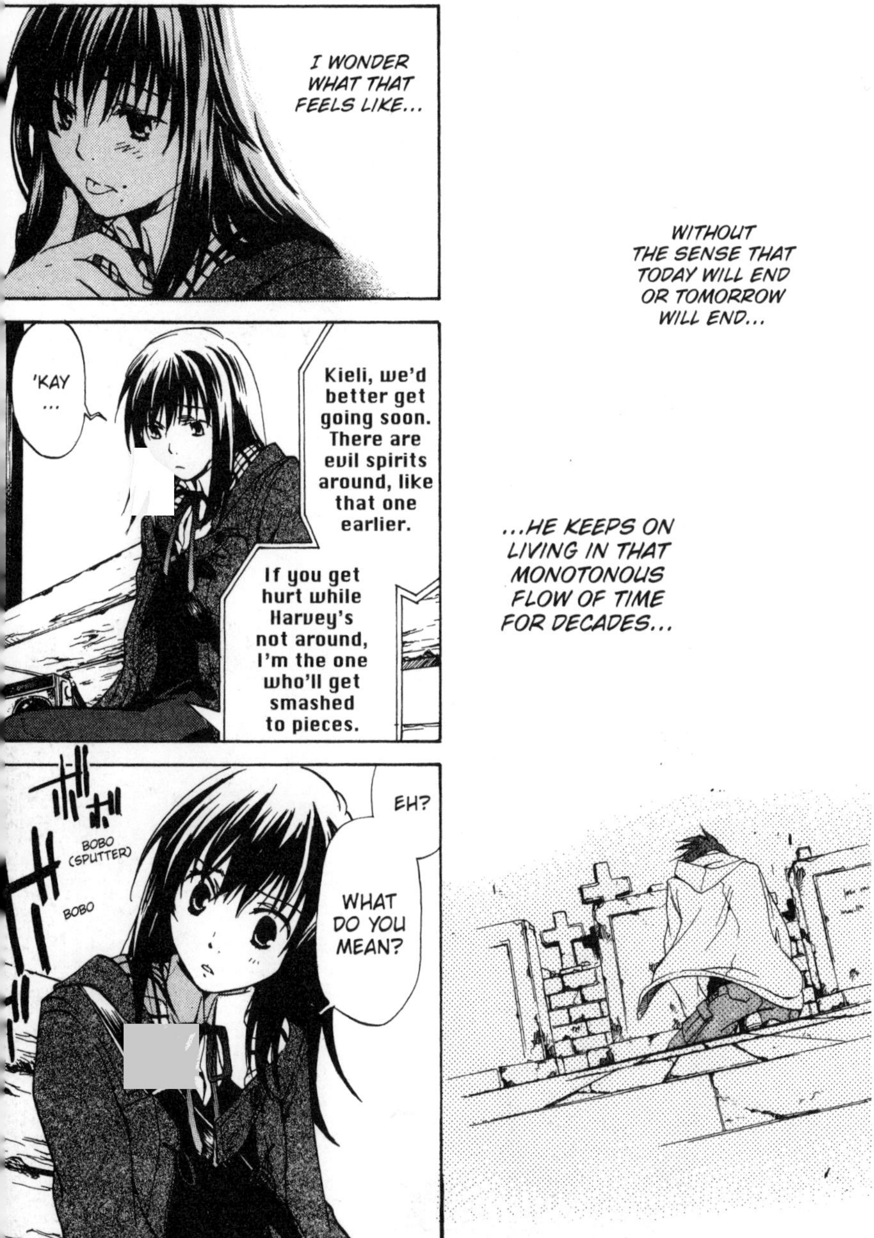
WITHOUT THE SENSE THAT TODAY WILL END OR TOMORROW WILL END...
...HE KEEPS ON LIVING IN THAT MONOTONOUS FLOW OF TIME FOR DECADES...
I WONDER WHAT THAT FEELS LIKE...
Kieli, we'd better get going soon. There are evil spirits around, like that one earlier.
If you get hurt while Harvey's not around, I'm the one who'll get smashed to pieces.
'KAY ...
EH?
WHAT DO YOU MEAN?
BOBO (SPUTTER)
BOBO

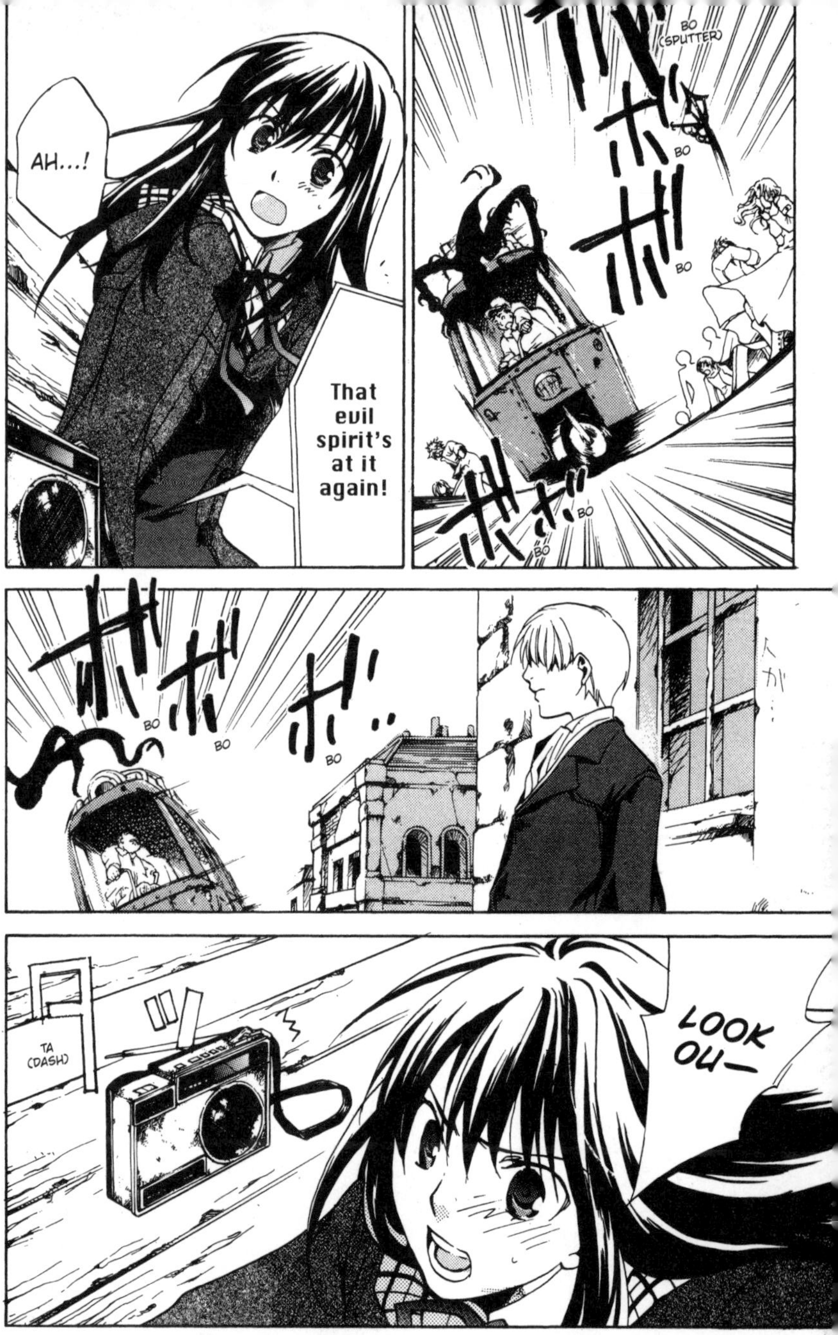
BO (SPUTTER)
BO
BO
BO
BO
AH...!
That evil spirit's at it again!
BO
BO
BO
LOOK OU—
TA (DASH)

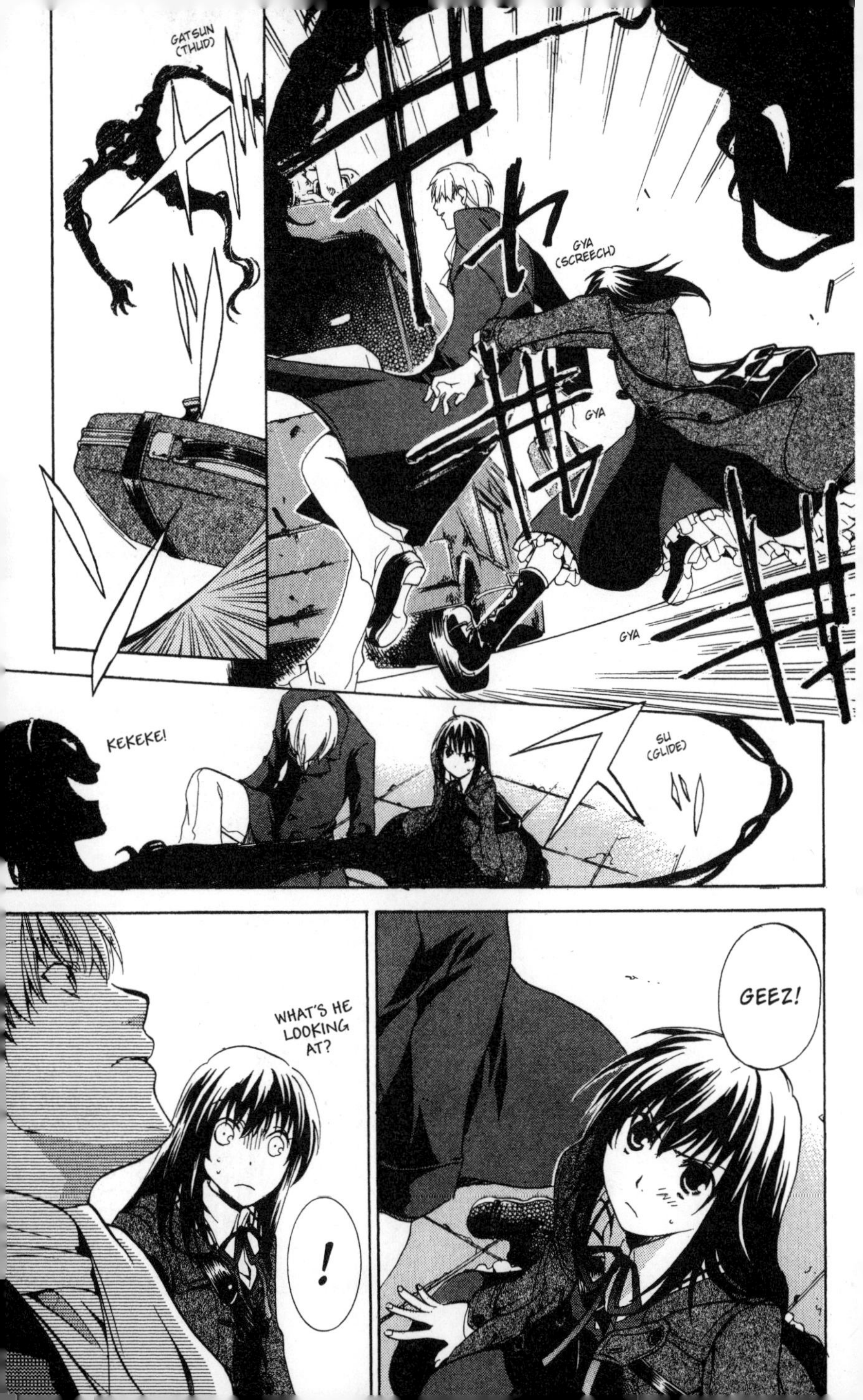
GYA (SCREECH)
GYA
GYA
GATSUN (THUD)
SU (GLIDE)
KEKEKE!
GEEZ!
WHAT'S HE LOOKING AT?
!

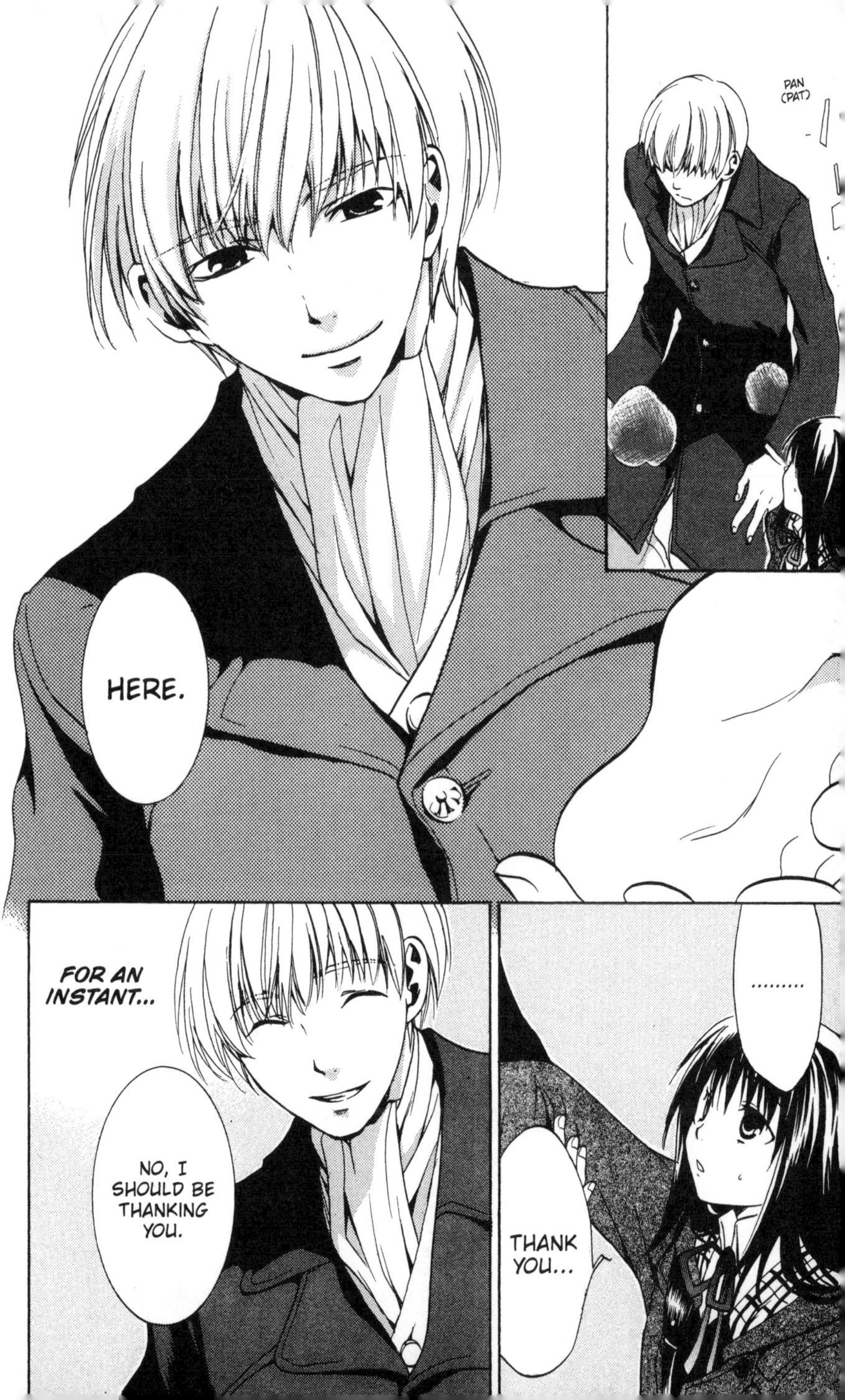
PAN
(PAT)
HERE.
....
THANK YOU...
FOR AN INSTANT...
NO, I SHOULD BE THANKING YOU.

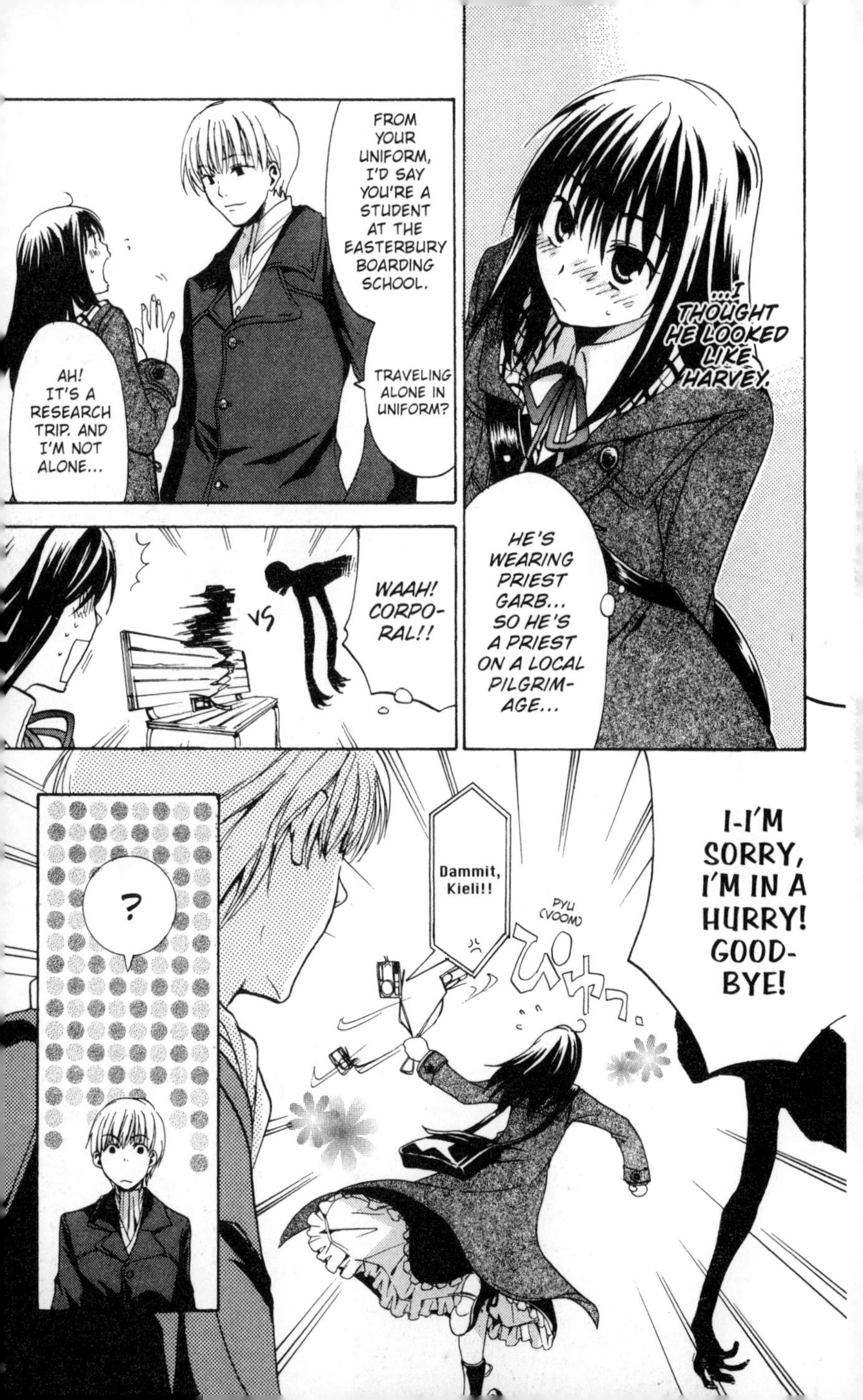

...I THOUGHT HE LOOKED LIKE HARVEY.
HE'S WEARING PRIEST GARB... SO HE'S A PRIEST ON A LOCAL PILGRIMAGE...
FROM YOUR UNIFORM, I'D SAY YOU'RE A STUDENT AT THE EASTERBURY BOARDING SCHOOL.
TRAVELING ALONE IN UNIFORM?
AH! IT'S A RESEARCH TRIP. AND I'M NOT ALONE...
WAAH! CORPORAL!!
VS
I-I'M SORRY, I'M IN A HURRY! GOOD-BYE!
PYU (VOOM)
Dammit, Kieli!!
?

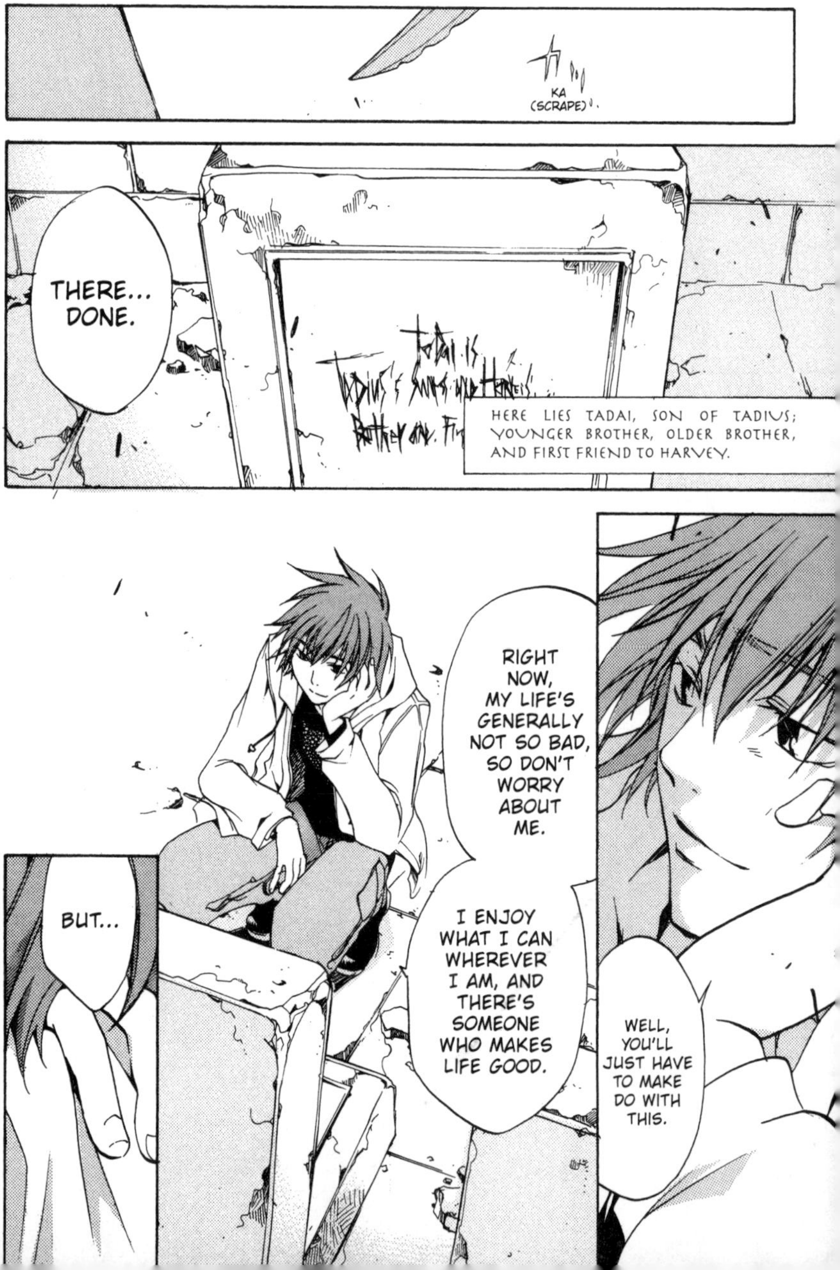
KA
(SCRAPE)
THERE... DONE.
HERE LIES TADAI, SON OF TADIUS; YOUNGER BROTHER, OLDER BROTHER, AND FIRST FRIEND TO HARVEY.
WELL, YOU'LL JUST HAVE TO MAKE DO WITH THIS.
RIGHT NOW, MY LIFE'S GENERALLY NOT SO BAD, SO DON'T WORRY ABOUT ME.
I ENJOY WHAT I CAN WHEREVER I AM, AND THERE'S SOMEONE WHO MAKES LIFE GOOD.
BUT...

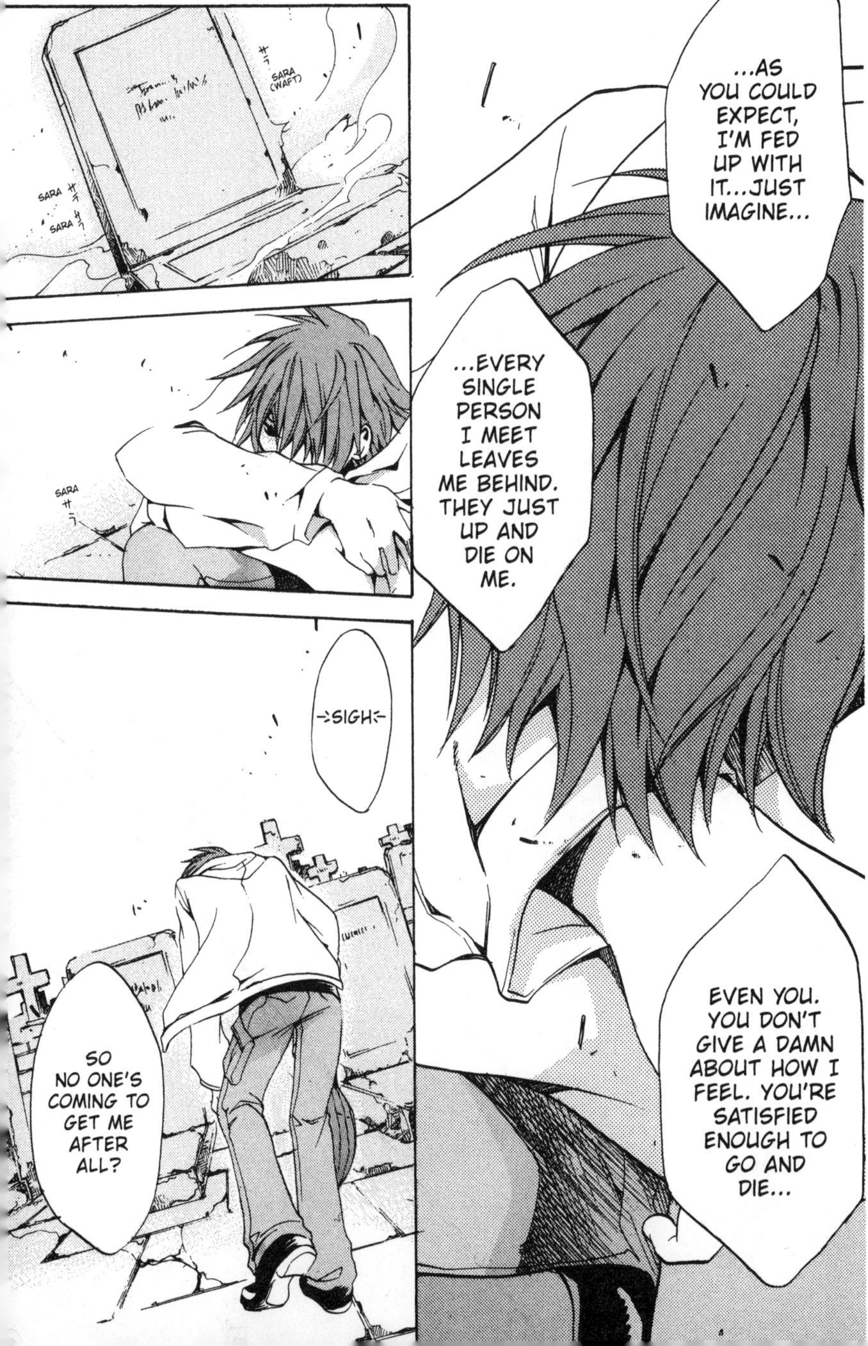
...AS YOU COULD EXPECT, I'M FED UP WITH IT...JUST IMAGINE...
...EVERY SINGLE PERSON I MEET LEAVES ME BEHIND. THEY JUST UP AND DIE ON ME.
EVEN YOU. YOU DON'T GIVE A DAMN ABOUT HOW I FEEL. YOU'RE SATISFIED ENOUGH TO GO AND DIE...
SARA (WAFT)
SARA
SARA
SARA
-SIGH-
SO NO ONE'S COMING TO GET ME AFTER ALL?

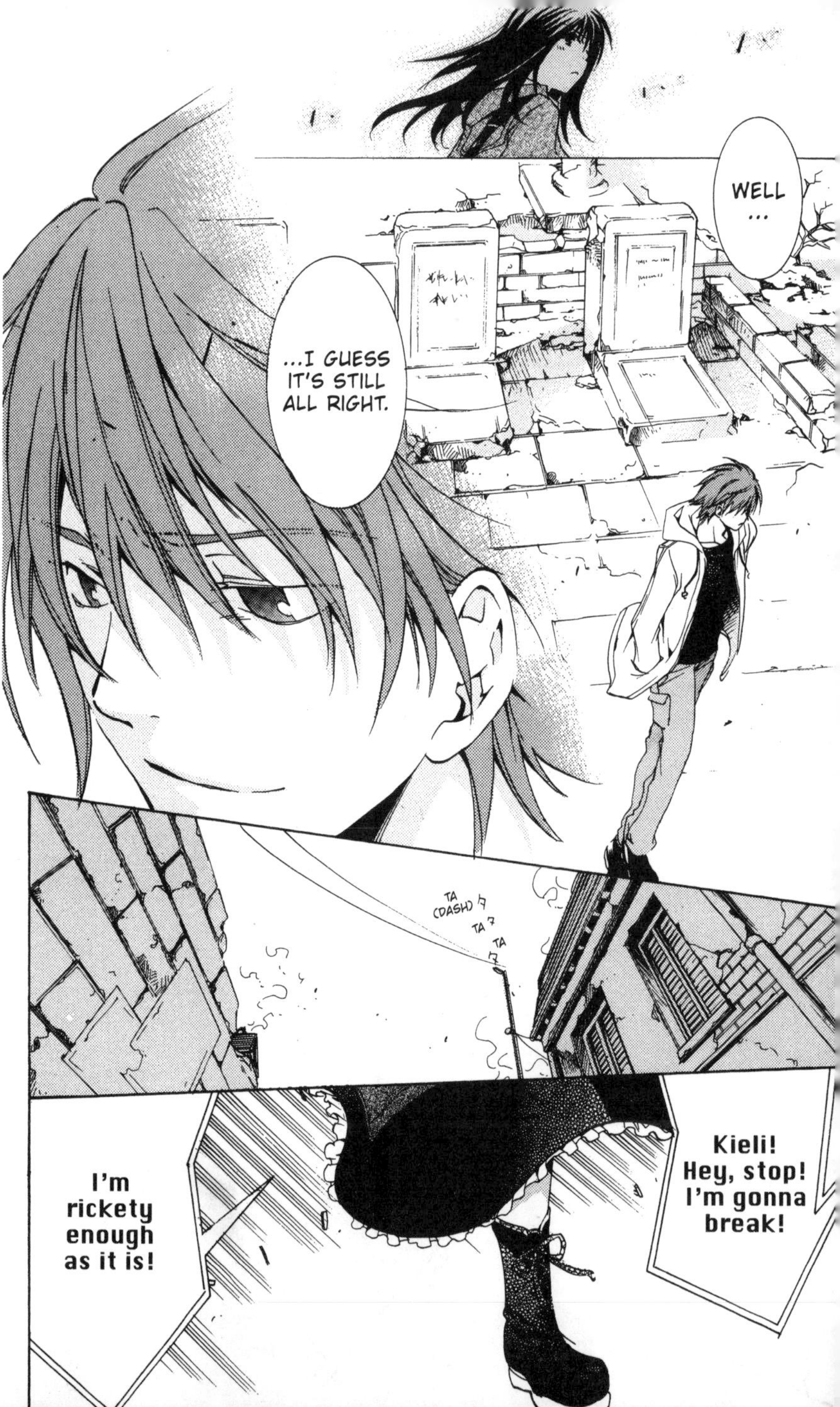
WELL...
...I GUESS IT'S STILL ALL RIGHT.
TA (DASH) タ
TA タ
TA タ
Kieli! Hey, stop! I'm gonna break!
I'm rickety enough as it is!

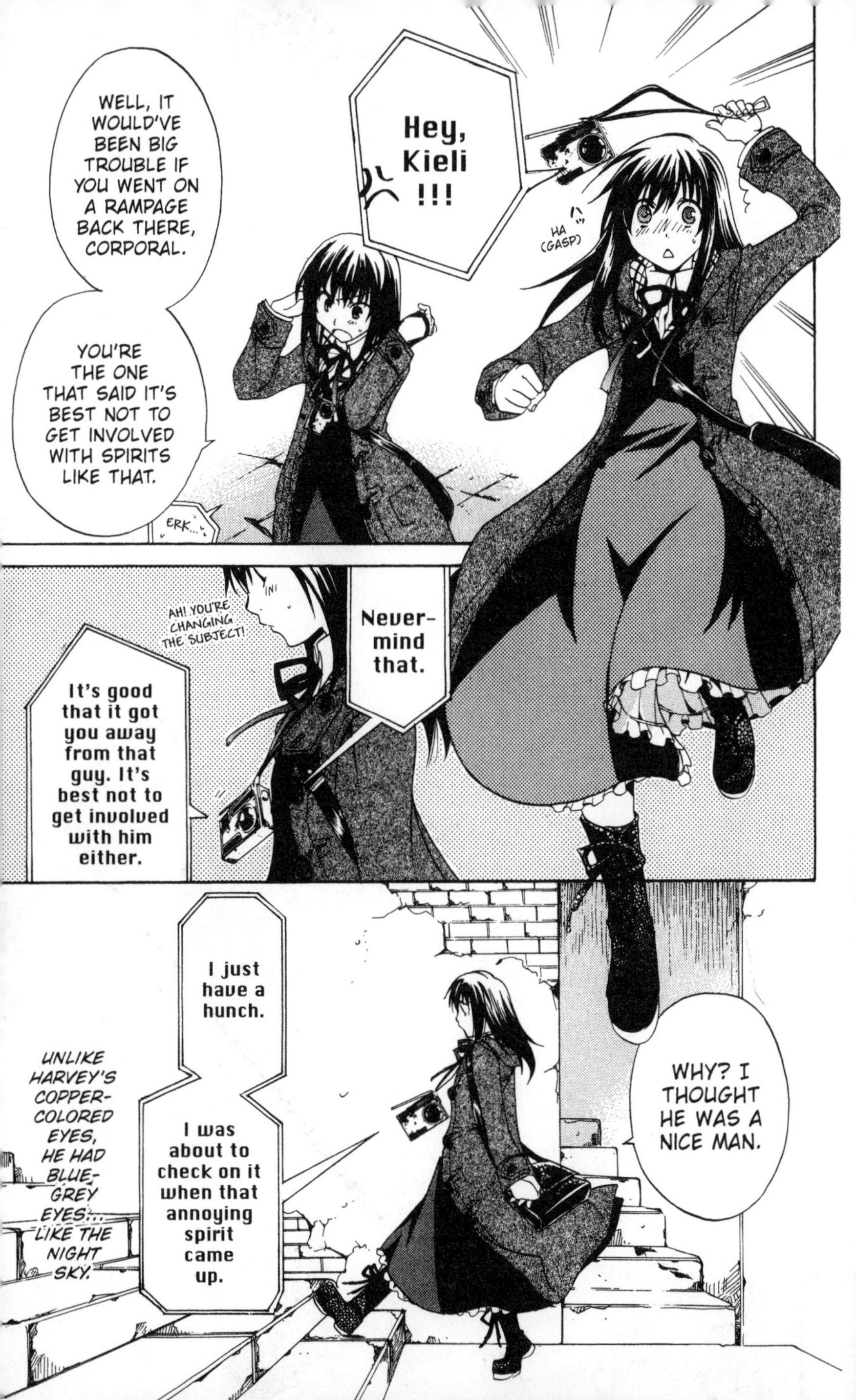
Hey, Kieli !!!
HA (GASP)
WELL, IT WOULD'VE BEEN BIG TROUBLE IF YOU WENT ON A RAMPAGE BACK THERE, CORPORAL.
YOU'RE THE ONE THAT SAID IT'S BEST NOT TO GET INVOLVED WITH SPIRITS LIKE THAT.
ERK...
Never-mind that.
AH! YOU'RE CHANGING THE SUBJECT!
It's good that it got you away from that guy. It's best not to get involved with him either.
WHY? I THOUGHT HE WAS A NICE MAN.
I just have a hunch.
I was about to check on it when that annoying spirit came up.
UNLIKE HARVEY'S COPPER-COLORED EYES, HE HAD BLUE-GREY EYES... LIKE THE NIGHT SKY.

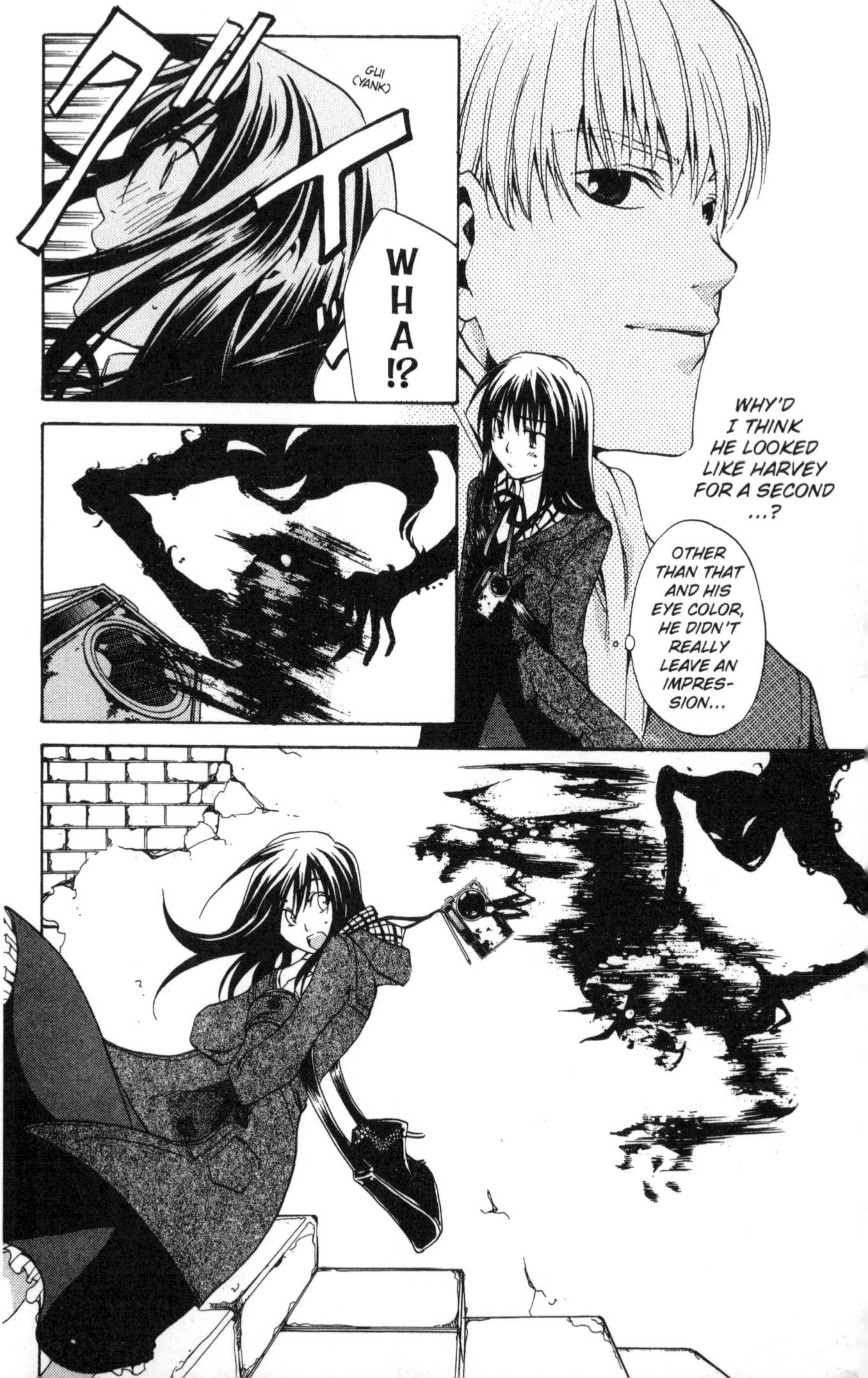
WHY'D I THINK HE LOOKED LIKE HARVEY FOR A SECOND ...?
OTHER THAN THAT AND HIS EYE COLOR, HE DIDN'T REALLY LEAVE AN IMPRES- SION...
GUI (YANK)
WHA!?

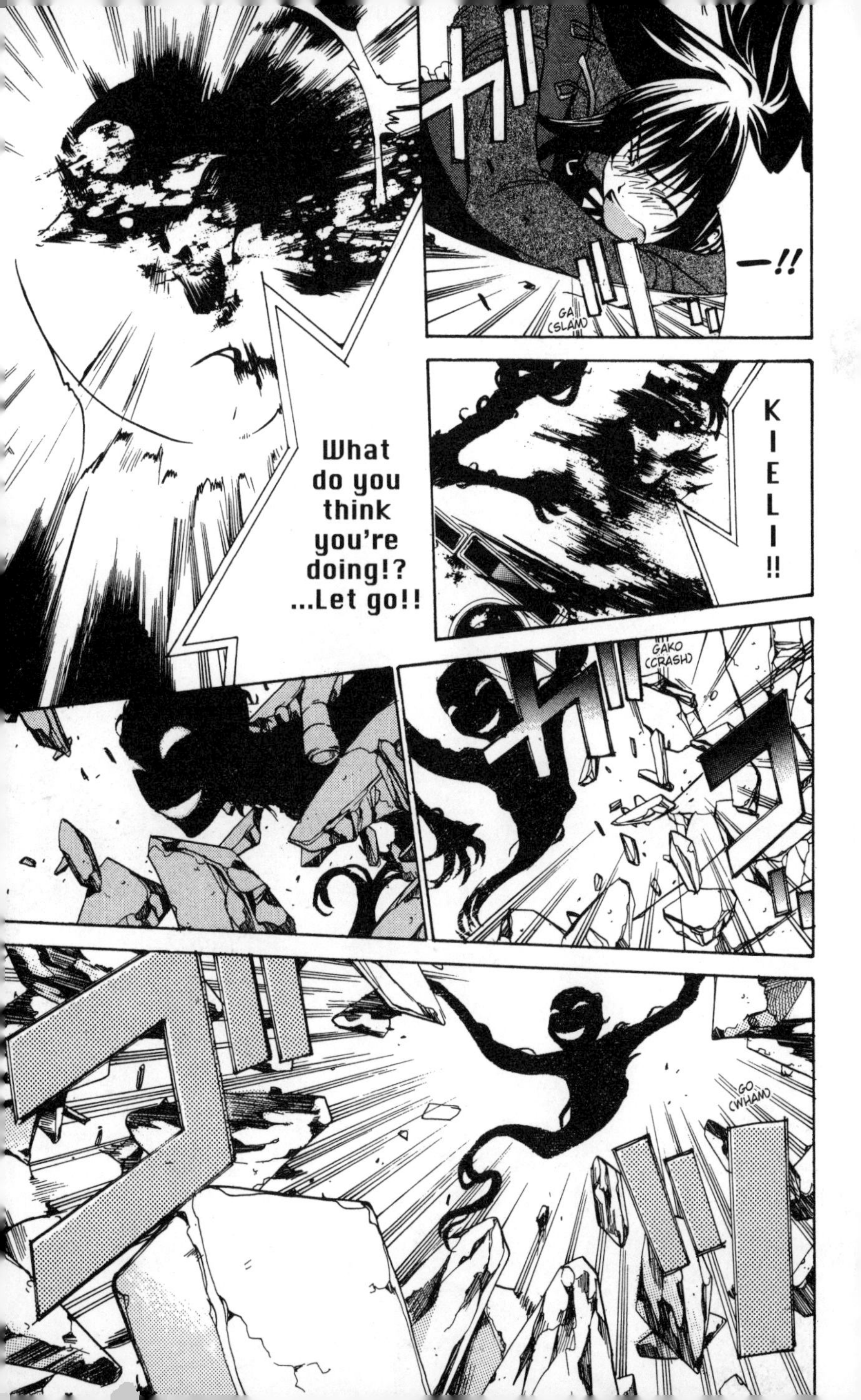
—!!
GA (SLAM)
KIELI!!
What do you think you're doing!? ...Let go!!
GAKO (CRASH)
GO (WHAM)

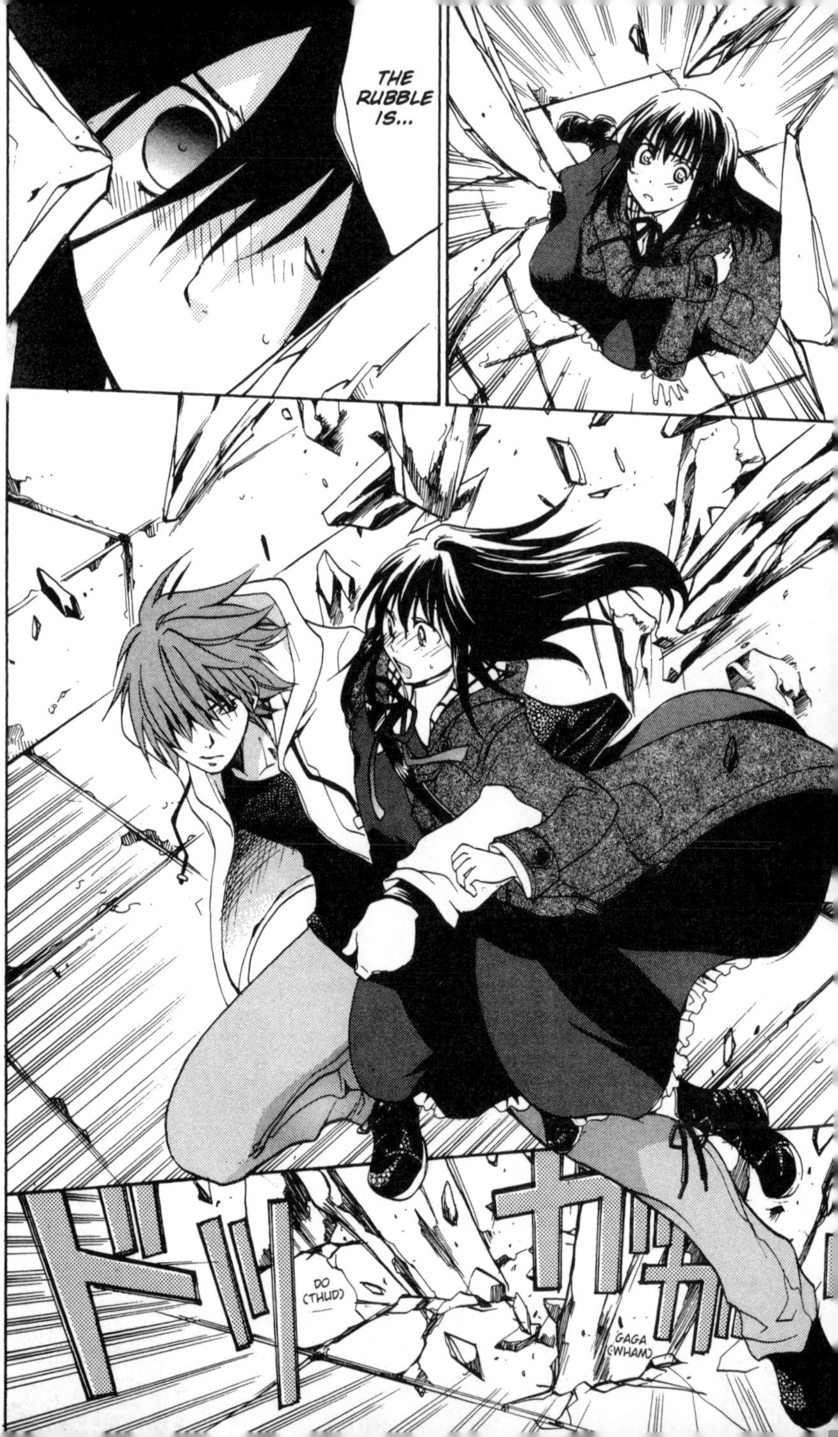
THE RUBBLE IS...
GAGA (WHAM)
DO (THUD)

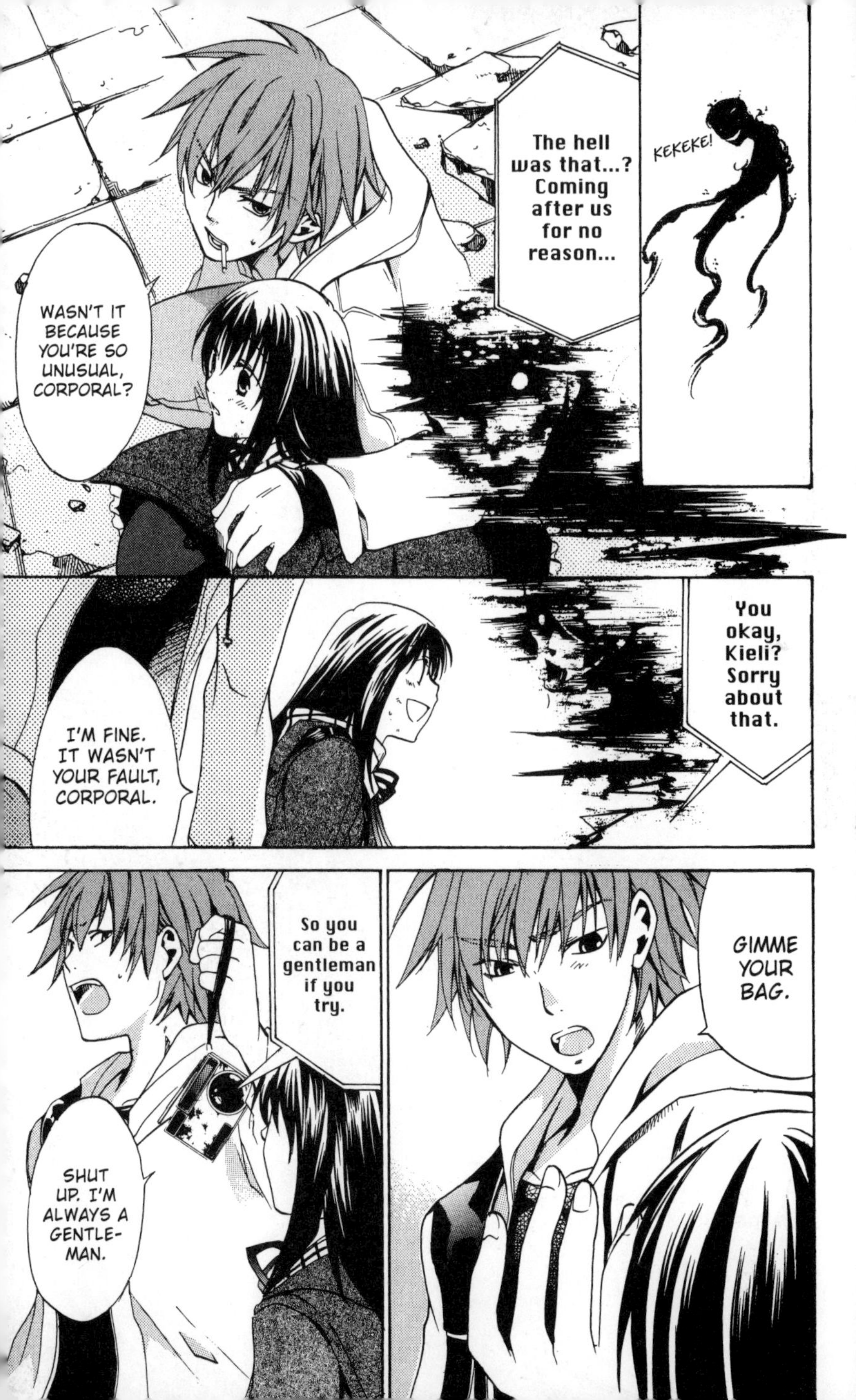
KEKEKE!
The hell was that...? Coming after us for no reason...
WASN'T IT BECAUSE YOU'RE SO UNUSUAL, CORPORAL?
You okay, Kieli? Sorry about that.
I'M FINE. IT WASN'T YOUR FAULT, CORPORAL.
GIMME YOUR BAG.
So you can be a gentleman if you try.
SHUT UP. I'M ALWAYS A GENTLE-MAN.

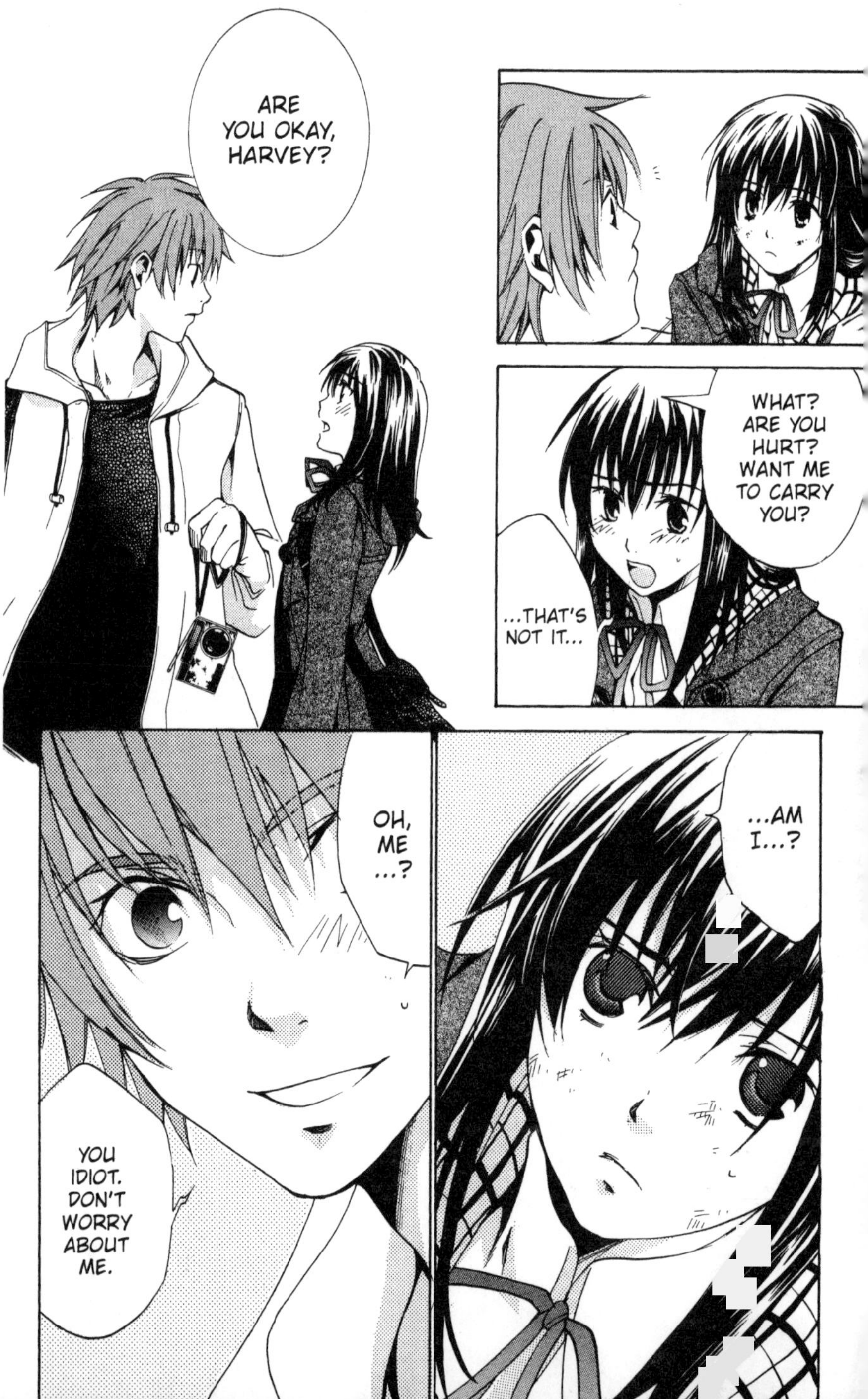
WHAT? ARE YOU HURT? WANT ME TO CARRY YOU?
...THAT'S NOT IT...
ARE YOU OKAY, HARVEY?
...AM I...?
OH, ME ...?
YOU IDIOT. DON'T WORRY ABOUT ME.

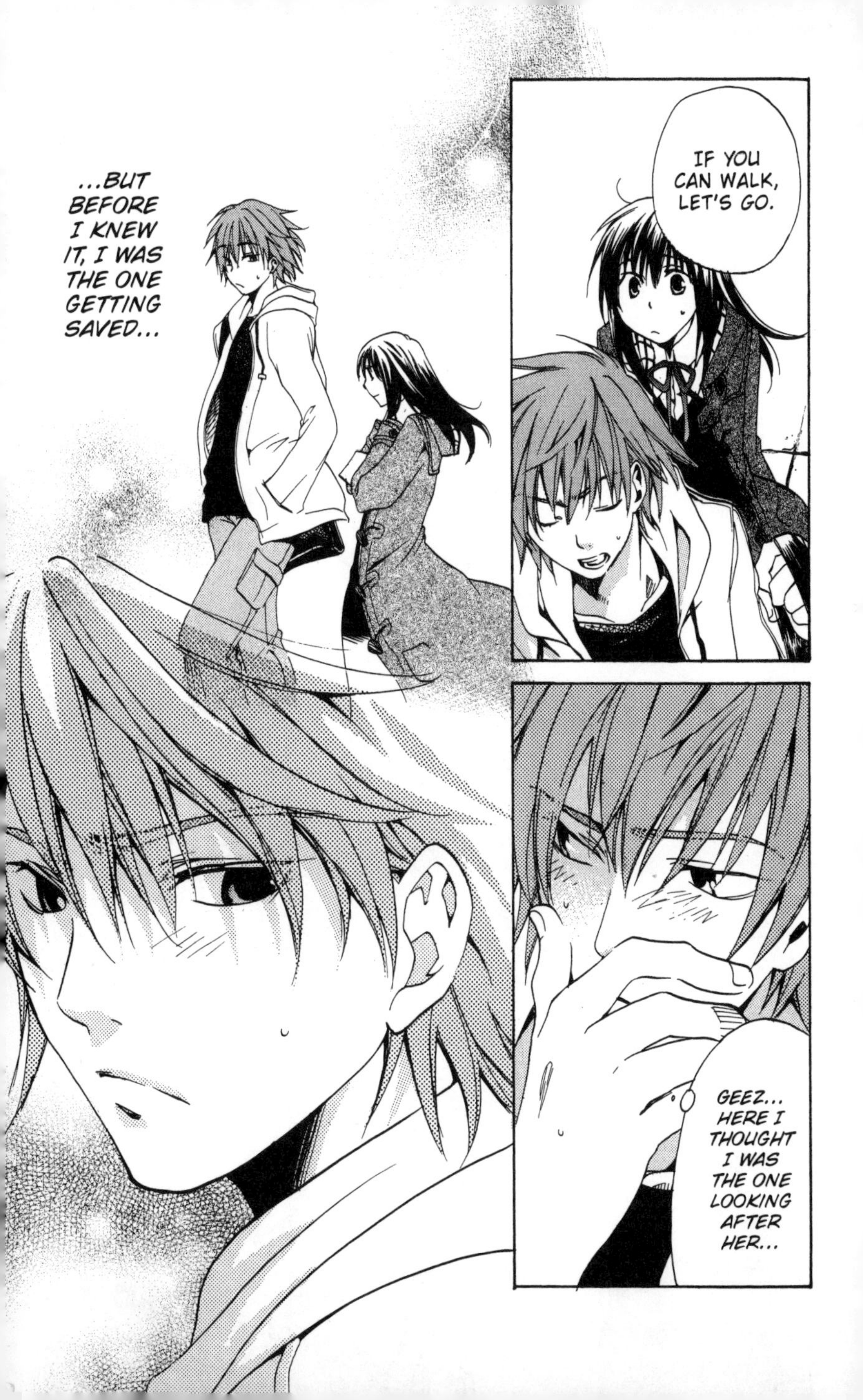
IF YOU CAN WALK, LET'S GO.
GEEZ... HERE I THOUGHT I WAS THE ONE LOOKING AFTER HER...
...BUT BEFORE I KNEW IT, I WAS THE ONE GETTING SAVED...

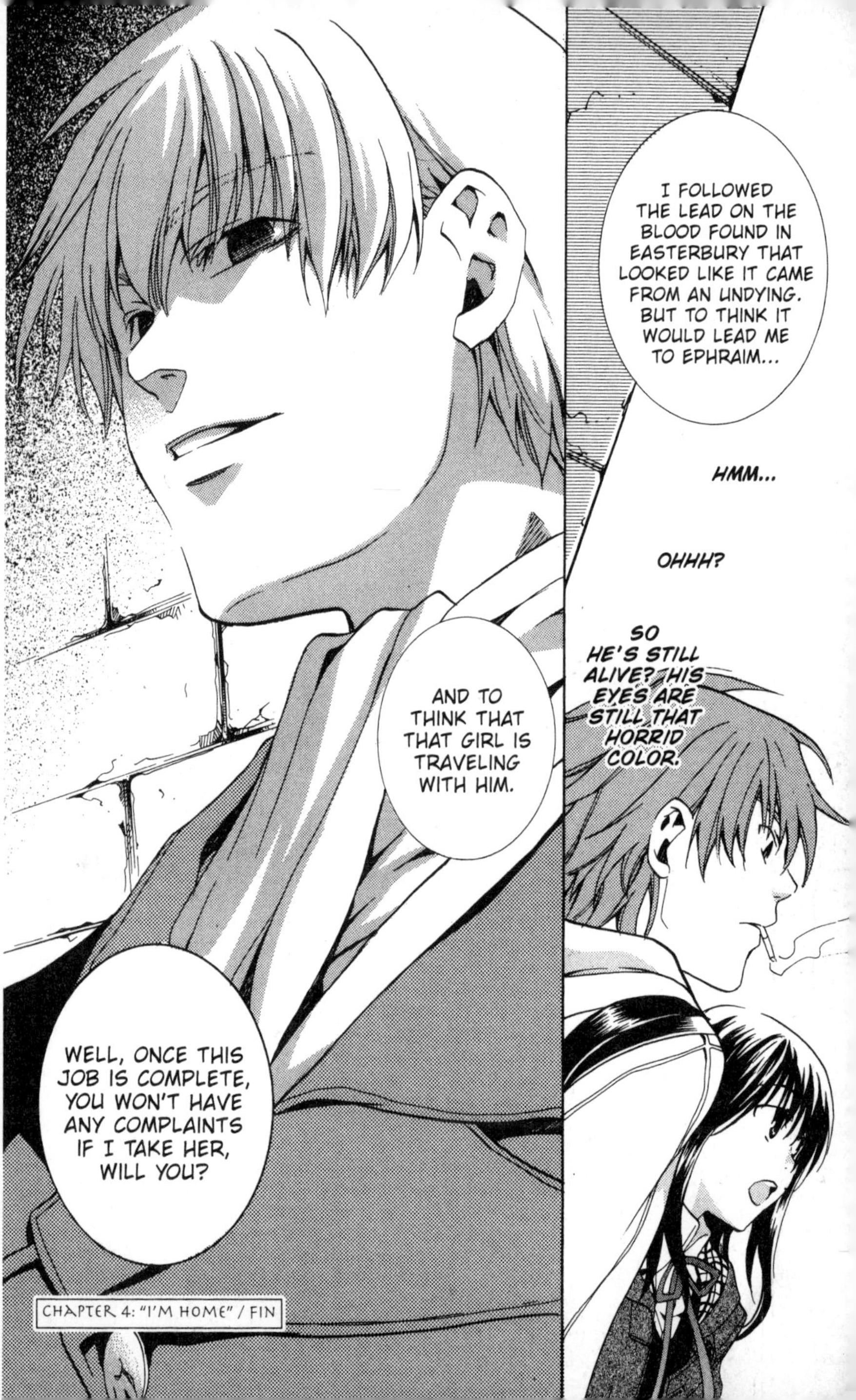
I FOLLOWED THE LEAD ON THE BLOOD FOUND IN EASTERBURY THAT LOOKED LIKE IT CAME FROM AN UNDYING. BUT TO THINK IT WOULD LEAD ME TO EPHRAIM...
HMM...
OHHH?
SO HE'S STILL ALIVE? HIS EYES ARE STILL THAT HORRID COLOR.
AND TO THINK THAT THAT GIRL IS TRAVELING WITH HIM.
WELL, ONCE THIS JOB IS COMPLETE, YOU WON'T HAVE ANY COMPLAINTS IF I TAKE HER, WILL YOU?
CHAPTER 4: "I'M HOME" / FIN

CHAPTER 5

THE DEAD SLEEP IN THE WILDERNESS

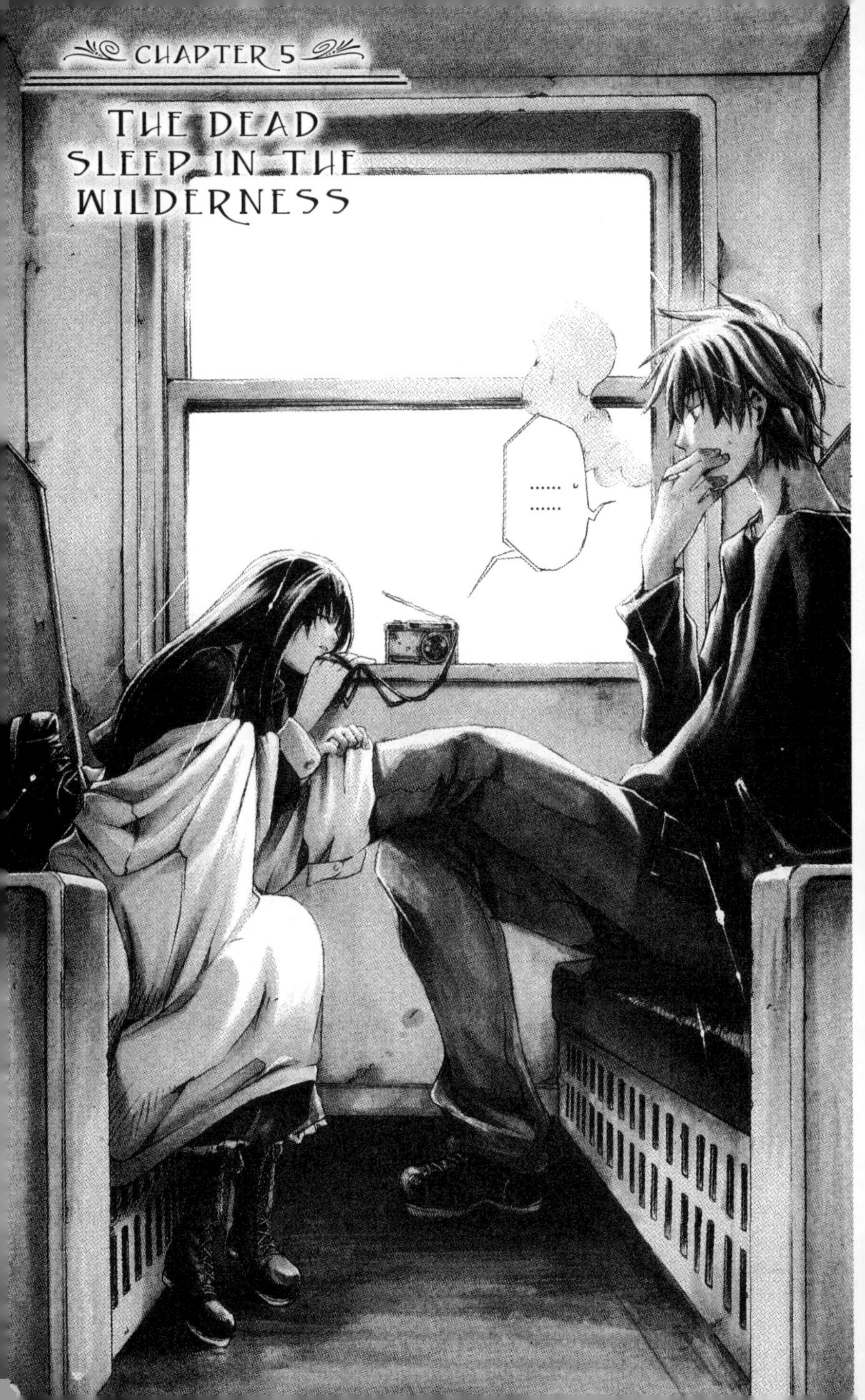
......
......

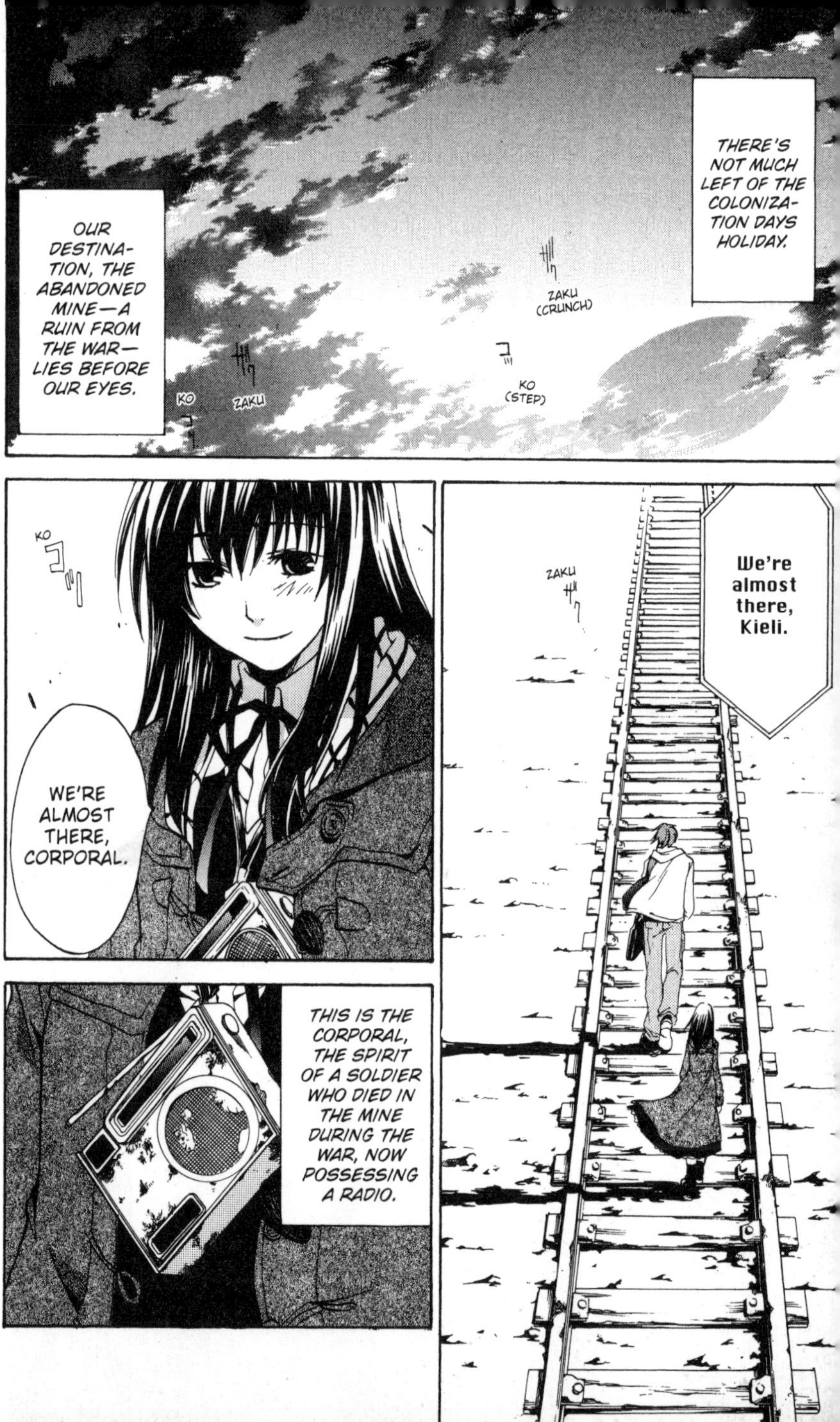
THERE'S NOT MUCH LEFT OF THE COLONIZATION DAYS HOLIDAY.
ZAKU (CRUNCH)
KO (STEP)
ZAKU
KO
OUR DESTINATION, THE ABANDONED MINE—A RUIN FROM THE WAR—LIES BEFORE OUR EYES.
We're almost there, Kieli.
ZAKU
KO
WE'RE ALMOST THERE, CORPORAL.
THIS IS THE CORPORAL, THE SPIRIT OF A SOLDIER WHO DIED IN THE MINE DURING THE WAR, NOW POSSESSING A RADIO.

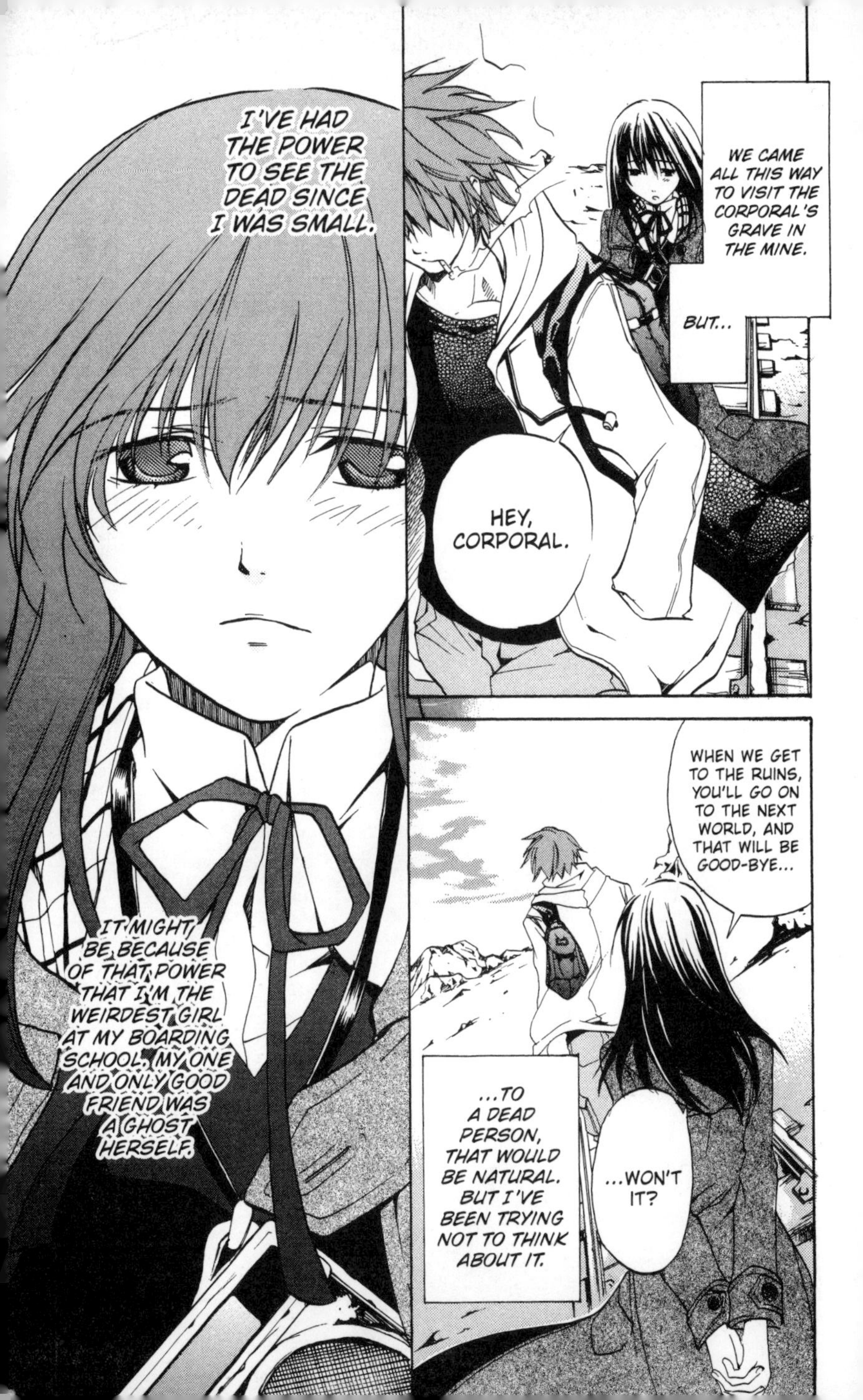
WE CAME ALL THIS WAY TO VISIT THE CORPORAL'S GRAVE IN THE MINE.
BUT...
HEY, CORPORAL.
WHEN WE GET TO THE RUINS, YOU'LL GO ON TO THE NEXT WORLD, AND THAT WILL BE GOOD-BYE...
...WON'T IT?
...TO A DEAD PERSON, THAT WOULD BE NATURAL. BUT I'VE BEEN TRYING NOT TO THINK ABOUT IT.
I'VE HAD THE POWER TO SEE THE DEAD SINCE I WAS SMALL.
IT MIGHT BE BECAUSE OF THAT POWER THAT I'M THE WEIRDEST GIRL AT MY BOARDING SCHOOL. MY ONE AND ONLY GOOD FRIEND WAS A GHOST HERSELF.

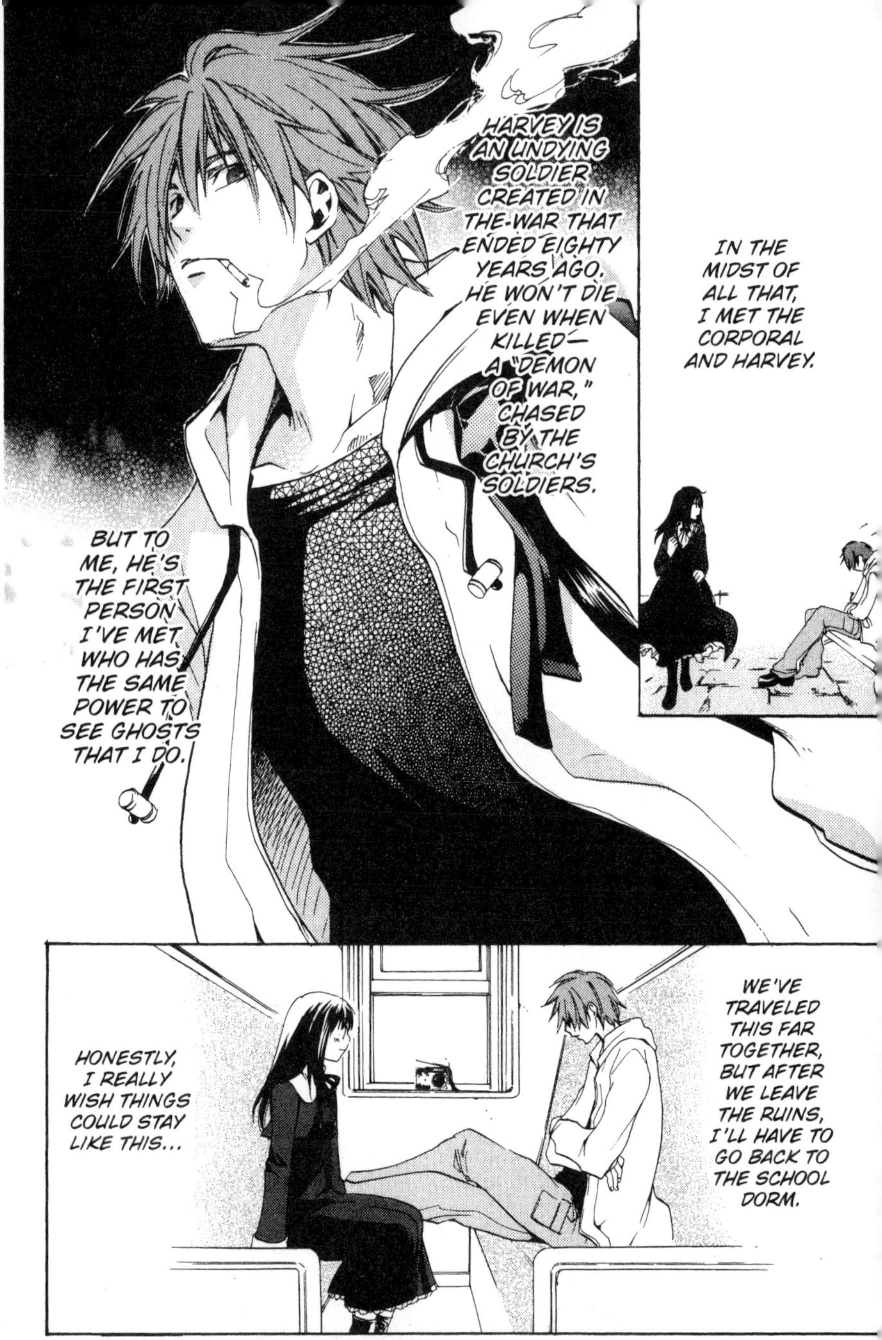
IN THE MIDST OF ALL THAT, I MET THE CORPORAL AND HARVEY.
HARVEY IS AN UNDYING SOLDIER CREATED IN THE WAR THAT ENDED EIGHTY YEARS AGO. HE WON'T DIE EVEN WHEN KILLED— A "DEMON OF WAR," CHASED BY THE CHURCH'S SOLDIERS.
BUT TO ME, HE'S THE FIRST PERSON I'VE MET WHO HAS THE SAME POWER TO SEE GHOSTS THAT I DO.
WE'VE TRAVELED THIS FAR TOGETHER, BUT AFTER WE LEAVE THE RUINS, I'LL HAVE TO GO BACK TO THE SCHOOL DORM.
HONESTLY, I REALLY WISH THINGS COULD STAY LIKE THIS...

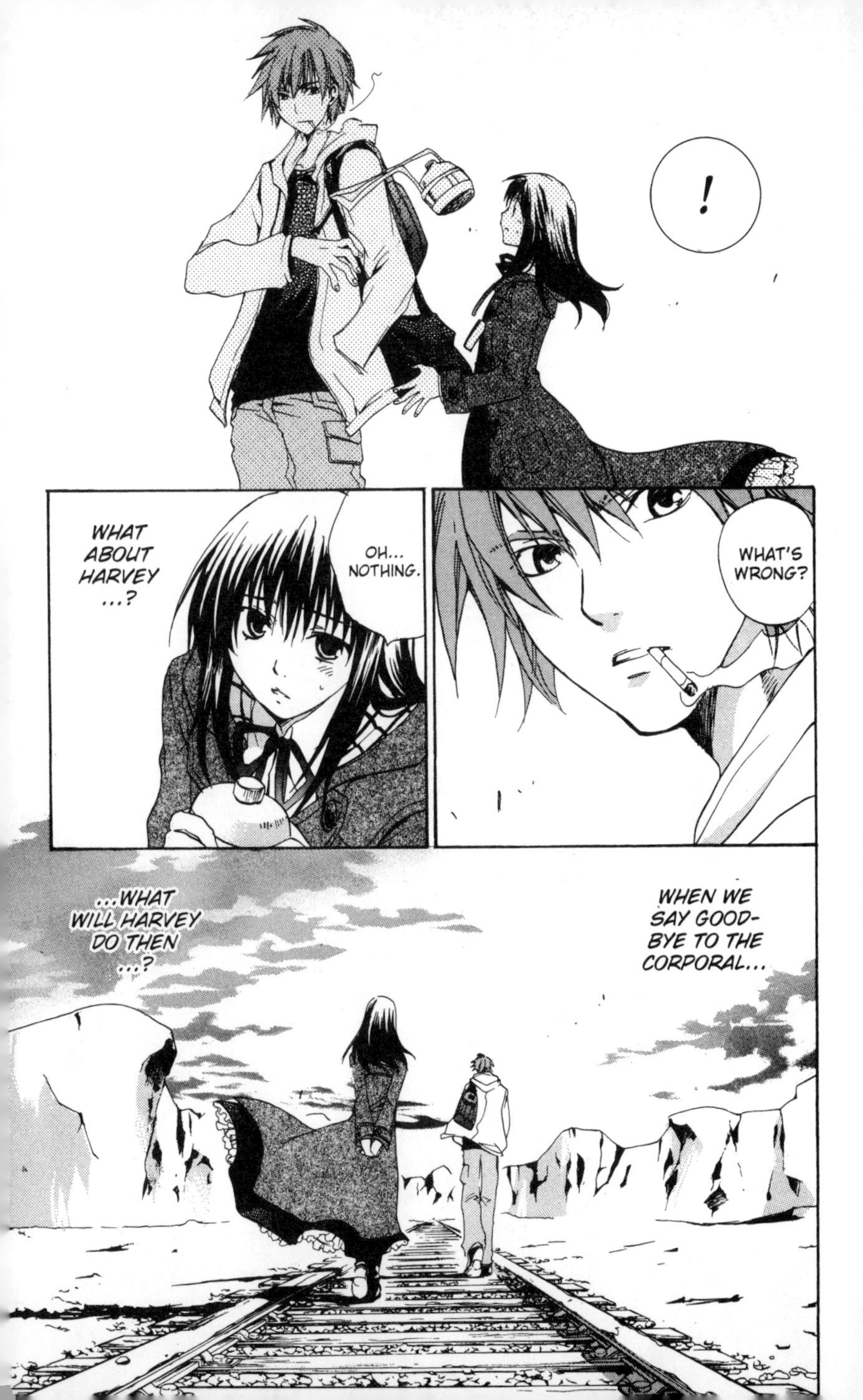
!
WHAT'S WRONG?
OH... NOTHING.
WHAT ABOUT HARVEY ...?
WHEN WE SAY GOOD-BYE TO THE CORPORAL...
...WHAT WILL HARVEY DO THEN ...?

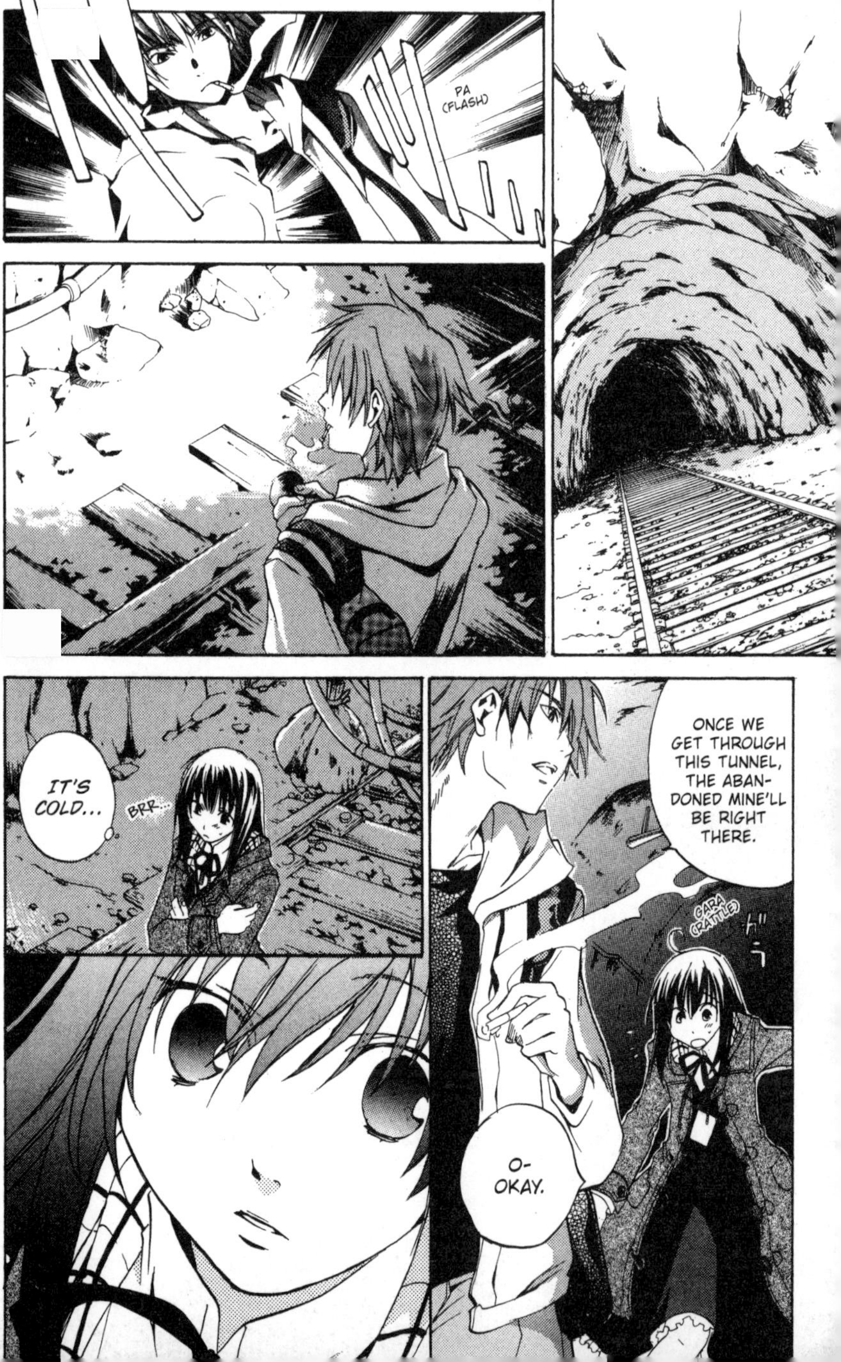
PA
(FLASH)
ONCE WE GET THROUGH THIS TUNNEL, THE ABAN-DONED MINE'LL BE RIGHT THERE.
CARA (RATTLE)
O-OKAY.
IT'S COLD...
BRR...

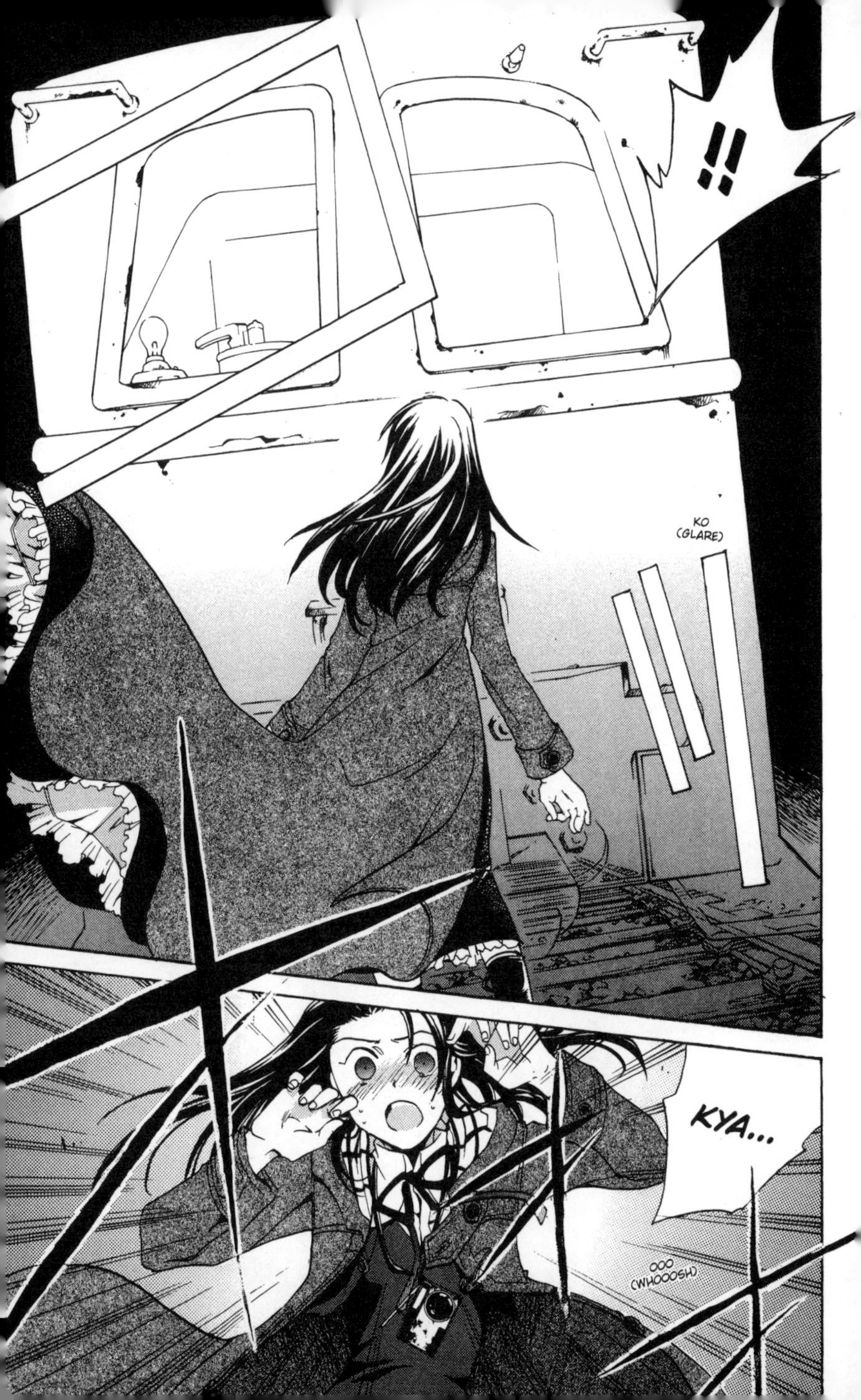
!!
KO (GLARE)
KYA...
OOO (WHOOOSH)

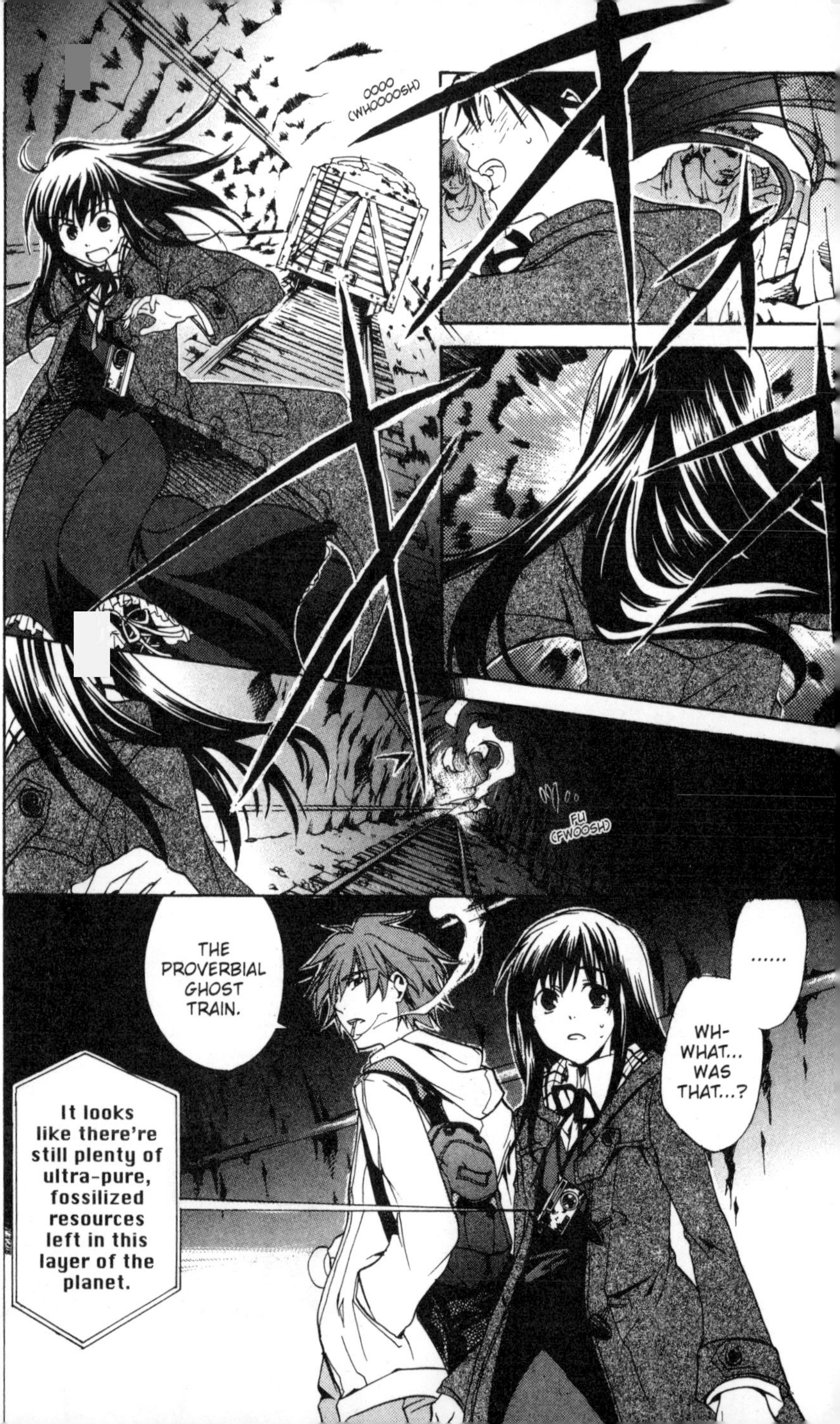
OOOO
(WHOOOOSH)
FU
(FWOOSH)
......
WH-
WHAT...
WAS
THAT...?
THE
PROVERBIAL
GHOST
TRAIN.
It looks like there're still plenty of ultra-pure, fossilized resources left in this layer of the planet.

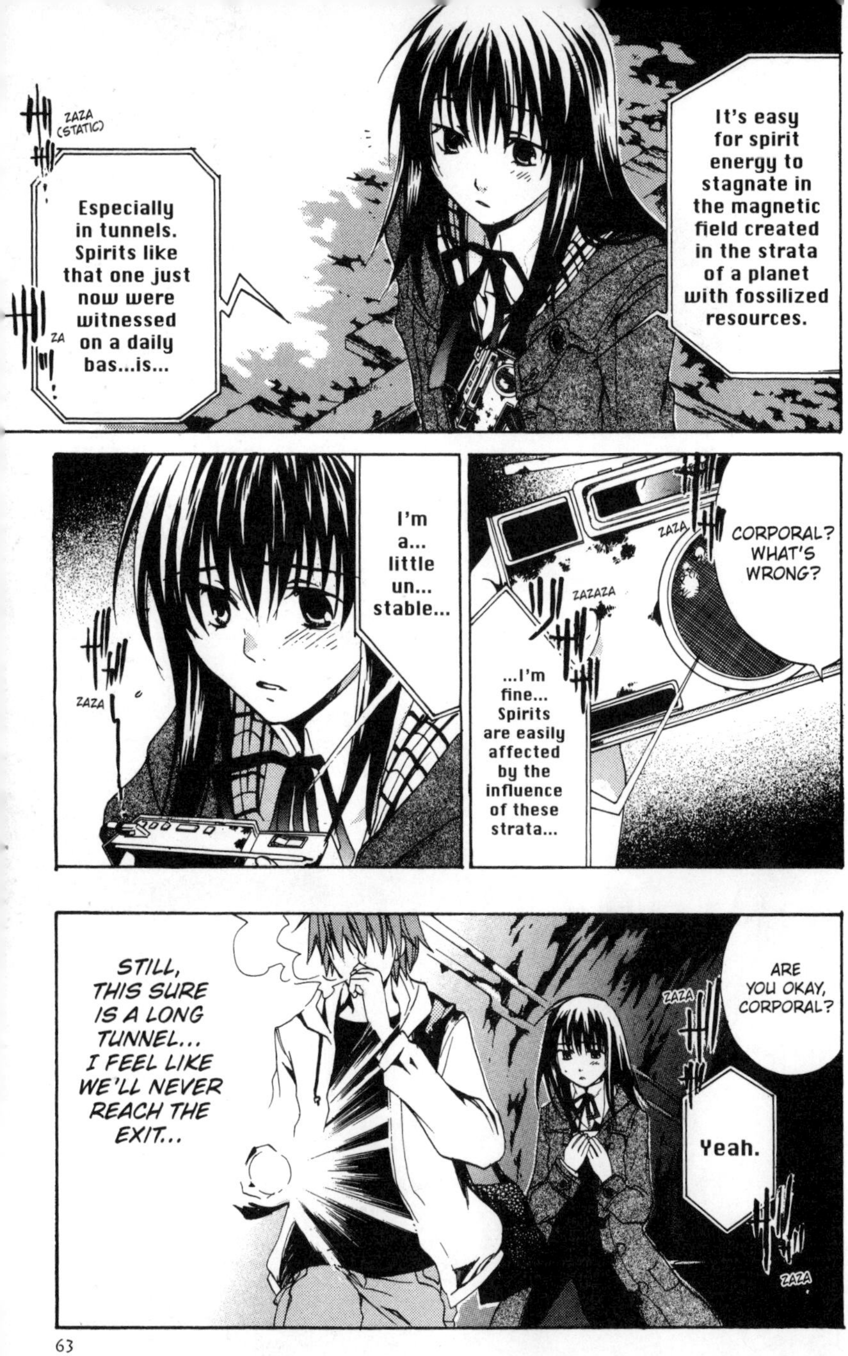
It's easy for spirit energy to stagnate in the magnetic field created in the strata of a planet with fossilized resources.
ZAZA (STATIC)
Especially in tunnels. Spirits like that one just now were witnessed on a daily bas...is...
ZA
CORPORAL? WHAT'S WRONG?
ZAZA
ZAZAZA
...I'm fine... Spirits are easily affected by the influence of these strata...
I'm a... little un... stable...
ZAZA
ARE YOU OKAY, CORPORAL?
ZAZA
Yeah.
ZAZA
STILL, THIS SURE IS A LONG TUNNEL... I FEEL LIKE WE'LL NEVER REACH THE EXIT...

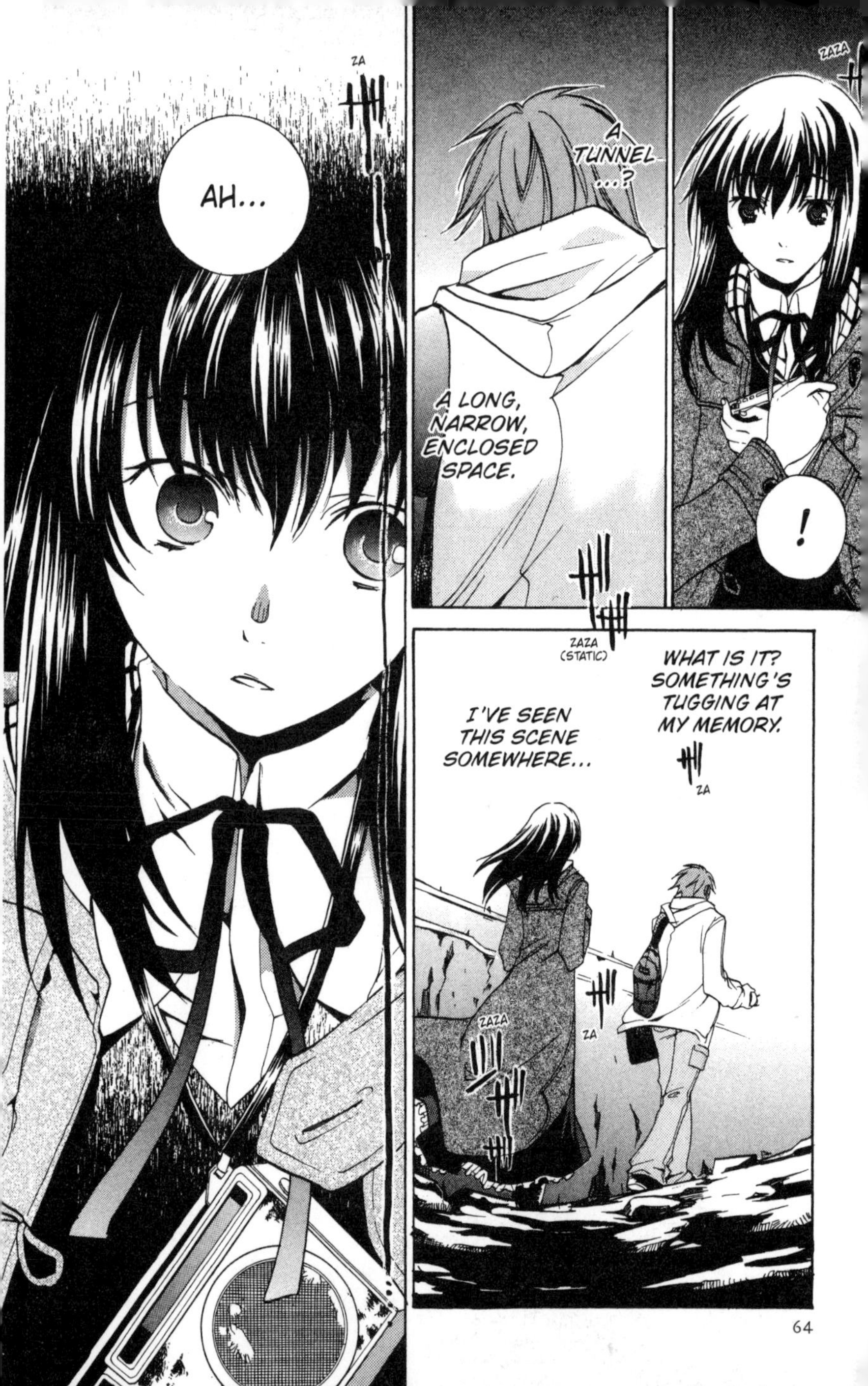
ZAZA
!
A TUNNEL ...?
A LONG, NARROW, ENCLOSED SPACE.
ZAZA (STATIC)
WHAT IS IT? SOMETHING'S TUGGING AT MY MEMORY.
I'VE SEEN THIS SCENE SOMEWHERE...
ZA
ZA
ZAZA
ZA
AH...

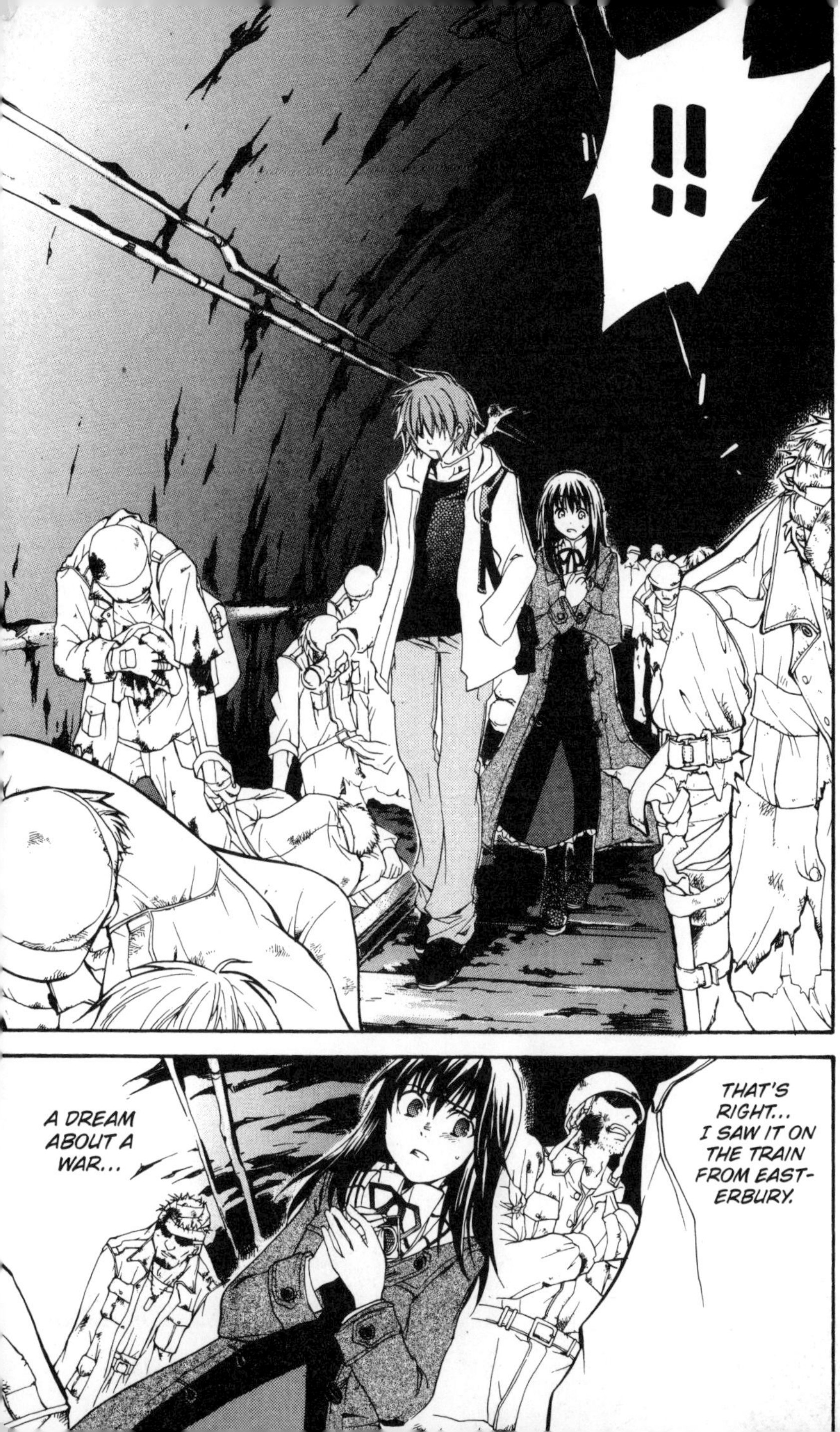
!!
THAT'S RIGHT... I SAW IT ON THE TRAIN FROM EAST-ERBURY.
A DREAM ABOUT A WAR...

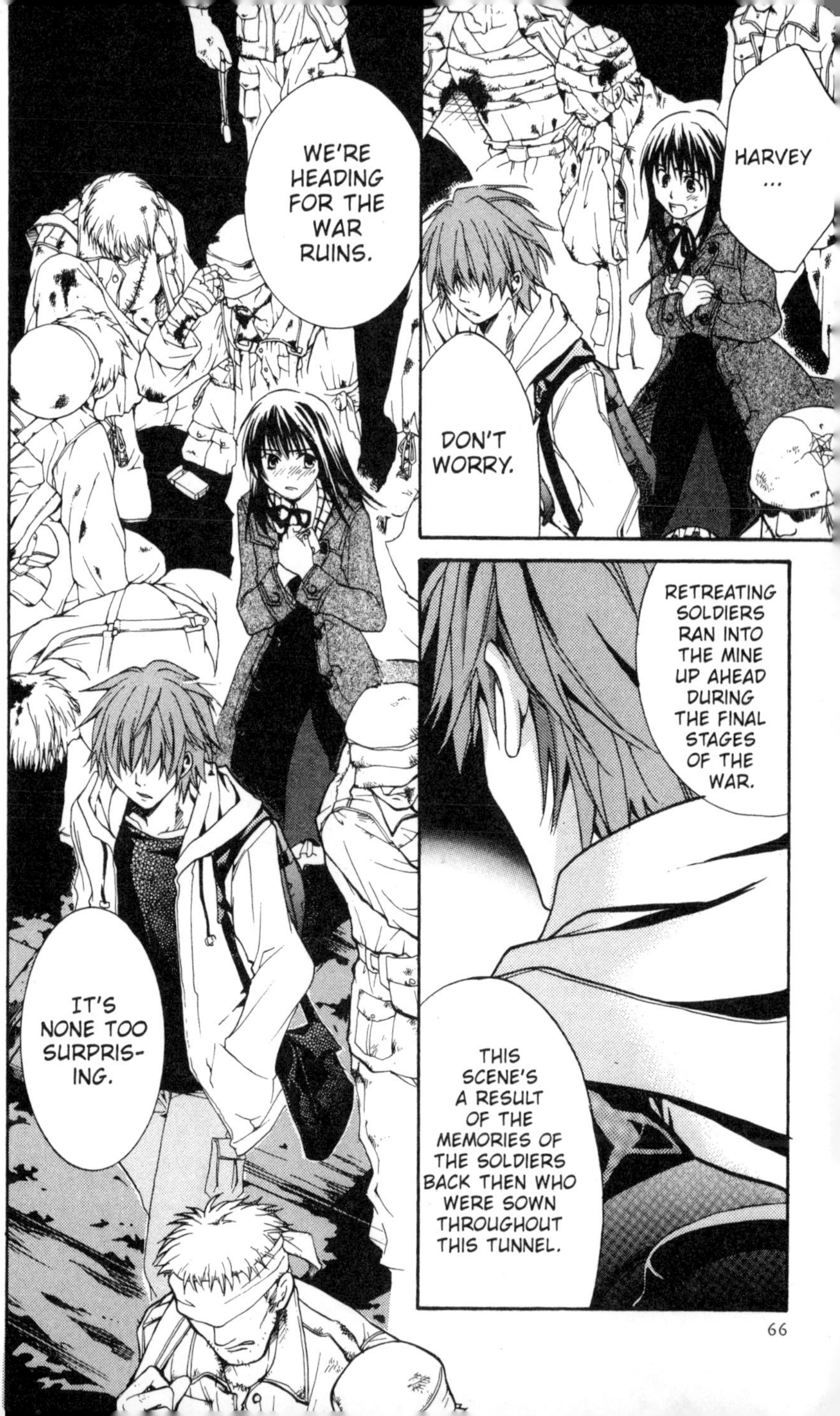
HARVEY ...
DON'T WORRY.
RETREATING SOLDIERS RAN INTO THE MINE UP AHEAD DURING THE FINAL STAGES OF THE WAR.
THIS SCENE'S A RESULT OF THE MEMORIES OF THE SOLDIERS BACK THEN WHO WERE SOWN THROUGHOUT THIS TUNNEL.
WE'RE HEADING FOR THE WAR RUINS.
IT'S NONE TOO SURPRIS-ING.

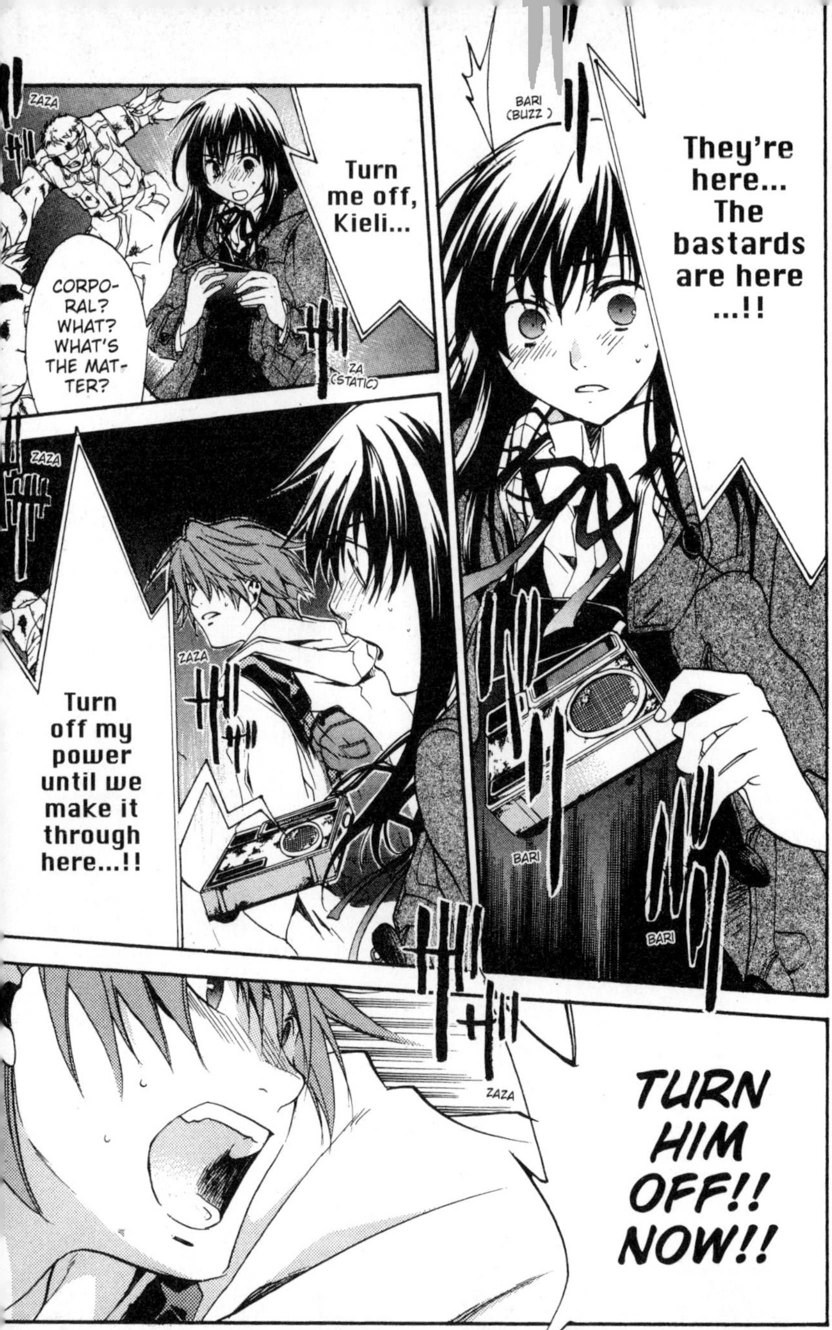
BARI (BUZZ)
They're here... The bastards are here ...!!
BARI
BARI
Turn me off, Kieli...
ZAZA
CORPO-RAL? WHAT? WHAT'S THE MAT-TER?
ZA (STATIC)
ZAZA
ZAZA
Turn off my power until we make it through here...!!
ZAZA
TURN HIM OFF!! NOW!!

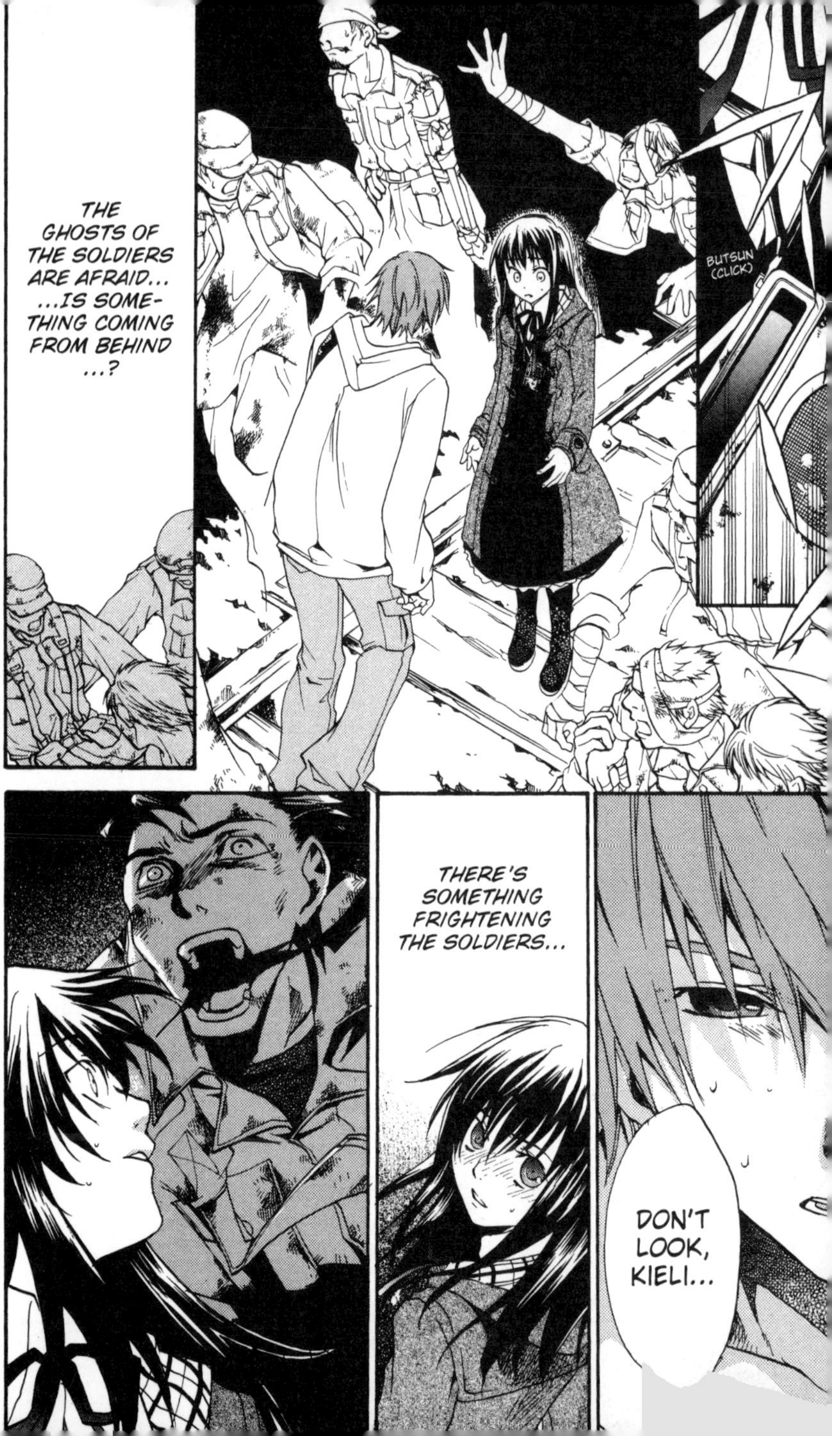
BUTSUN (CLICK)
THE GHOSTS OF THE SOLDIERS ARE AFRAID... ...IS SOME-THING COMING FROM BEHIND ...?
DON'T LOOK, KIELI...
THERE'S SOMETHING FRIGHTENING THE SOLDIERS...

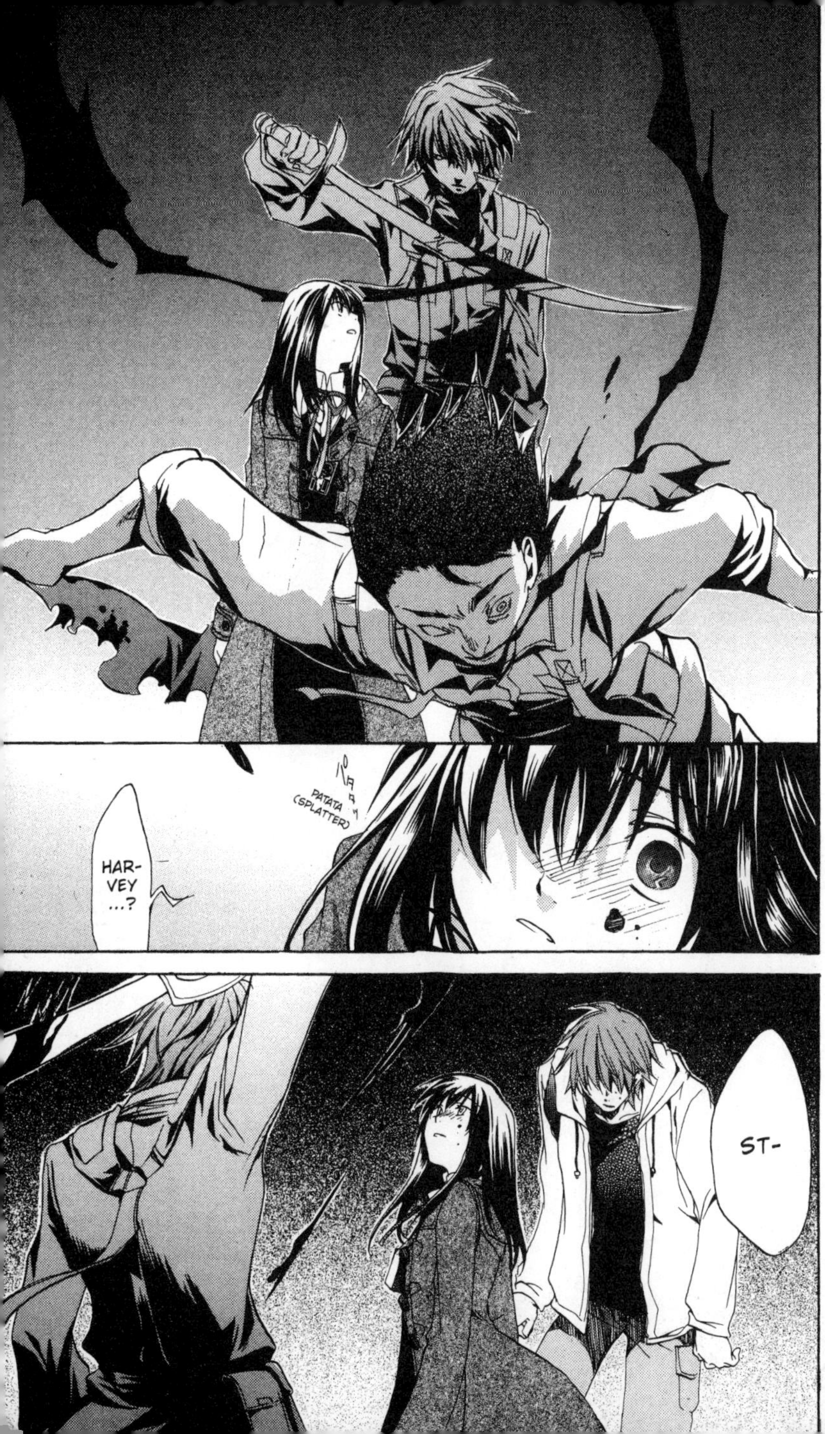
PATATA (SPLATTER)
HAR-VEY ...?
ST-

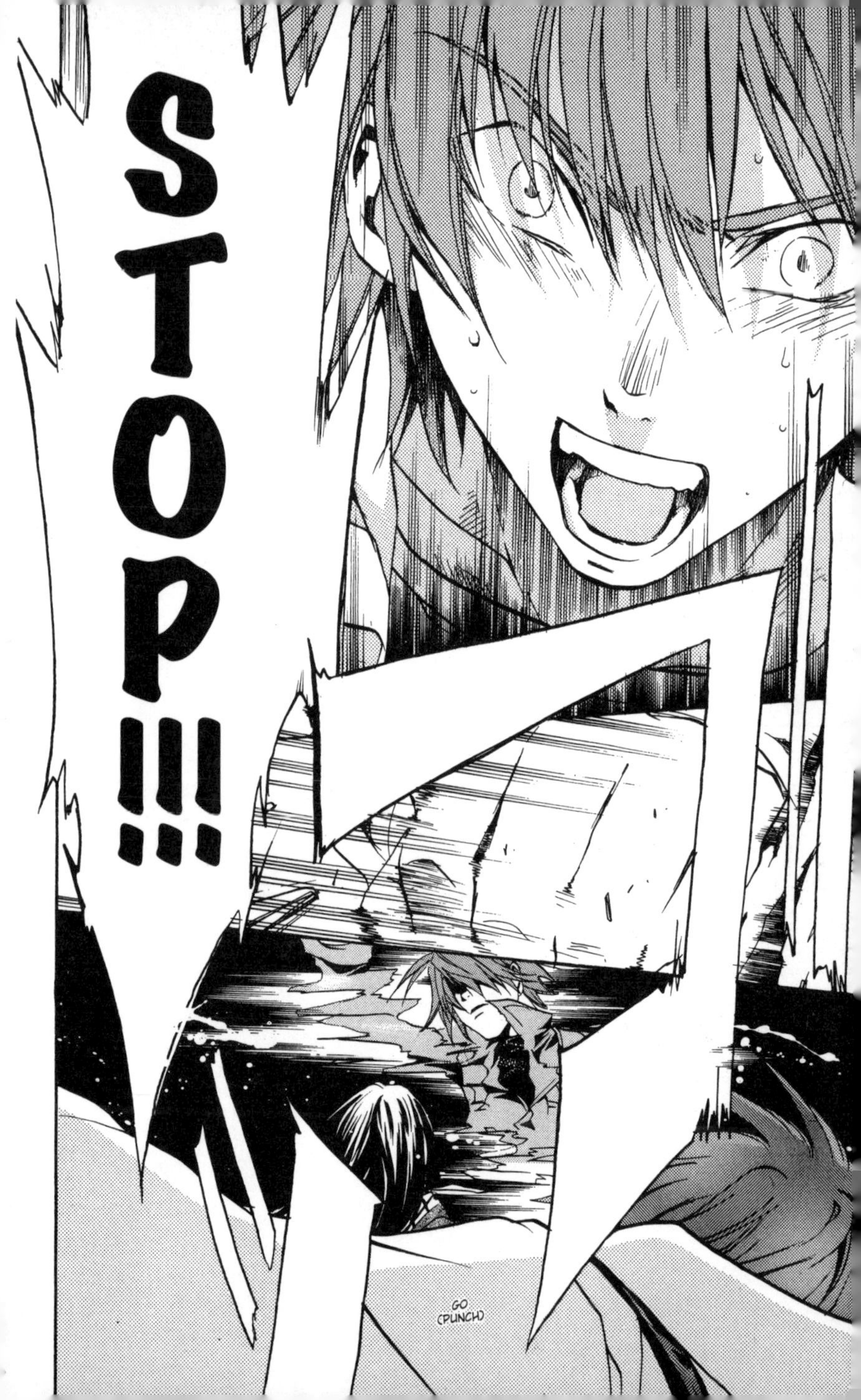
STOP!!!
GO (PUNCH)

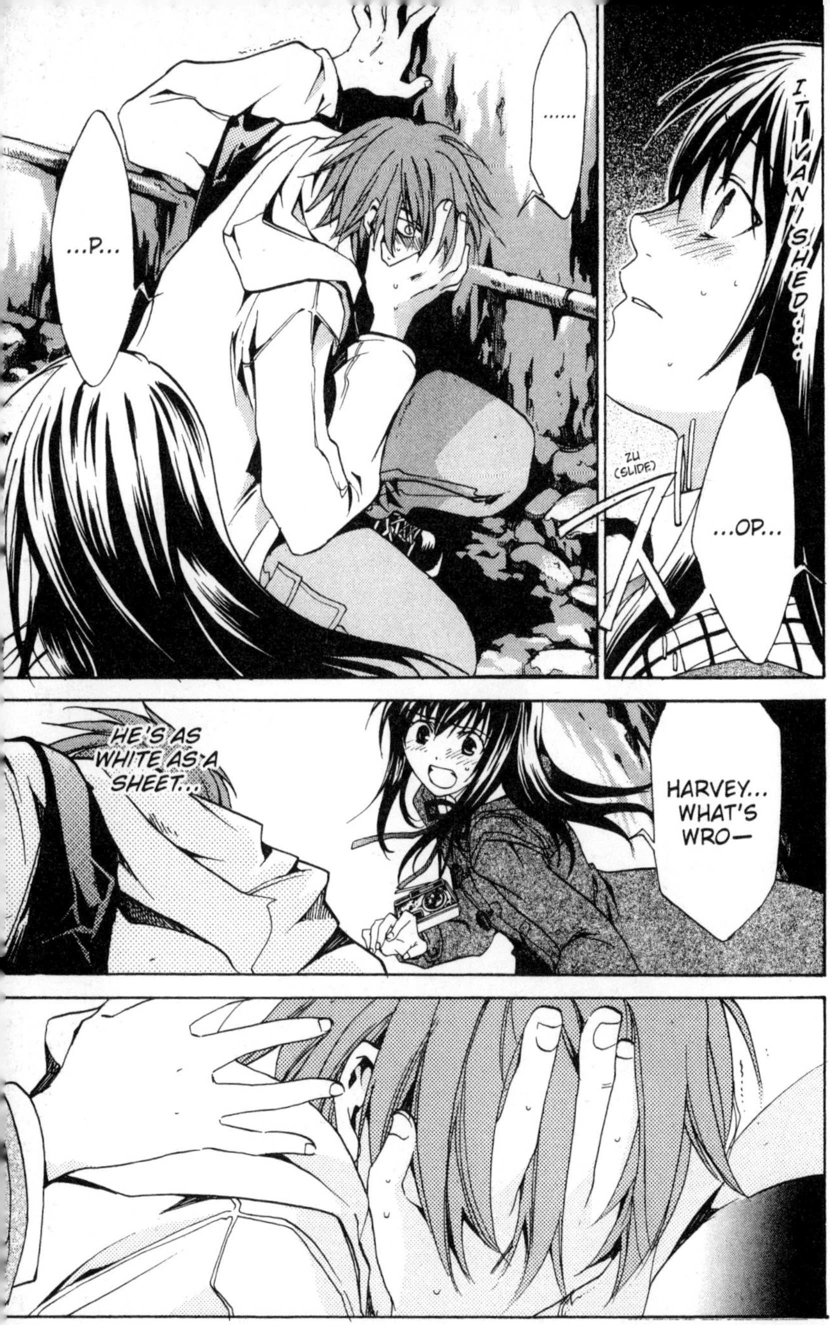
IT VANISHED...
ZU (SLIDE)
...OP...
......
...P...
HARVEY... WHAT'S WRO—
HE'S AS WHITE AS A SHEET...

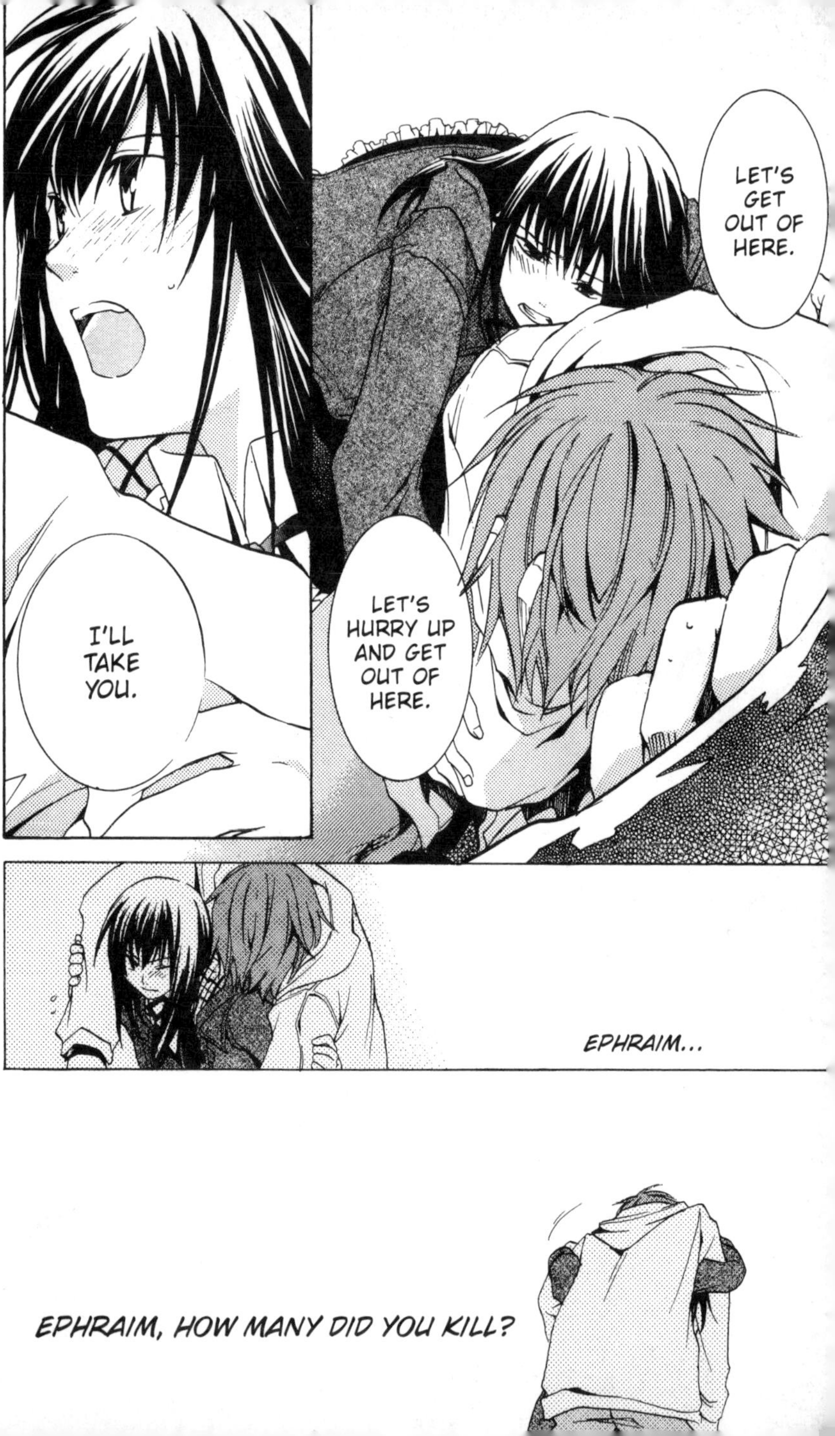
LET'S GET OUT OF HERE.
LET'S HURRY UP AND GET OUT OF HERE.
I'LL TAKE YOU.
EPHRAIM...
EPHRAIM, HOW MANY DID YOU KILL?

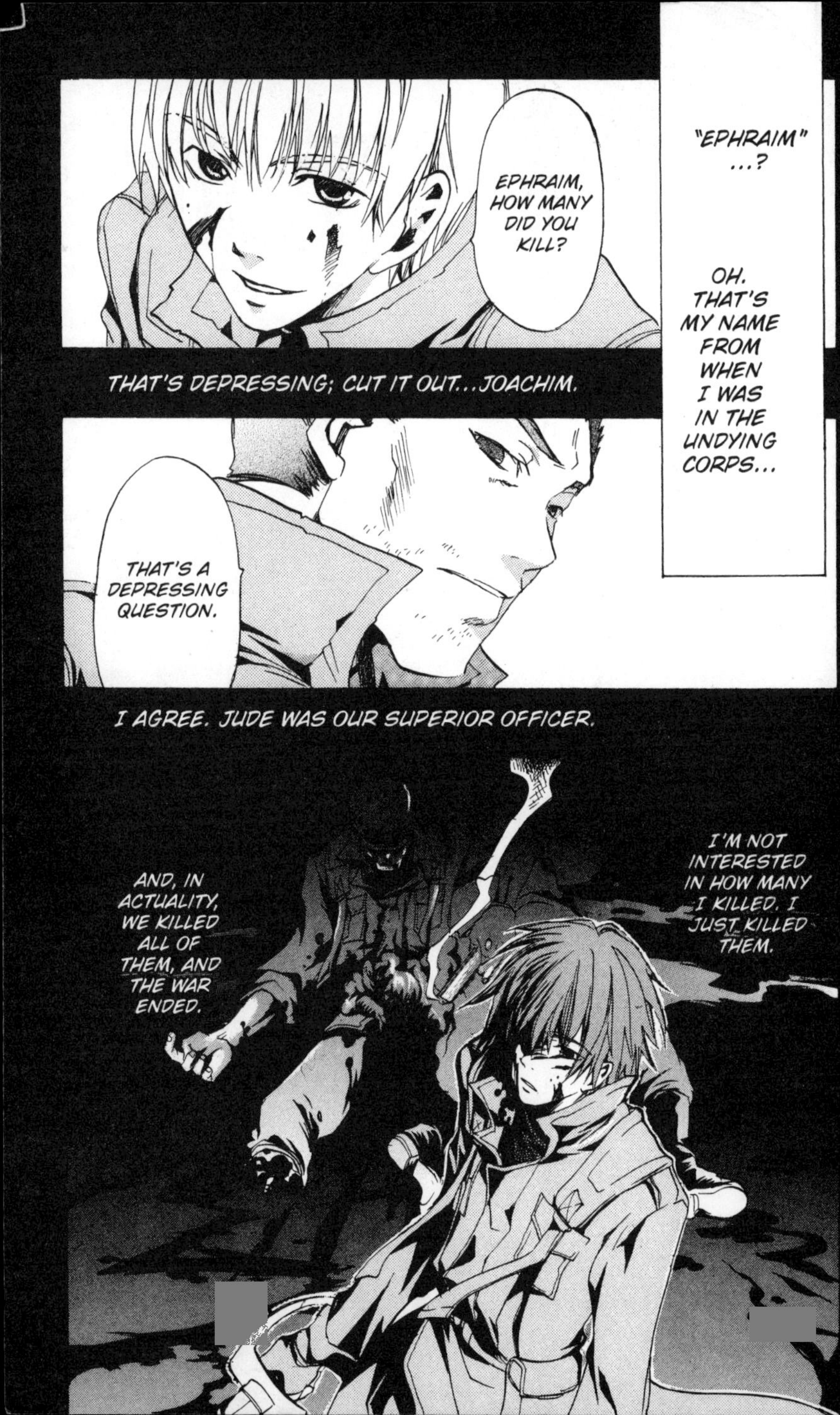
"EPHRAIM" ...?
OH. THAT'S MY NAME FROM WHEN I WAS IN THE UNDYING CORPS...
EPHRAIM, HOW MANY DID YOU KILL?
THAT'S DEPRESSING; CUT IT OUT...JOACHIM.
THAT'S A DEPRESSING QUESTION.
I AGREE. JUDE WAS OUR SUPERIOR OFFICER.
I'M NOT INTERESTED IN HOW MANY I KILLED. I JUST KILLED THEM.
AND, IN ACTUALITY, WE KILLED ALL OF THEM, AND THE WAR ENDED.

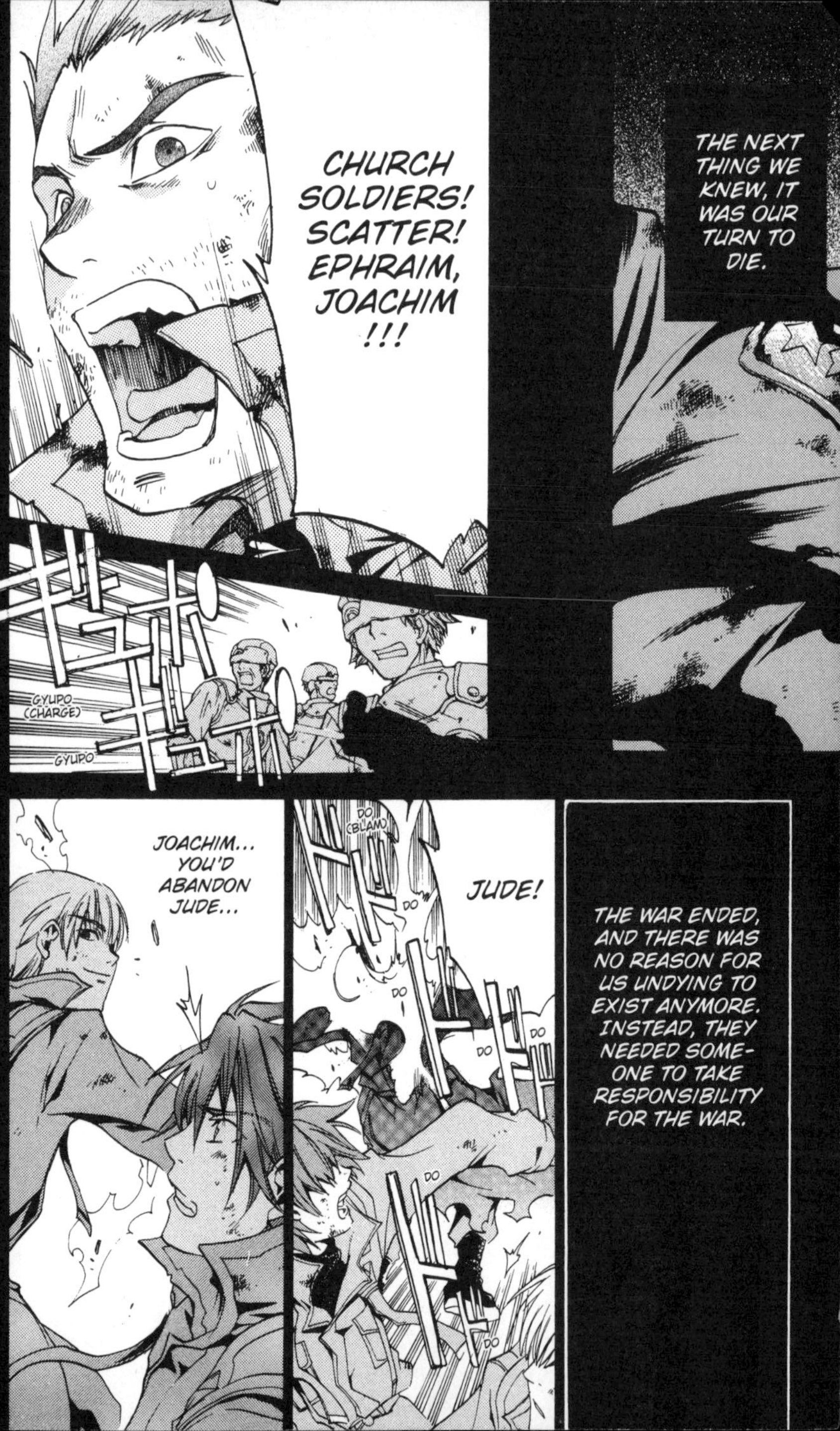
THE NEXT THING WE KNEW, IT WAS OUR TURN TO DIE.
CHURCH SOLDIERS! SCATTER! EPHRAIM, JOACHIM !!!
GYUPO (CHARGE)
GYUPO
THE WAR ENDED, AND THERE WAS NO REASON FOR US UNDYING TO EXIST ANYMORE. INSTEAD, THEY NEEDED SOME-ONE TO TAKE RESPONSIBILITY FOR THE WAR.
DO (BLAM)
JUDE!
DO
DO
DO
DO
DO
DO
JOACHIM... YOU'D ABANDON JUDE...

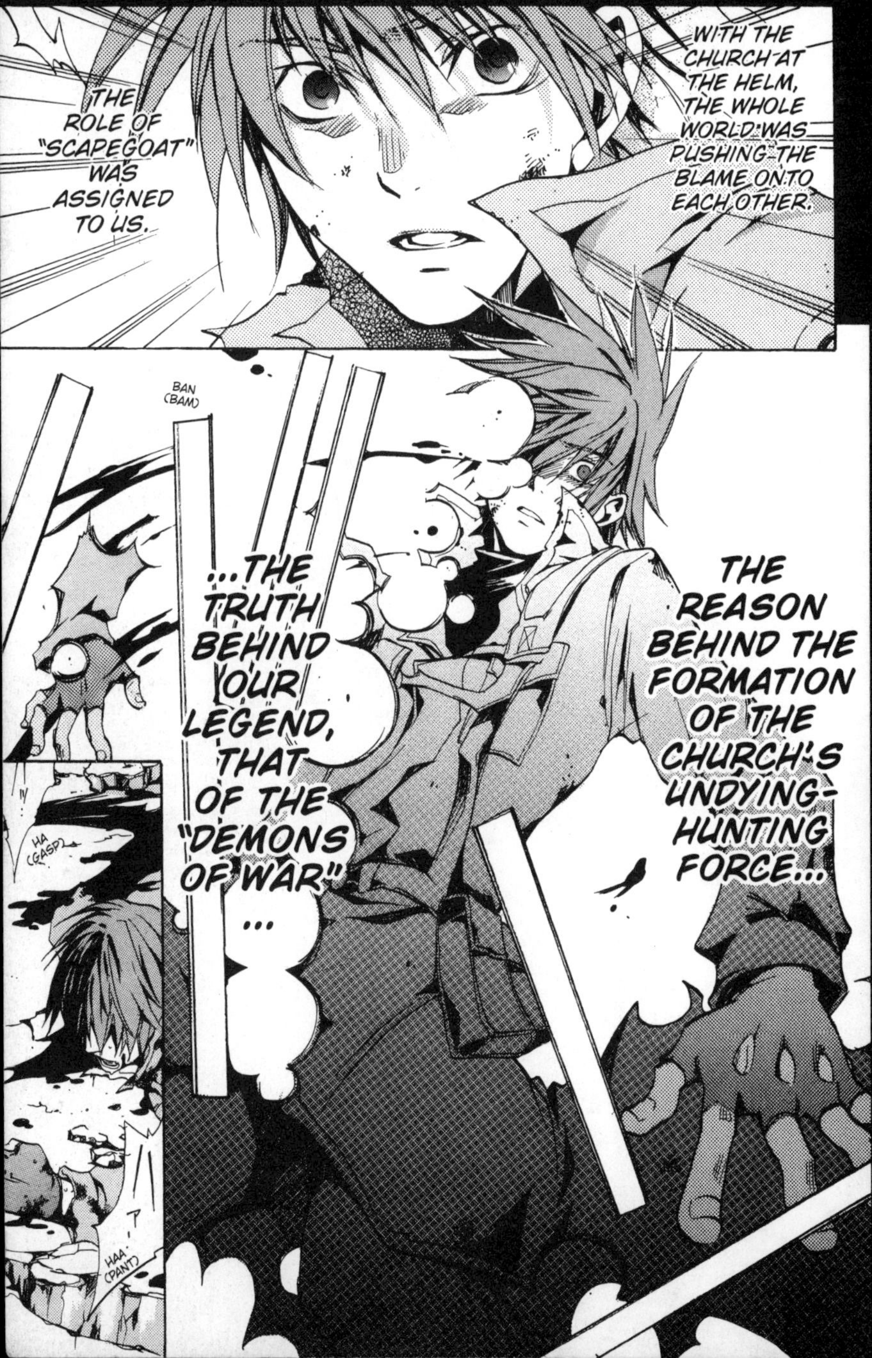
WITH THE CHURCH AT THE HELM, THE WHOLE WORLD WAS PUSHING THE BLAME ONTO EACH OTHER.
THE ROLE OF "SCAPEGOAT" WAS ASSIGNED TO US.
BAN (BAM)
THE REASON BEHIND THE FORMATION OF THE CHURCH'S UNDYING-HUNTING FORCE...
...THE TRUTH BEHIND OUR LEGEND, THAT OF THE "DEMONS OF WAR"...
HA (GASP)
HAA (PANT)

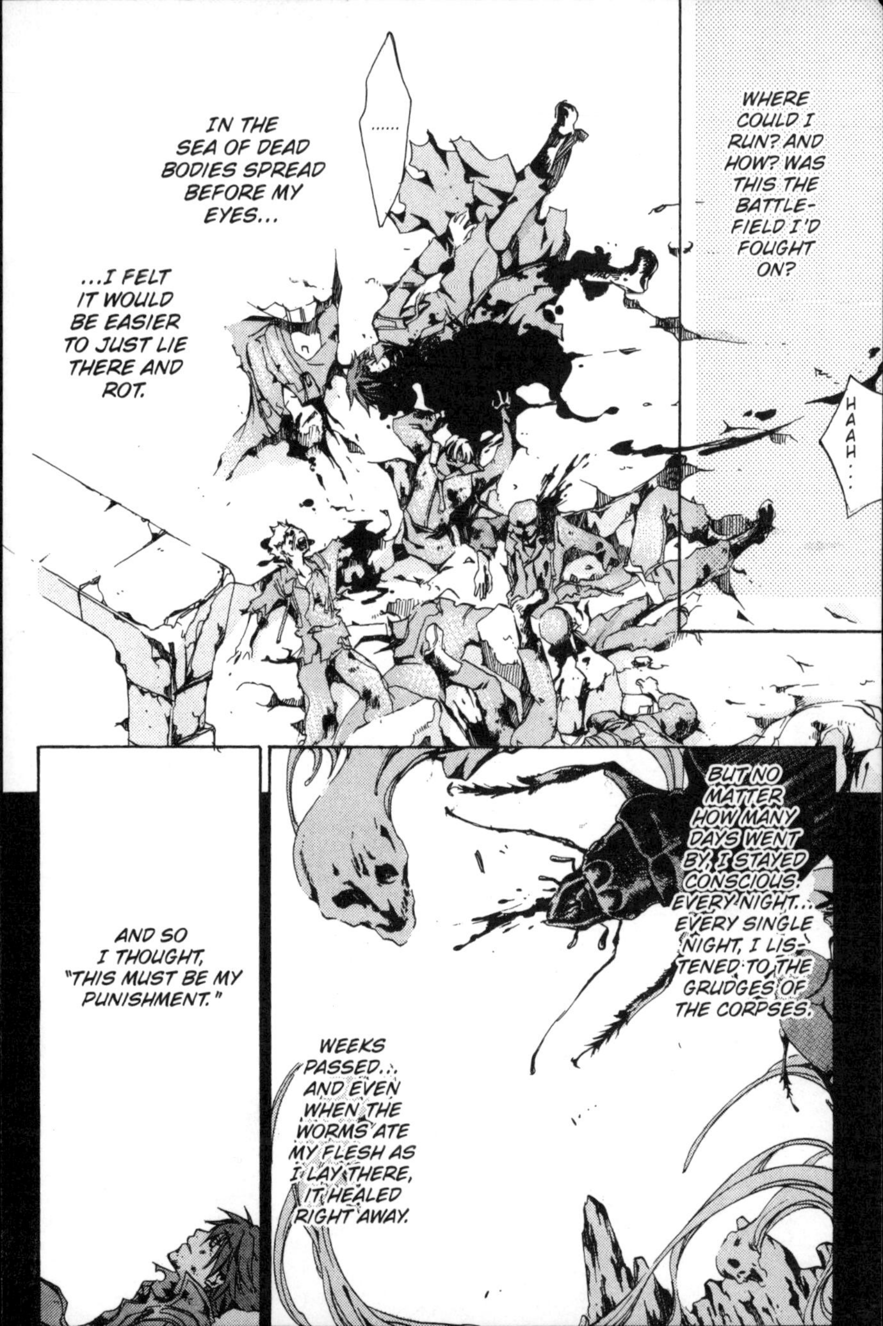
WHERE COULD I RUN? AND HOW? WAS THIS THE BATTLE-FIELD I'D FOUGHT ON?
HAAH...
......
IN THE SEA OF DEAD BODIES SPREAD BEFORE MY EYES...
...I FELT IT WOULD BE EASIER TO JUST LIE THERE AND ROT.
BUT NO MATTER HOW MANY DAYS WENT BY, I STAYED CONSCIOUS. EVERY NIGHT... EVERY SINGLE NIGHT, I LISTENED TO THE GRUDGES OF THE CORPSES.
WEEKS PASSED... AND EVEN WHEN THE WORMS ATE MY FLESH AS I LAY THERE, IT HEALED RIGHT AWAY.
AND SO I THOUGHT, "THIS MUST BE MY PUNISHMENT."

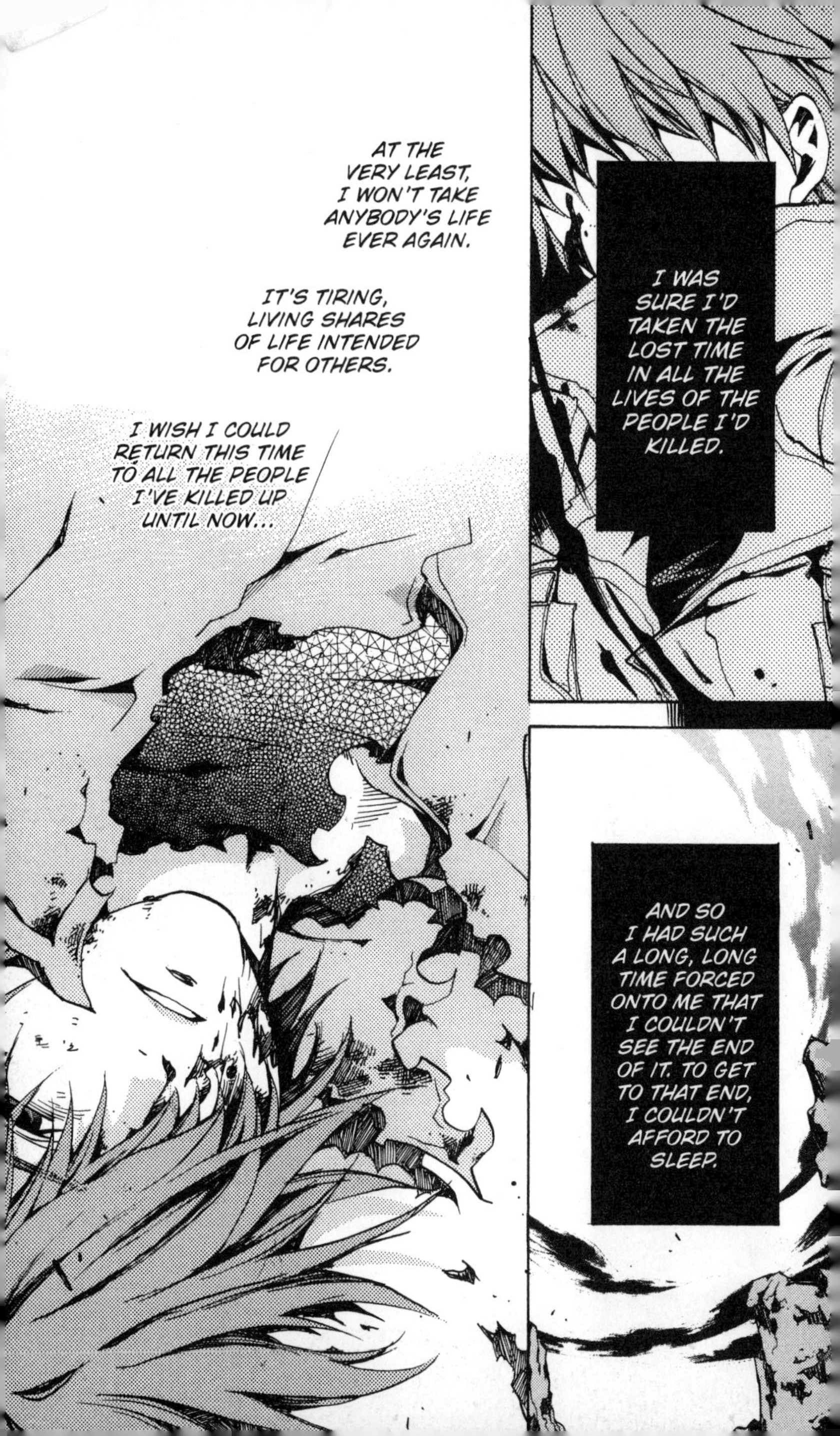
I WAS SURE I'D TAKEN THE LOST TIME IN ALL THE LIVES OF THE PEOPLE I'D KILLED.
AND SO I HAD SUCH A LONG, LONG TIME FORCED ONTO ME THAT I COULDN'T SEE THE END OF IT. TO GET TO THAT END, I COULDN'T AFFORD TO SLEEP.
AT THE VERY LEAST, I WON'T TAKE ANYBODY'S LIFE EVER AGAIN.
IT'S TIRING, LIVING SHARES OF LIFE INTENDED FOR OTHERS.
I WISH I COULD RETURN THIS TIME TO ALL THE PEOPLE I'VE KILLED UP UNTIL NOW...

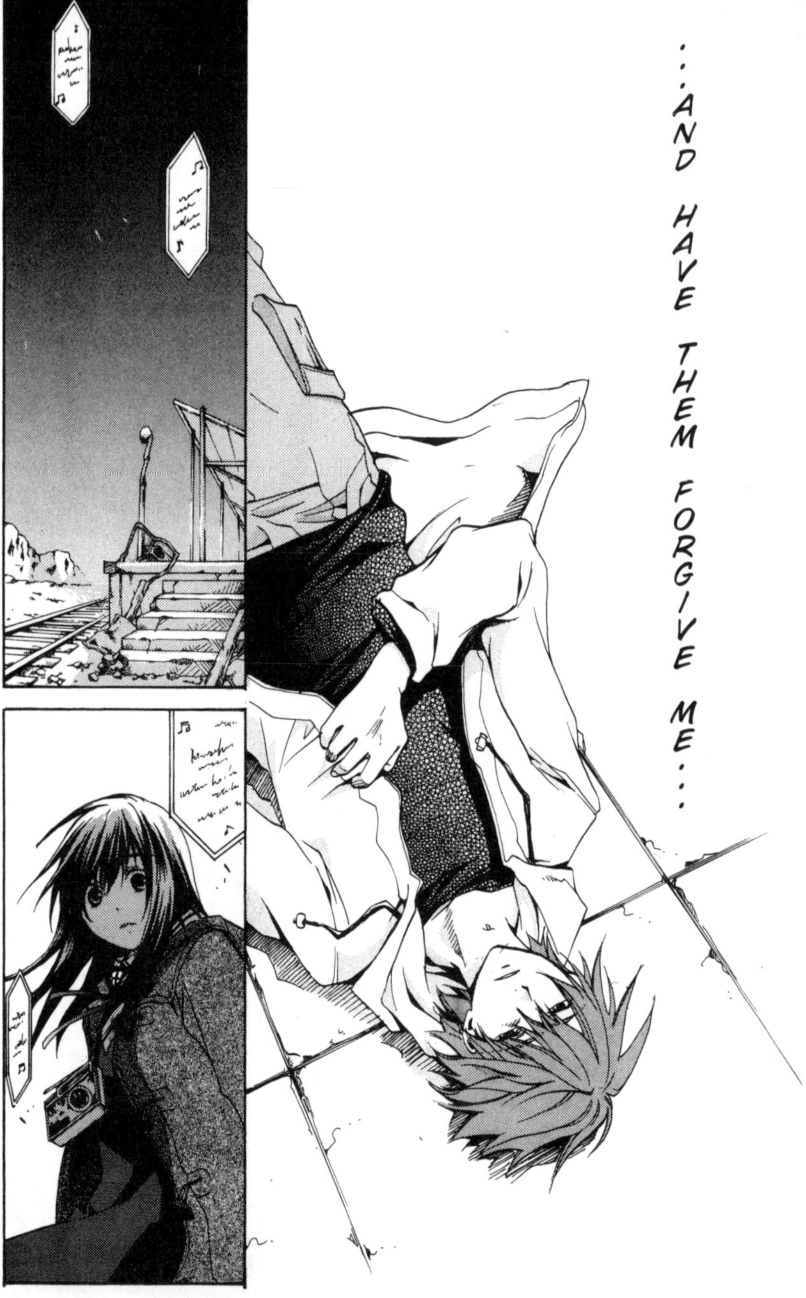
...AND HAVE THEM FORGIVE ME...

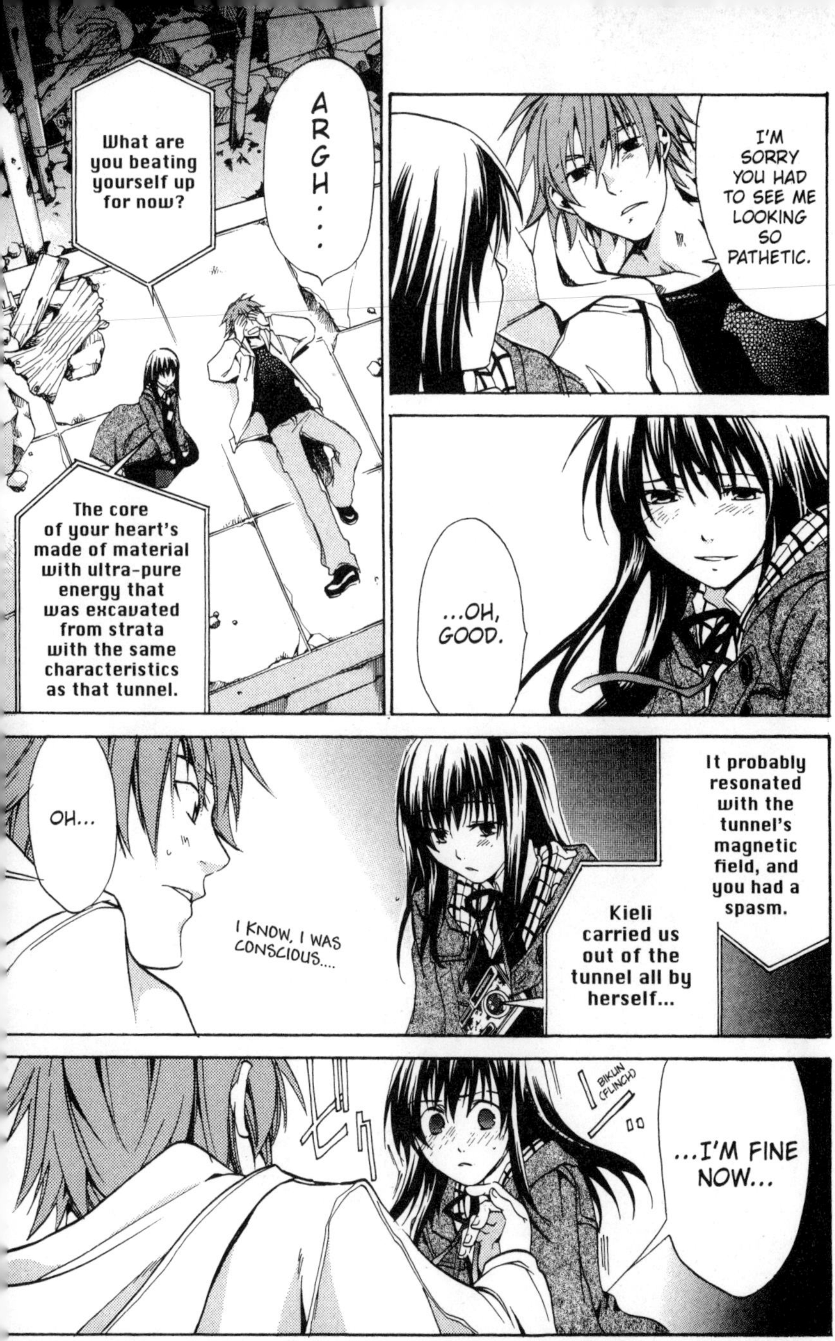
I'M SORRY YOU HAD TO SEE ME LOOKING SO PATHETIC.
...OH, GOOD.
ARGH...
What are you beating yourself up for now?
The core of your heart's made of material with ultra-pure energy that was excavated from strata with the same characteristics as that tunnel.
It probably resonated with the tunnel's magnetic field, and you had a spasm.
Kieli carried us out of the tunnel all by herself...
I KNOW, I WAS CONSCIOUS....
OH...
BIKUN (FLINCH)
...I'M FINE NOW...

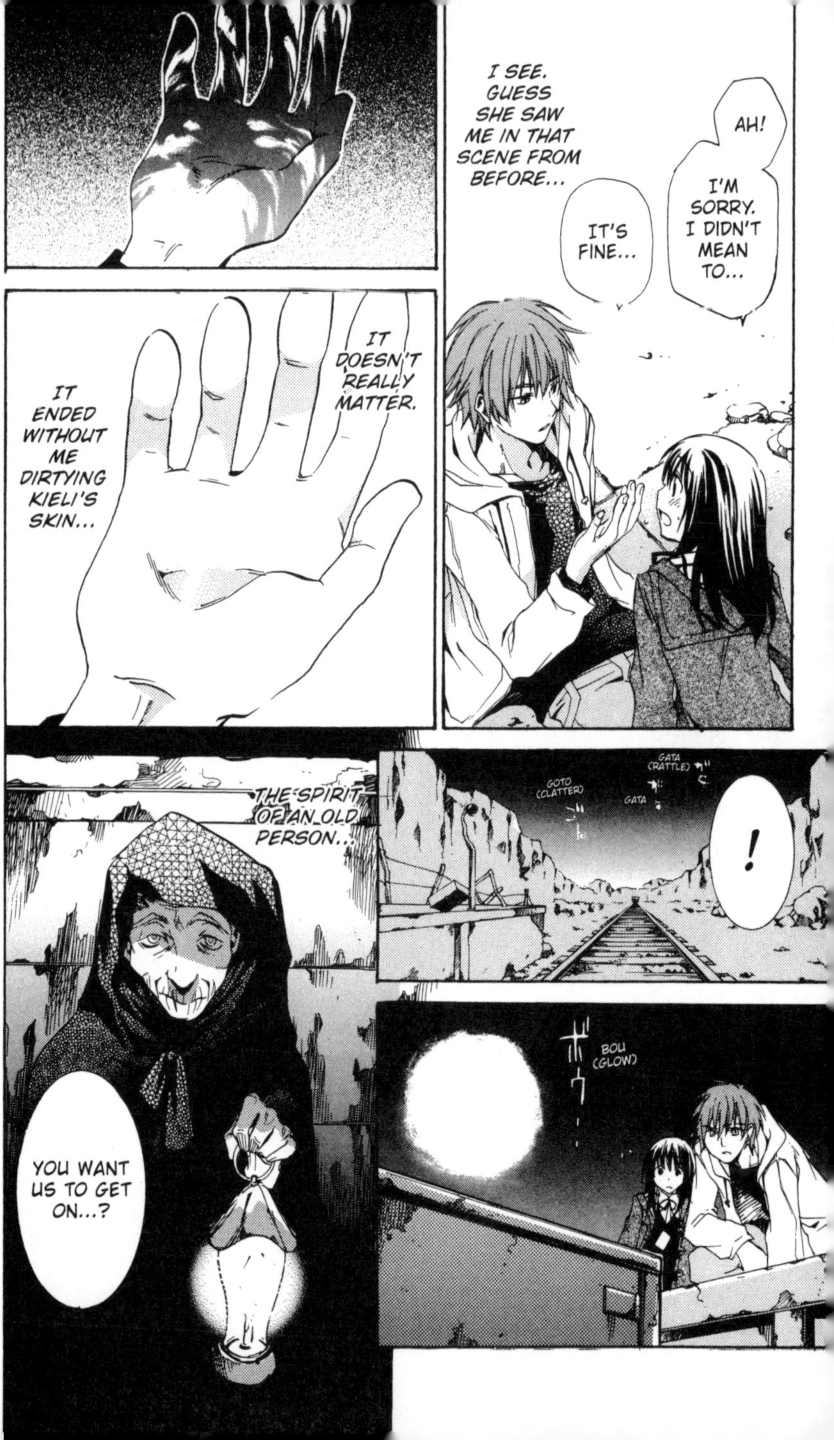
AH!
I'M SORRY. I DIDN'T MEAN TO...
IT'S FINE...
I SEE. GUESS SHE SAW ME IN THAT SCENE FROM BEFORE...
IT DOESN'T REALLY MATTER.
IT ENDED WITHOUT ME DIRTYING KIELI'S SKIN...
!
GATA (RATTLE)
GATA
GOTO (CLATTER)
BOU (GLOW)
THE SPIRIT OF AN OLD PERSON...
YOU WANT US TO GET ON...?

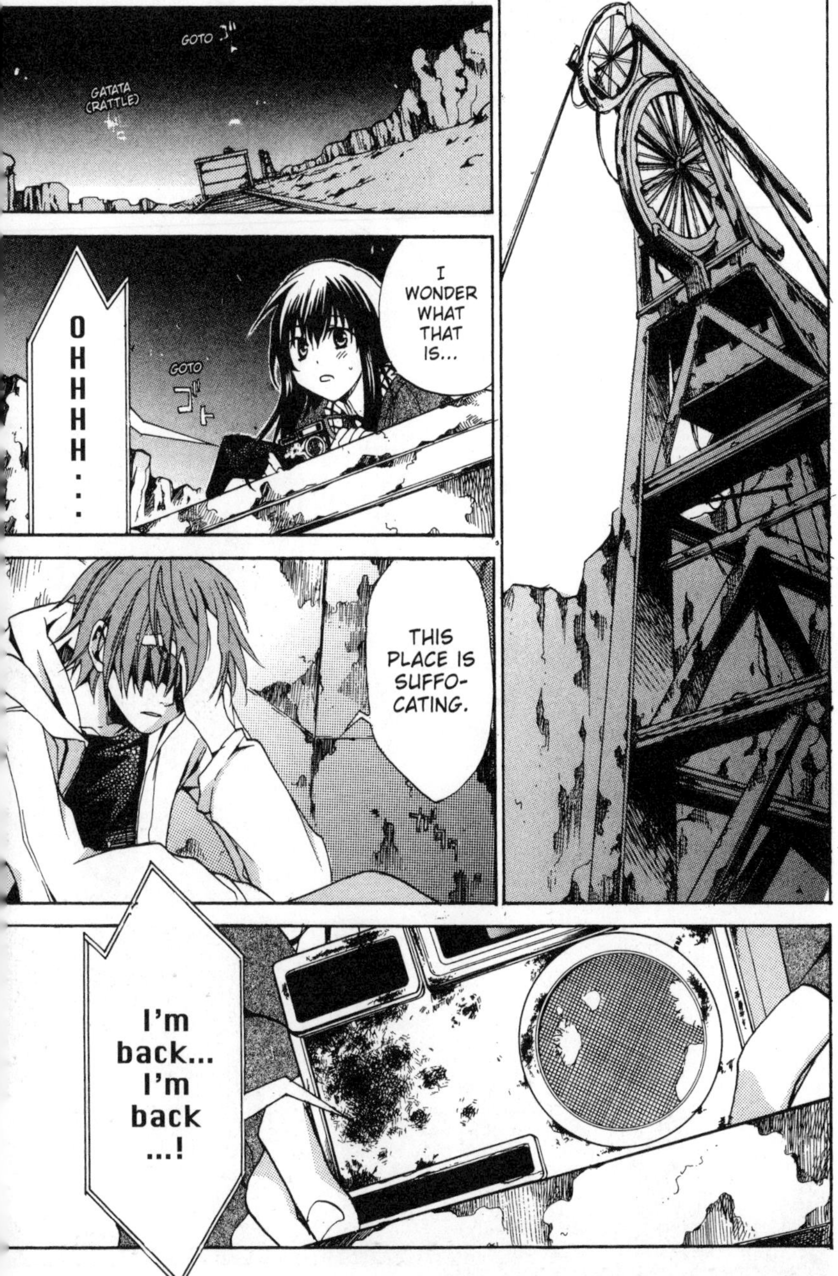
GOTO
GATATA (RATTLE)
I WONDER WHAT THAT IS...
GOTO
OHHHH...
THIS PLACE IS SUFFO-CATING.
I'm back... I'm back ...!

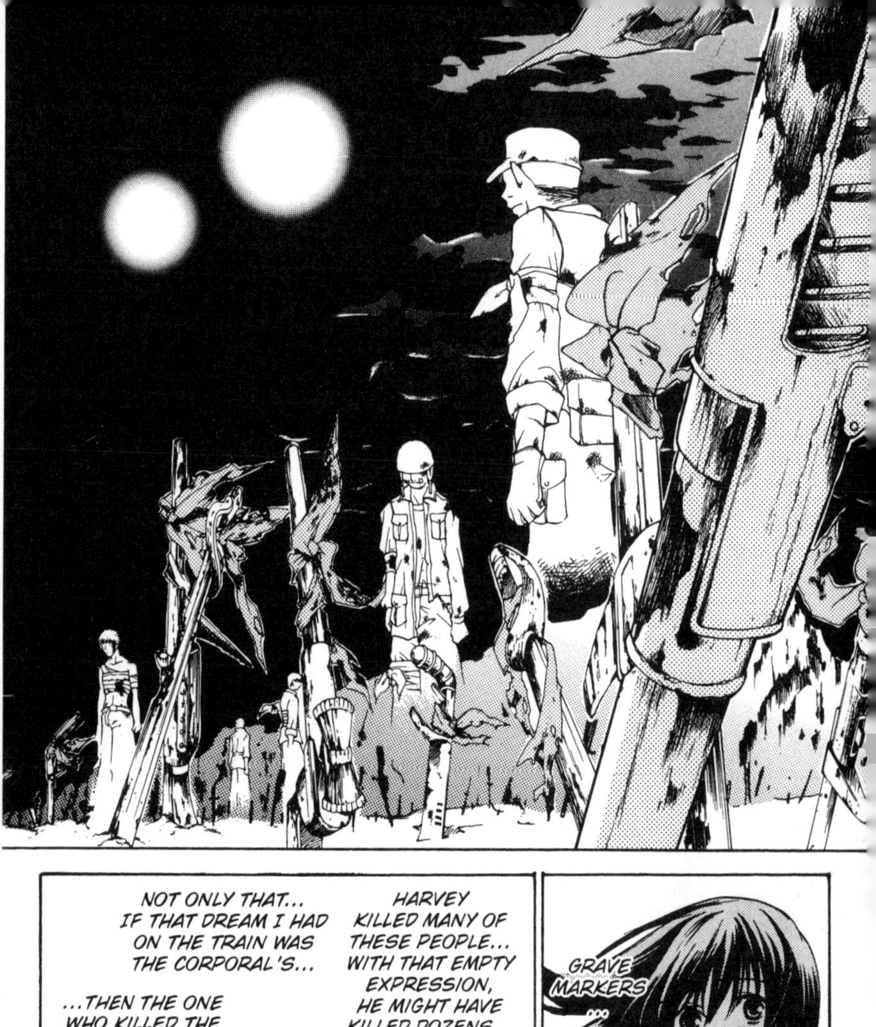

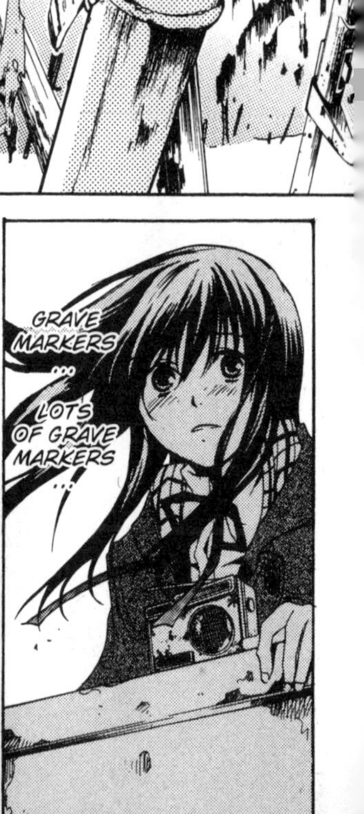
GRAVE MARKERS...
LOTS OF GRAVE MARKERS...

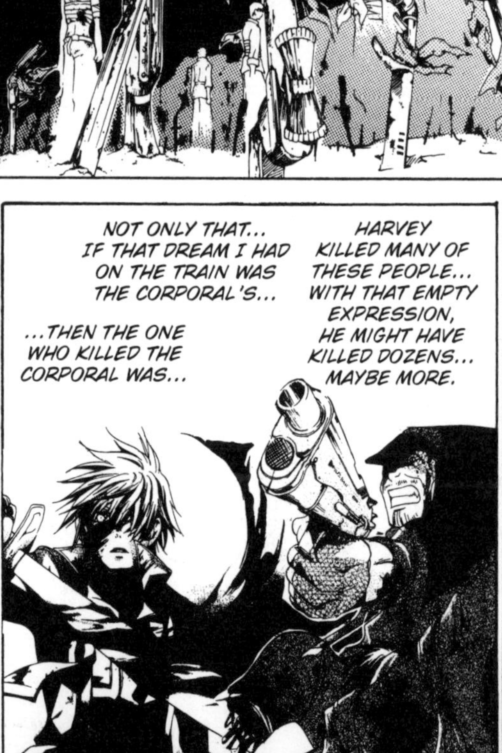
HARVEY KILLED MANY OF THESE PEOPLE... WITH THAT EMPTY EXPRESSION, HE MIGHT HAVE KILLED DOZENS... MAYBE MORE.
NOT ONLY THAT... IF THAT DREAM I HAD ON THE TRAIN WAS THE CORPORAL'S...
...THEN THE ONE WHO KILLED THE CORPORAL WAS...

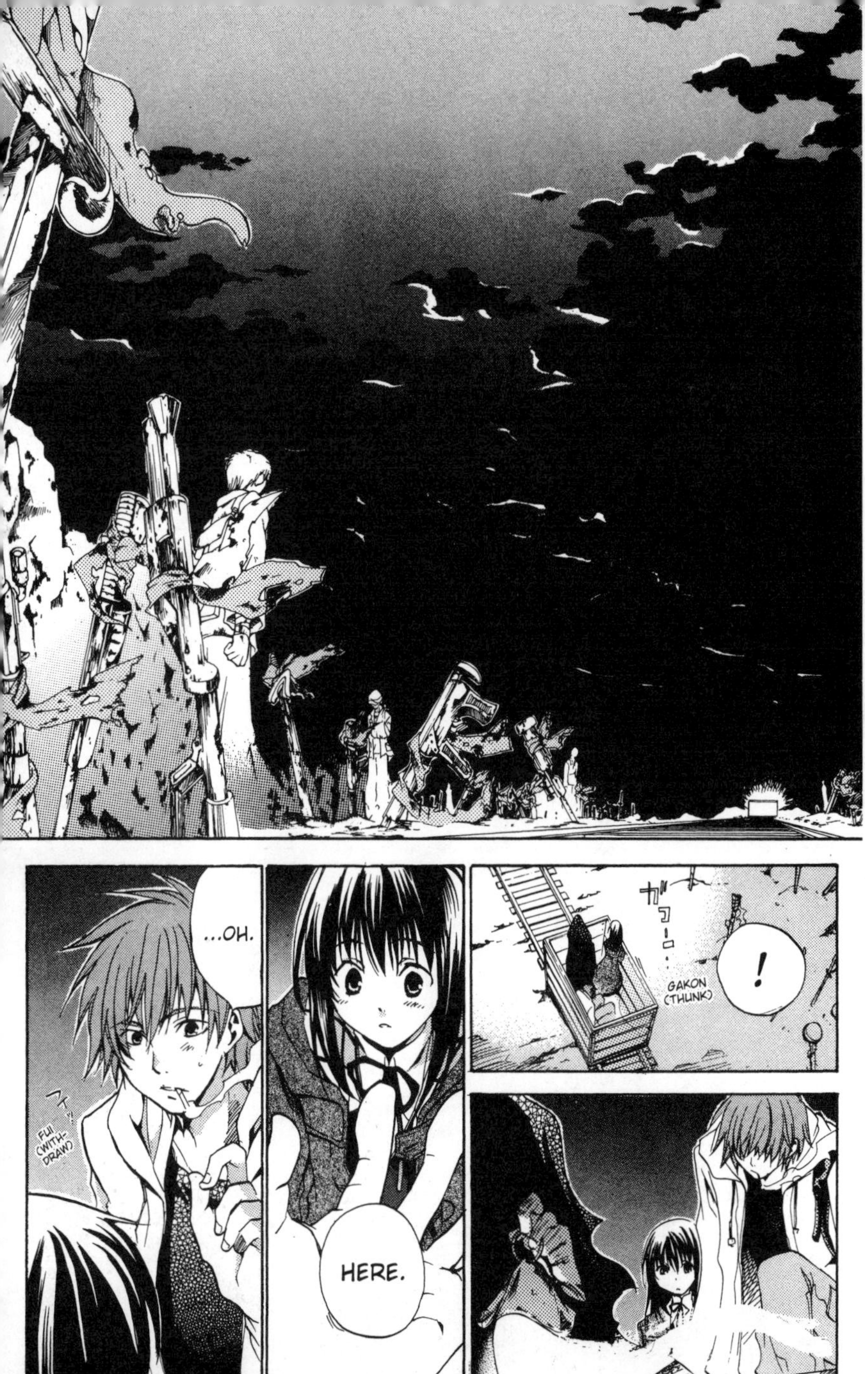

GAKON (THUNK)
!
HERE.
...OH.
FUI (WITH-DRAW)

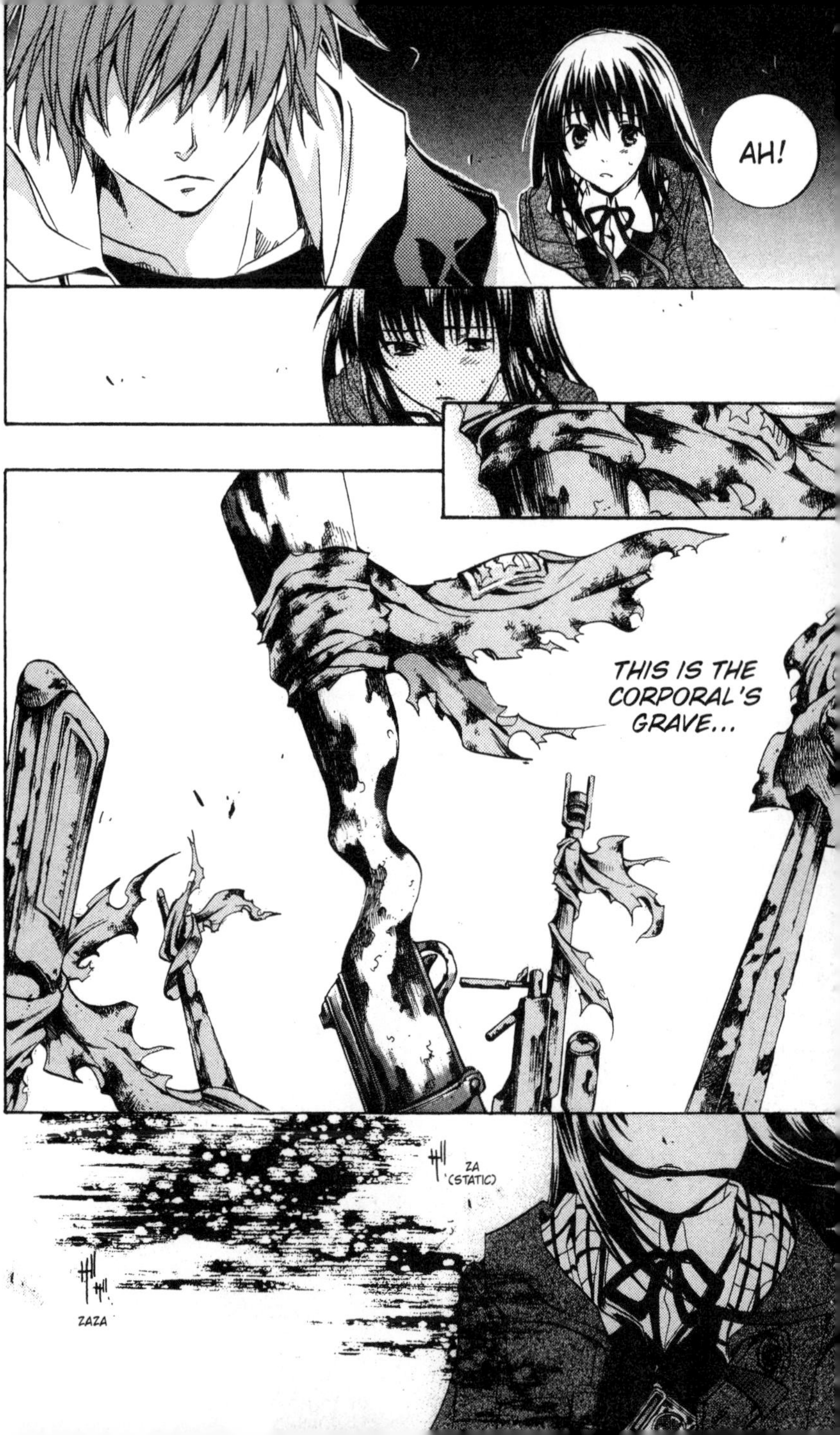
AH!
THIS IS THE CORPORAL'S GRAVE...
ZA (STATIC)
ZAZA

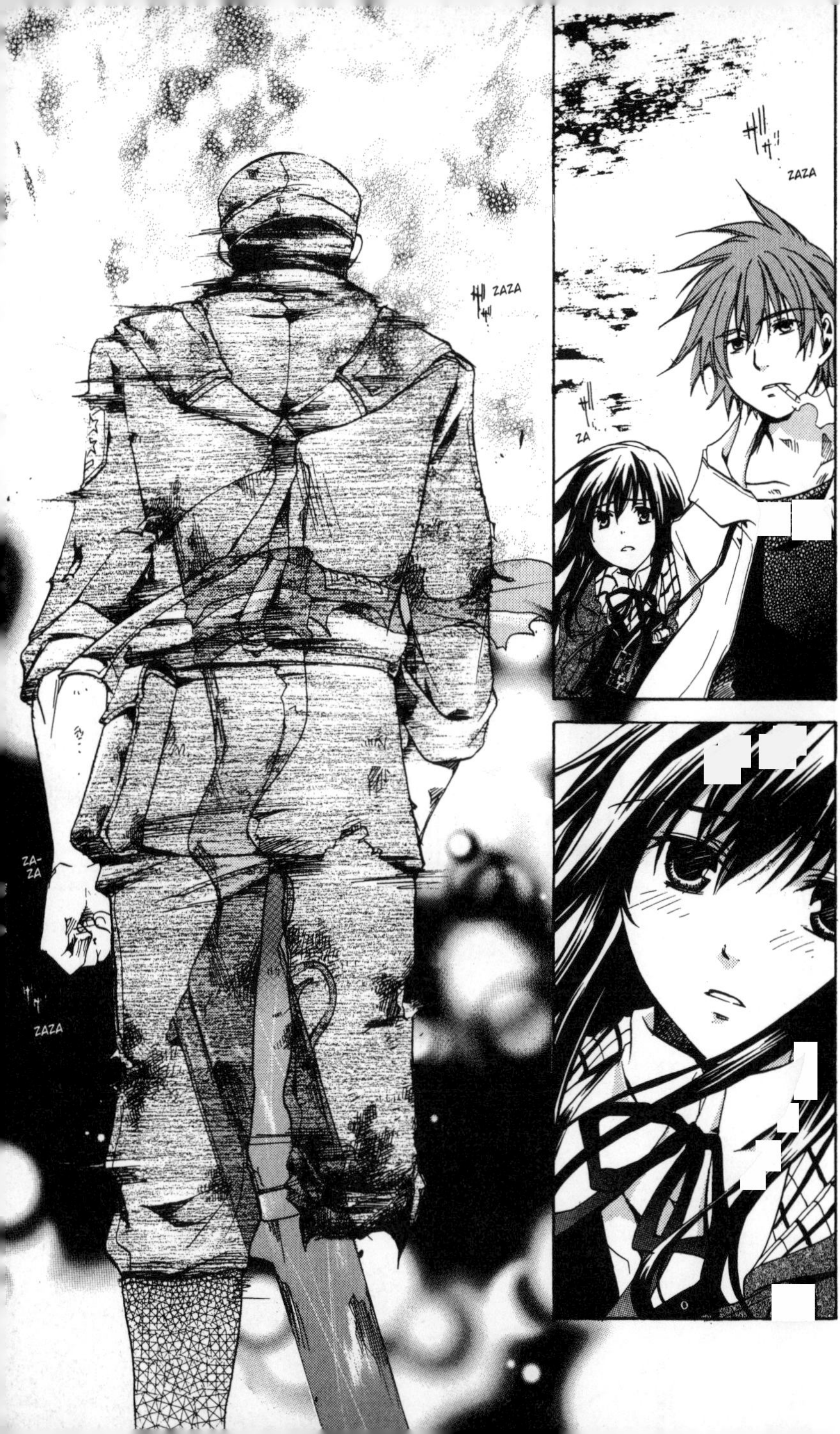
ZAZA
ZA
ZAZA
ZA-ZA
ZAZA

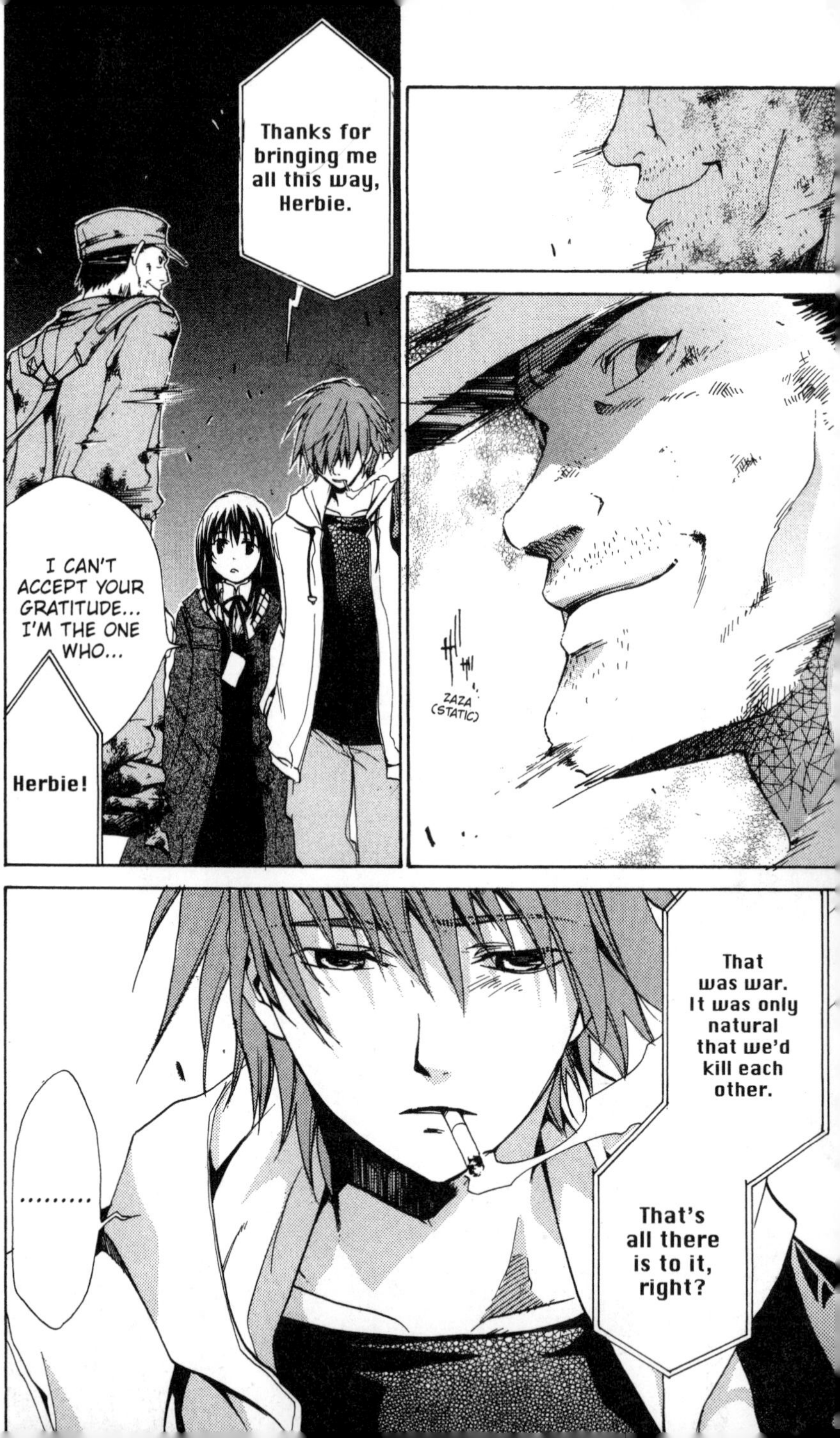
ZAZA (STATIC)
Thanks for bringing me all this way, Herbie.
I CAN'T ACCEPT YOUR GRATITUDE... I'M THE ONE WHO...
Herbie!
That was war. It was only natural that we'd kill each other.
That's all there is to it, right?
....

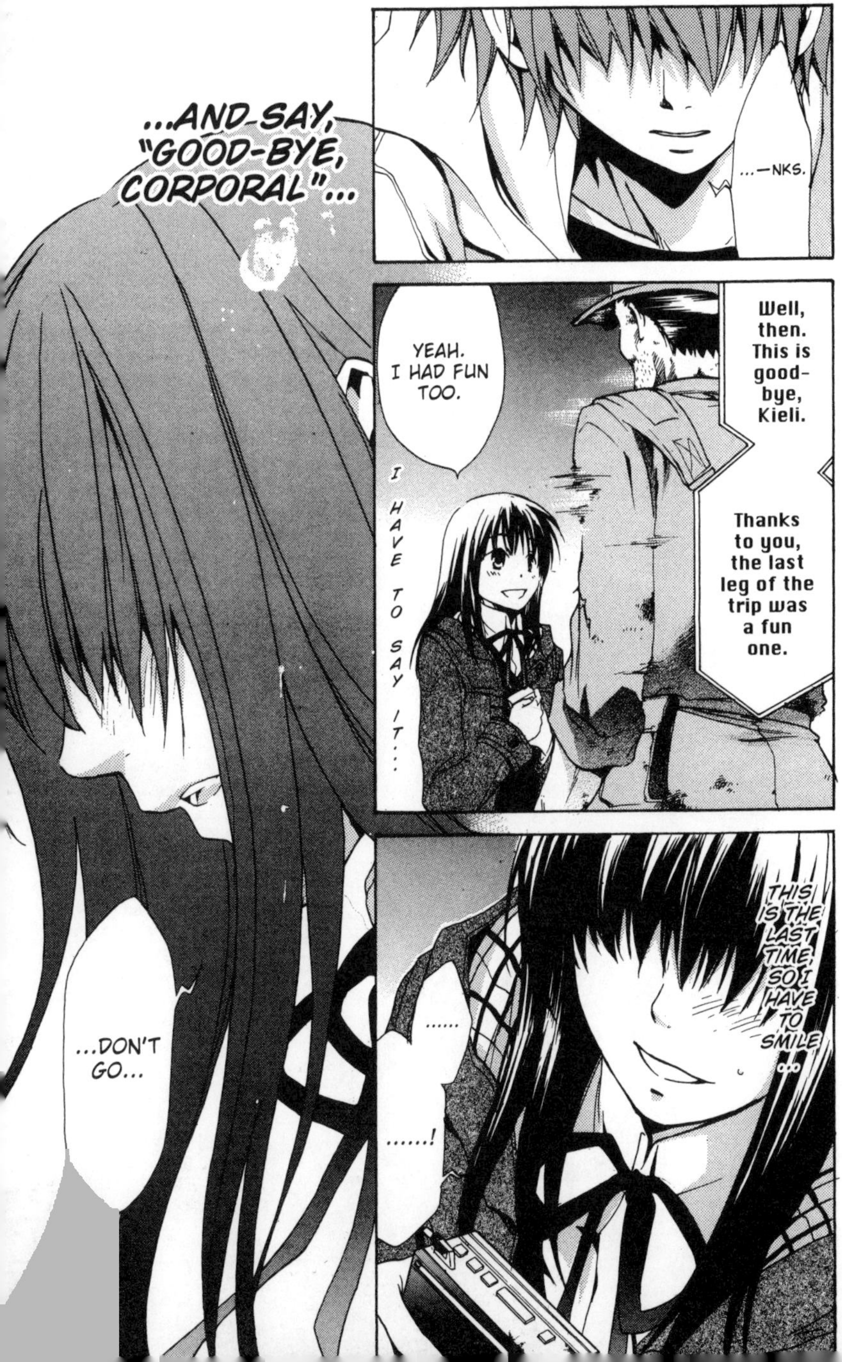
...—NKS.
Well, then. This is good-bye, Kieli.
Thanks to you, the last leg of the trip was a fun one.
YEAH. I HAD FUN TOO.
I HAVE TO SAY IT...
THIS IS THE LAST TIME, SO I HAVE TO SMILE...
......
......!
...AND SAY, "GOOD-BYE, CORPORAL"...
...DON'T GO...

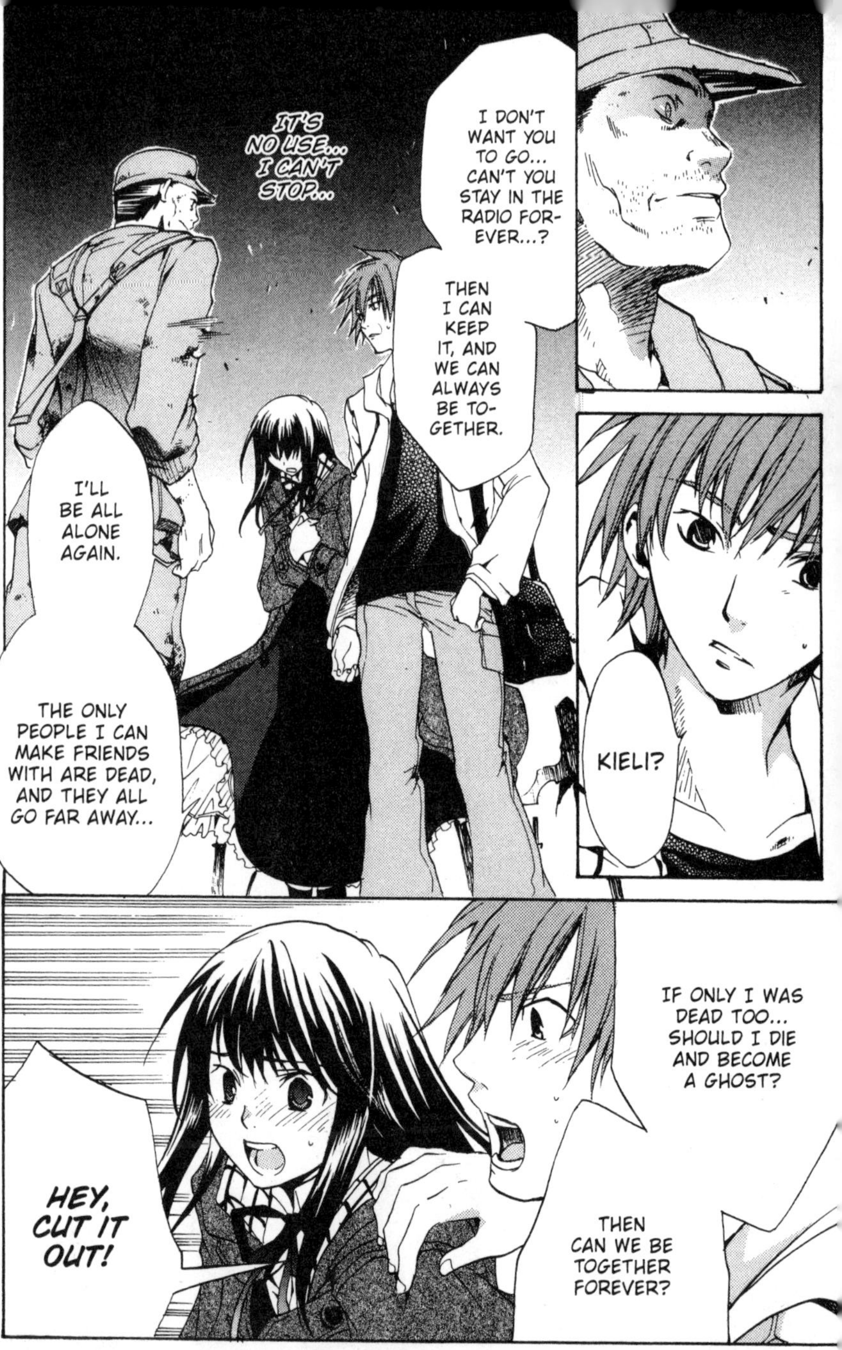

KIELI?
I DON'T WANT YOU TO GO... CAN'T YOU STAY IN THE RADIO FOR-EVER...?
THEN I CAN KEEP IT, AND WE CAN ALWAYS BE TO-GETHER.
IT'S NO USE... I CAN'T STOP...
I'LL BE ALL ALONE AGAIN.
THE ONLY PEOPLE I CAN MAKE FRIENDS WITH ARE DEAD, AND THEY ALL GO FAR AWAY...
IF ONLY I WAS DEAD TOO... SHOULD I DIE AND BECOME A GHOST?
THEN CAN WE BE TOGETHER FOREVER?
HEY, CUT IT OUT!

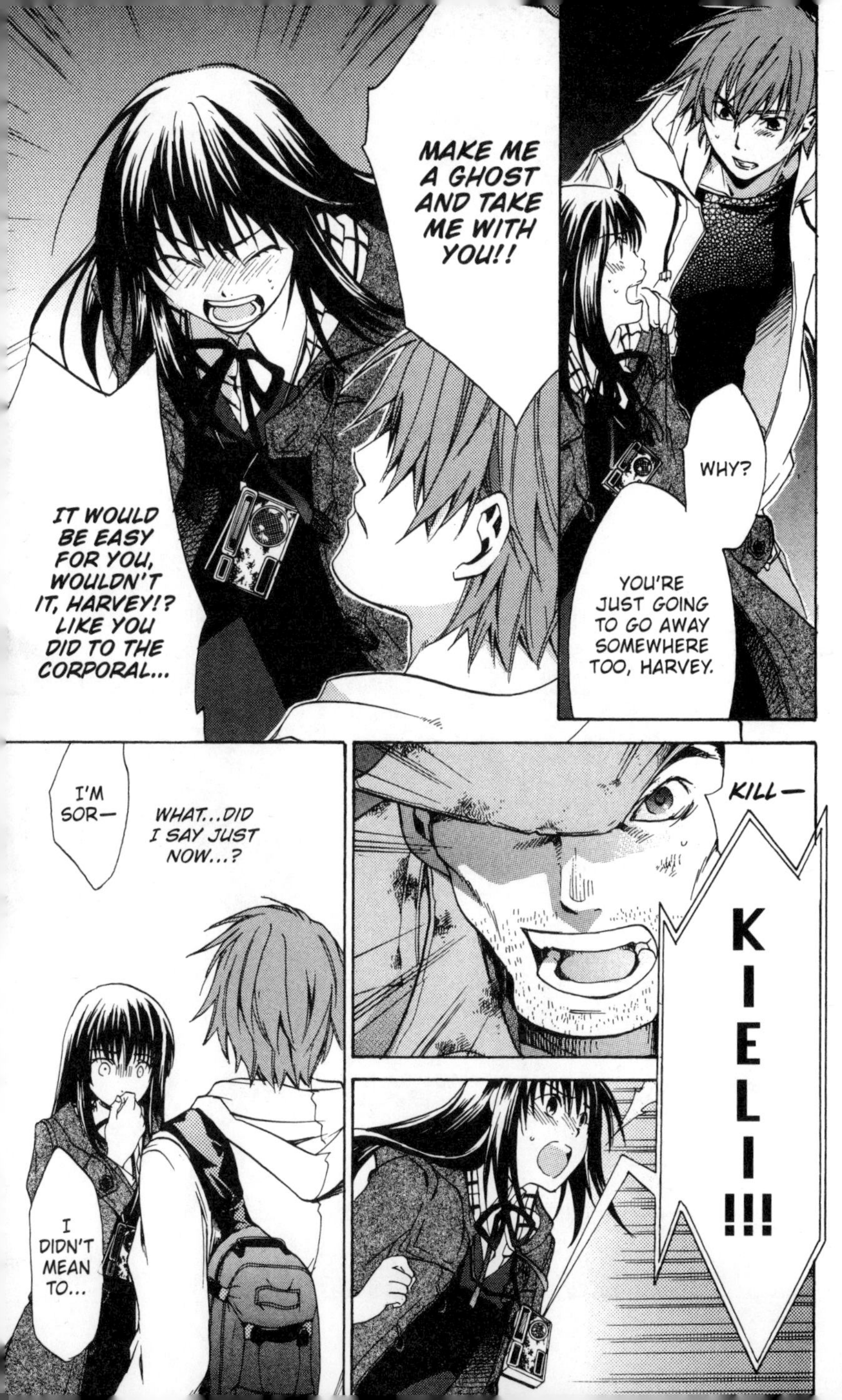
WHY?
YOU'RE JUST GOING TO GO AWAY SOMEWHERE TOO, HARVEY.
MAKE ME A GHOST AND TAKE ME WITH YOU!!
IT WOULD BE EASY FOR YOU, WOULDN'T IT, HARVEY!? LIKE YOU DID TO THE CORPORAL...
KILL—
KIELI!!!
WHAT...DID I SAY JUST NOW...?
I'M SOR—
I DIDN'T MEAN TO...

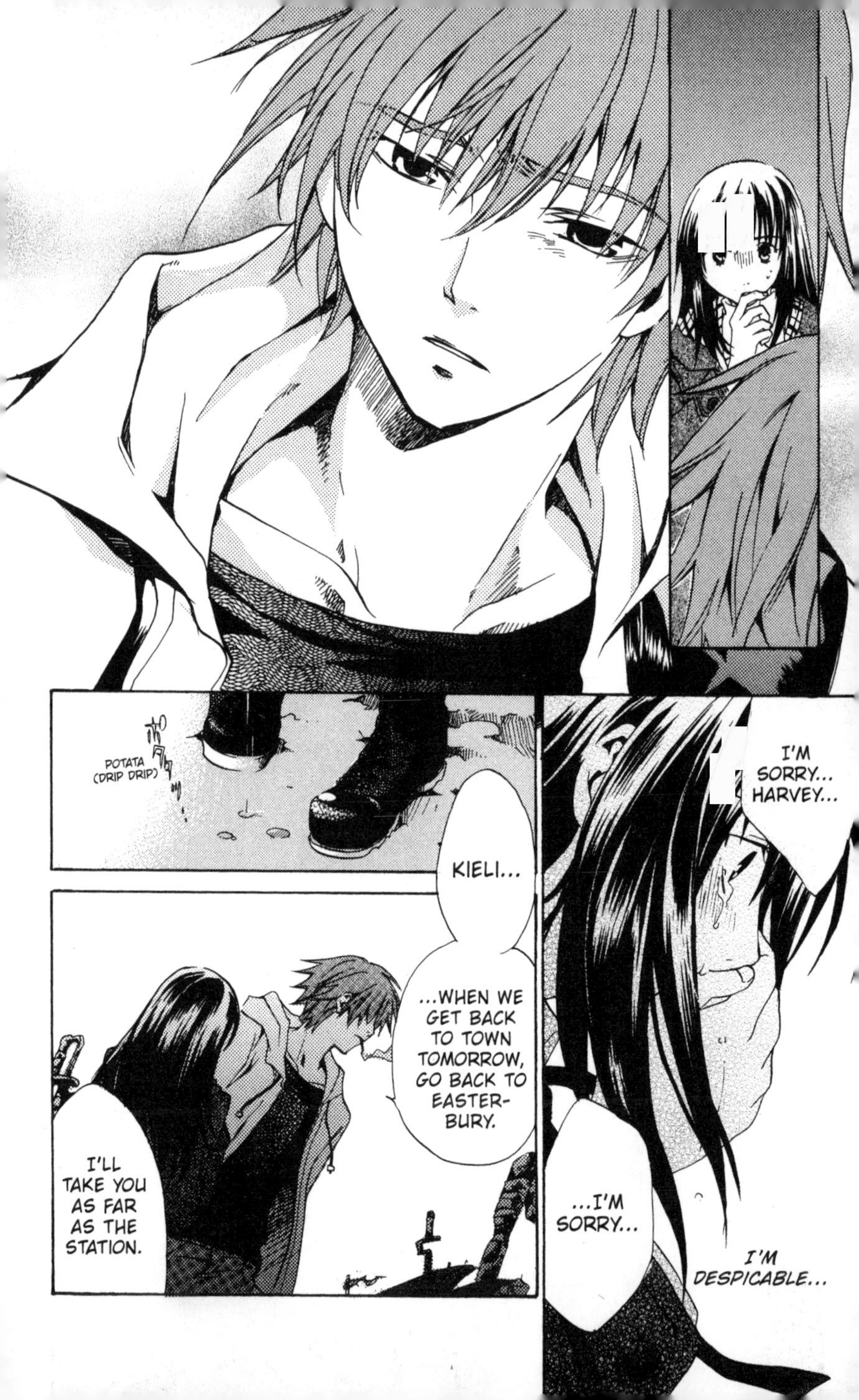
I'M SORRY... HARVEY...
...I'M SORRY...
I'M DESPICABLE...
POTATA (DRIP DRIP)
KIELI...
...WHEN WE GET BACK TO TOWN TOMORROW, GO BACK TO EASTER-BURY.
I'LL TAKE YOU AS FAR AS THE STATION.

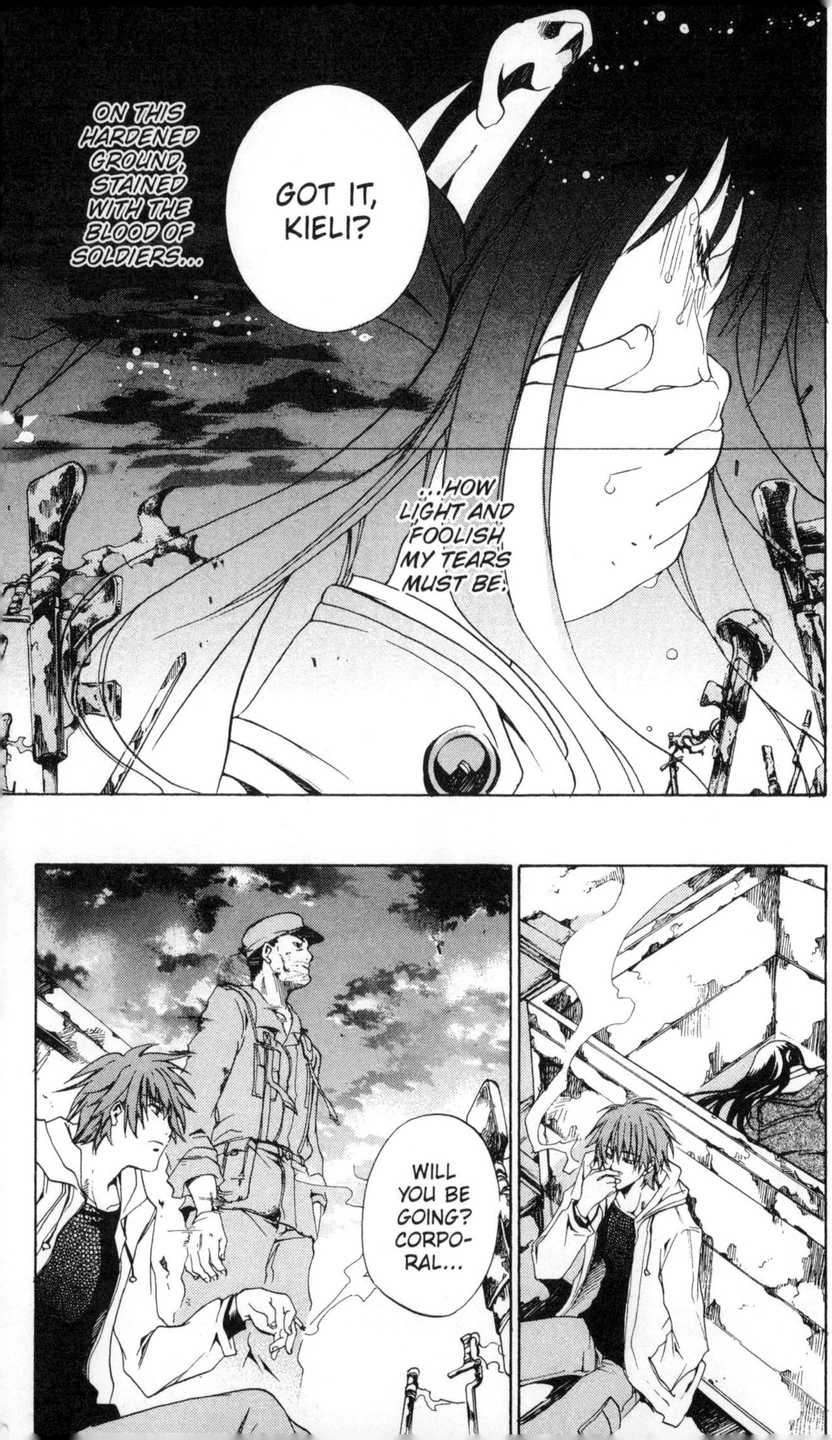
GOT IT, KIELI?
ON THIS HARDENED GROUND, STAINED WITH THE BLOOD OF SOLDIERS...
...HOW LIGHT AND FOOLISH MY TEARS MUST BE.
WILL YOU BE GOING? CORPORAL...

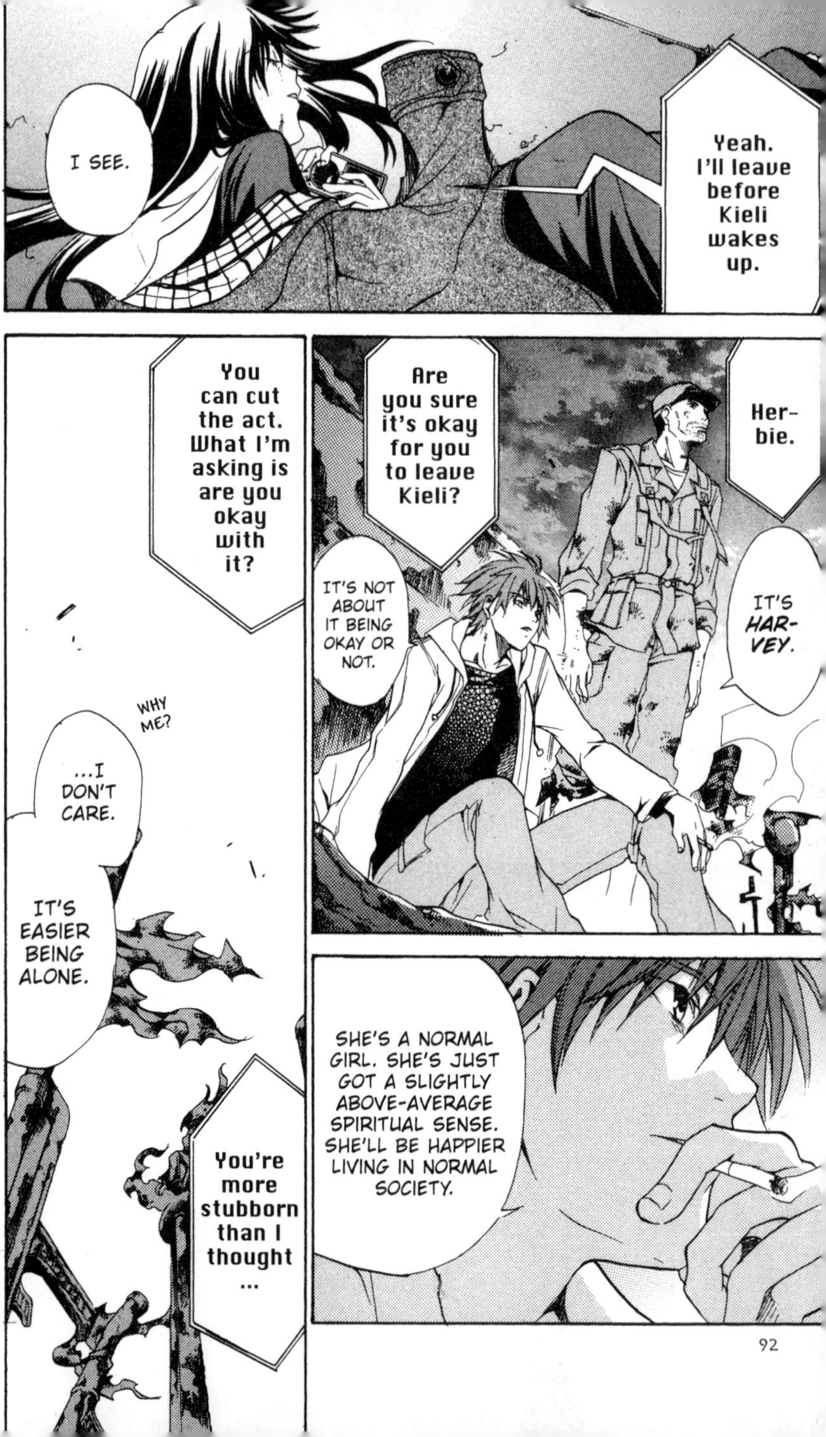

Yeah. I'll leave before Kieli wakes up.
I SEE.
Her-bie.
IT'S *HARVEY*.
Are you sure it's okay for you to leave Kieli?
IT'S NOT ABOUT IT BEING OKAY OR NOT.
SHE'S A NORMAL GIRL. SHE'S JUST GOT A SLIGHTLY ABOVE-AVERAGE SPIRITUAL SENSE. SHE'LL BE HAPPIER LIVING IN NORMAL SOCIETY.
You can cut the act. What I'm asking is are you okay with it?
WHY ME?
...I DON'T CARE.
IT'S EASIER BEING ALONE.
You're more stubborn than I thought...

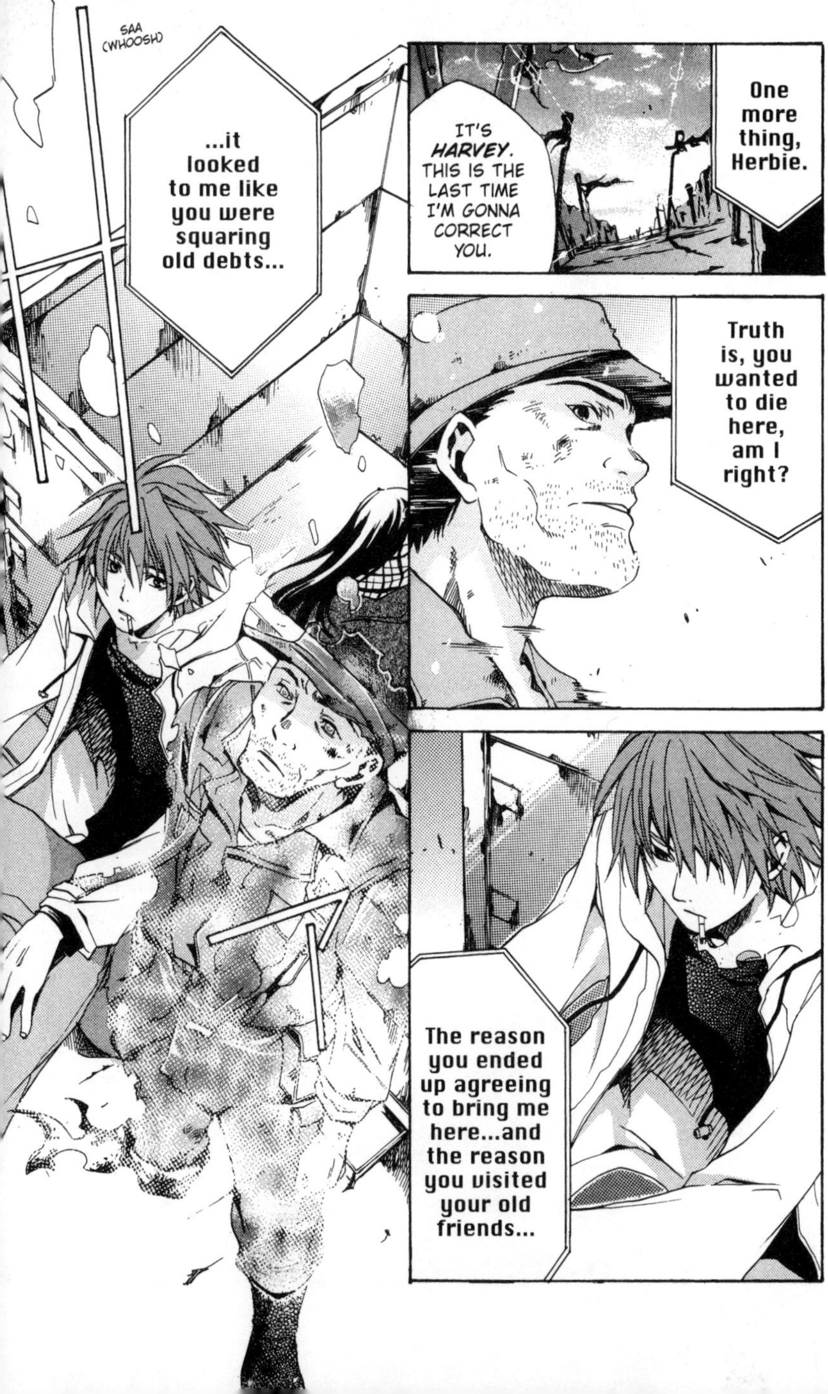
One more thing, Herbie.
IT'S HARVEY. THIS IS THE LAST TIME I'M GONNA CORRECT YOU.
Truth is, you wanted to die here, am I right?
The reason you ended up agreeing to bring me here...and the reason you visited your old friends...
SAA (WHOOSH)
...it looked to me like you were squaring old debts...

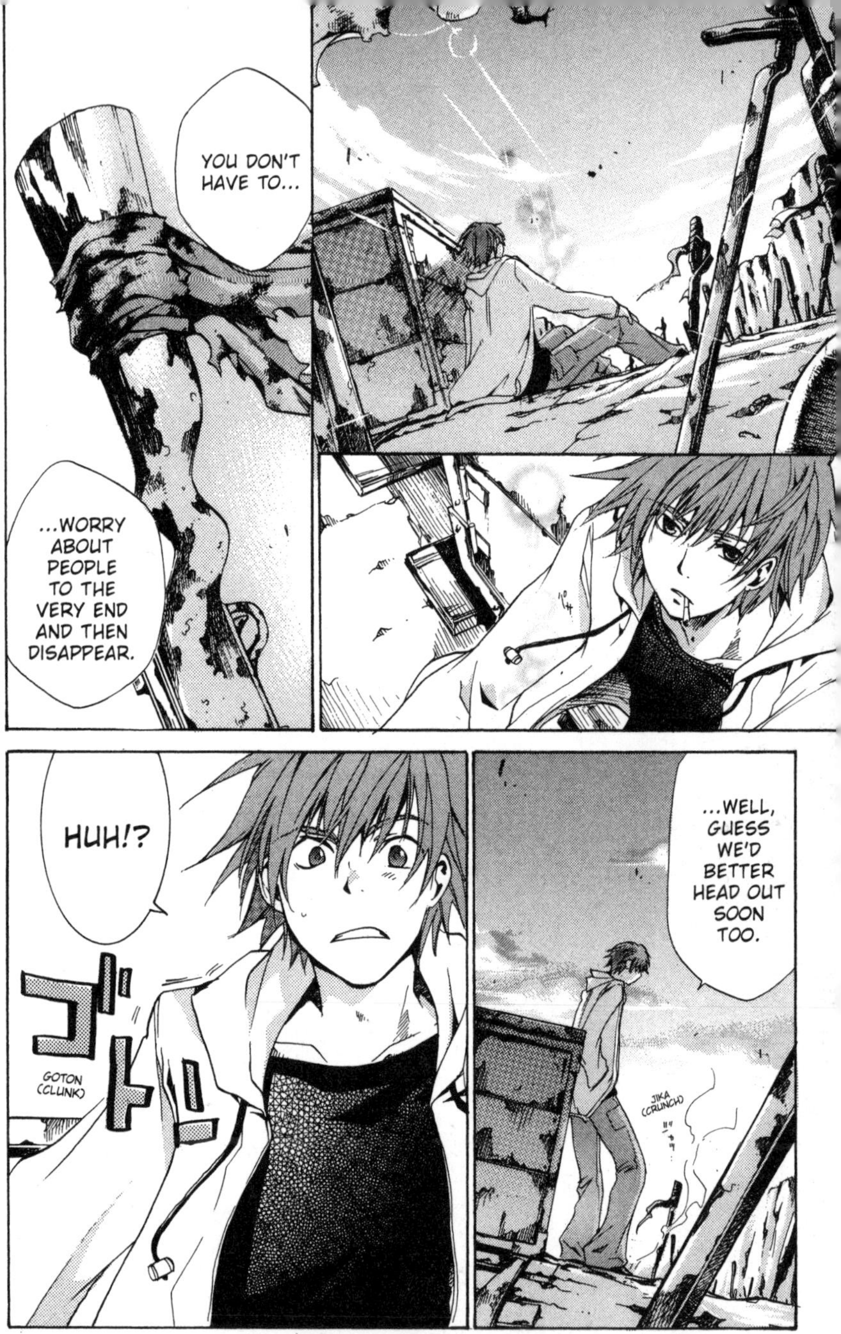
YOU DON'T HAVE TO...
...WORRY ABOUT PEOPLE TO THE VERY END AND THEN DISAPPEAR.
...WELL, GUESS WE'D BETTER HEAD OUT SOON TOO.
JIKA (CRUNCH)
HUH!?
ゴトン
GOTON (CLUNK)

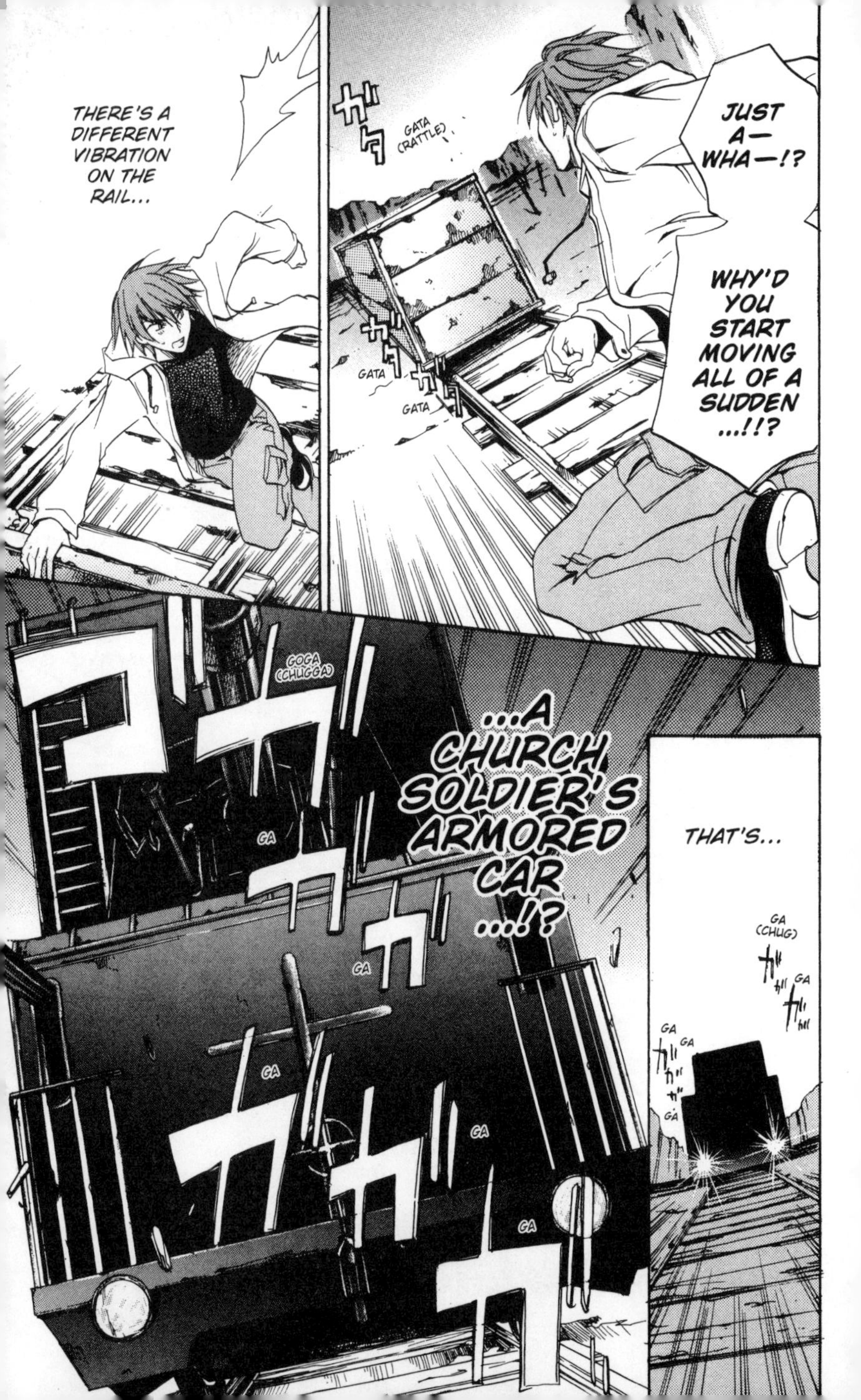
JUST A— WHA—!?
GATA (RATTLE)
GATA
GATA
WHY'D YOU START MOVING ALL OF A SUDDEN ...!!?
THERE'S A DIFFERENT VIBRATION ON THE RAIL...
THAT'S...
GA (CHUG)
GA
GA
GA
GA
GOGA (CHUGGA)
...A CHURCH SOLDIER'S ARMORED CAR ...!?
GA
GA
GA
GA
GA

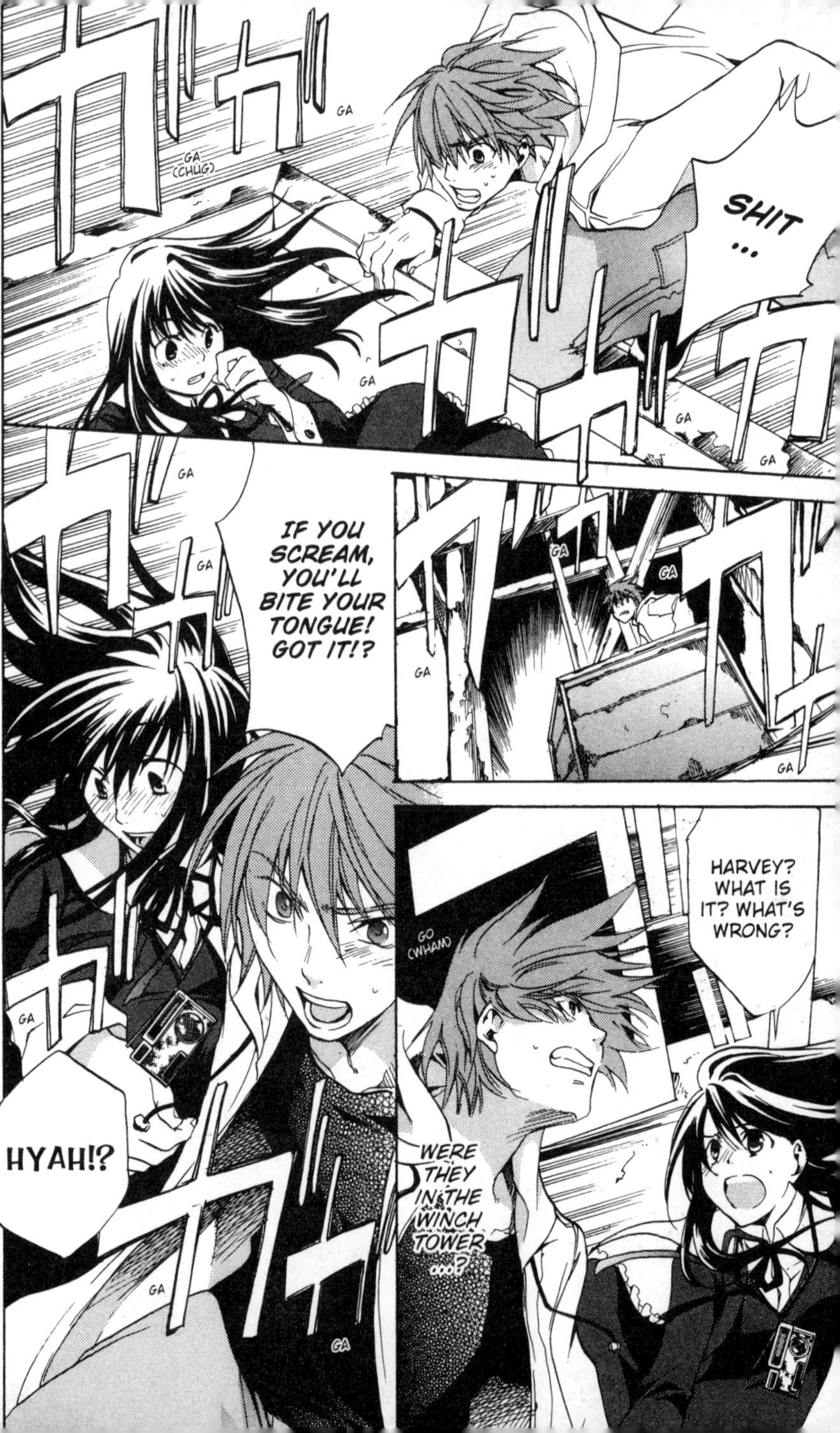
SHIT ...
GA
GA (CHUG)
GA
GA
GA
GA
GA
GA
GA
HARVEY? WHAT IS IT? WHAT'S WRONG?
GO (WHAM)
WERE THEY IN THE WINCH TOWER ...?
GA
IF YOU SCREAM, YOU'LL BITE YOUR TONGUE! GOT IT!?
GA
GA
HYAH!?
GA
GA

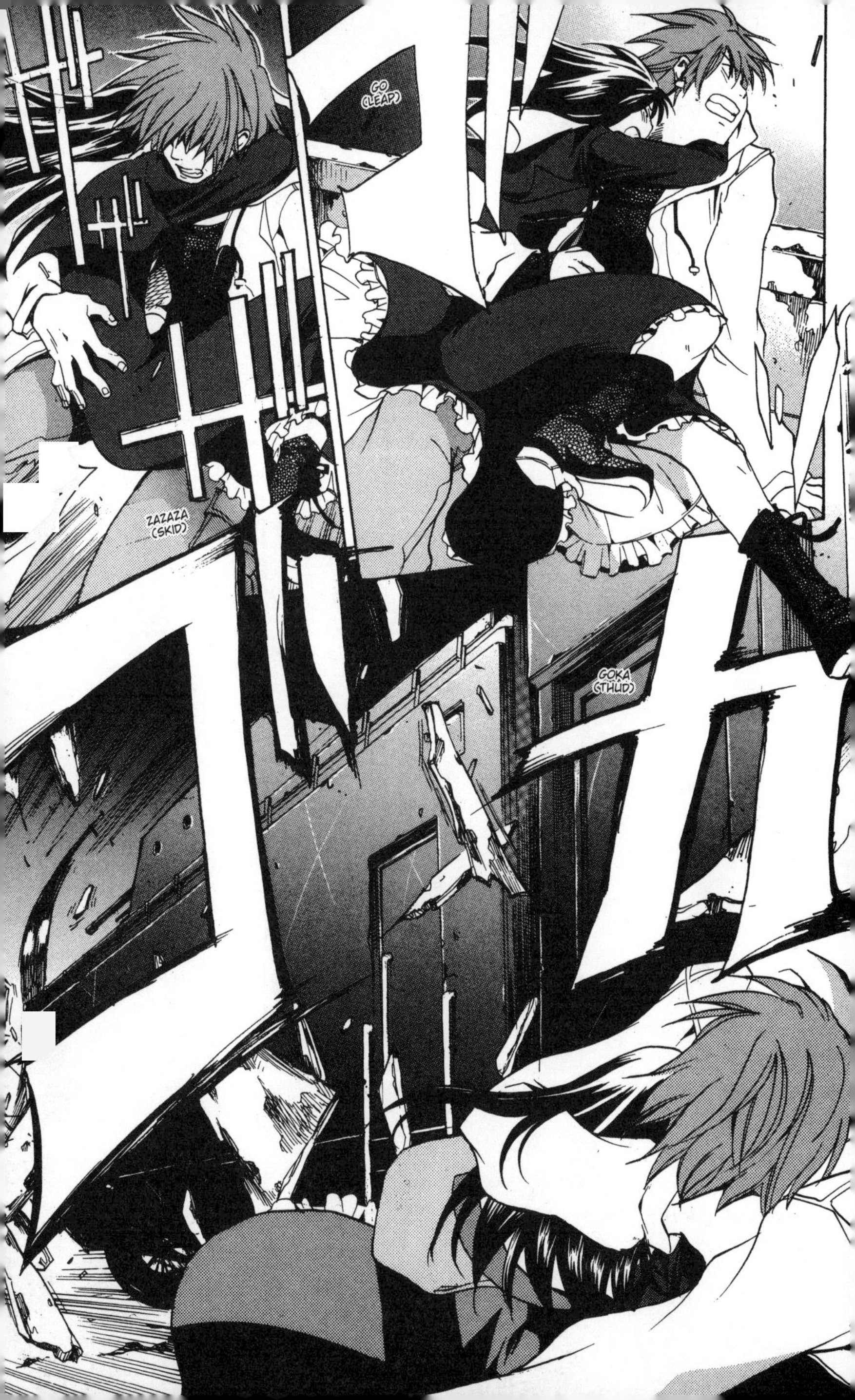
GO (LEAP)
ZAZAZA (SKID)
GOKA (THUD)

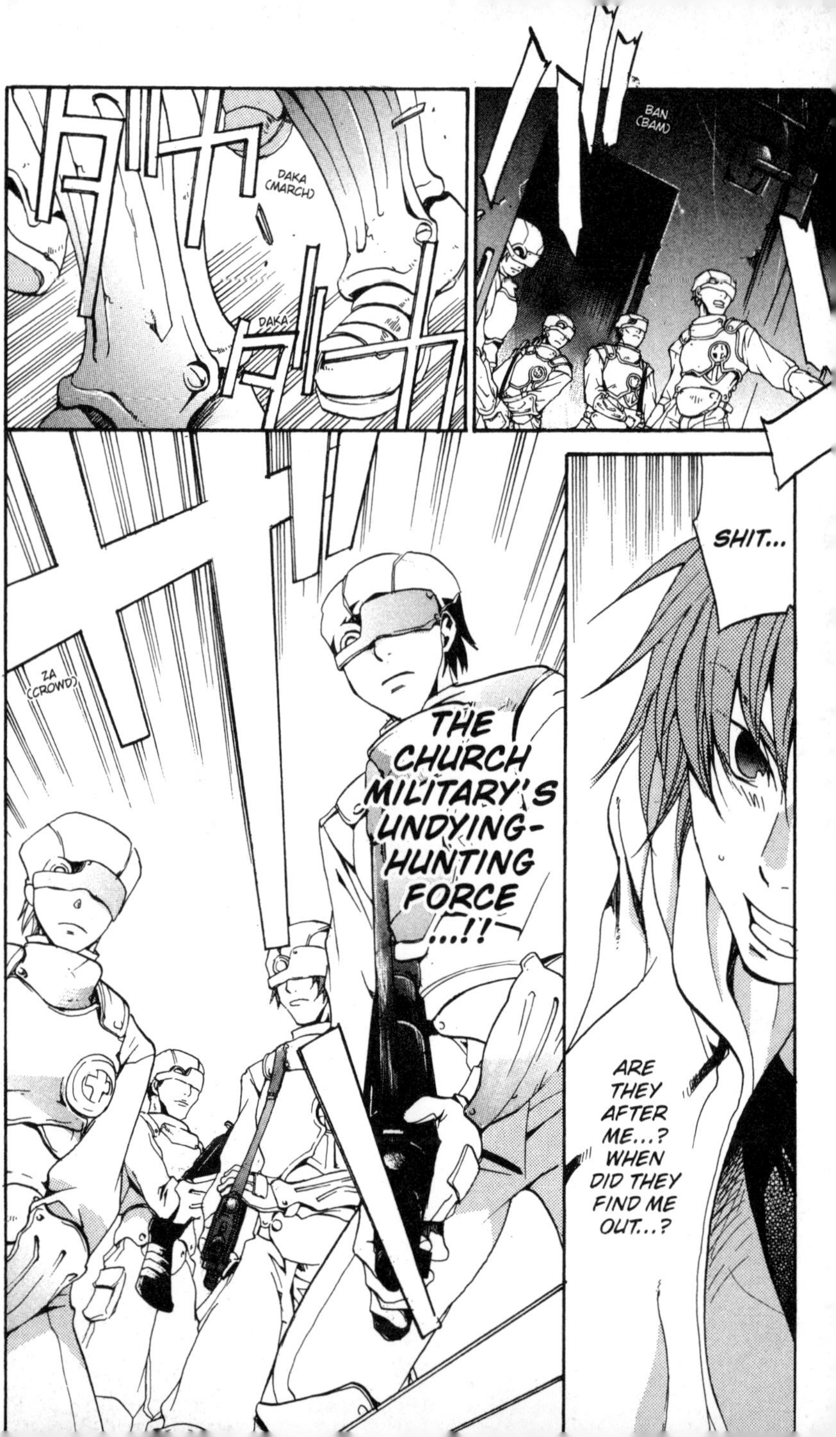
BAN
(BAM)
DAKA
(MARCH)
DAKA
SHIT...
ARE THEY AFTER ME...? WHEN DID THEY FIND ME OUT...?
ZA
(CROWD)
THE CHURCH MILITARY'S UNDYING-HUNTING FORCE ...!!

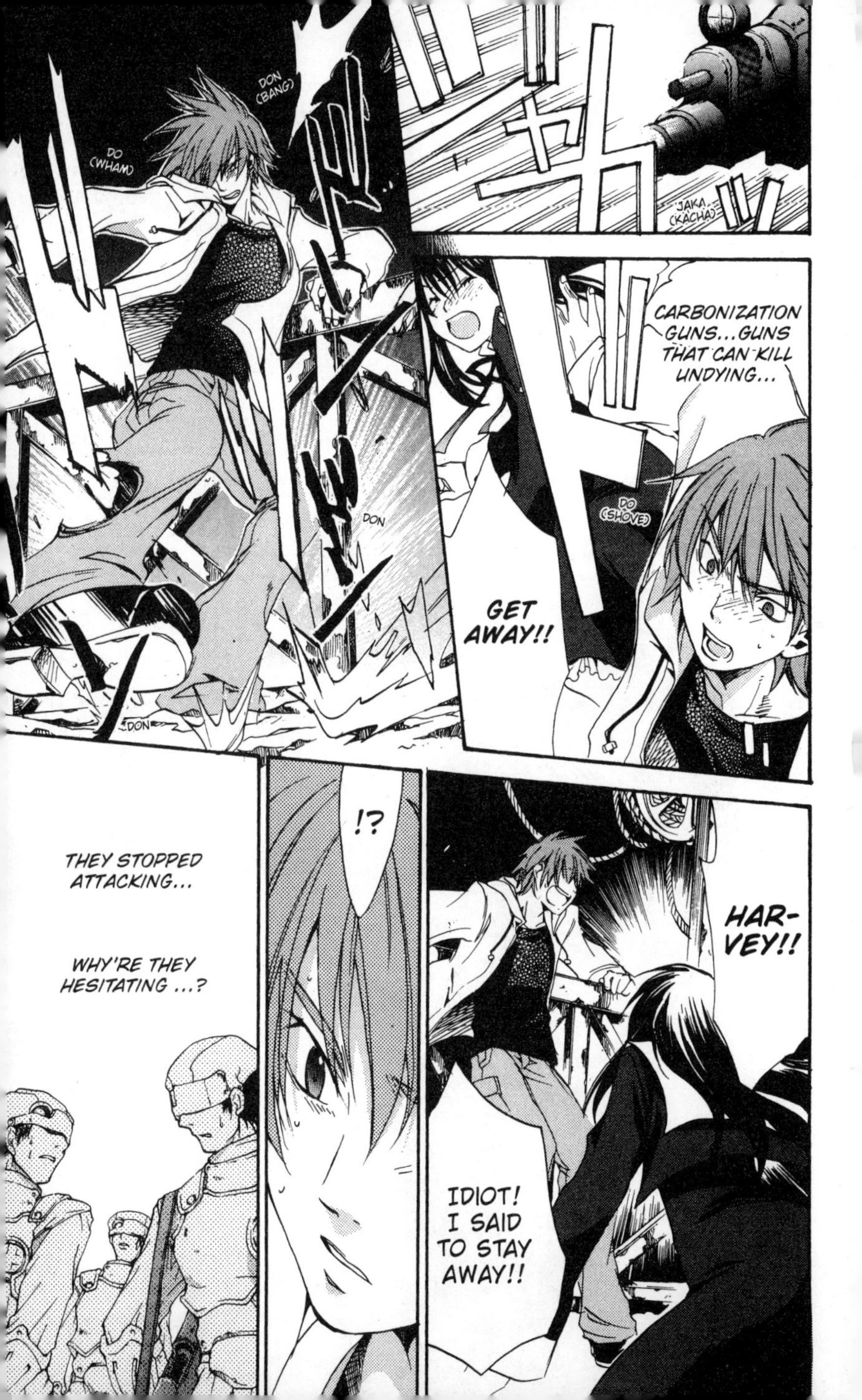
JAKA (KACHA)
CARBONIZATION GUNS...GUNS THAT CAN KILL UNDYING...
DO (SHOVE)
GET AWAY!!
DON (BANG)
DO (WHAM)
DON
DON
HAR-VEY!!
IDIOT! I SAID TO STAY AWAY!!
!?
THEY STOPPED ATTACKING...
WHY'RE THEY HESITATING ...?

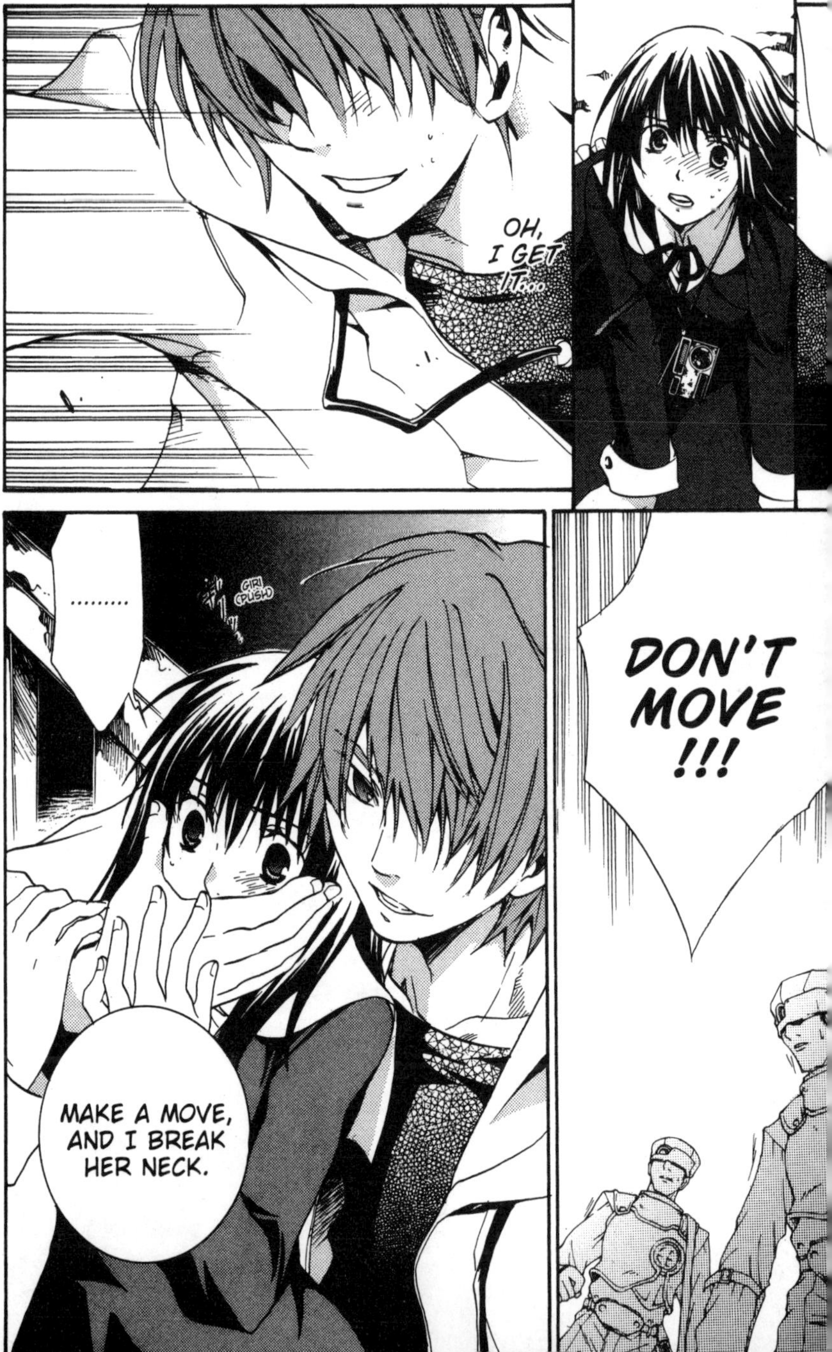
OH, I GET IT...
....
GIRI (PUSH)
DON'T MOVE !!!
MAKE A MOVE, AND I BREAK HER NECK.

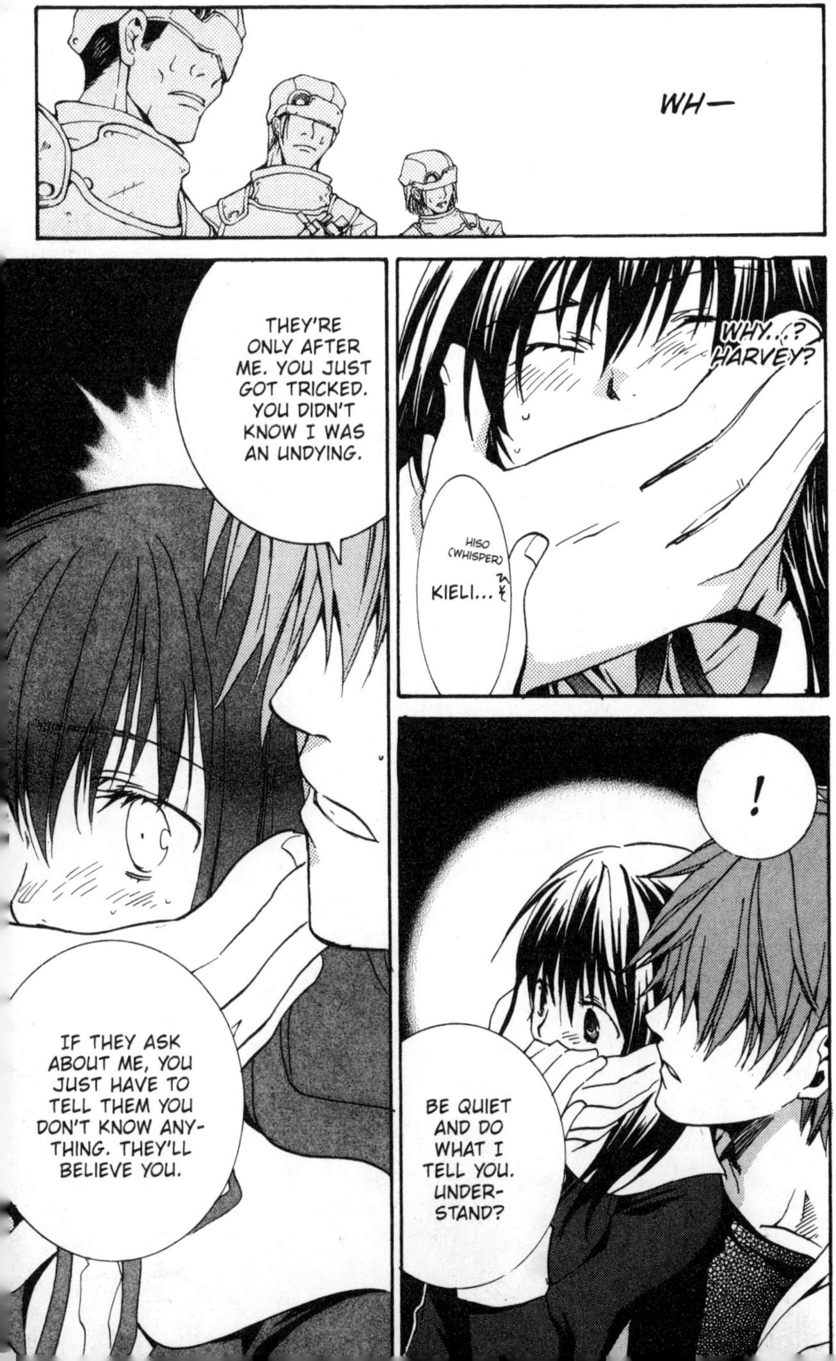
WH—
WHY...? HARVEY?
HISO (WHISPER)
KIELI...
!
BE QUIET AND DO WHAT I TELL YOU. UNDERSTAND?
THEY'RE ONLY AFTER ME. YOU JUST GOT TRICKED. YOU DIDN'T KNOW I WAS AN UNDYING.
IF THEY ASK ABOUT ME, YOU JUST HAVE TO TELL THEM YOU DON'T KNOW ANYTHING. THEY'LL BELIEVE YOU.

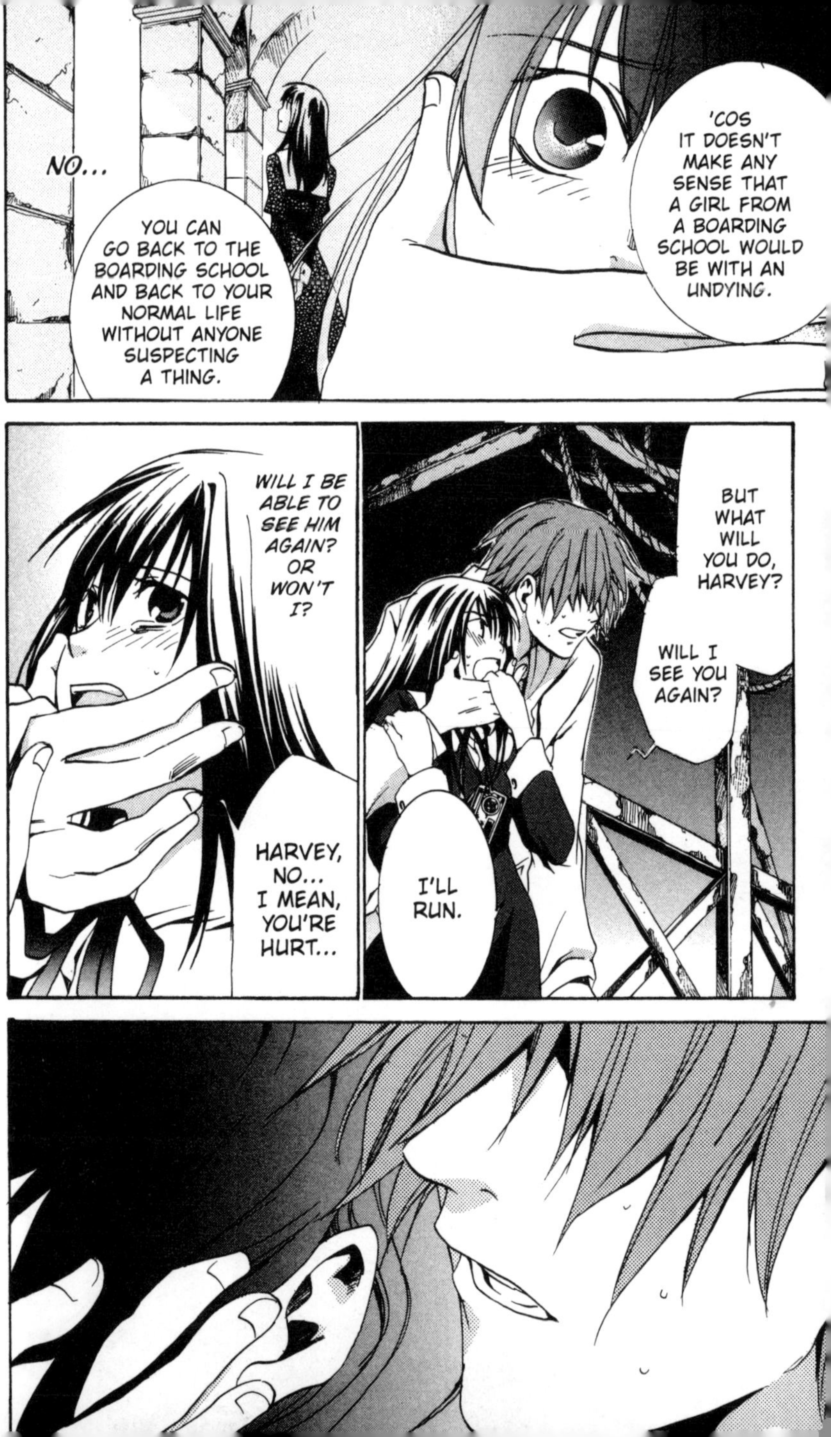

'COS IT DOESN'T MAKE ANY SENSE THAT A GIRL FROM A BOARDING SCHOOL WOULD BE WITH AN UNDYING.
NO...
YOU CAN GO BACK TO THE BOARDING SCHOOL AND BACK TO YOUR NORMAL LIFE WITHOUT ANYONE SUSPECTING A THING.
BUT WHAT WILL YOU DO, HARVEY?
WILL I SEE YOU AGAIN?
I'LL RUN.
WILL I BE ABLE TO SEE HIM AGAIN? OR WON'T I?
HARVEY, NO... I MEAN, YOU'RE HURT...

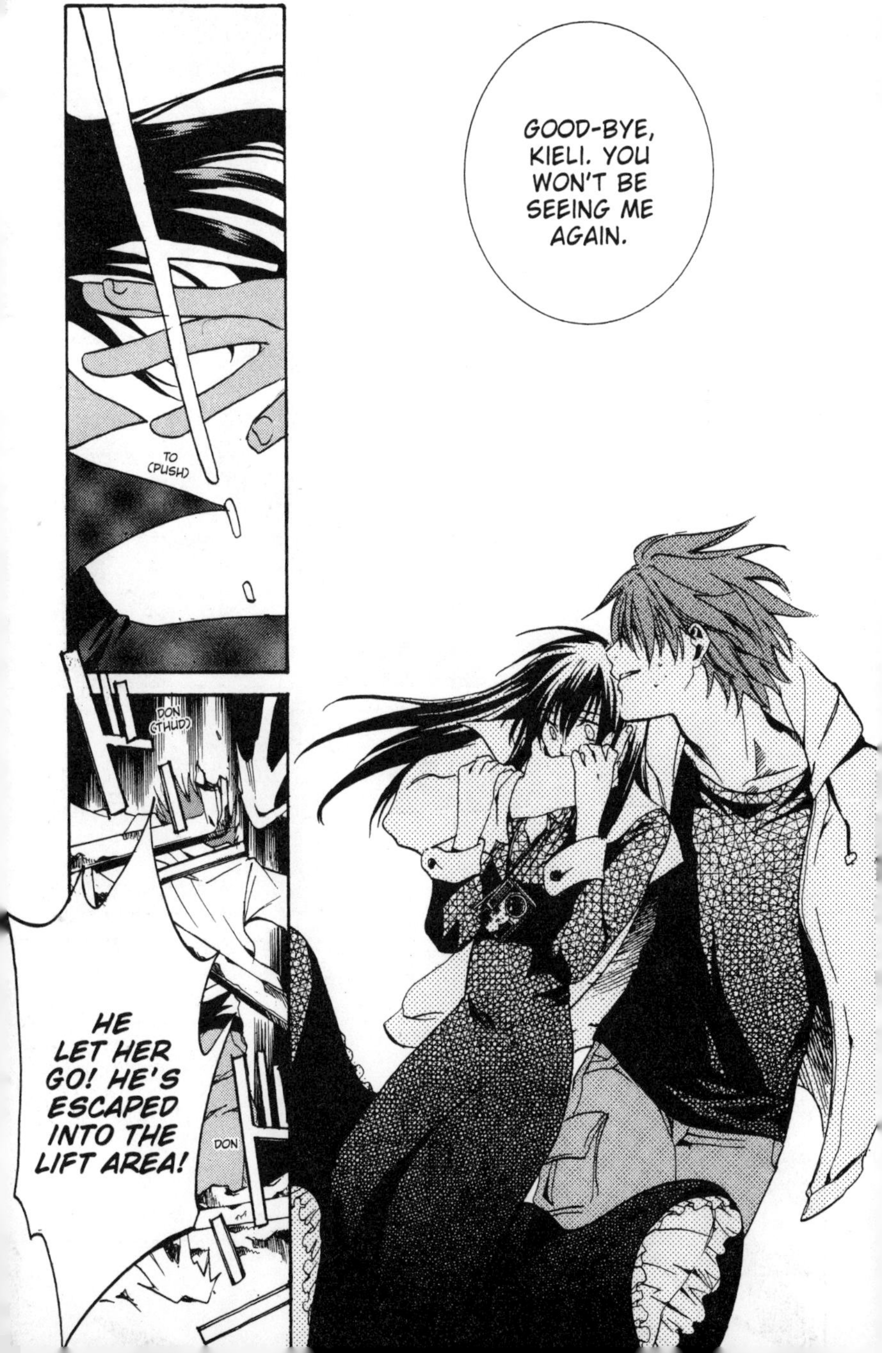
GOOD-BYE, KIELI. YOU WON'T BE SEEING ME AGAIN.
TO (PUSH)
DON (THUD)
HE LET HER GO! HE'S ESCAPED INTO THE LIFT AREA!
DON

RAISE THE LIFT!!
ARE YOU OKAY!?
GOOD-BYE, KIELI. YOU WON'T BE SEEING ME AGAIN.
HEY!
GOOD-BYE, KIELI. YOU WON'T BE SEEING ME AGAIN.

GOOD-BYE, KIELI.

CHAPTER 5: THE DEAD SLEEP IN THE WILDERNESS / FIN

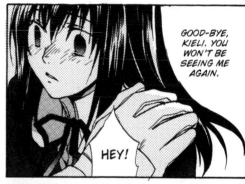

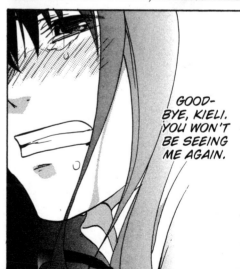

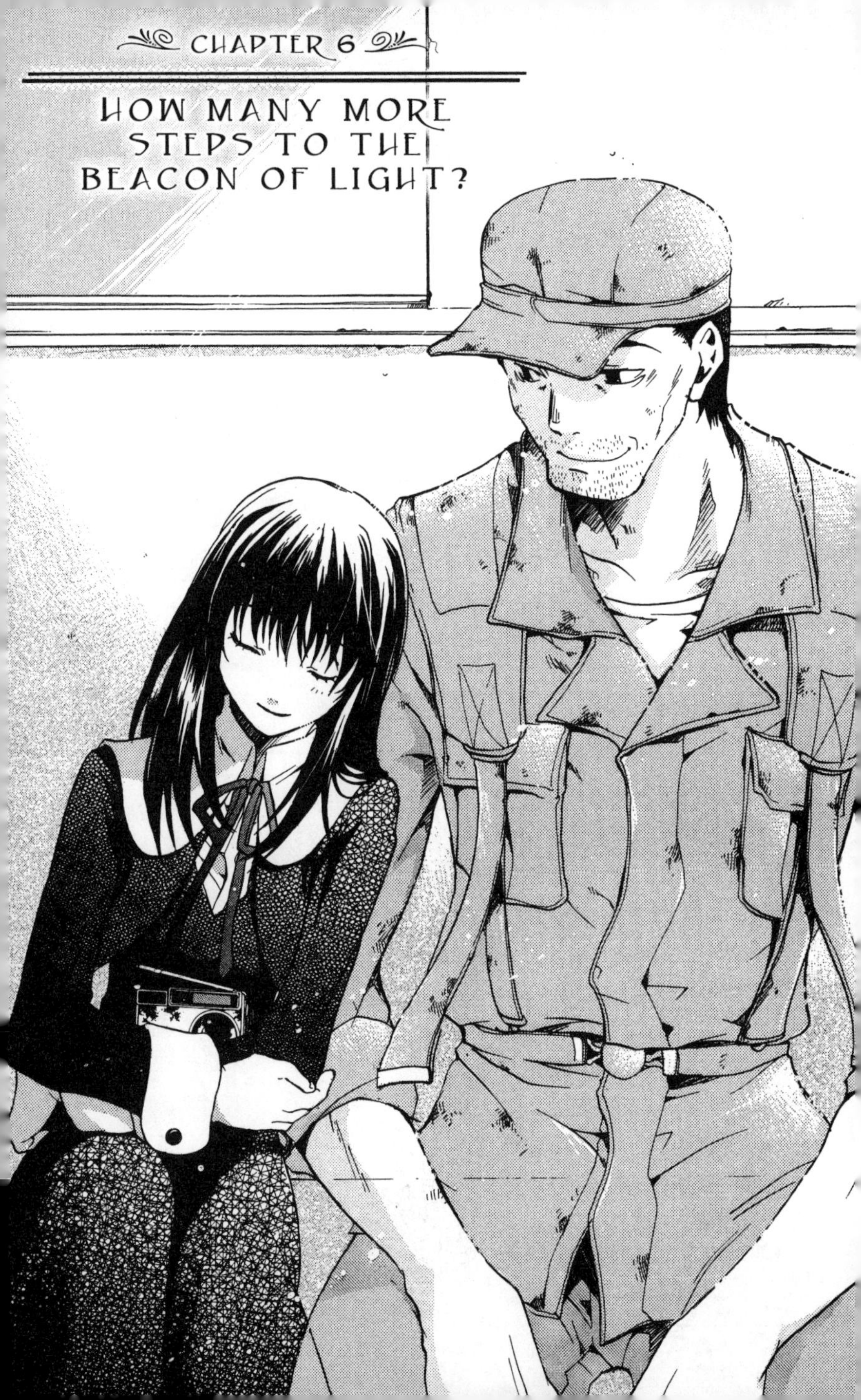
CHAPTER 6
HOW MANY MORE STEPS TO THE BEACON OF LIGHT?

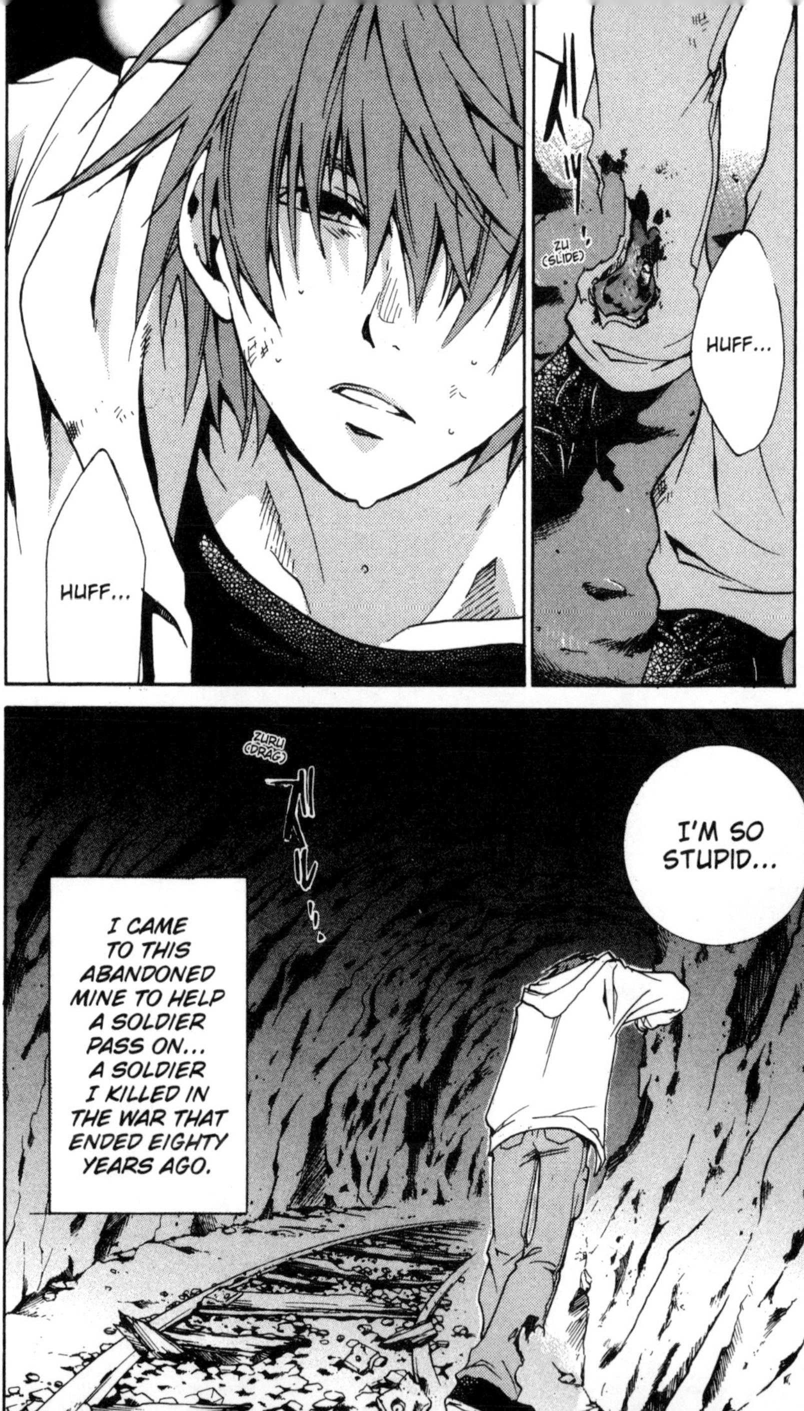
ZU (SLIDE)
HUFF...
HUFF...
I'M SO STUPID...
ZURU (DRAG)
I CAME TO THIS ABANDONED MINE TO HELP A SOLDIER PASS ON... A SOLDIER I KILLED IN THE WAR THAT ENDED EIGHTY YEARS AGO.

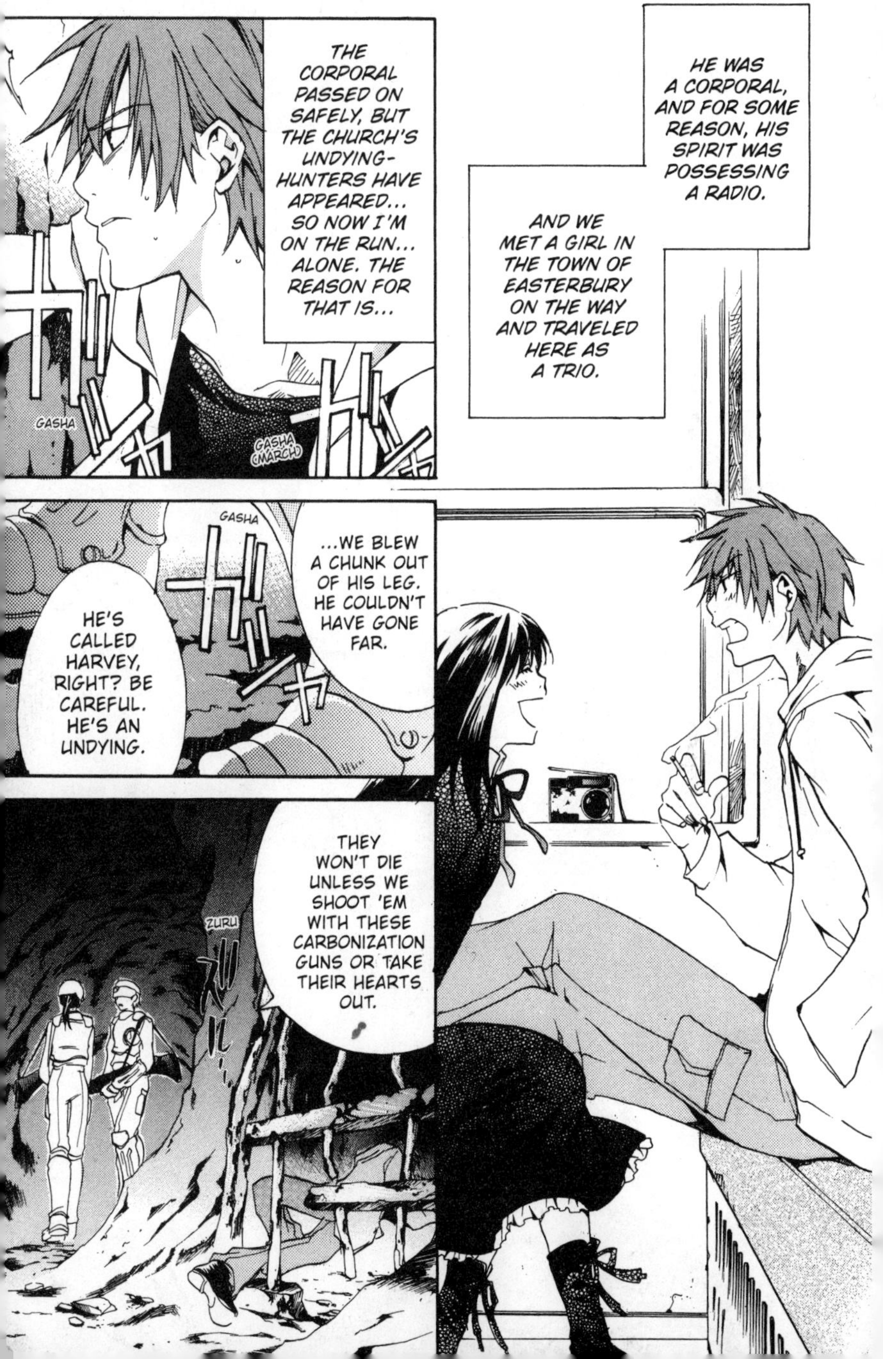
HE WAS A CORPORAL, AND FOR SOME REASON, HIS SPIRIT WAS POSSESSING A RADIO.
AND WE MET A GIRL IN THE TOWN OF EASTERBURY ON THE WAY AND TRAVELED HERE AS A TRIO.
THE CORPORAL PASSED ON SAFELY, BUT THE CHURCH'S UNDYING-HUNTERS HAVE APPEARED... SO NOW I'M ON THE RUN... ALONE. THE REASON FOR THAT IS...
GASHA (MARCH)
GASHA
GASHA
...WE BLEW A CHUNK OUT OF HIS LEG. HE COULDN'T HAVE GONE FAR.
HE'S CALLED HARVEY, RIGHT? BE CAREFUL. HE'S AN UNDYING.
THEY WON'T DIE UNLESS WE SHOOT 'EM WITH THESE CARBONIZATION GUNS OR TAKE THEIR HEARTS OUT.
ZURU

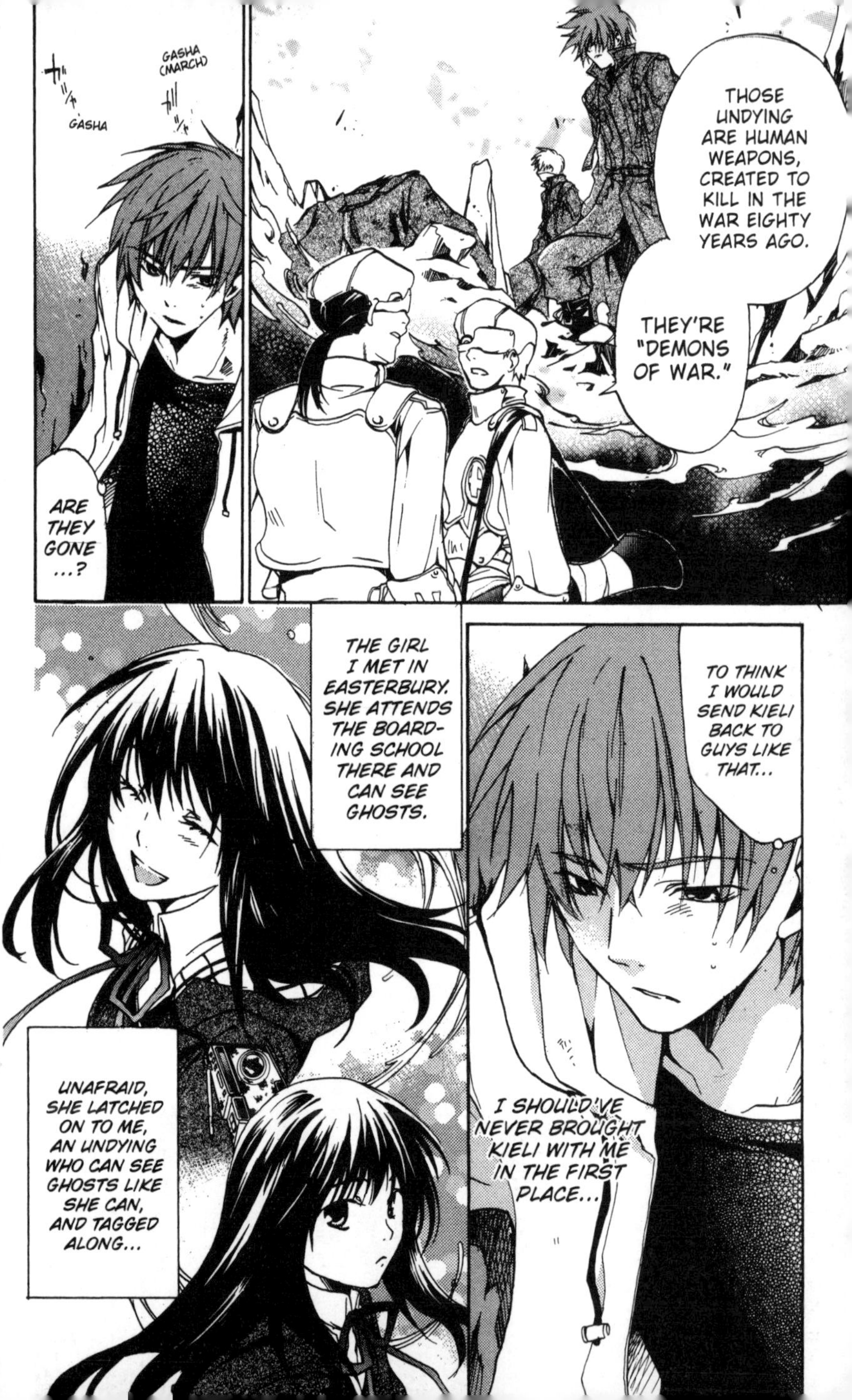
THOSE UNDYING ARE HUMAN WEAPONS, CREATED TO KILL IN THE WAR EIGHTY YEARS AGO.
THEY'RE "DEMONS OF WAR."
GASHA (MARCH)
GASHA
ARE THEY GONE ...?
TO THINK I WOULD SEND KIELI BACK TO GUYS LIKE THAT...
I SHOULD'VE NEVER BROUGHT KIELI WITH ME IN THE FIRST PLACE...
THE GIRL I MET IN EASTERBURY. SHE ATTENDS THE BOARDING SCHOOL THERE AND CAN SEE GHOSTS.
UNAFRAID, SHE LATCHED ON TO ME, AN UNDYING WHO CAN SEE GHOSTS LIKE SHE CAN, AND TAGGED ALONG...

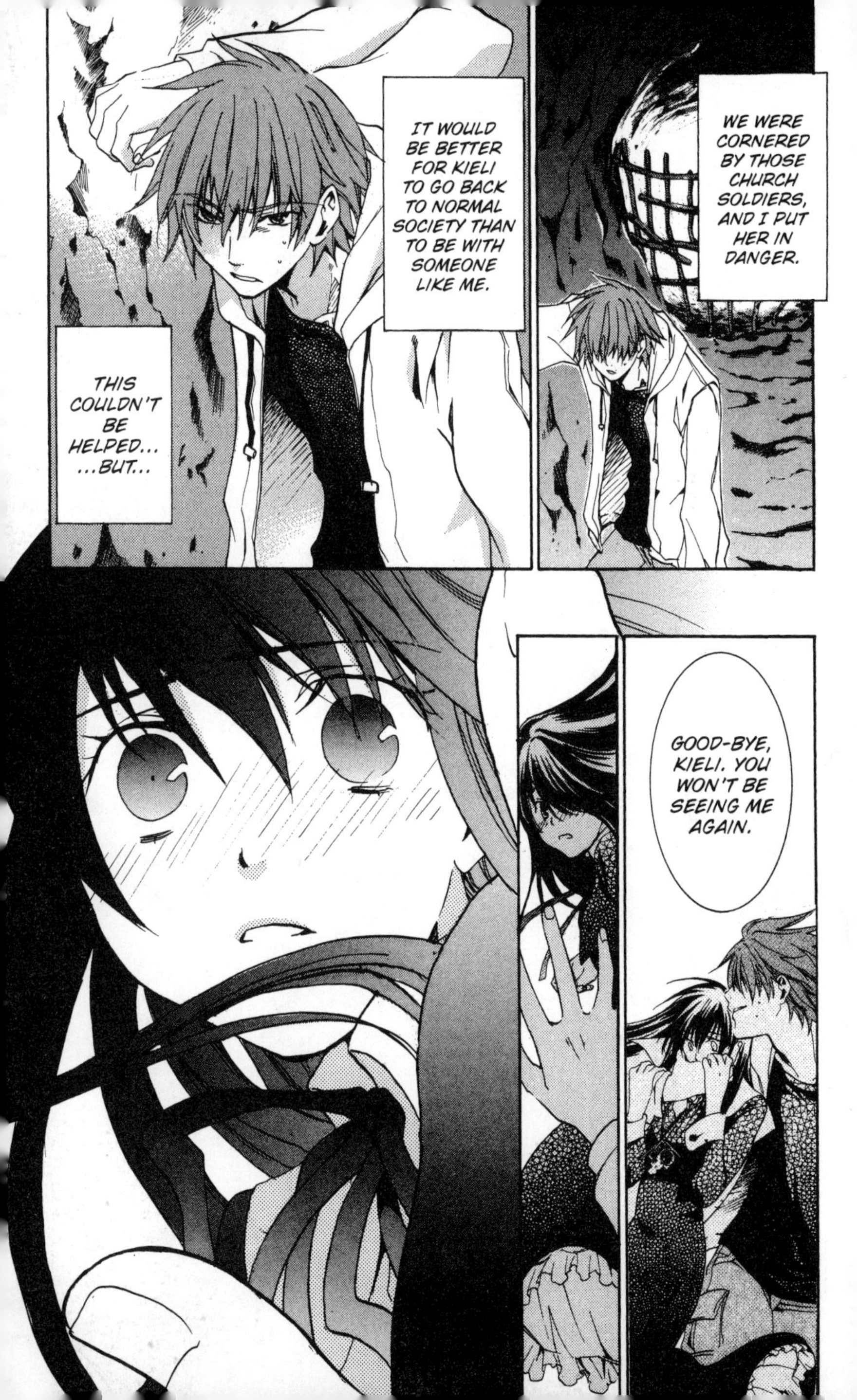
WE WERE CORNERED BY THOSE CHURCH SOLDIERS, AND I PUT HER IN DANGER.
IT WOULD BE BETTER FOR KIELI TO GO BACK TO NORMAL SOCIETY THAN TO BE WITH SOMEONE LIKE ME.
THIS COULDN'T BE HELPED... ...BUT...
GOOD-BYE, KIELI. YOU WON'T BE SEEING ME AGAIN.

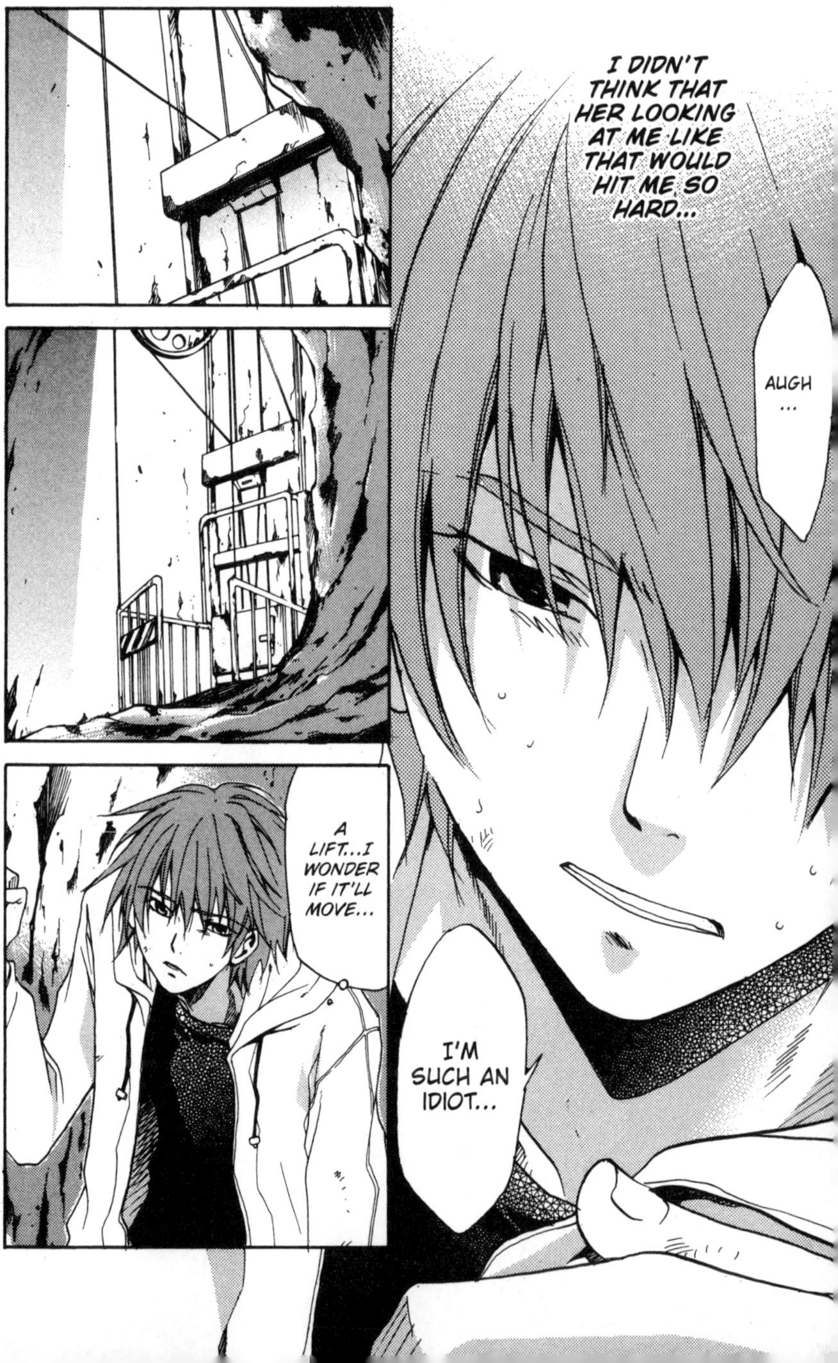

I DIDN'T THINK THAT HER LOOKING AT ME LIKE THAT WOULD HIT ME SO HARD...
AUGH ...
I'M SUCH AN IDIOT...
A LIFT...I WONDER IF IT'LL MOVE...

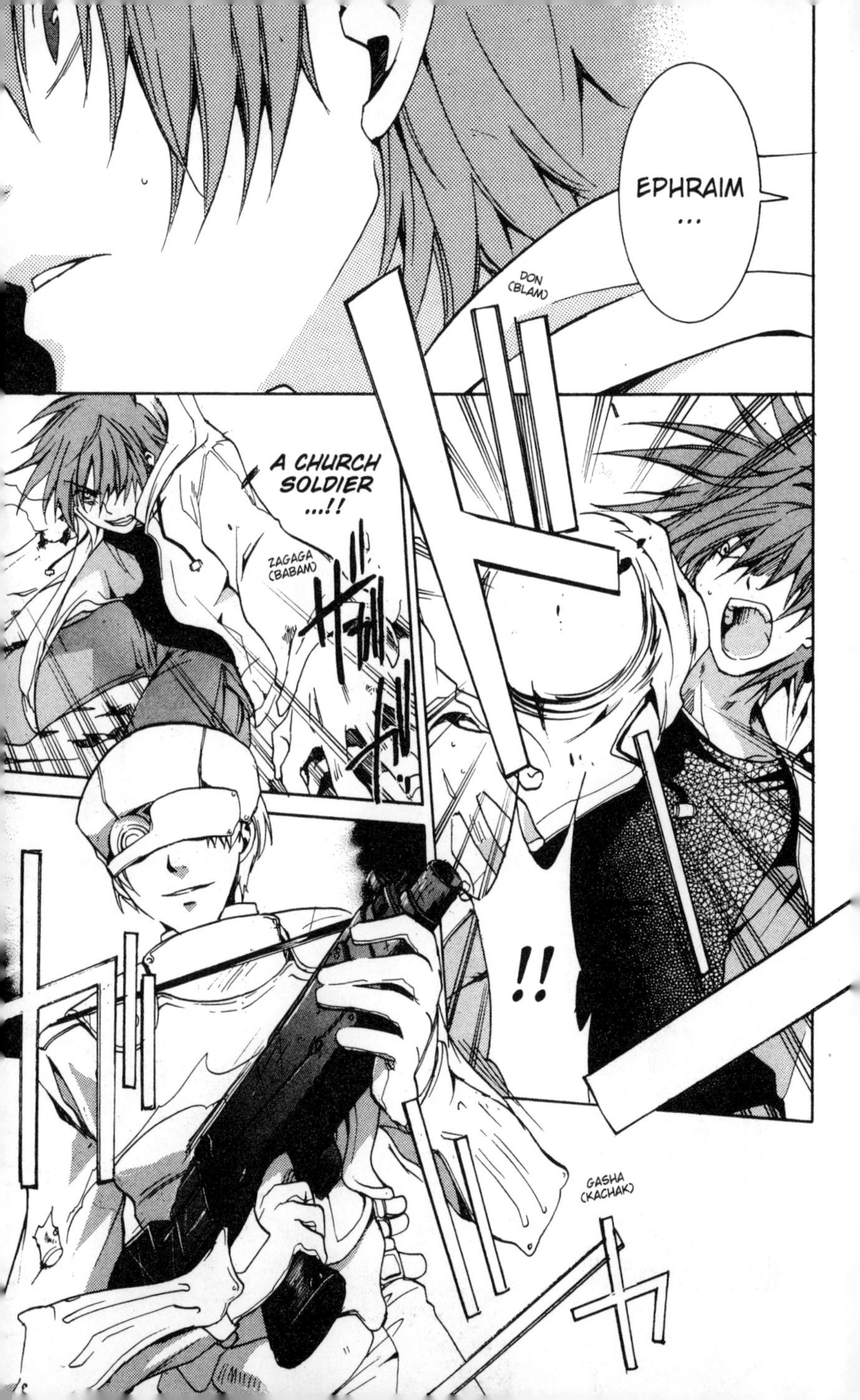
EPHRAIM
...
DON
(BLAM)
A CHURCH SOLDIER ...!!
ZAGAGA
(BABAM)
!!
GASHA
(KACHAK)

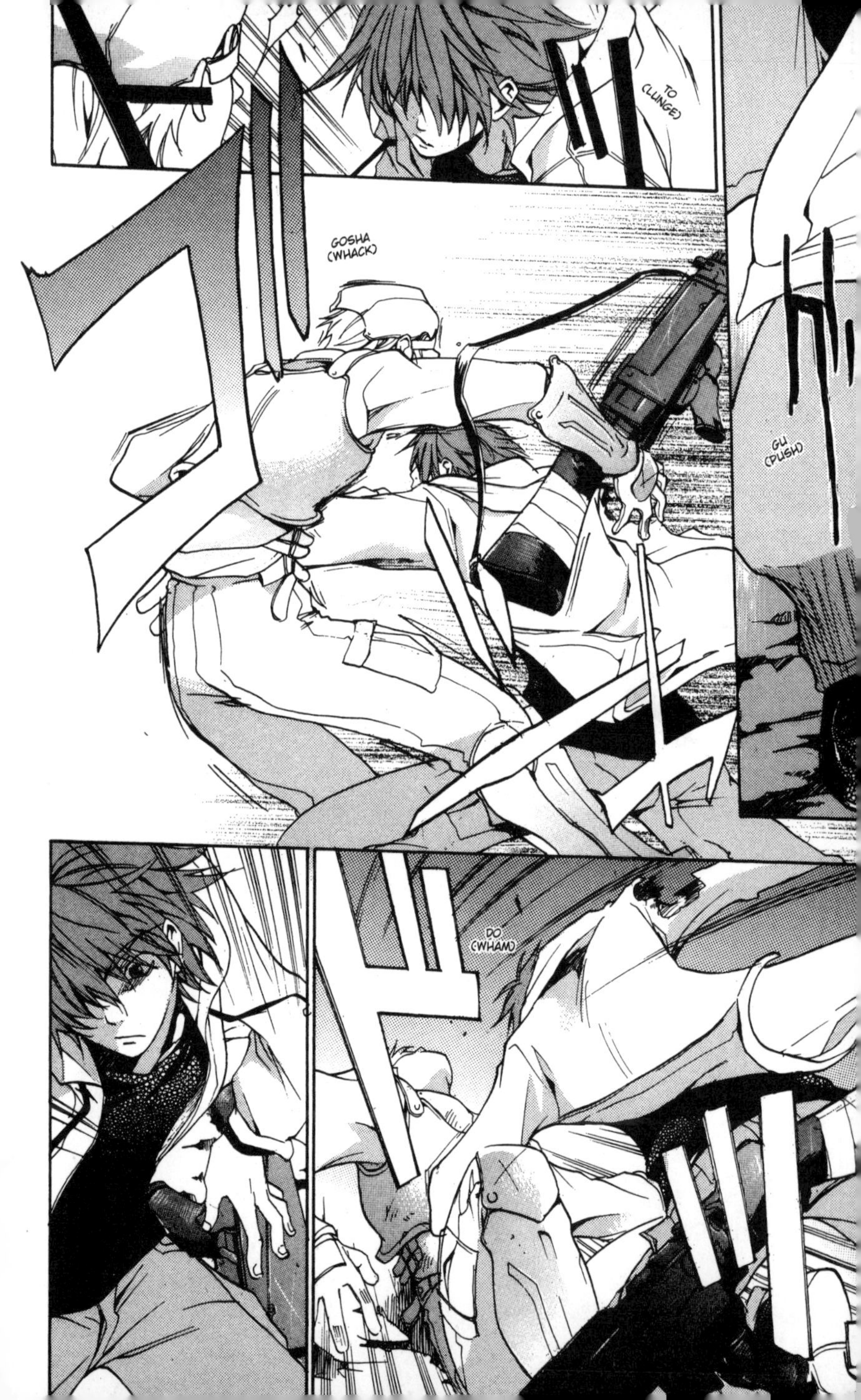
TO
(LUNGE)
GU
(PUSH)
GOSHA
(WHACK)
DO
(WHAM)

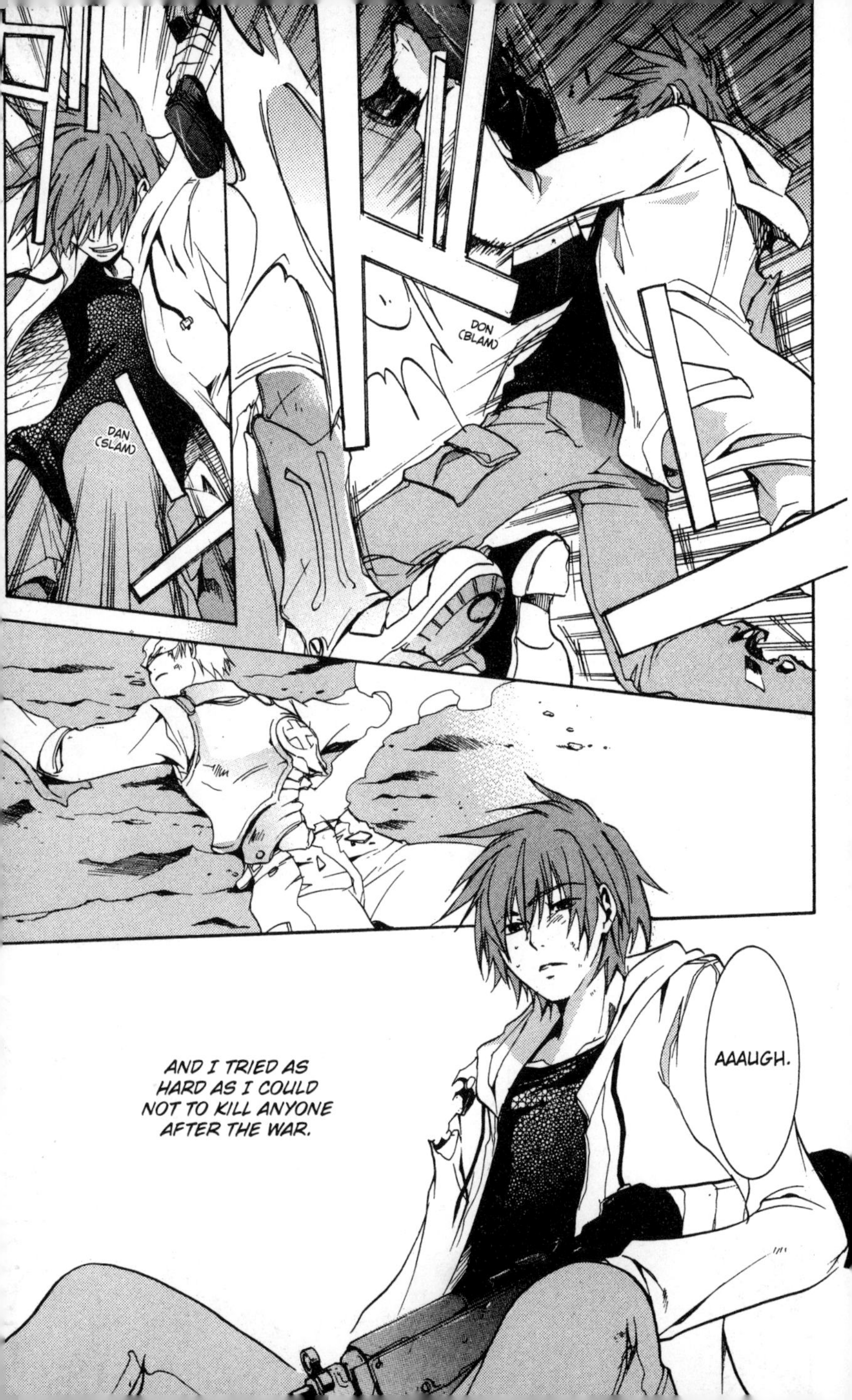
DON (BLAM)
DAN (SLAM)
AAAUGH.
AND I TRIED AS HARD AS I COULD NOT TO KILL ANYONE AFTER THE WAR.

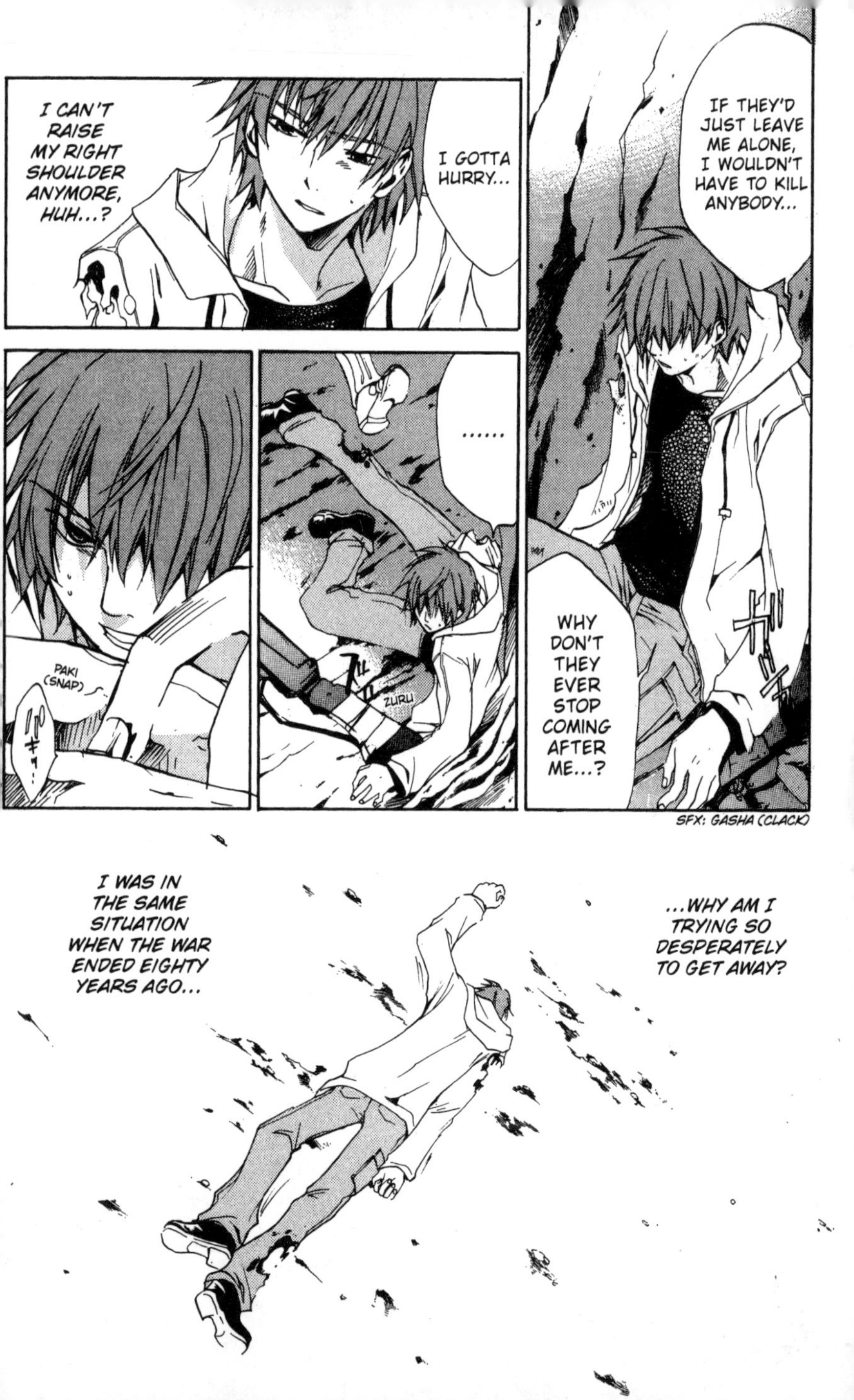
IF THEY'D JUST LEAVE ME ALONE, I WOULDN'T HAVE TO KILL ANYBODY...
WHY DON'T THEY EVER STOP COMING AFTER ME...?
SFX: GASHA (CLACK)
I GOTTA HURRY...
I CAN'T RAISE MY RIGHT SHOULDER ANYMORE, HUH...?
......
ZURU
PAKI (SNAP)
...WHY AM I TRYING SO DESPERATELY TO GET AWAY?
I WAS IN THE SAME SITUATION WHEN THE WAR ENDED EIGHTY YEARS AGO...

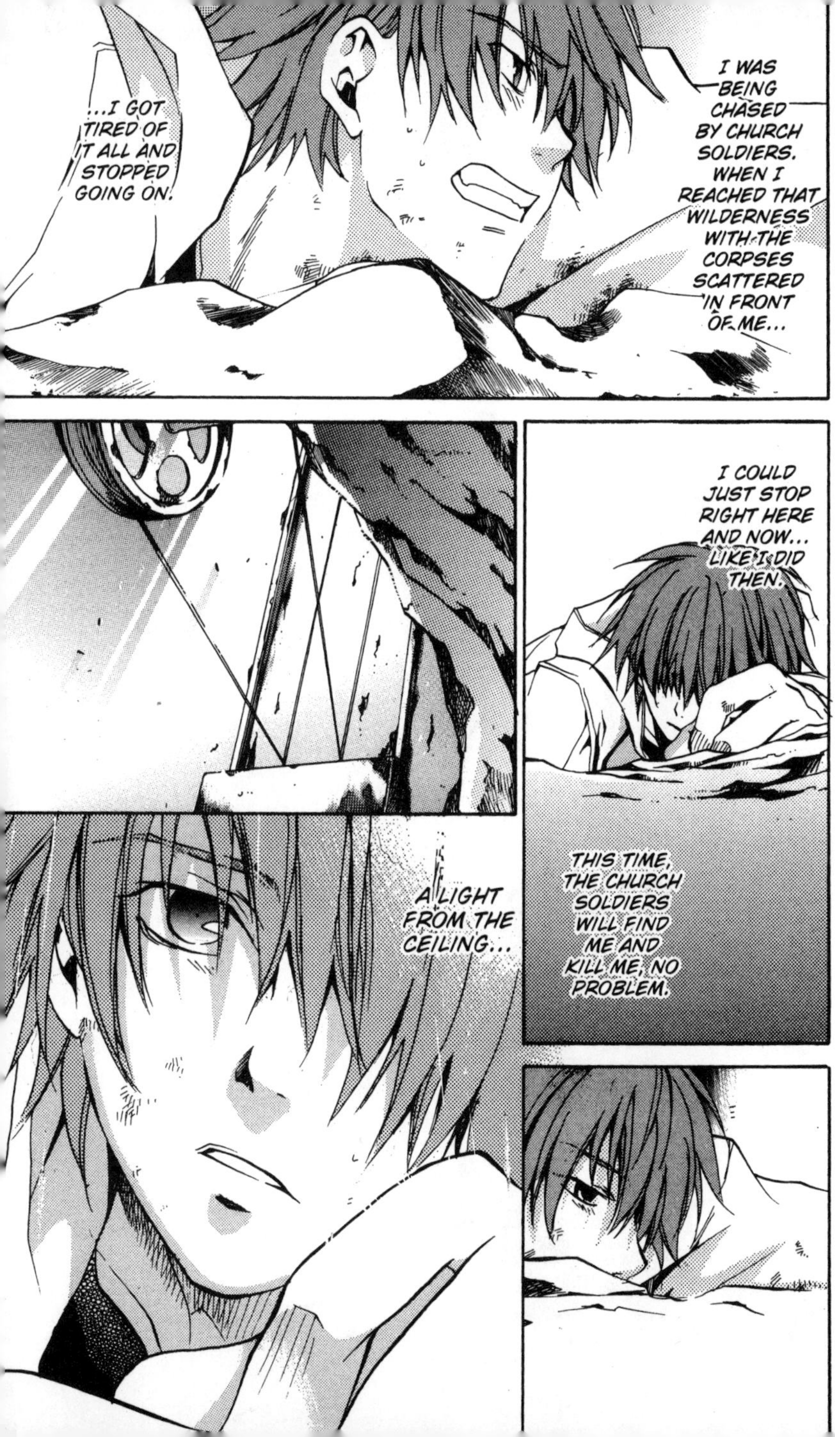
I WAS BEING CHASED BY CHURCH SOLDIERS. WHEN I REACHED THAT WILDERNESS WITH THE CORPSES SCATTERED IN FRONT OF ME...
...I GOT TIRED OF IT ALL AND STOPPED GOING ON.
I COULD JUST STOP RIGHT HERE AND NOW... LIKE I DID THEN.
THIS TIME, THE CHURCH SOLDIERS WILL FIND ME AND KILL ME, NO PROBLEM.
A LIGHT FROM THE CEILING...

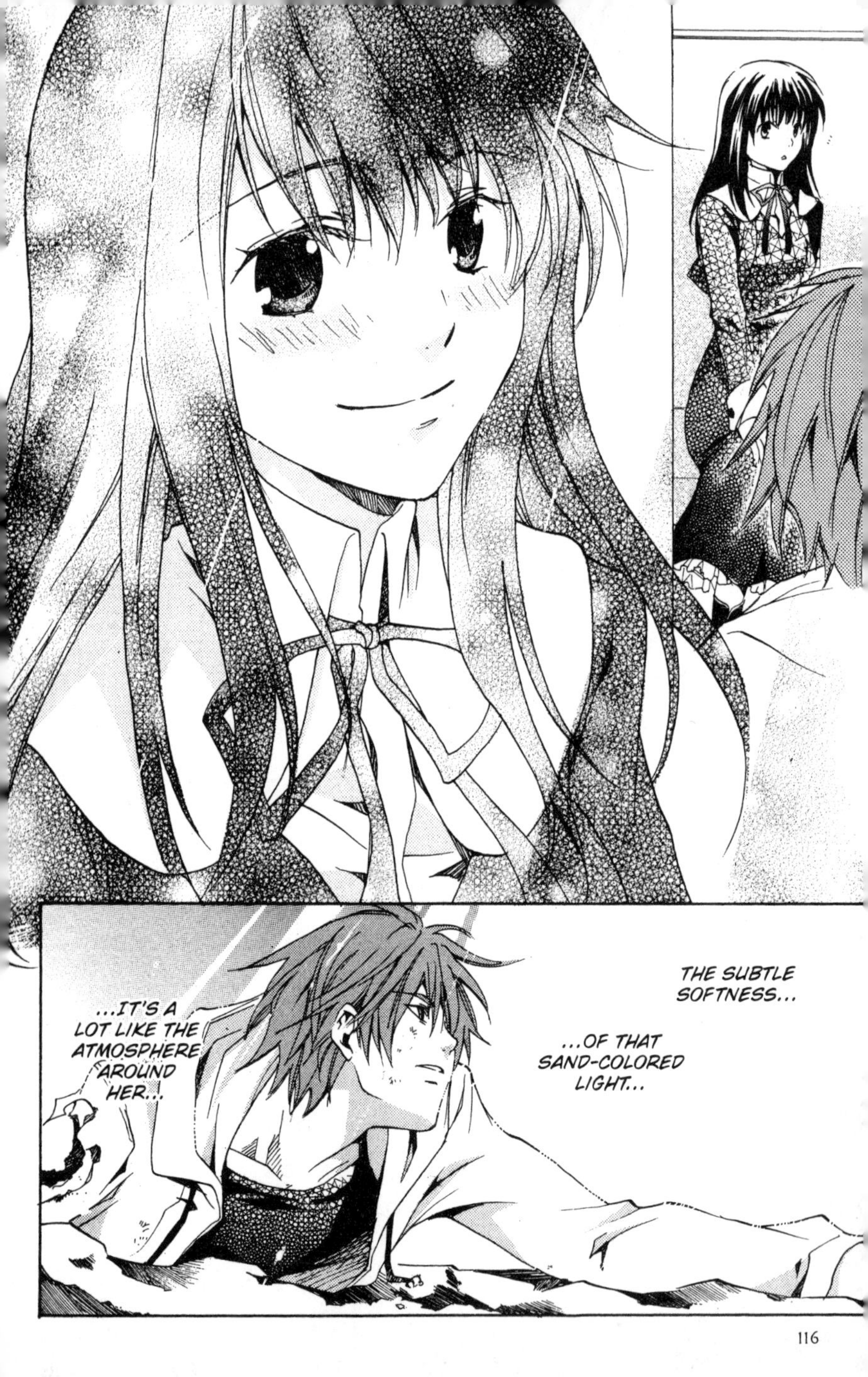
THE SUBTLE SOFTNESS...
...OF THAT SAND-COLORED LIGHT...
...IT'S A LOT LIKE THE ATMOSPHERE AROUND HER...

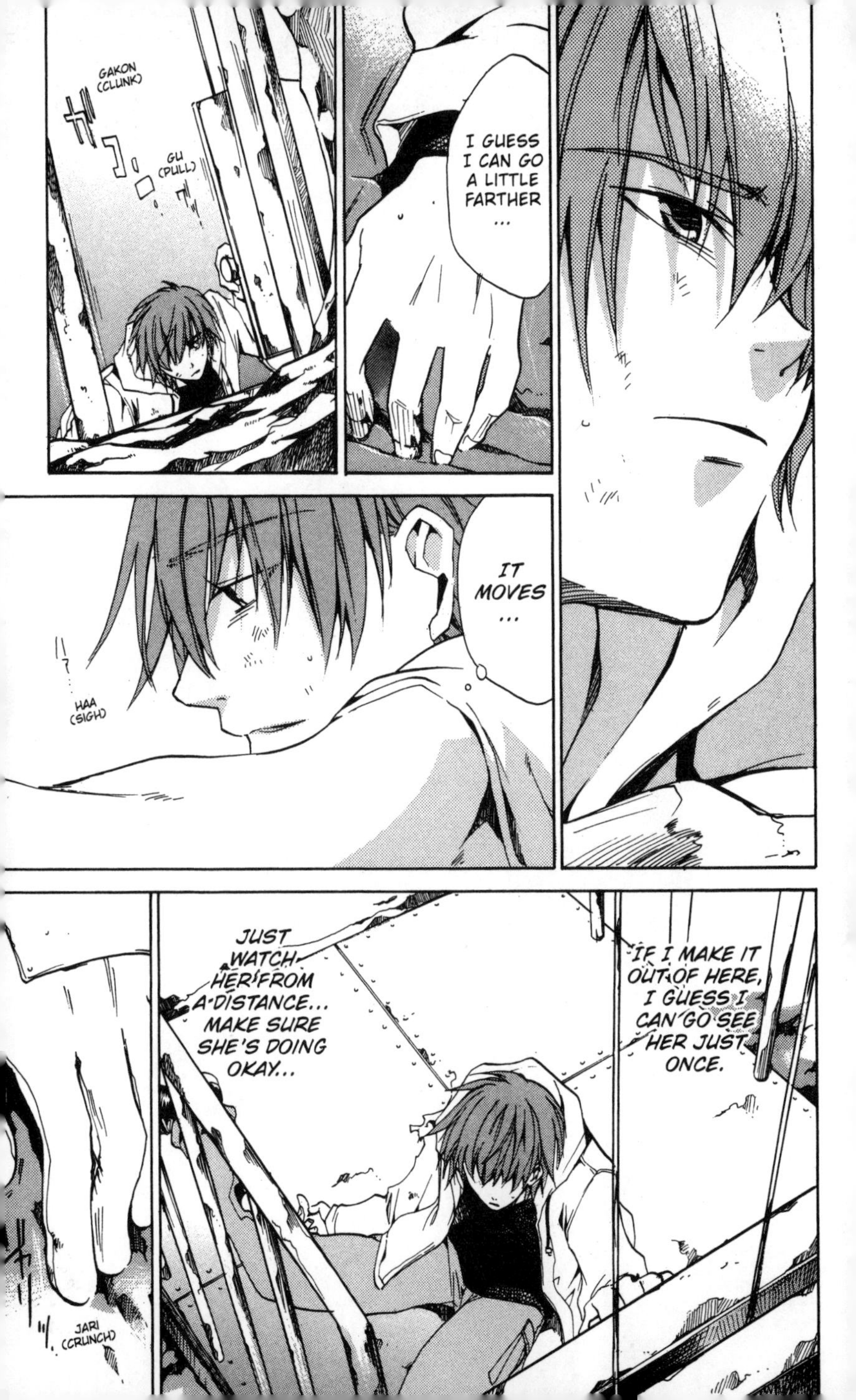
I GUESS I CAN GO A LITTLE FARTHER ...
GAKON (CLUNK)
GU (PULL)
IT MOVES ...
HAA (SIGH)
IF I MAKE IT OUT OF HERE, I GUESS I CAN GO SEE HER JUST ONCE.
JUST WATCH HER FROM A DISTANCE... MAKE SURE SHE'S DOING OKAY...
JARI (CRUNCH)

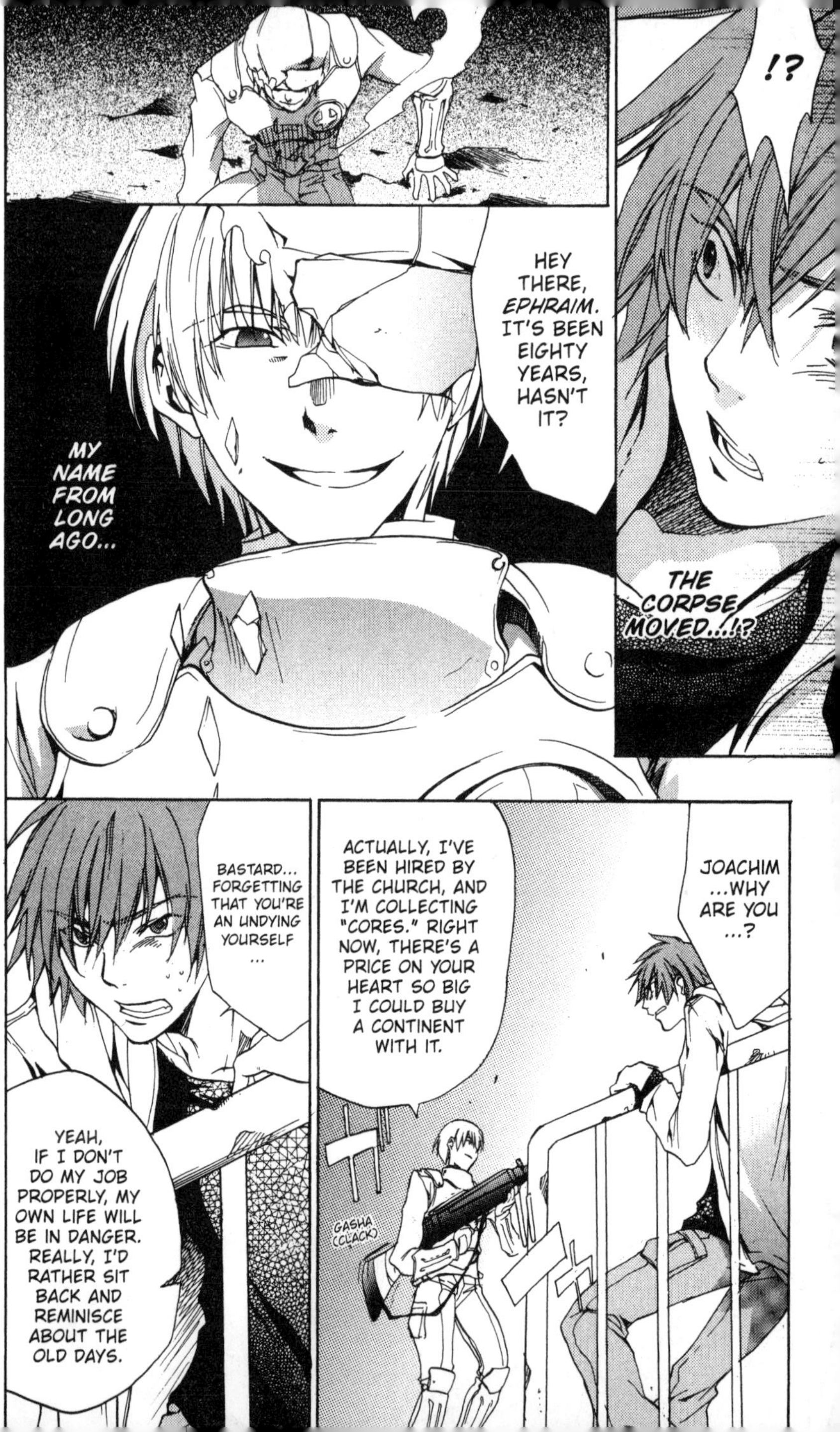
!?
THE CORPSE MOVED...!?
HEY THERE, EPHRAIM. IT'S BEEN EIGHTY YEARS, HASN'T IT?
MY NAME FROM LONG AGO...
JOACHIM ...WHY ARE YOU ...?
ACTUALLY, I'VE BEEN HIRED BY THE CHURCH, AND I'M COLLECTING "CORES." RIGHT NOW, THERE'S A PRICE ON YOUR HEART SO BIG I COULD BUY A CONTINENT WITH IT.
GASHA (CLACK)
BASTARD... FORGETTING THAT YOU'RE AN UNDYING YOURSELF ...
YEAH, IF I DON'T DO MY JOB PROPERLY, MY OWN LIFE WILL BE IN DANGER. REALLY, I'D RATHER SIT BACK AND REMINISCE ABOUT THE OLD DAYS.

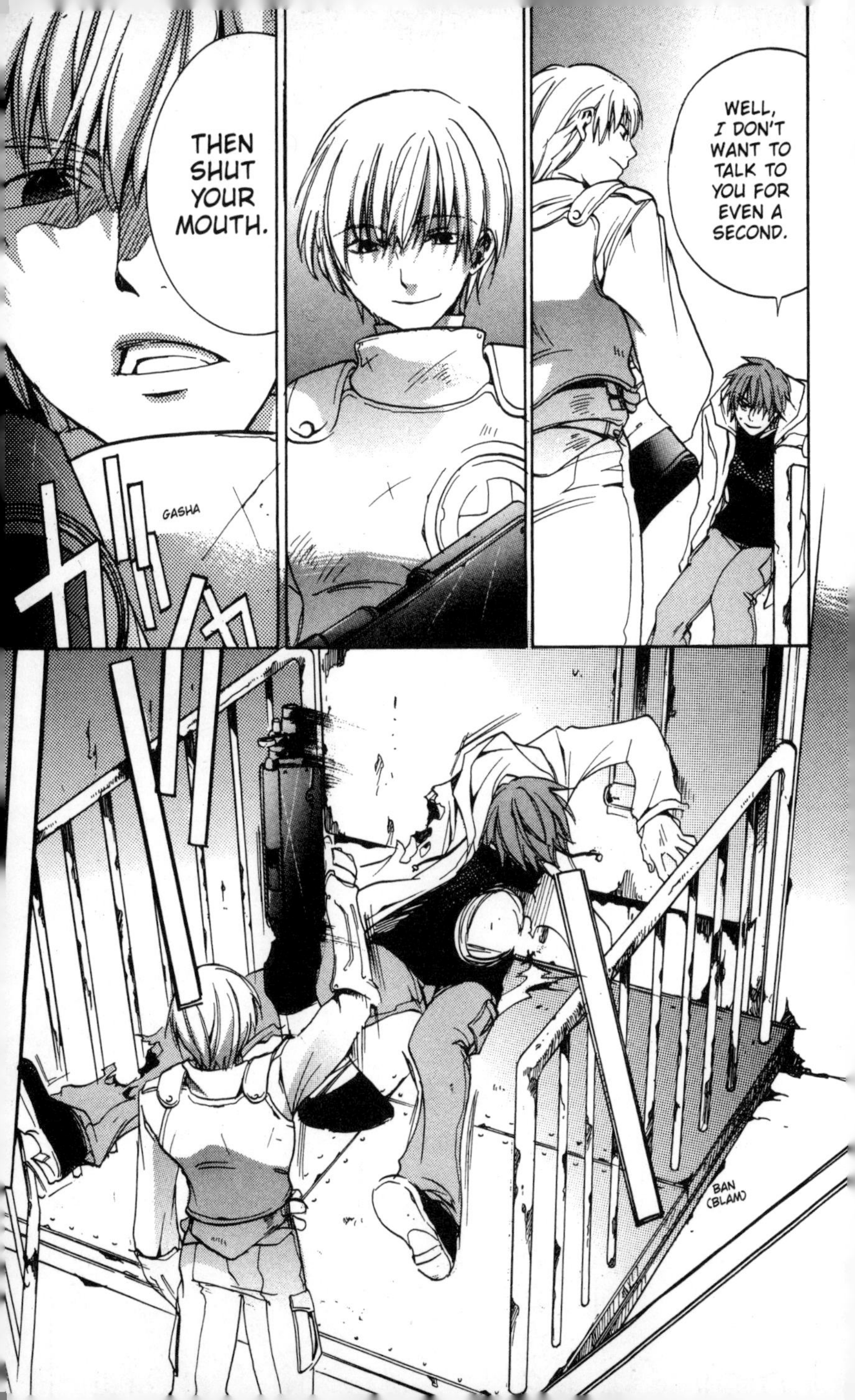
WELL, I DON'T WANT TO TALK TO YOU FOR EVEN A SECOND.
THEN SHUT YOUR MOUTH.
GASHA
BAN (BLAM)

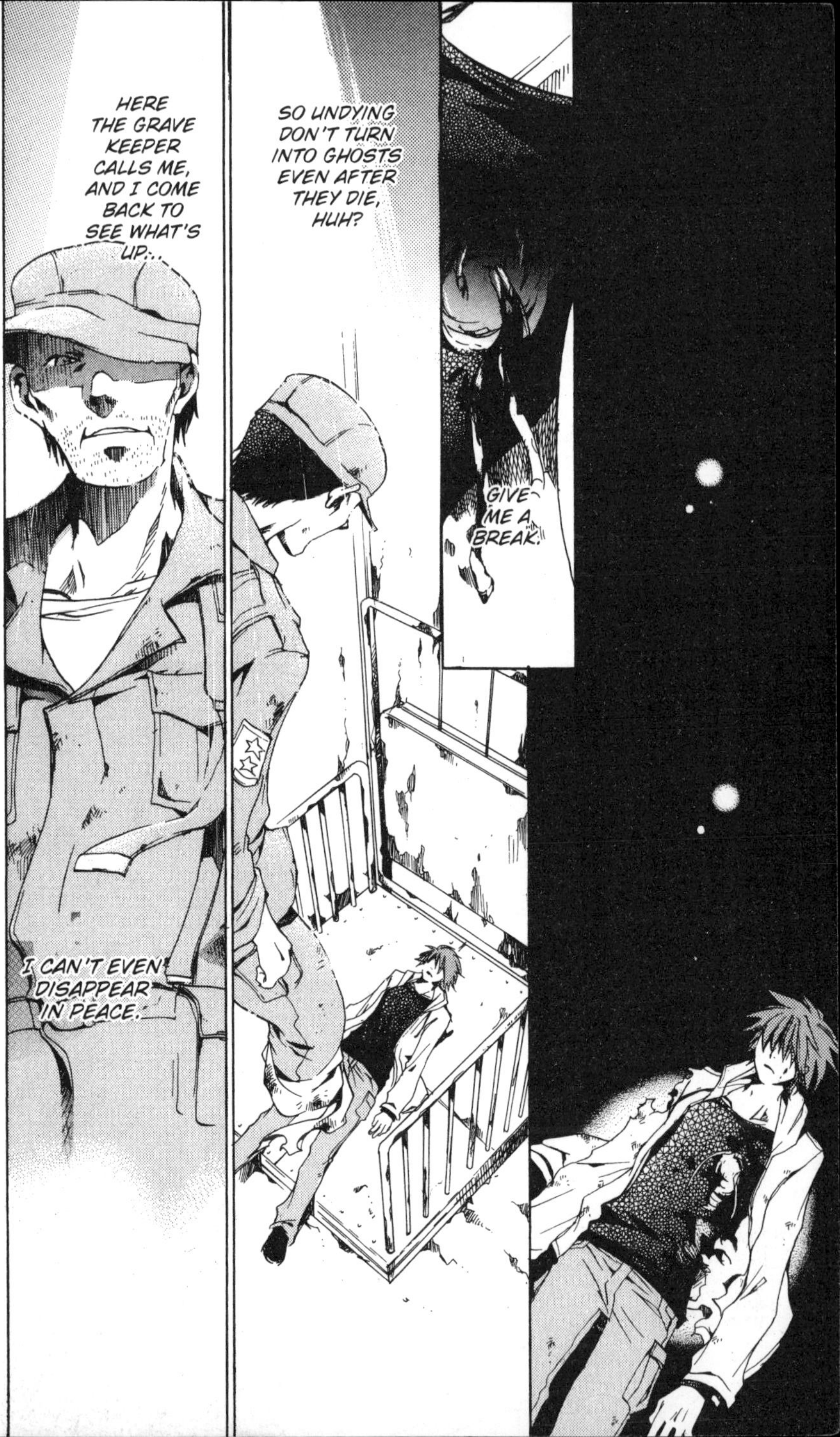
GIVE ME A BREAK.
SO UNDYING DON'T TURN INTO GHOSTS EVEN AFTER THEY DIE, HUH?
HERE THE GRAVE KEEPER CALLS ME, AND I COME BACK TO SEE WHAT'S UP...
I CAN'T EVEN DISAPPEAR IN PEACE.

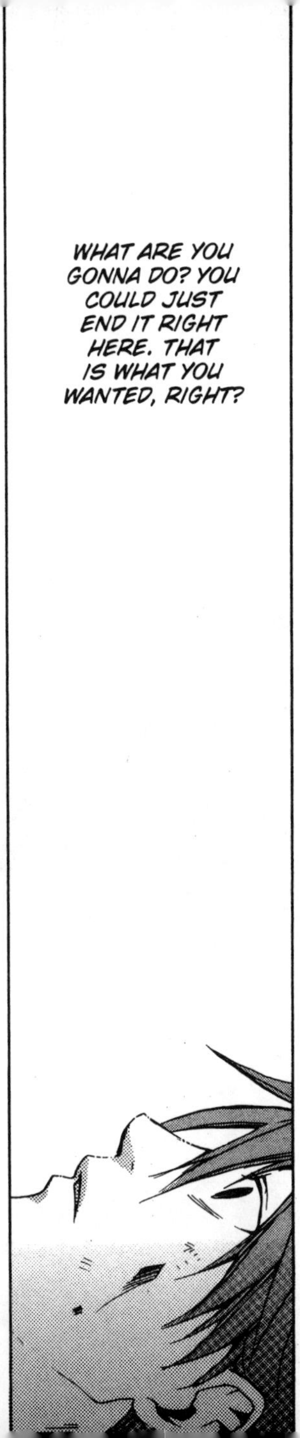
WHAT ARE YOU GONNA DO? YOU COULD JUST END IT RIGHT HERE. THAT IS WHAT YOU WANTED, RIGHT?
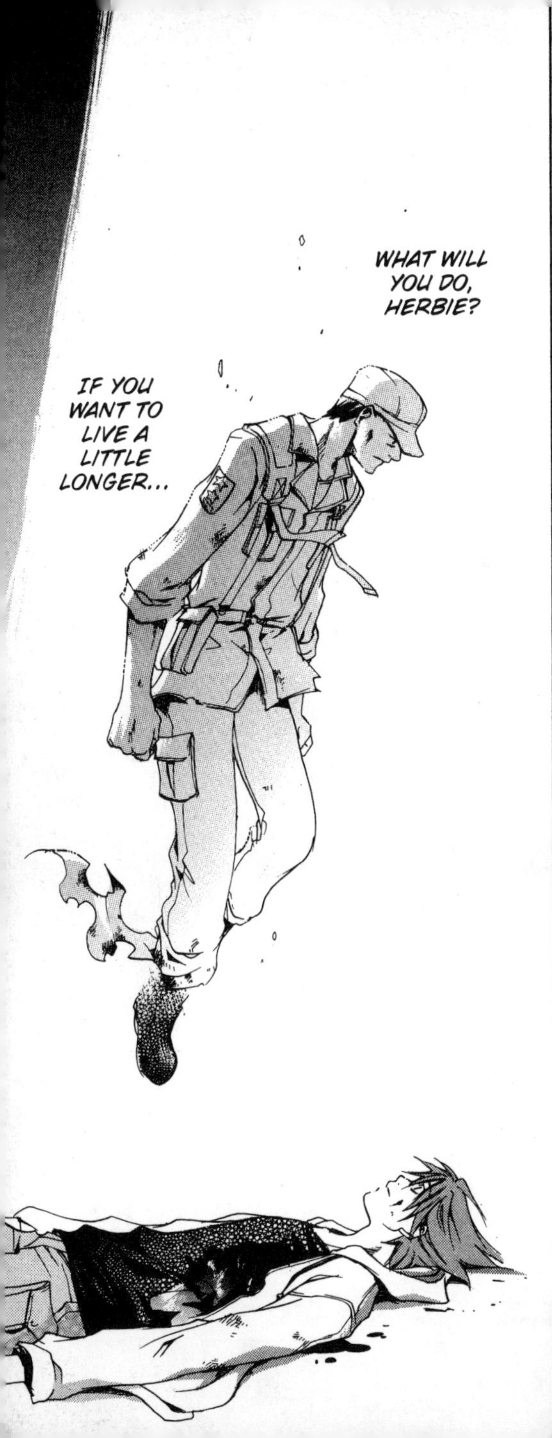
WHAT WILL YOU DO, HERBIE?
IF YOU WANT TO LIVE A LITTLE LONGER...

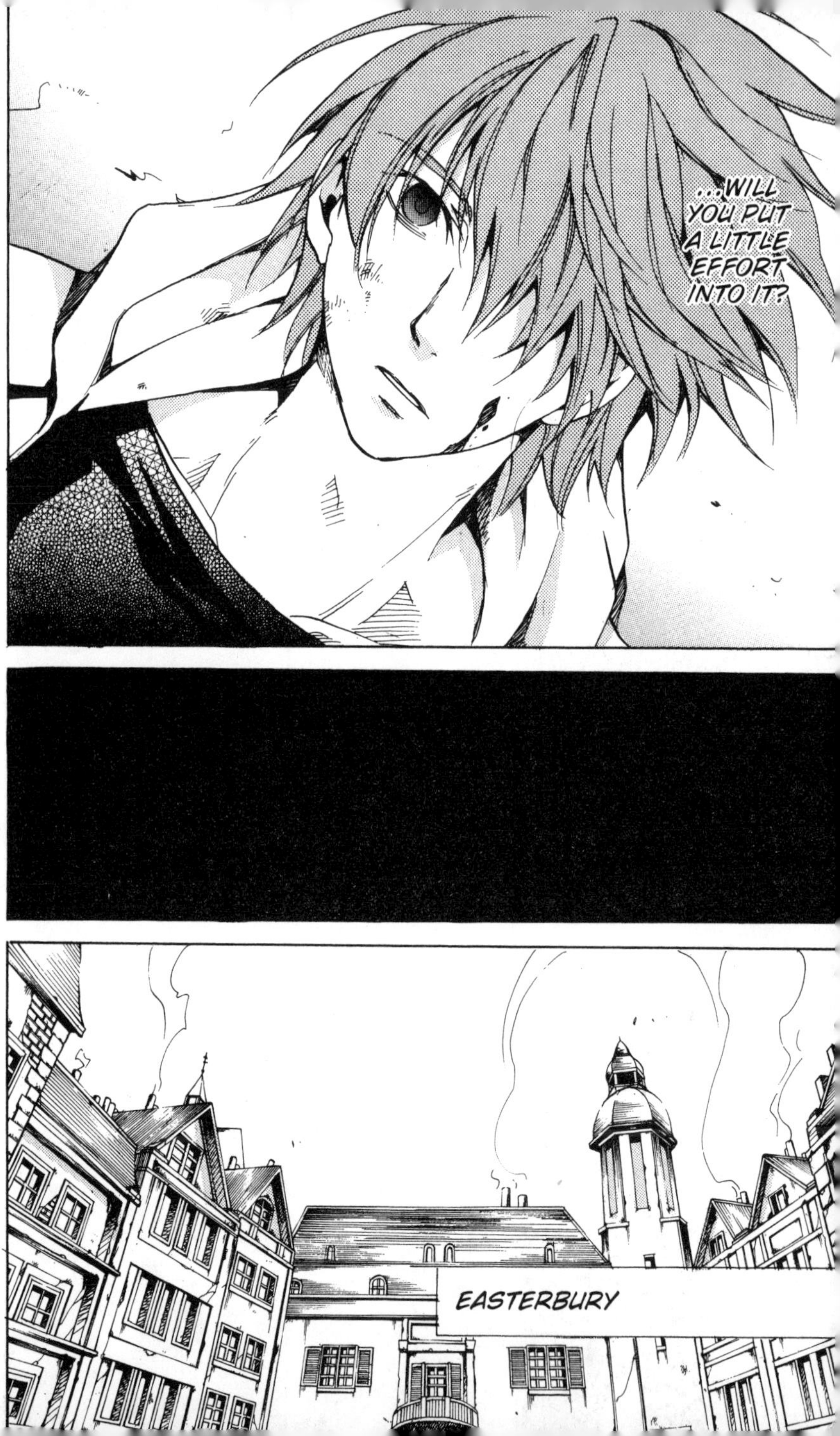
...WILL YOU PUT A LITTLE EFFORT INTO IT?
EASTERBURY

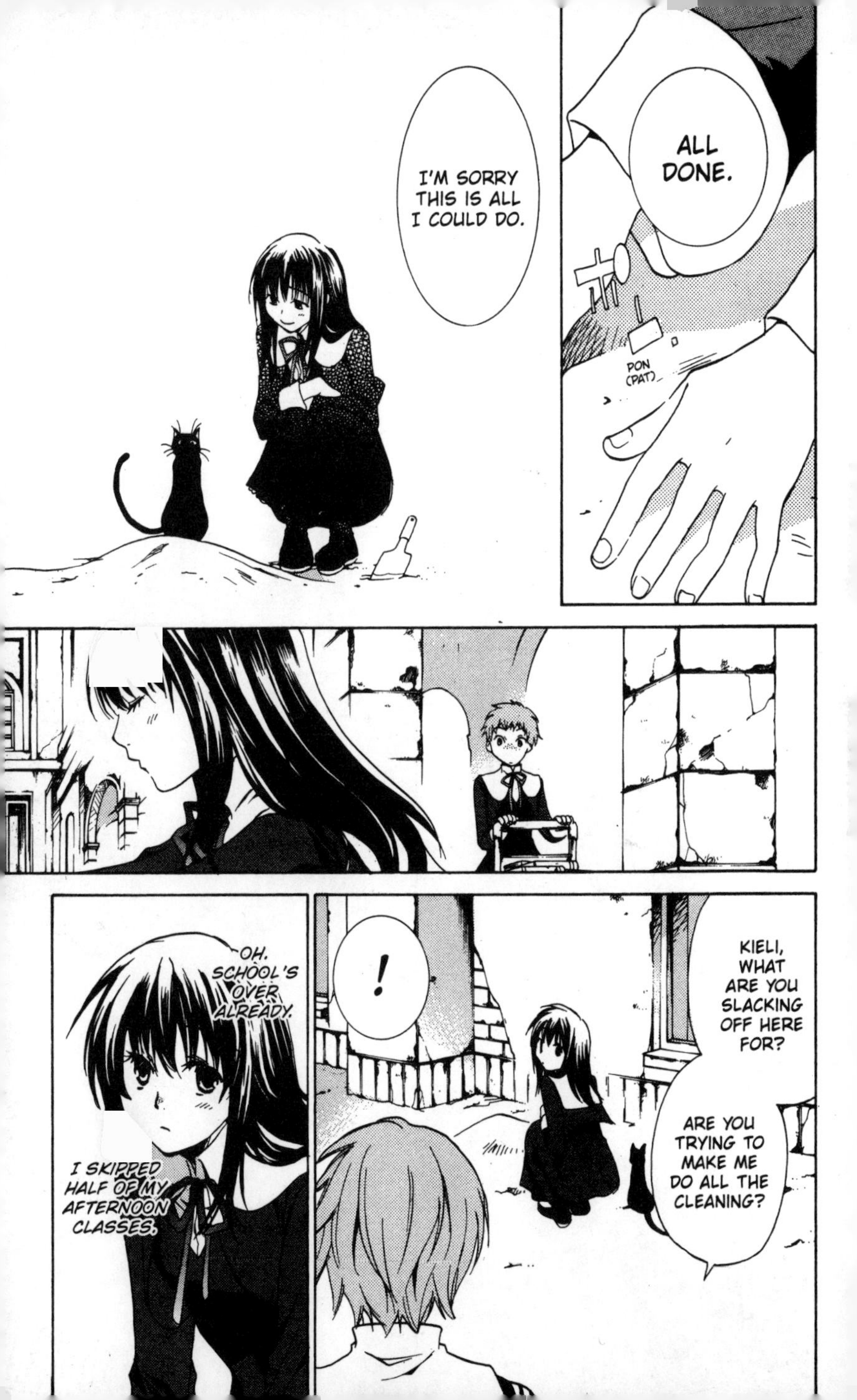
ALL DONE.
PON (PAT)
I'M SORRY THIS IS ALL I COULD DO.
KIELI, WHAT ARE YOU SLACKING OFF HERE FOR?
!
ARE YOU TRYING TO MAKE ME DO ALL THE CLEANING?
OH. SCHOOL'S OVER ALREADY.
I SKIPPED HALF OF MY AFTERNOON CLASSES.

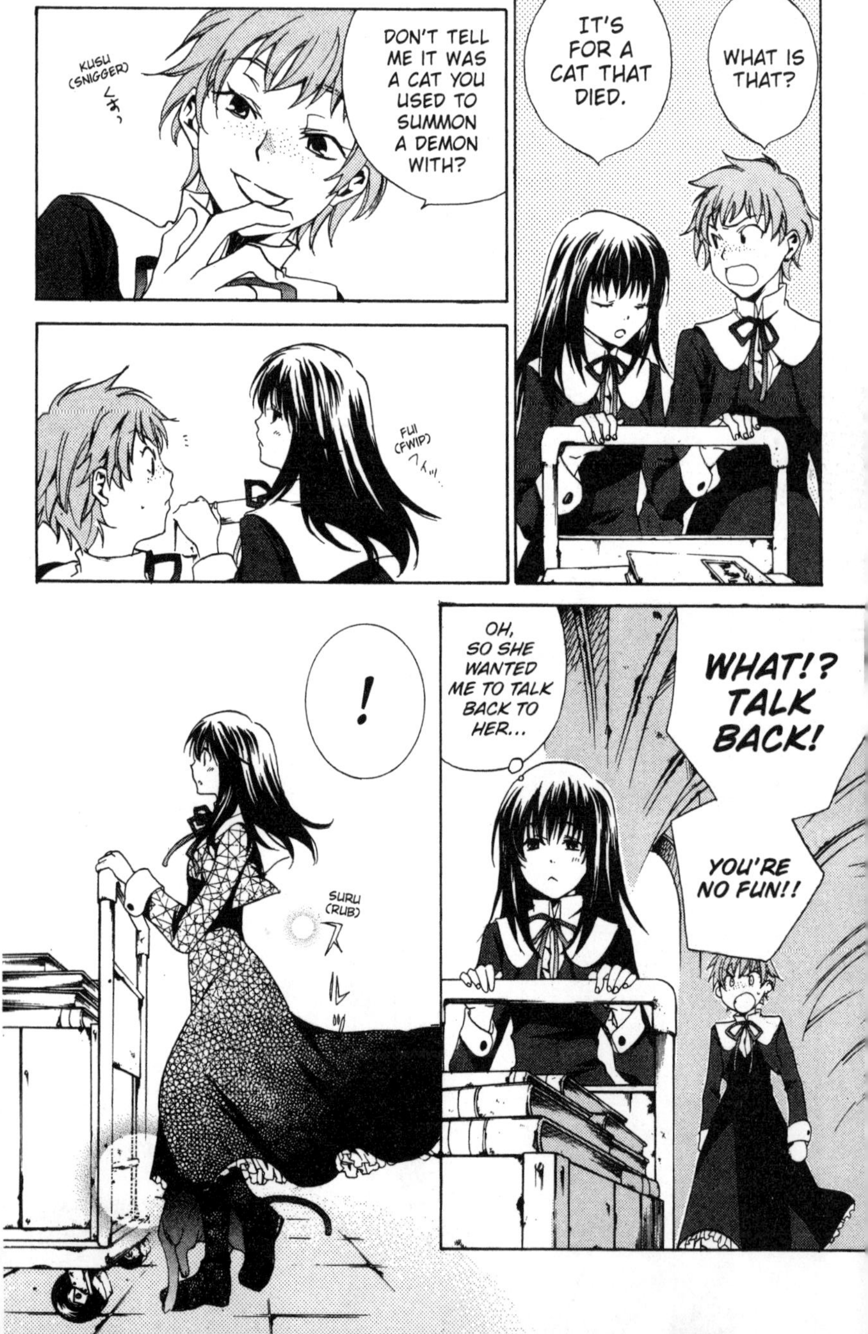
WHAT IS THAT?
IT'S FOR A CAT THAT DIED.
DON'T TELL ME IT WAS A CAT YOU USED TO SUMMON A DEMON WITH?
KUSU (SNIGGER)
FUI (FWIP)
WHAT!? TALK BACK!
YOU'RE NO FUN!!
OH, SO SHE WANTED ME TO TALK BACK TO HER...
!
SURU (RUB)

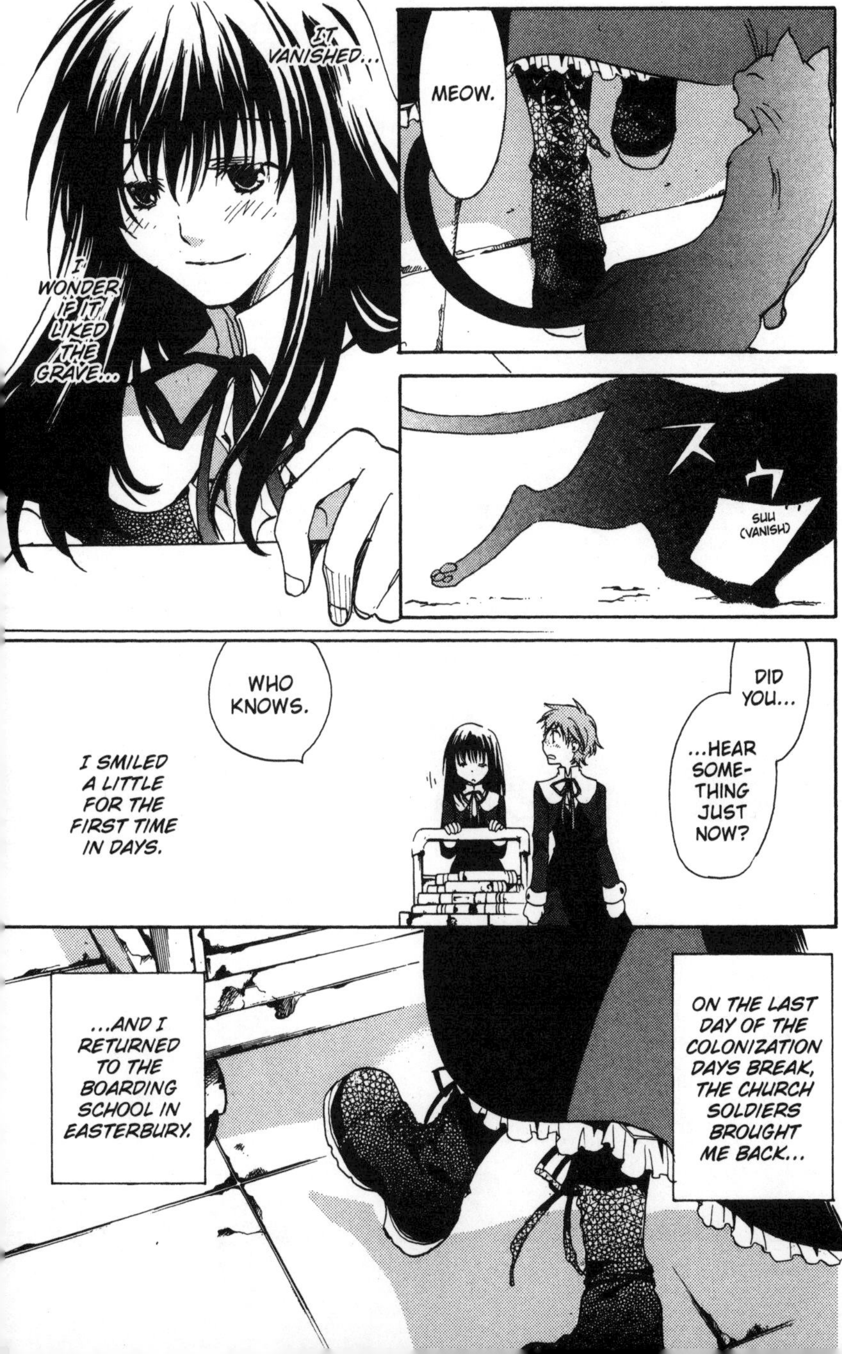
MEOW.
スウ
SUU (VANISH)
IT VANISHED...
I WONDER IF IT LIKED THE GRAVE...
DID YOU... ...HEAR SOMETHING JUST NOW?
WHO KNOWS.
I SMILED A LITTLE FOR THE FIRST TIME IN DAYS.
ON THE LAST DAY OF THE COLONIZATION DAYS BREAK, THE CHURCH SOLDIERS BROUGHT ME BACK...
...AND I RETURNED TO THE BOARDING SCHOOL IN EASTERBURY.

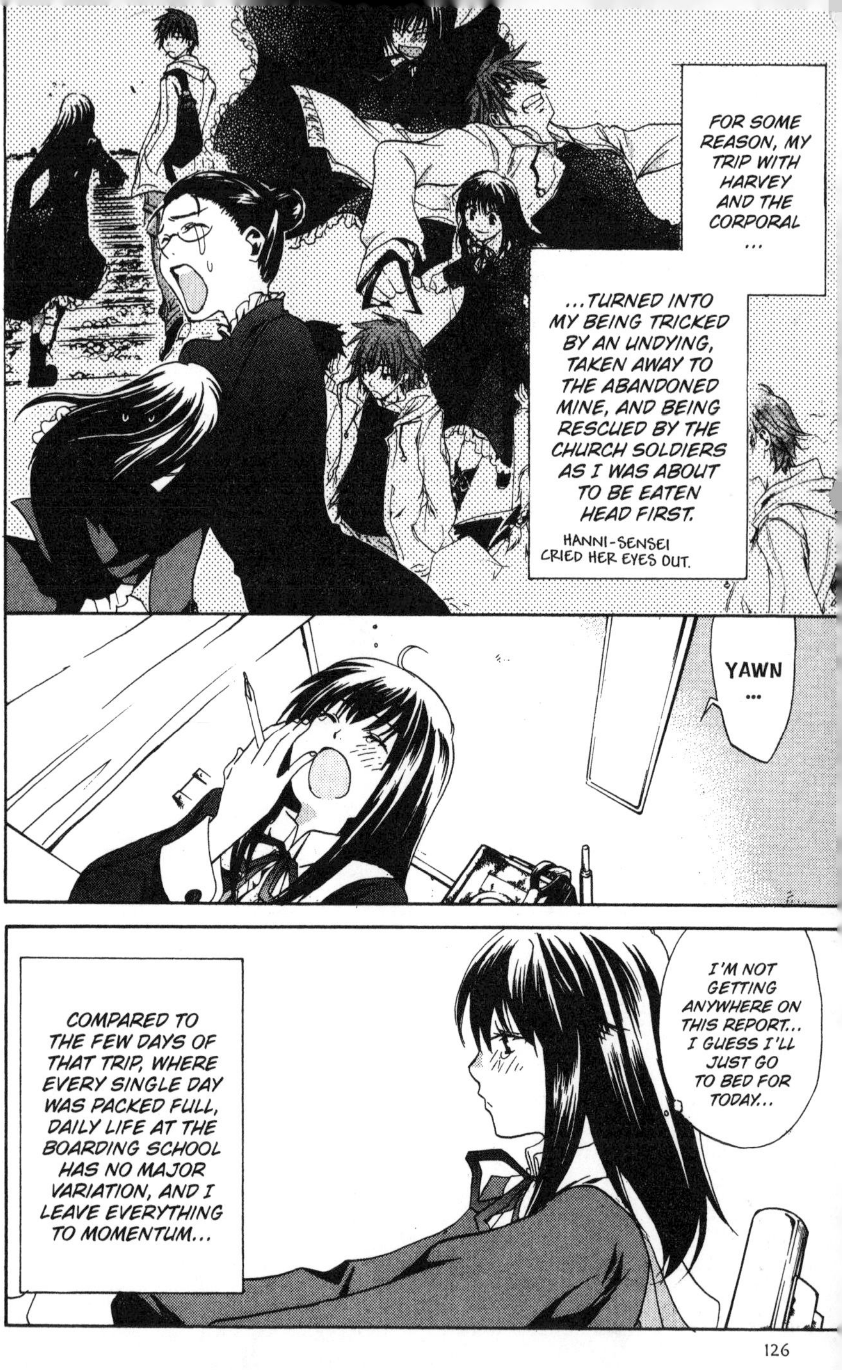
FOR SOME REASON, MY TRIP WITH HARVEY AND THE CORPORAL ...
...TURNED INTO MY BEING TRICKED BY AN UNDYING, TAKEN AWAY TO THE ABANDONED MINE, AND BEING RESCUED BY THE CHURCH SOLDIERS AS I WAS ABOUT TO BE EATEN HEAD FIRST.
HANNI-SENSEI CRIED HER EYES OUT.
YAWN ...
I'M NOT GETTING ANYWHERE ON THIS REPORT... I GUESS I'LL JUST GO TO BED FOR TODAY...
COMPARED TO THE FEW DAYS OF THAT TRIP, WHERE EVERY SINGLE DAY WAS PACKED FULL, DAILY LIFE AT THE BOARDING SCHOOL HAS NO MAJOR VARIATION, AND I LEAVE EVERYTHING TO MOMENTUM...

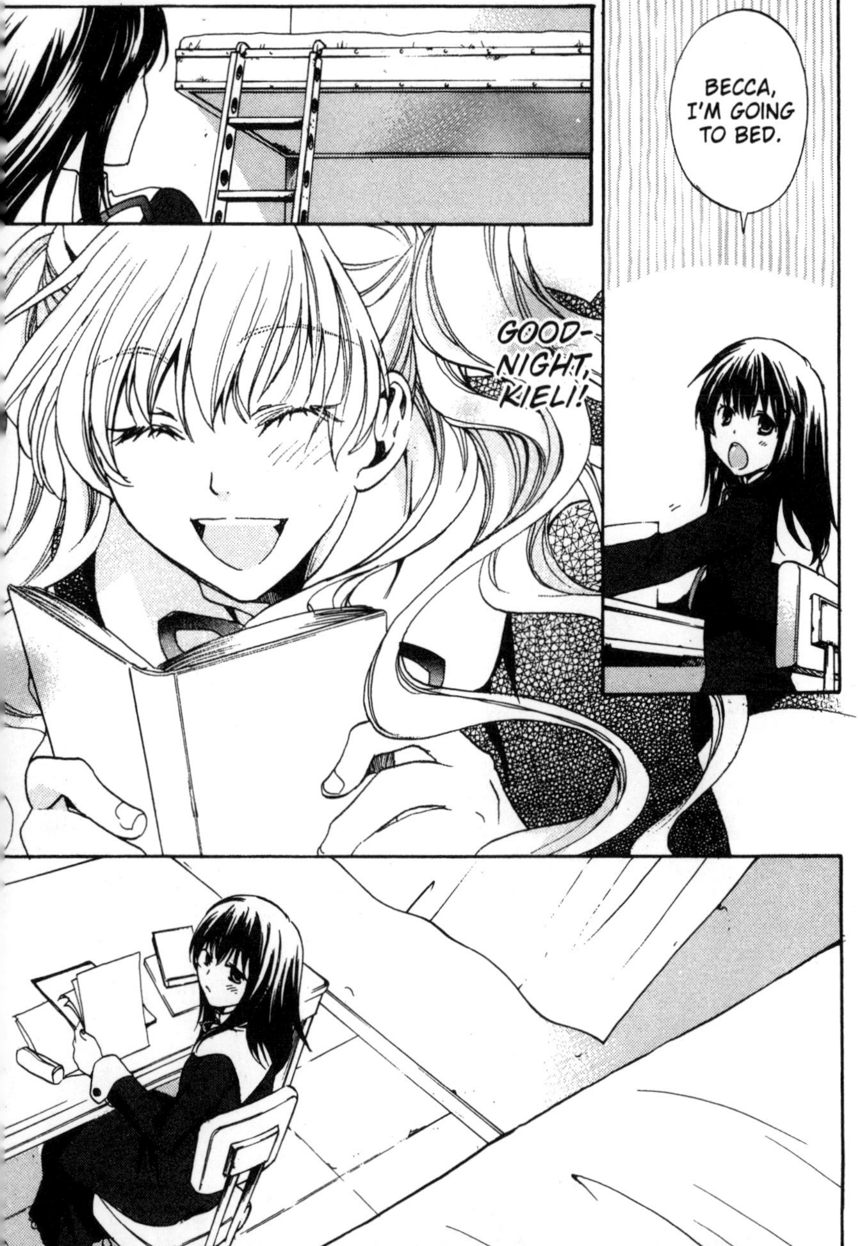
BECCA, I'M GOING TO BED.
GOOD-NIGHT, KIELI!

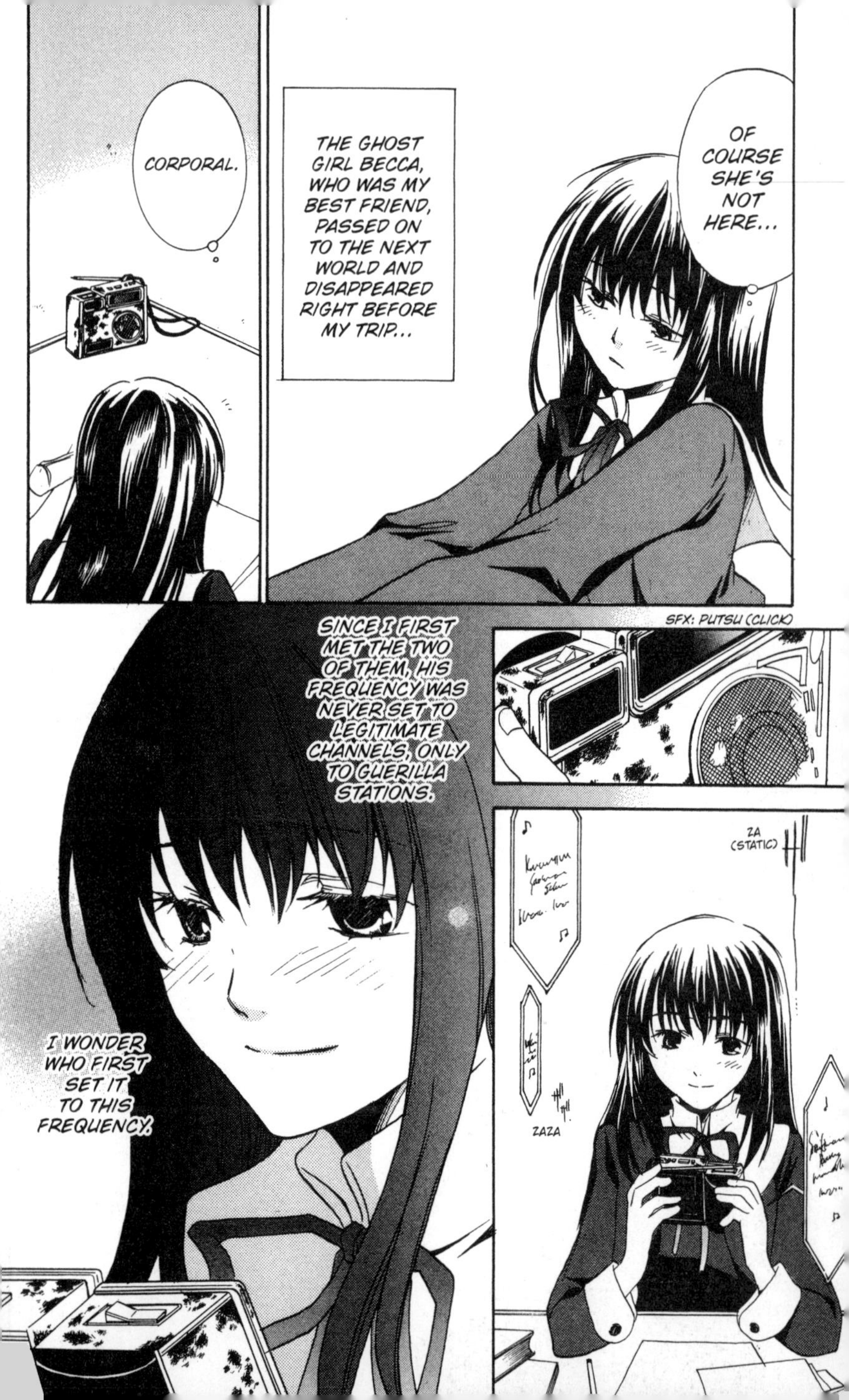
OF COURSE SHE'S NOT HERE...
THE GHOST GIRL BECCA, WHO WAS MY BEST FRIEND, PASSED ON TO THE NEXT WORLD AND DISAPPEARED RIGHT BEFORE MY TRIP...
CORPORAL.
SFX: PUTSU (CLICK)
ZA (STATIC)
ZAZA
SINCE I FIRST MET THE TWO OF THEM, HIS FREQUENCY WAS NEVER SET TO LEGITIMATE CHANNELS, ONLY TO GUERILLA STATIONS.
I WONDER WHO FIRST SET IT TO THIS FREQUENCY.

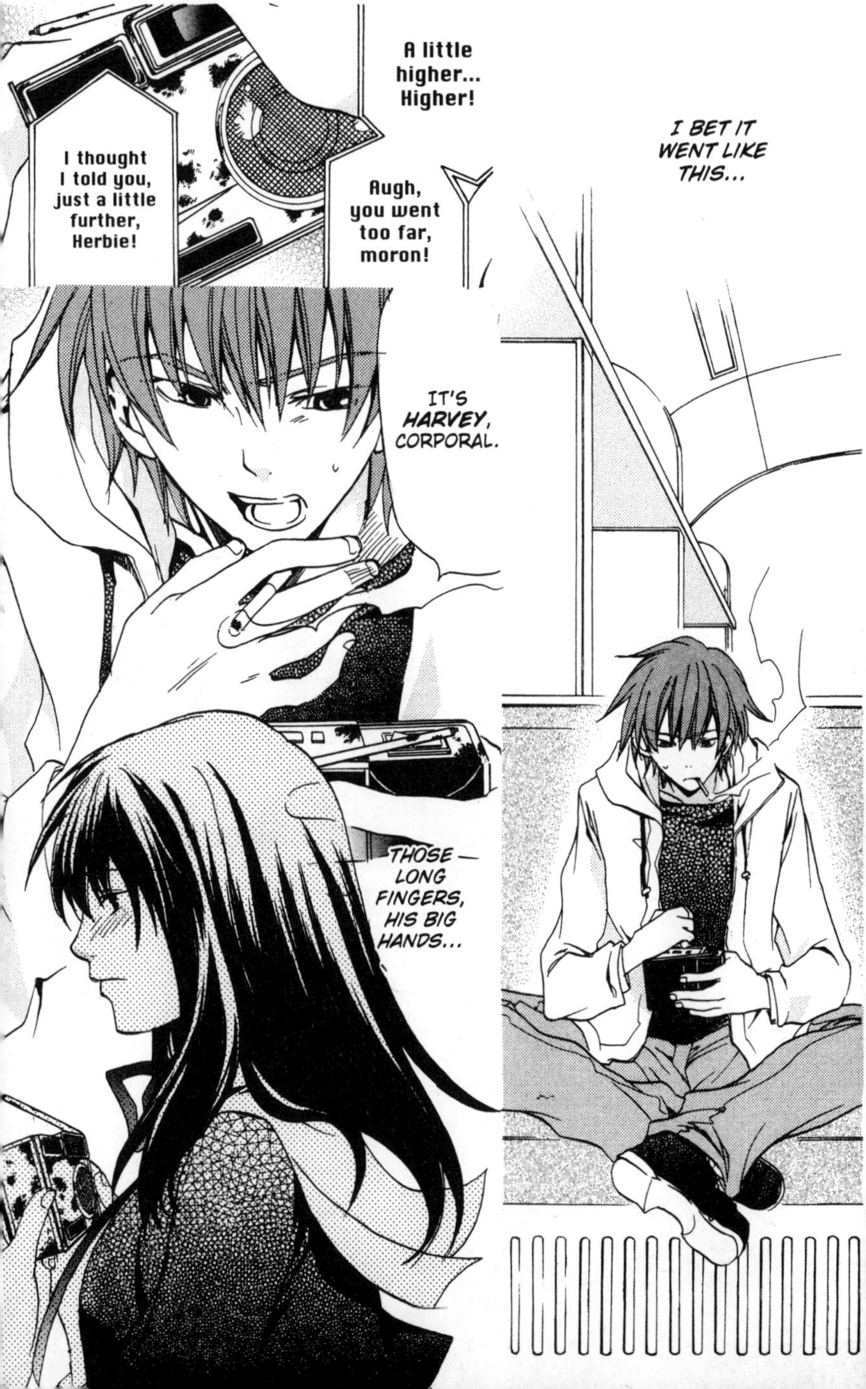
I BET IT WENT LIKE THIS...
A little higher... Higher!
Augh, you went too far, moron!
I thought I told you, just a little further, Herbie!
IT'S HARVEY, CORPORAL.
THOSE— LONG FINGERS, HIS BIG HANDS...

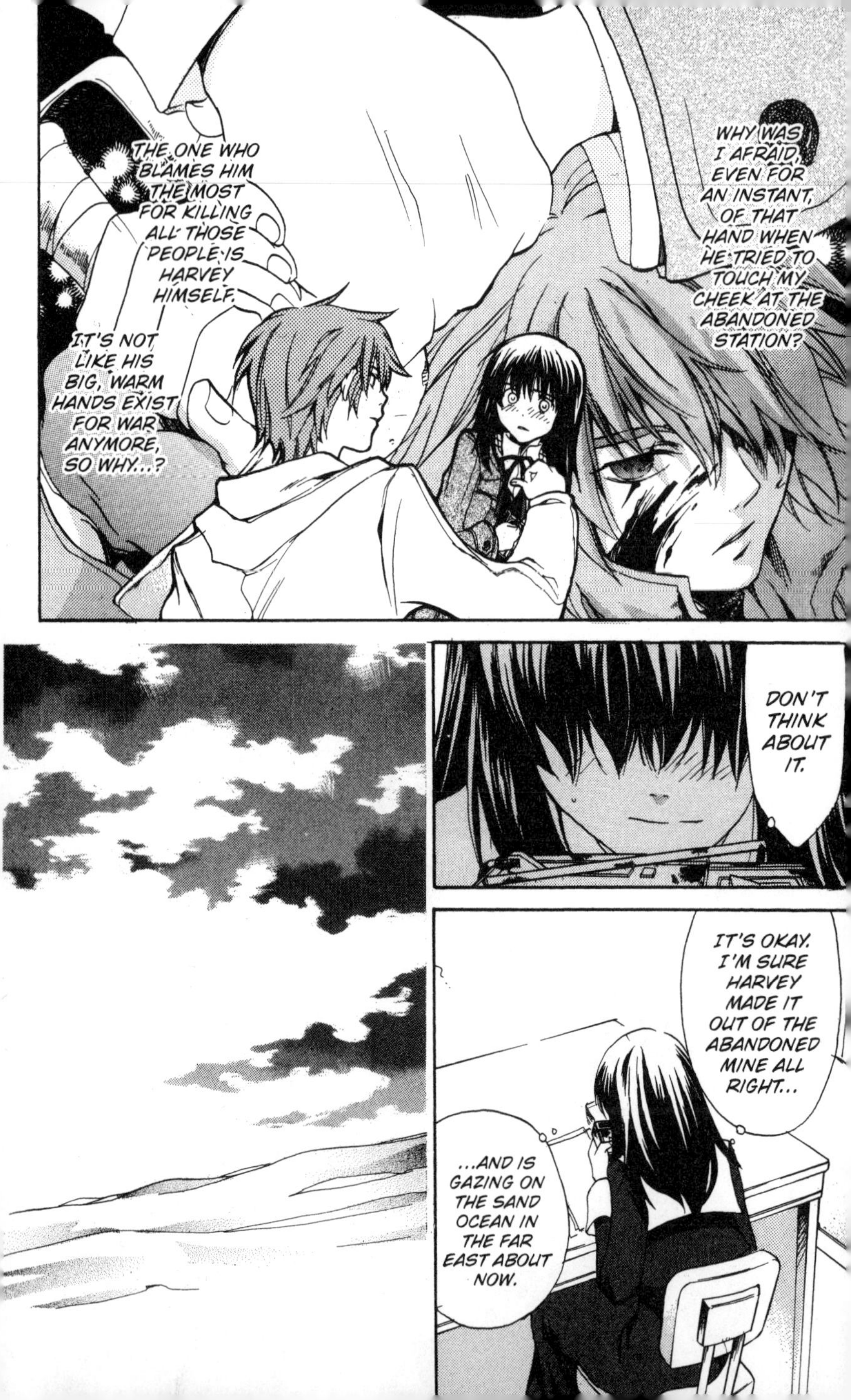
WHY WAS I AFRAID, EVEN FOR AN INSTANT, OF THAT HAND WHEN HE TRIED TO TOUCH MY CHEEK AT THE ABANDONED STATION?
THE ONE WHO BLAMES HIM THE MOST FOR KILLING ALL THOSE PEOPLE IS HARVEY HIMSELF.
IT'S NOT LIKE HIS BIG, WARM HANDS EXIST FOR WAR ANYMORE, SO WHY...?
DON'T THINK ABOUT IT.
IT'S OKAY. I'M SURE HARVEY MADE IT OUT OF THE ABANDONED MINE ALL RIGHT...
...AND IS GAZING ON THE SAND OCEAN IN THE FAR EAST ABOUT NOW.

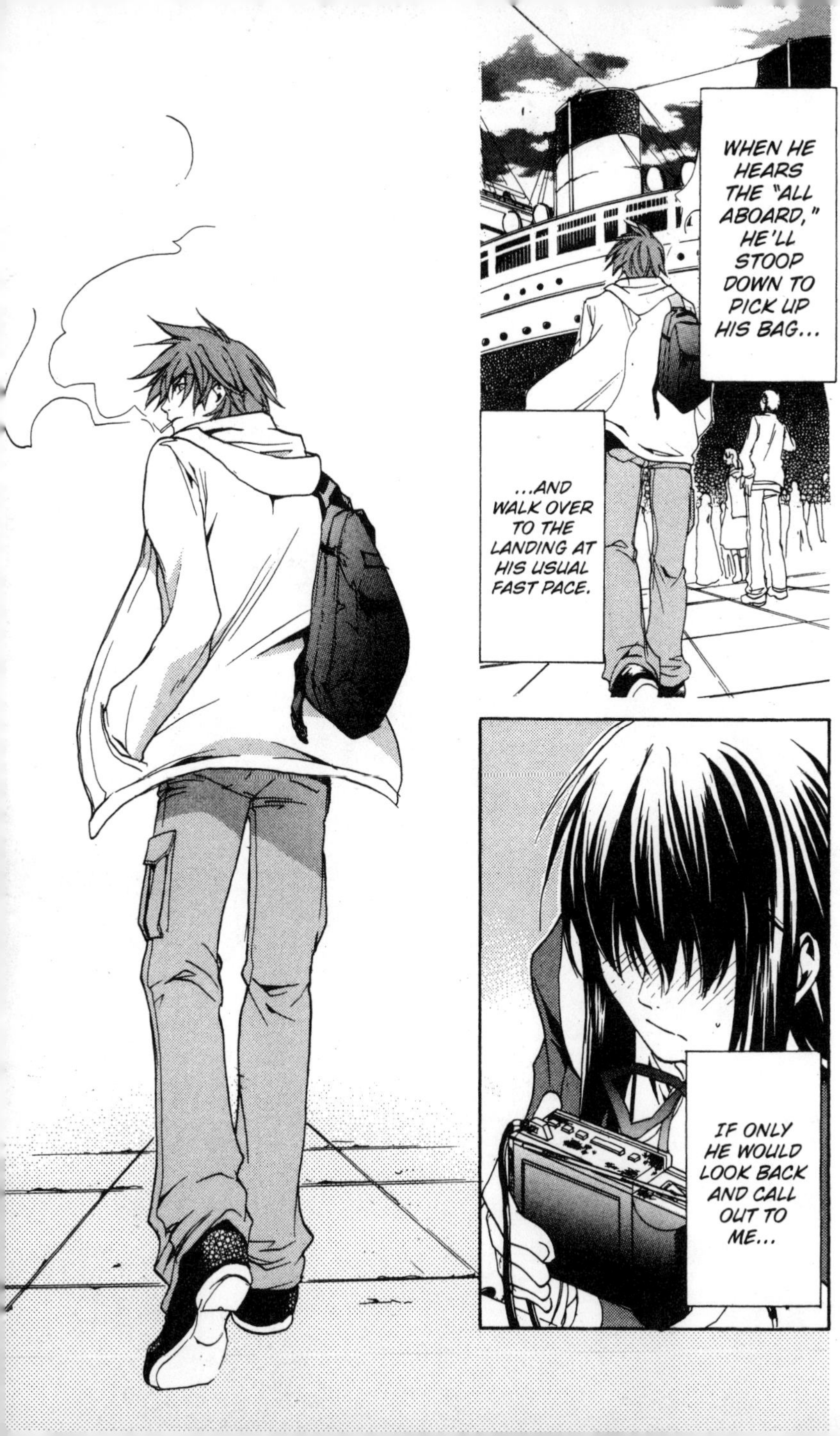
WHEN HE HEARS THE "ALL ABOARD," HE'LL STOOP DOWN TO PICK UP HIS BAG...
...AND WALK OVER TO THE LANDING AT HIS USUAL FAST PACE.
IF ONLY HE WOULD LOOK BACK AND CALL OUT TO ME...

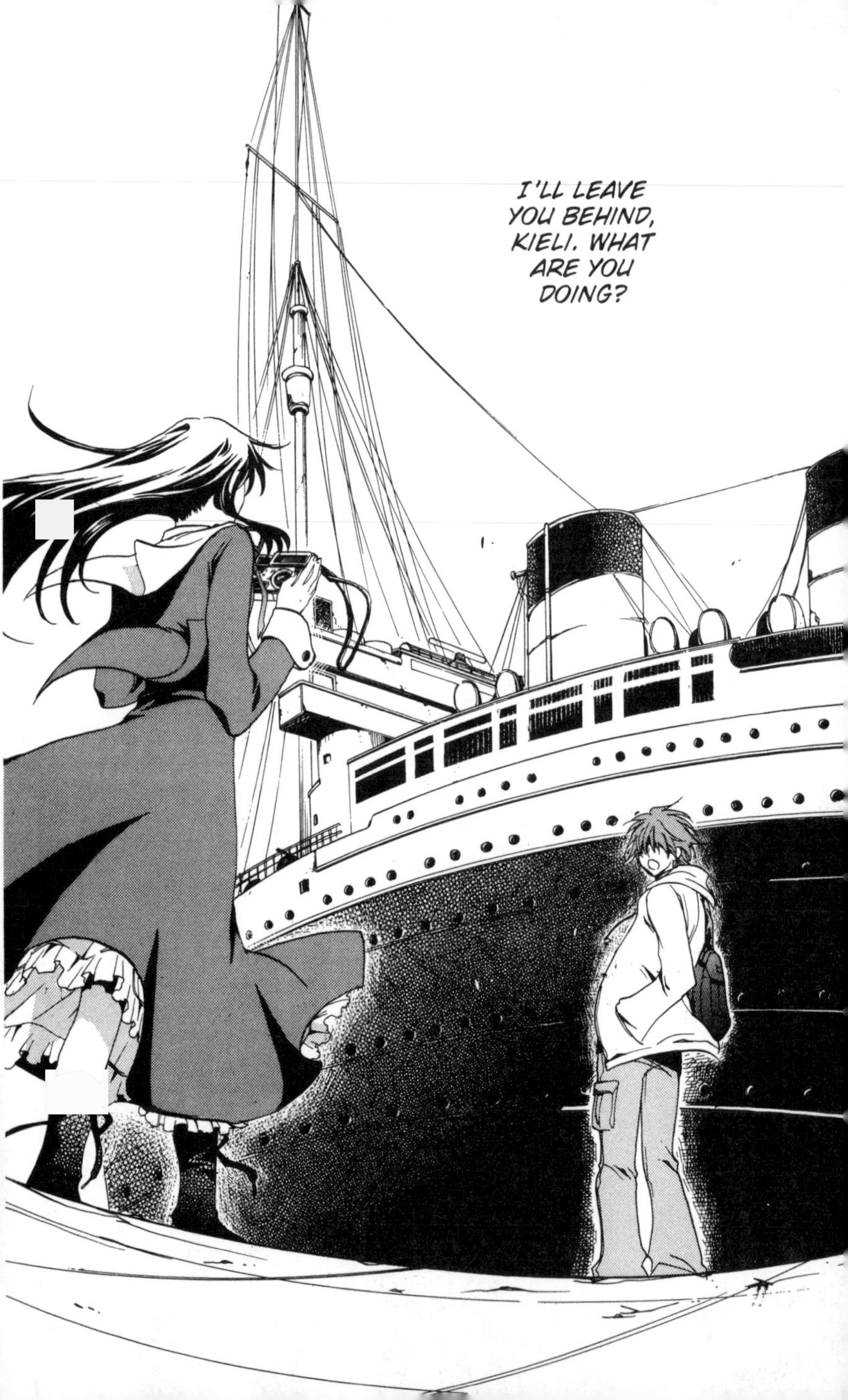
I'LL LEAVE YOU BEHIND, KIELI. WHAT ARE YOU DOING?

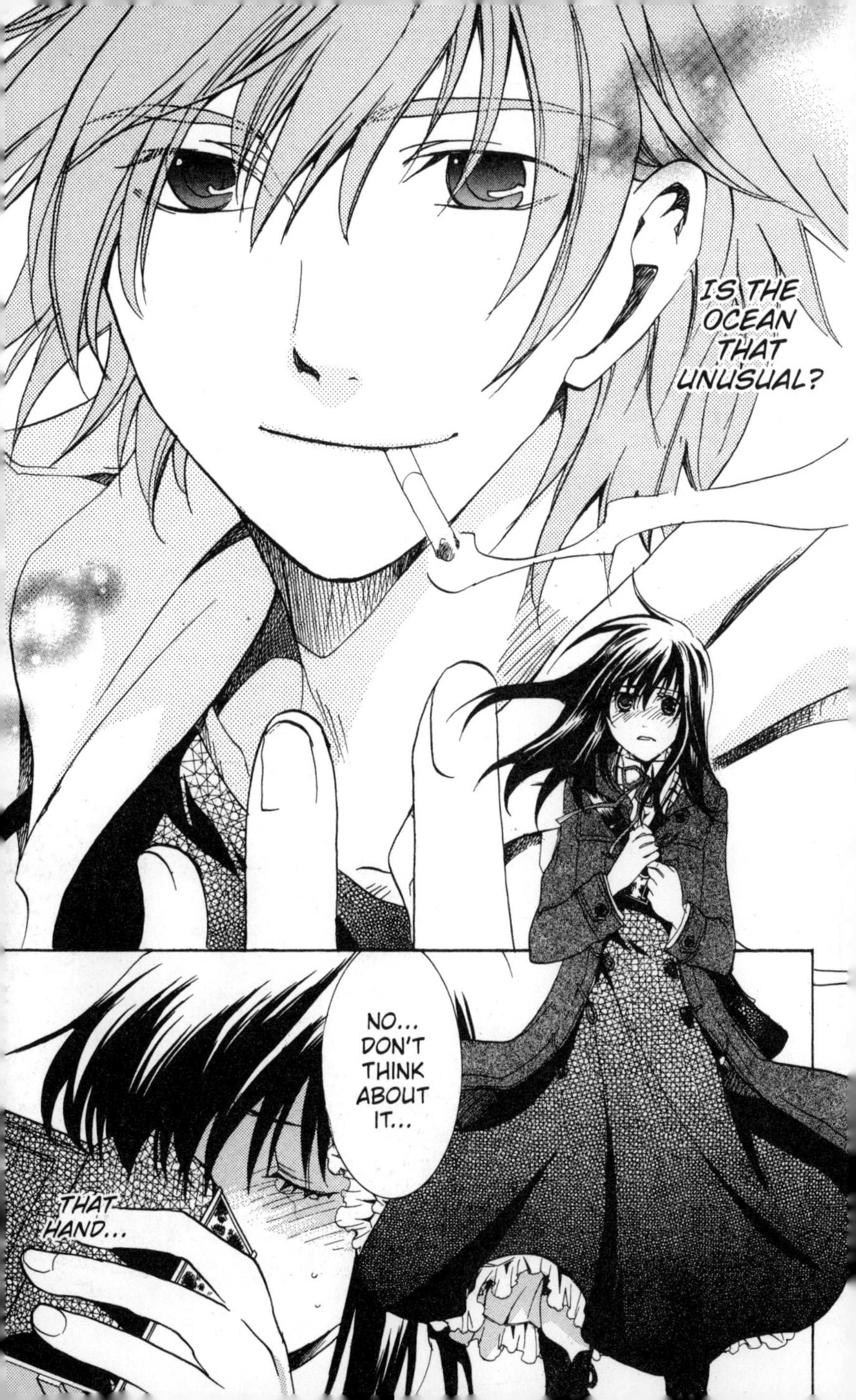
IS THE OCEAN THAT UNUSUAL?
NO... DON'T THINK ABOUT IT...
THAT HAND...

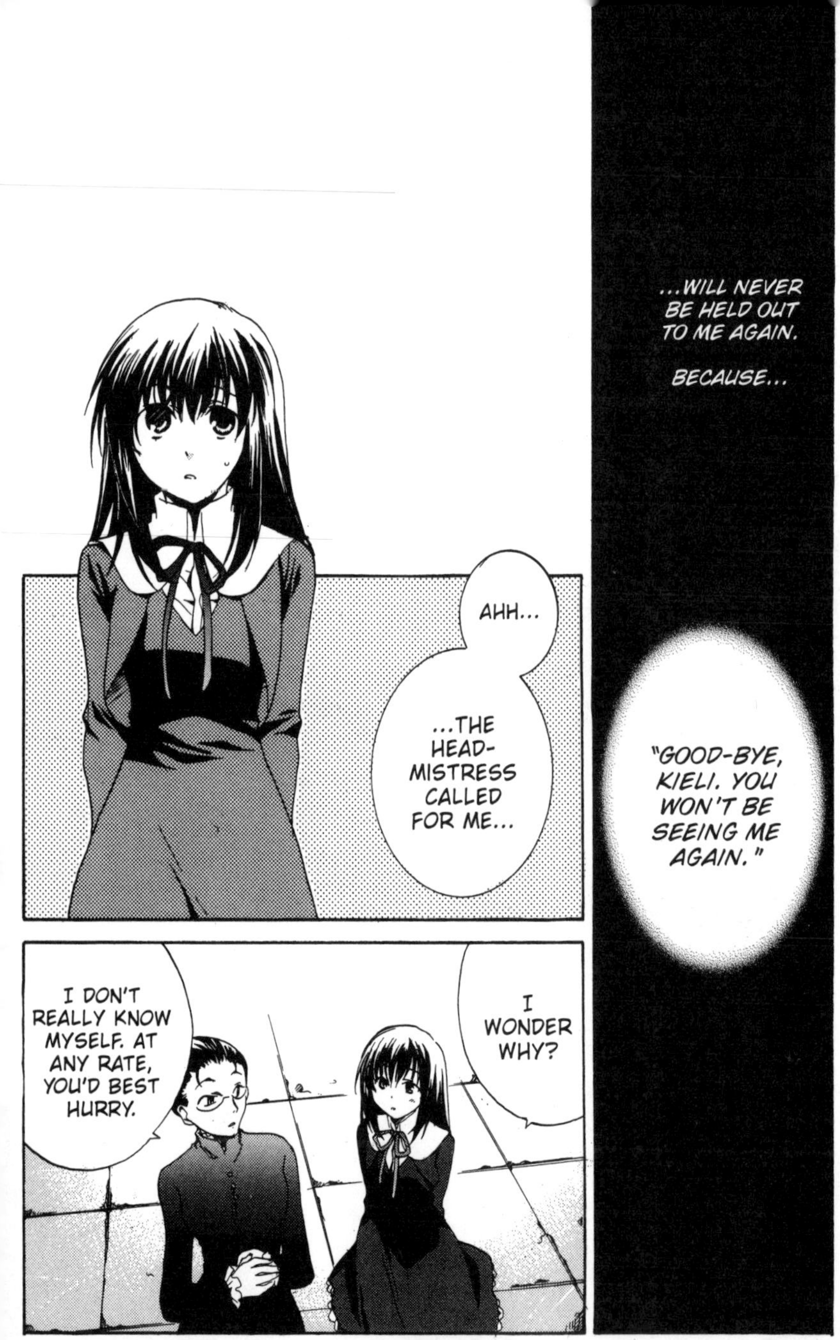
...WILL NEVER BE HELD OUT TO ME AGAIN.
BECAUSE...
"GOOD-BYE, KIELI. YOU WON'T BE SEEING ME AGAIN."
AHH...
...THE HEAD-MISTRESS CALLED FOR ME...
I WONDER WHY?
I DON'T REALLY KNOW MYSELF. AT ANY RATE, YOU'D BEST HURRY.

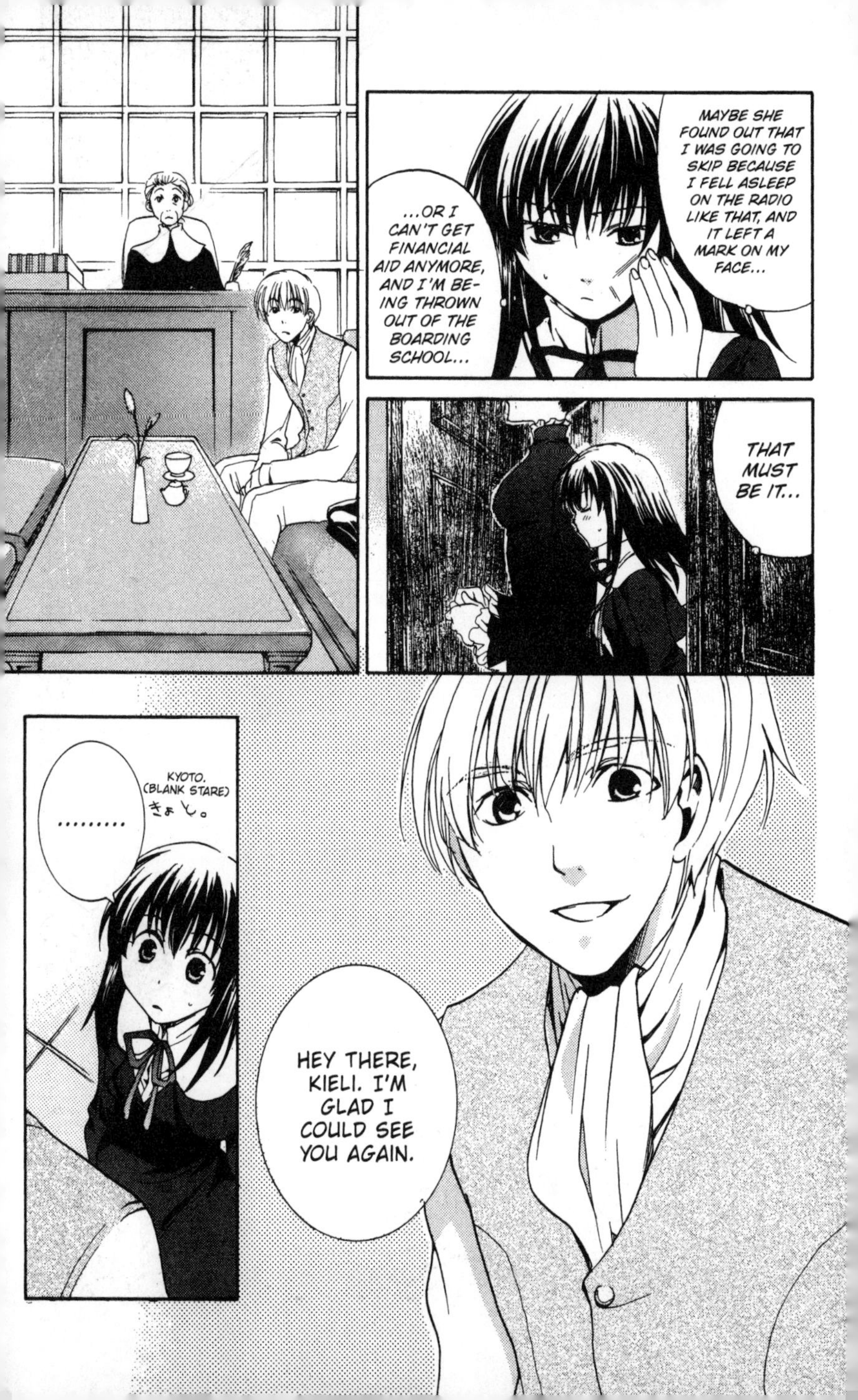
MAYBE SHE FOUND OUT THAT I WAS GOING TO SKIP BECAUSE I FELL ASLEEP ON THE RADIO LIKE THAT, AND IT LEFT A MARK ON MY FACE...
...OR I CAN'T GET FINANCIAL AID ANYMORE, AND I'M BE-ING THROWN OUT OF THE BOARDING SCHOOL...
THAT MUST BE IT...
HEY THERE, KIELI. I'M GLAD I COULD SEE YOU AGAIN.
....
KYOTO. (BLANK STARE)
きょと。

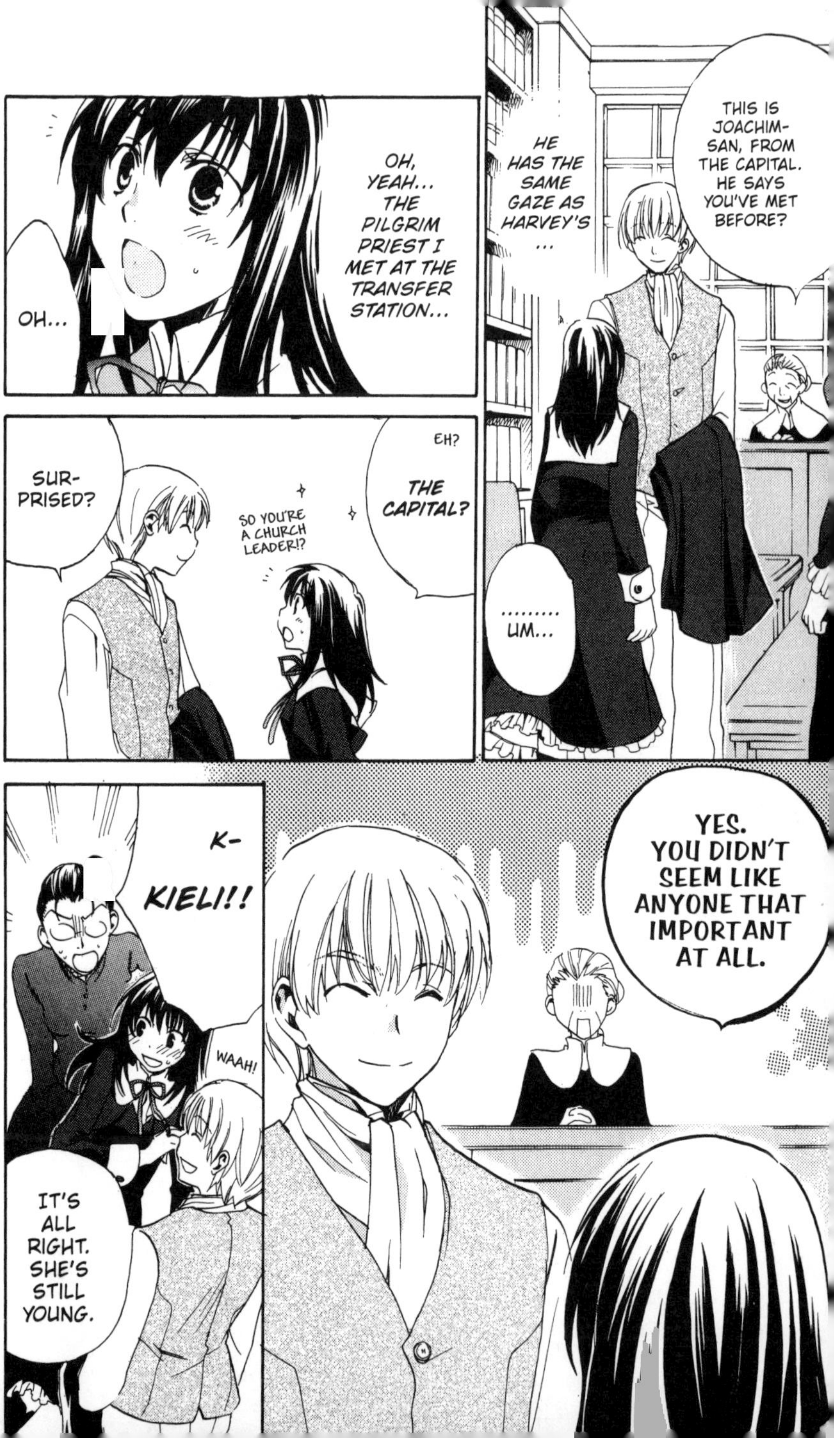
THIS IS JOACHIM-SAN, FROM THE CAPITAL. HE SAYS YOU'VE MET BEFORE?
HE HAS THE SAME GAZE AS HARVEY'S...
....
UM...
OH, YEAH... THE PILGRIM PRIEST I MET AT THE TRANSFER STATION...
OH...
EH?
THE CAPITAL?
SO YOU'RE A CHURCH LEADER!?
SUR-PRISED?
YES. YOU DIDN'T SEEM LIKE ANYONE THAT IMPORTANT AT ALL.
K-
KIELI!!
WAAH!
IT'S ALL RIGHT. SHE'S STILL YOUNG.

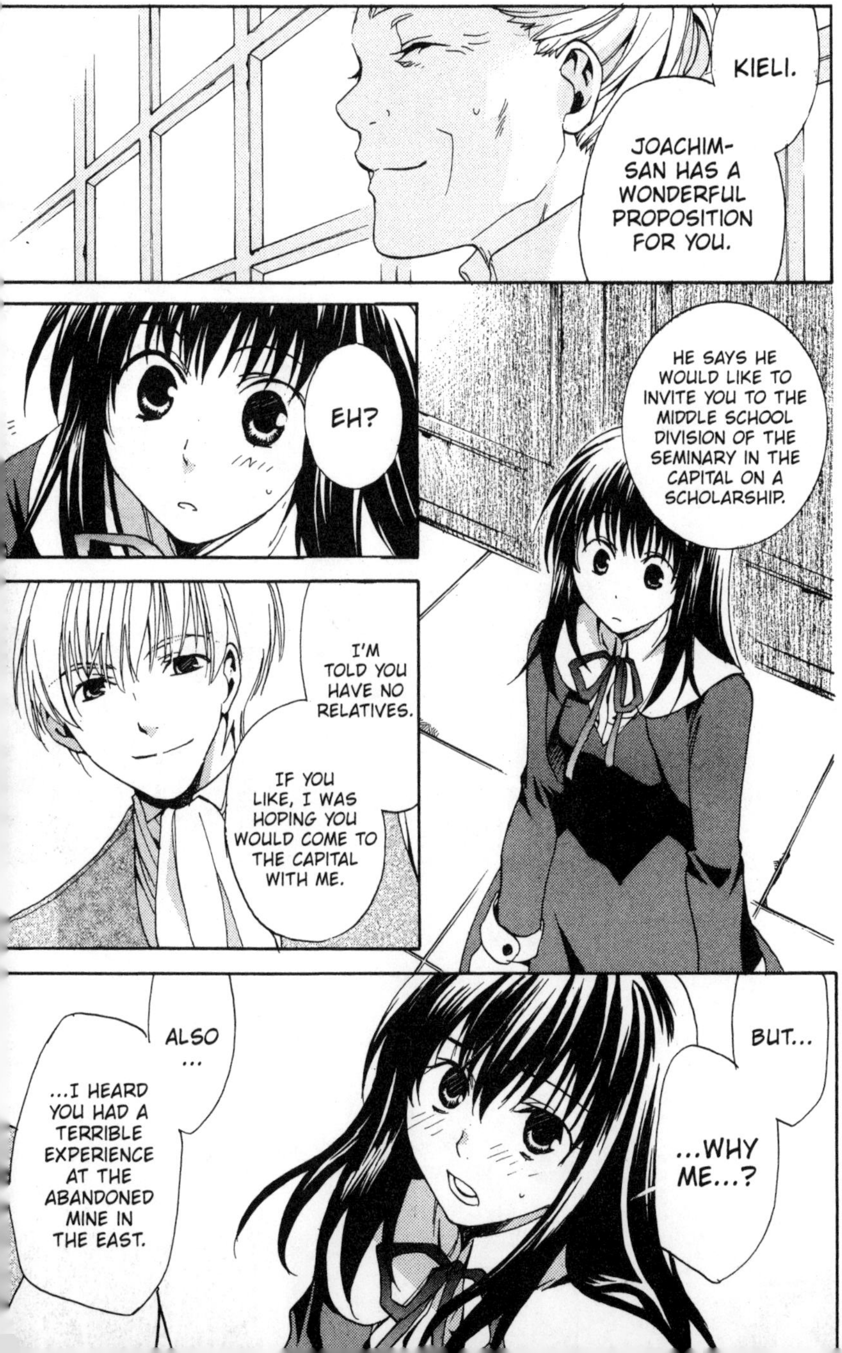
KIELI.
JOACHIM-SAN HAS A WONDERFUL PROPOSITION FOR YOU.
HE SAYS HE WOULD LIKE TO INVITE YOU TO THE MIDDLE SCHOOL DIVISION OF THE SEMINARY IN THE CAPITAL ON A SCHOLARSHIP.
EH?
I'M TOLD YOU HAVE NO RELATIVES.
IF YOU LIKE, I WAS HOPING YOU WOULD COME TO THE CAPITAL WITH ME.
BUT...
...WHY ME...?
ALSO ...
...I HEARD YOU HAD A TERRIBLE EXPERIENCE AT THE ABANDONED MINE IN THE EAST.

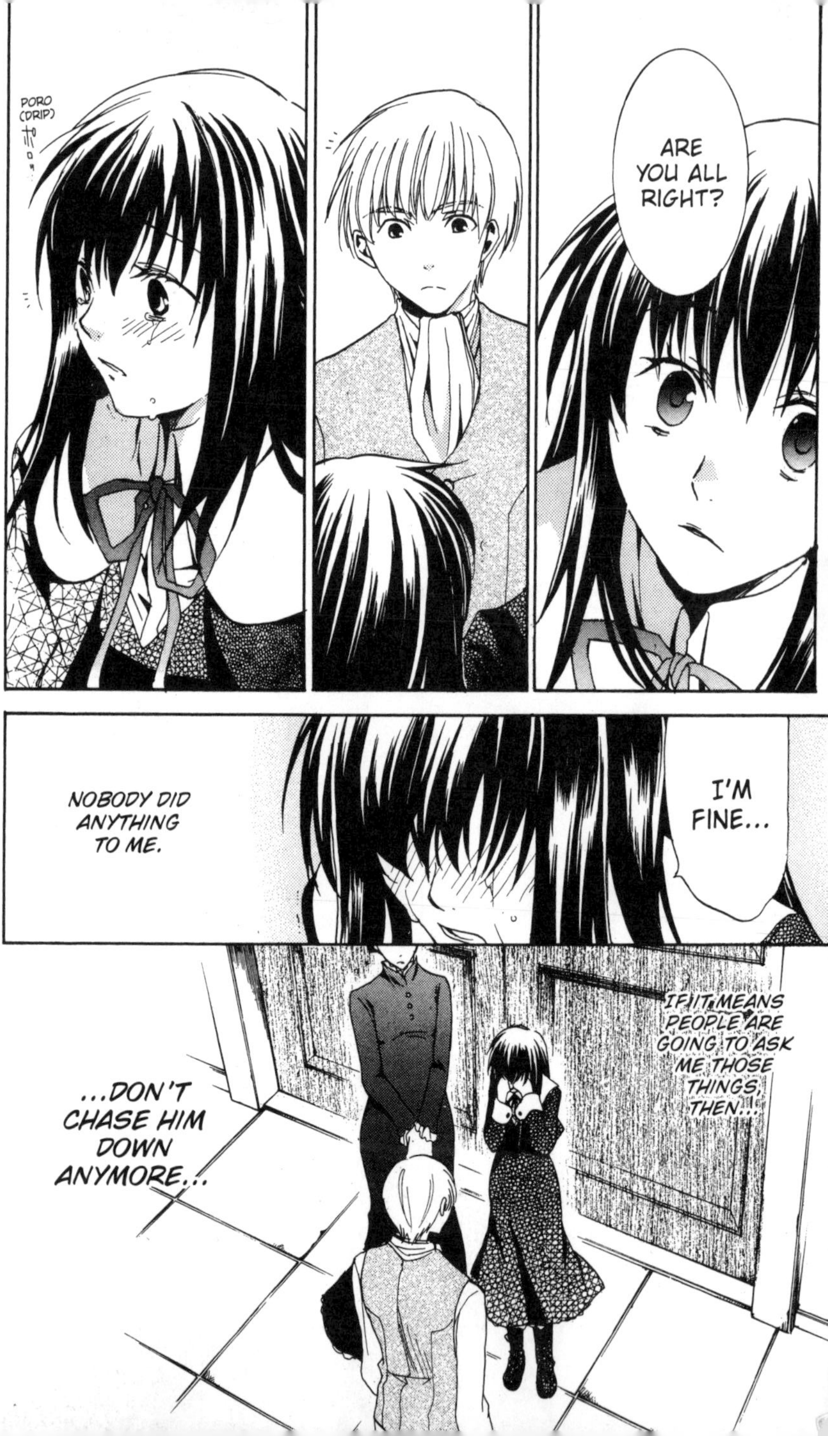
ARE YOU ALL RIGHT?
PORO (DRIP)
I'M FINE...
NOBODY DID ANYTHING TO ME.
IF IT MEANS PEOPLE ARE GOING TO ASK ME THOSE THINGS, THEN..!
...DON'T CHASE HIM DOWN ANYMORE...

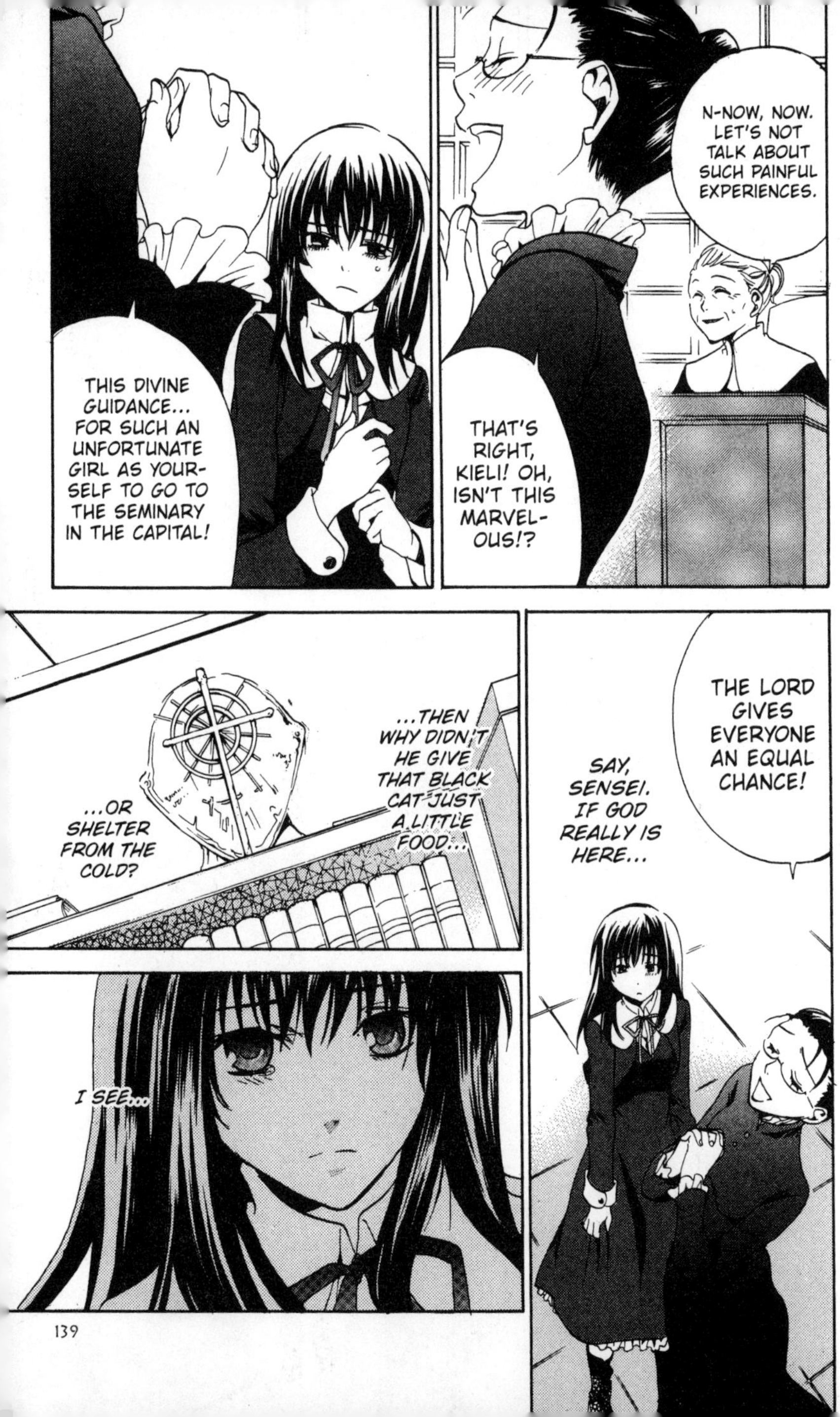
N-NOW, NOW. LET'S NOT TALK ABOUT SUCH PAINFUL EXPERIENCES.
THAT'S RIGHT, KIELI! OH, ISN'T THIS MARVEL-OUS!?
THIS DIVINE GUIDANCE... FOR SUCH AN UNFORTUNATE GIRL AS YOUR-SELF TO GO TO THE SEMINARY IN THE CAPITAL!
THE LORD GIVES EVERYONE AN EQUAL CHANCE!
SAY, SENSEI. IF GOD REALLY IS HERE...
...THEN WHY DIDN'T HE GIVE THAT BLACK CAT JUST A LITTLE FOOD...
...OR SHELTER FROM THE COLD?
I SEE...

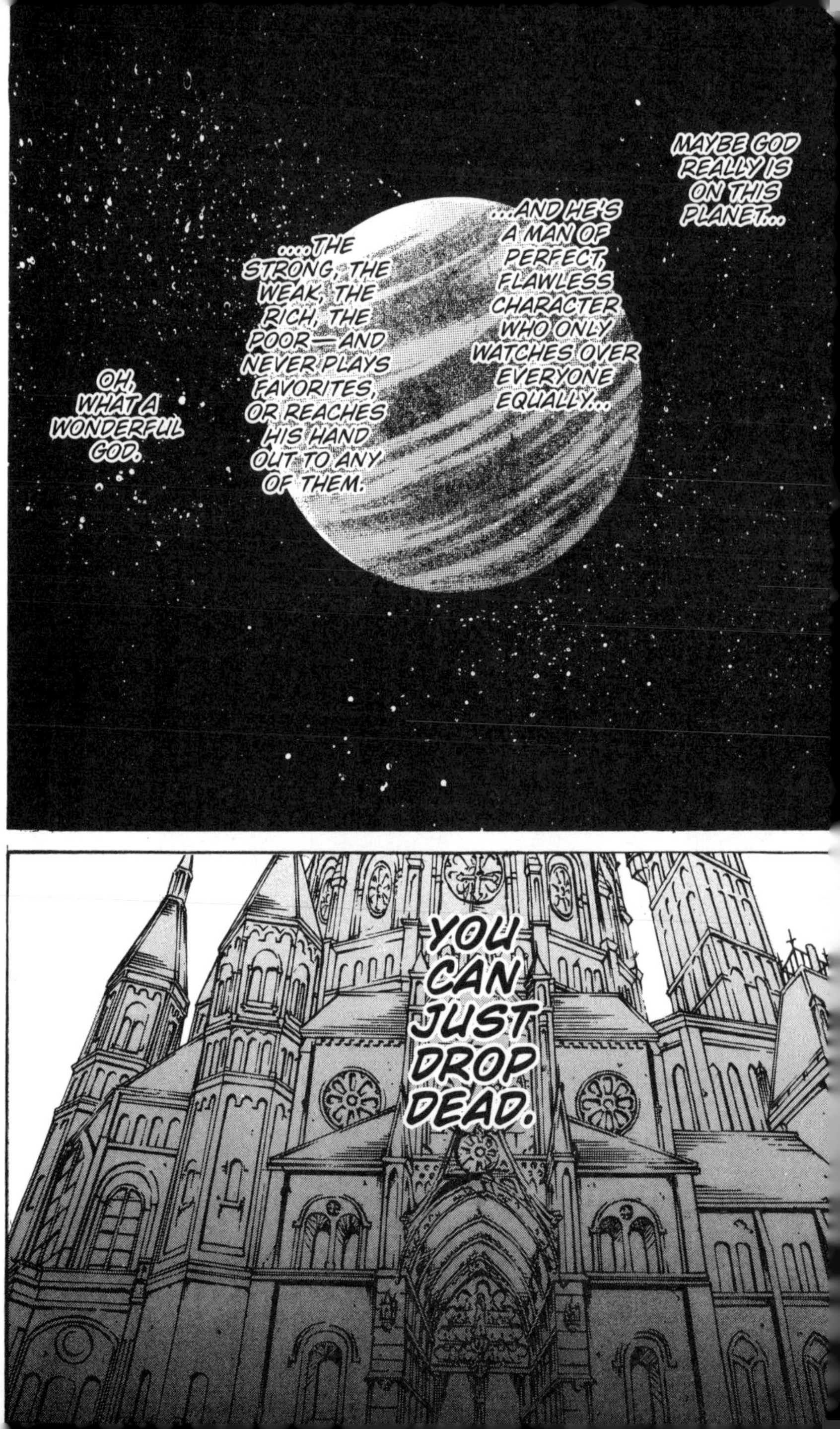
MAYBE GOD REALLY IS ON THIS PLANET...
...AND HE'S A MAN OF PERFECT, FLAWLESS CHARACTER WHO ONLY WATCHES OVER EVERYONE EQUALLY...
...THE STRONG, THE WEAK, THE RICH, THE POOR—AND NEVER PLAYS FAVORITES, OR REACHES HIS HAND OUT TO ANY OF THEM.
OH, WHAT A WONDERFUL GOD.
YOU CAN JUST DROP DEAD.

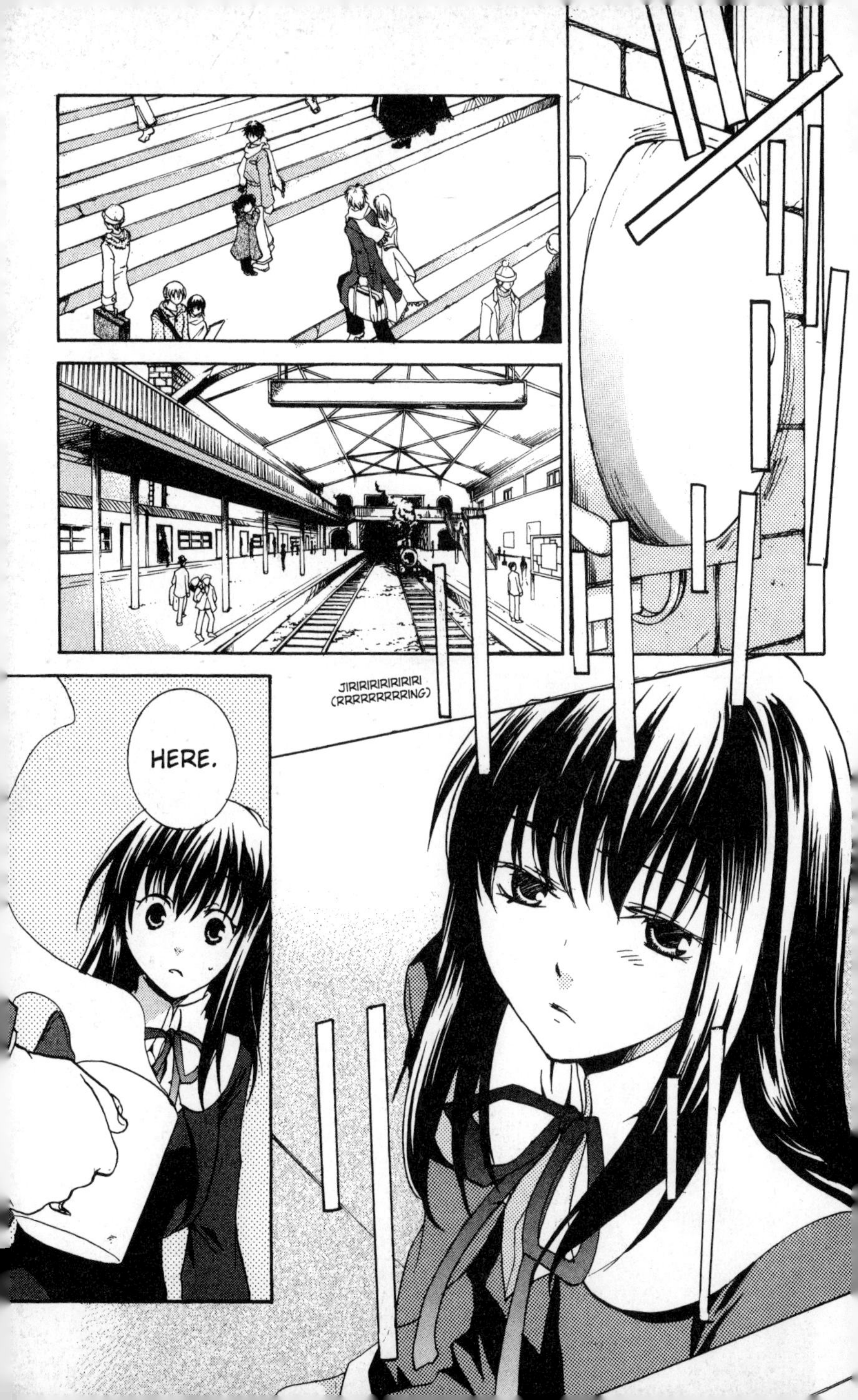
JIRIRIRIRIRIRIRI (RRRRRRRRRRING)
HERE.

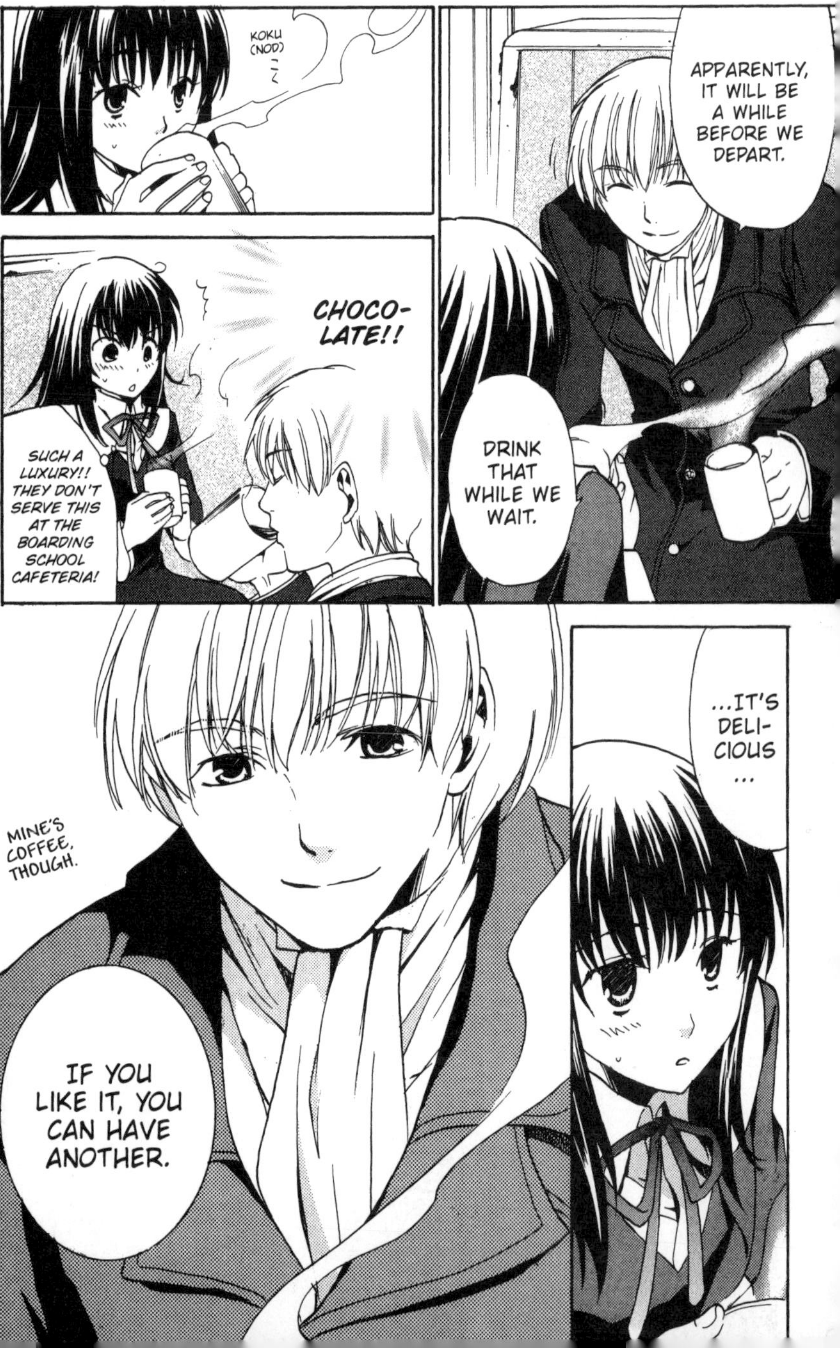
APPARENTLY, IT WILL BE A WHILE BEFORE WE DEPART.
DRINK THAT WHILE WE WAIT.
KOKU (NOD)
CHOCO-LATE!!
SUCH A LUXURY!! THEY DON'T SERVE THIS AT THE BOARDING SCHOOL CAFETERIA!
...IT'S DELI-CIOUS...
MINE'S COFFEE, THOUGH.
IF YOU LIKE IT, YOU CAN HAVE ANOTHER.

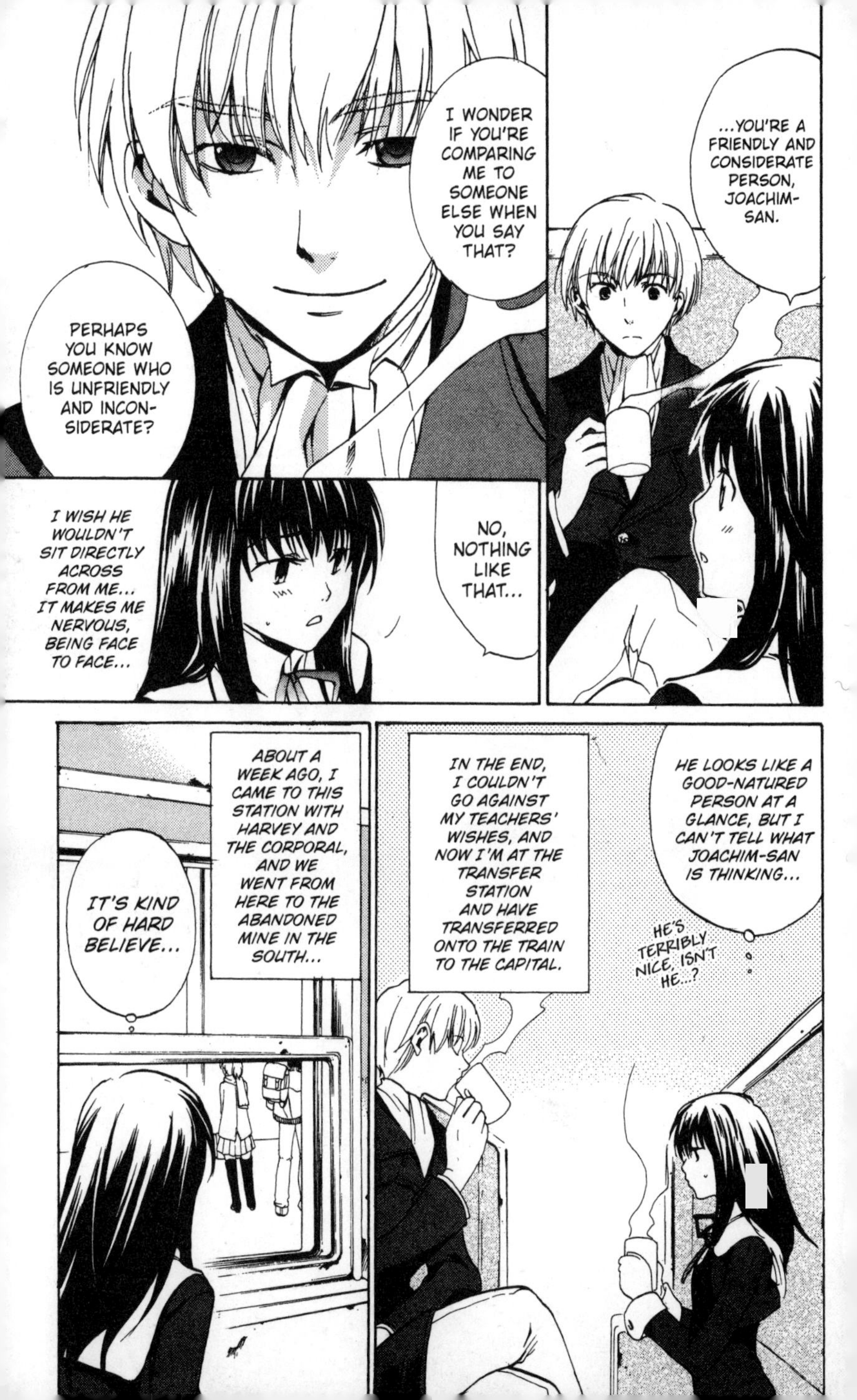
...YOU'RE A FRIENDLY AND CONSIDERATE PERSON, JOACHIM-SAN.
I WONDER IF YOU'RE COMPARING ME TO SOMEONE ELSE WHEN YOU SAY THAT?
PERHAPS YOU KNOW SOMEONE WHO IS UNFRIENDLY AND INCON-SIDERATE?
NO, NOTHING LIKE THAT...
I WISH HE WOULDN'T SIT DIRECTLY ACROSS FROM ME... IT MAKES ME NERVOUS, BEING FACE TO FACE...
HE LOOKS LIKE A GOOD-NATURED PERSON AT A GLANCE, BUT I CAN'T TELL WHAT JOACHIM-SAN IS THINKING...
HE'S TERRIBLY NICE, ISN'T HE...?
IN THE END, I COULDN'T GO AGAINST MY TEACHERS' WISHES, AND NOW I'M AT THE TRANSFER STATION AND HAVE TRANSFERRED ONTO THE TRAIN TO THE CAPITAL.
ABOUT A WEEK AGO, I CAME TO THIS STATION WITH HARVEY AND THE CORPORAL, AND WE WENT FROM HERE TO THE ABANDONED MINE IN THE SOUTH...
IT'S KIND OF HARD BELIEVE...

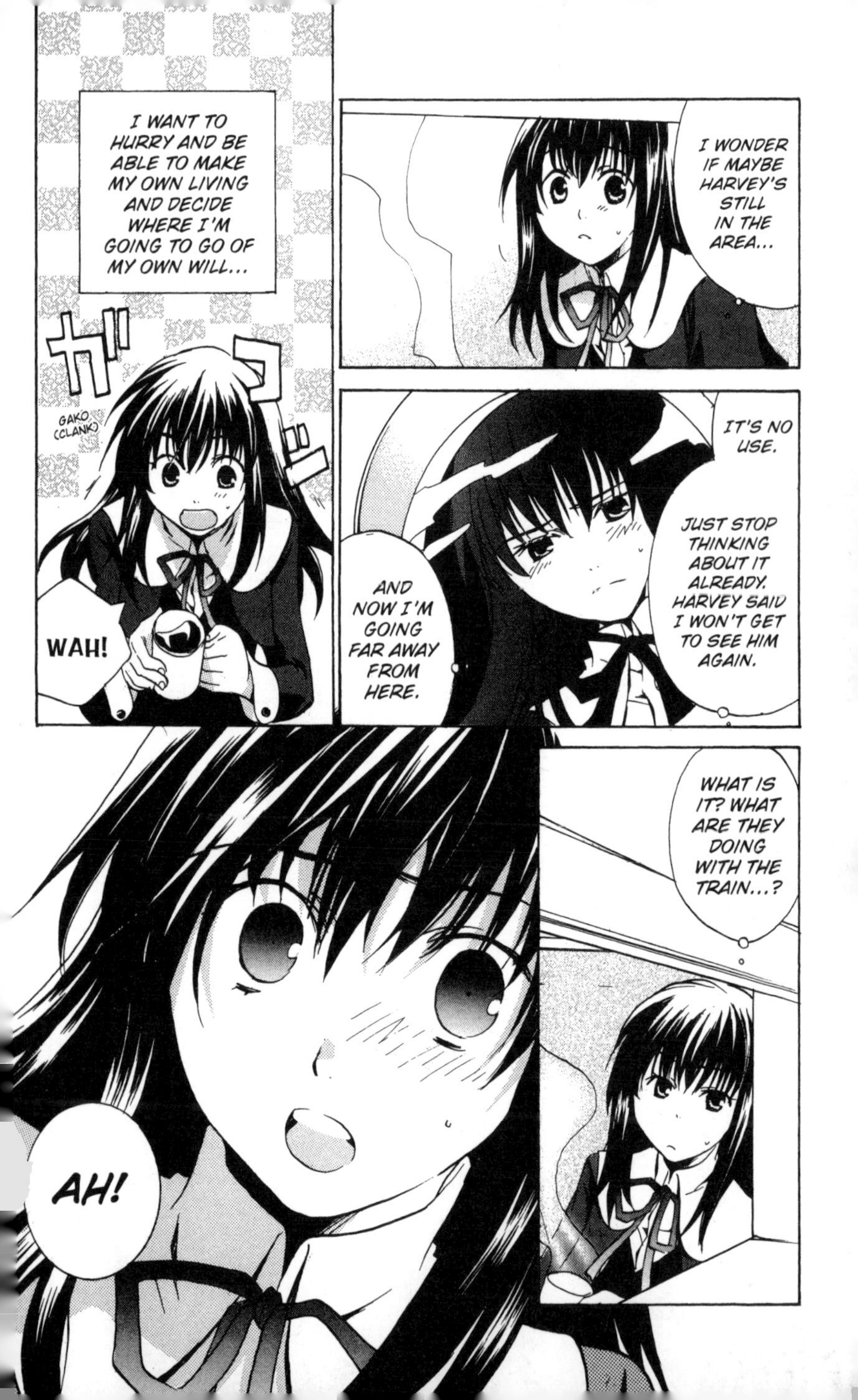
I WONDER IF MAYBE HARVEY'S STILL IN THE AREA...
IT'S NO USE.
JUST STOP THINKING ABOUT IT ALREADY. HARVEY SAID I WON'T GET TO SEE HIM AGAIN.
AND NOW I'M GOING FAR AWAY FROM HERE.
I WANT TO HURRY AND BE ABLE TO MAKE MY OWN LIVING AND DECIDE WHERE I'M GOING TO GO OF MY OWN WILL...
ガコッ
GAKO (CLANK)
WAH!
WHAT IS IT? WHAT ARE THEY DOING WITH THE TRAIN...?
AH!

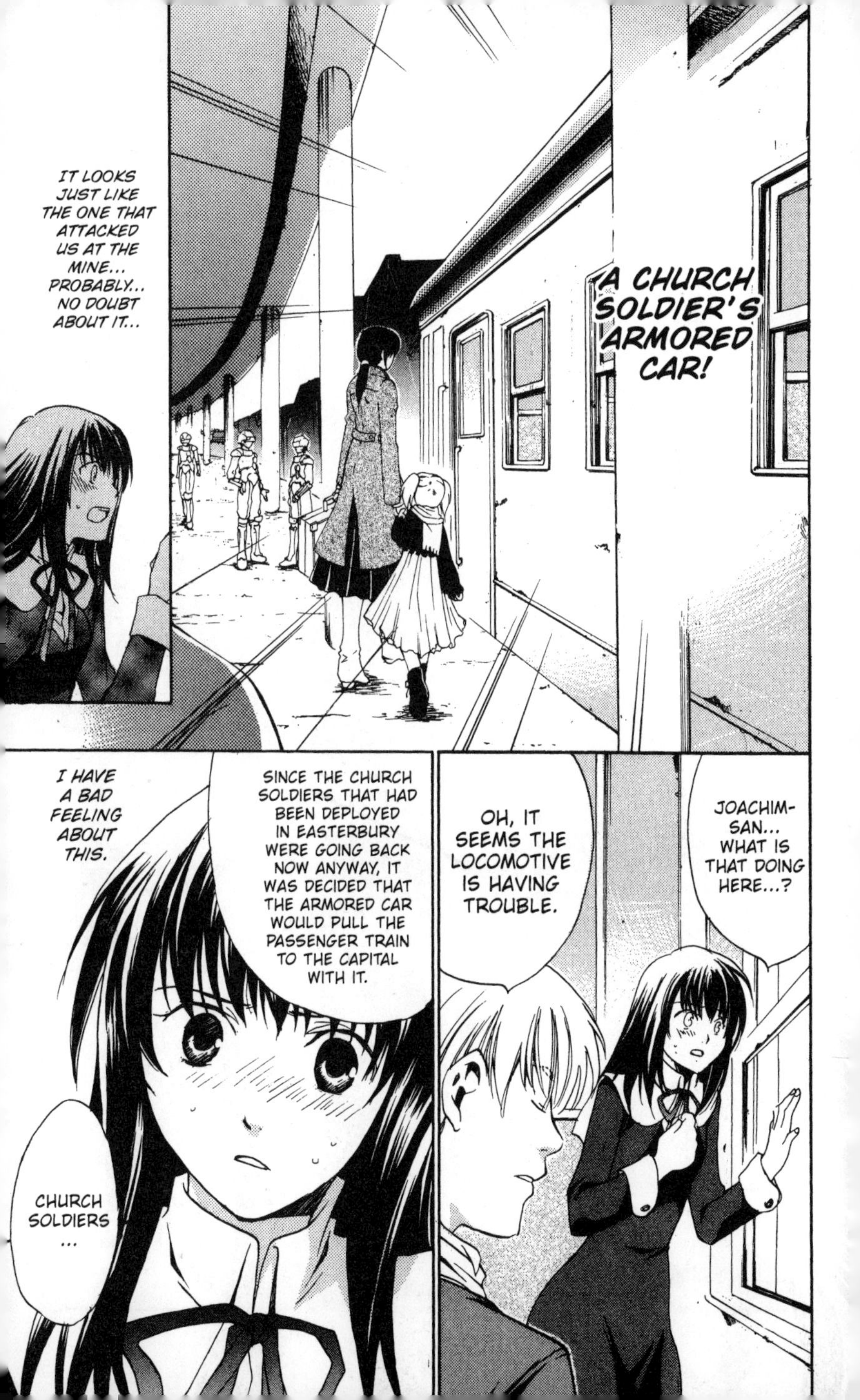
A CHURCH SOLDIER'S ARMORED CAR!
IT LOOKS JUST LIKE THE ONE THAT ATTACKED US AT THE MINE... PROBABLY... NO DOUBT ABOUT IT...
JOACHIM-SAN... WHAT IS THAT DOING HERE...?
OH, IT SEEMS THE LOCOMOTIVE IS HAVING TROUBLE.
SINCE THE CHURCH SOLDIERS THAT HAD BEEN DEPLOYED IN EASTERBURY WERE GOING BACK NOW ANYWAY, IT WAS DECIDED THAT THE ARMORED CAR WOULD PULL THE PASSENGER TRAIN TO THE CAPITAL WITH IT.
I HAVE A BAD FEELING ABOUT THIS.
CHURCH SOLDIERS ...

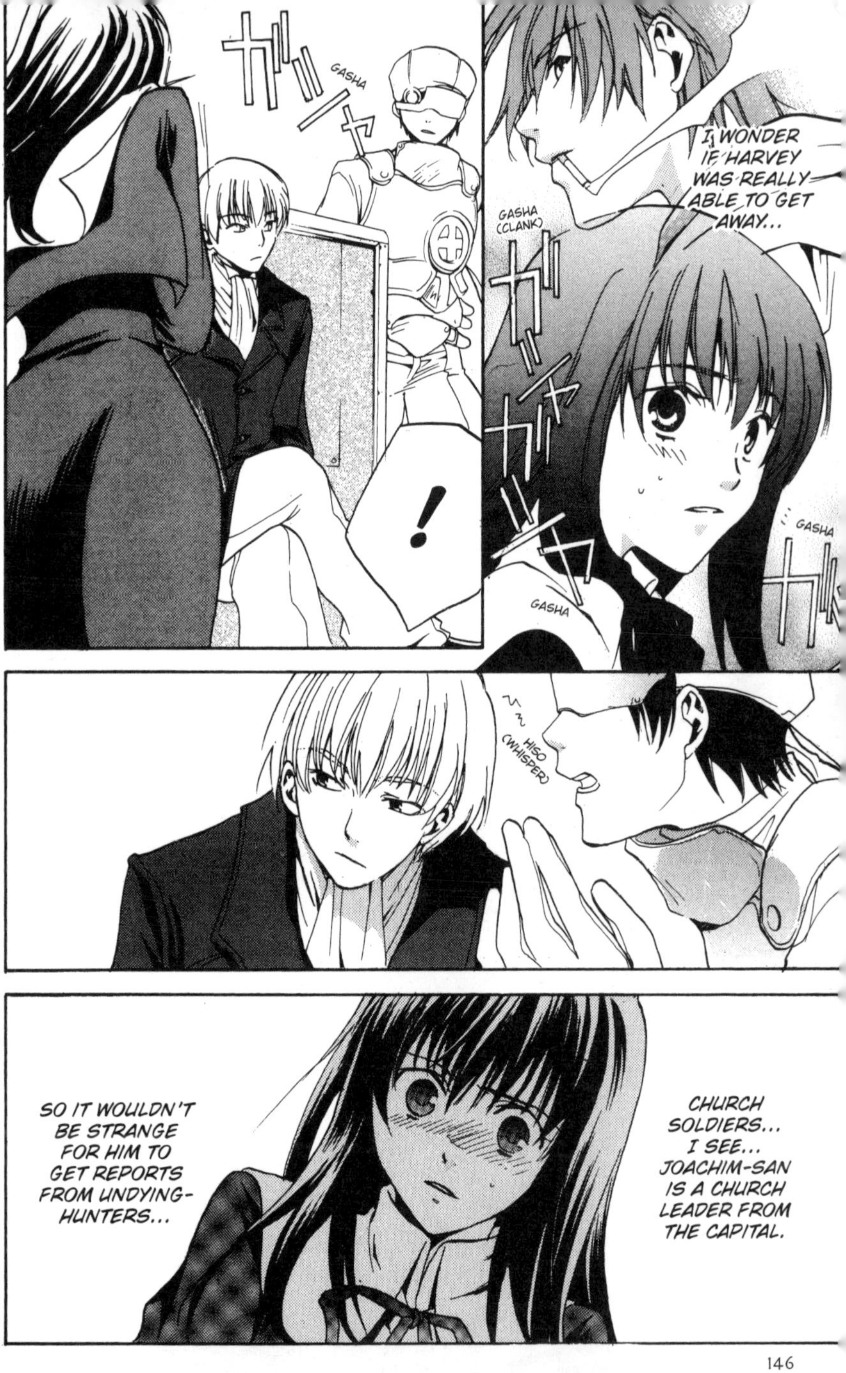
I WONDER IF HARVEY WAS REALLY ABLE TO GET AWAY...
GASHA
GASHA (CLANK)
GASHA
GASHA
!
HISO (WHISPER)
CHURCH SOLDIERS... I SEE... JOACHIM-SAN IS A CHURCH LEADER FROM THE CAPITAL.
SO IT WOULDN'T BE STRANGE FOR HIM TO GET REPORTS FROM UNDYING-HUNTERS...

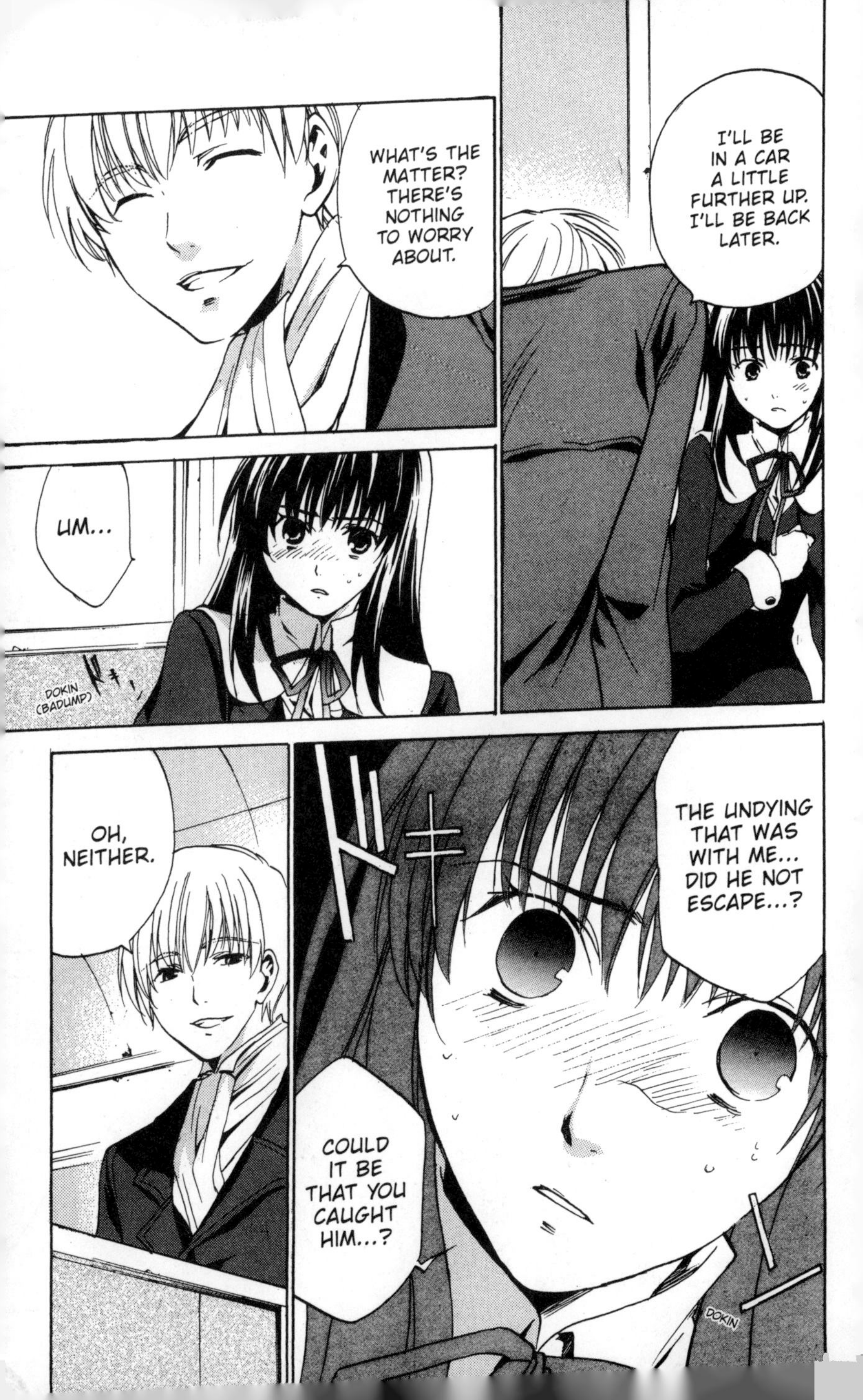
I'LL BE IN A CAR A LITTLE FURTHER UP. I'LL BE BACK LATER.
WHAT'S THE MATTER? THERE'S NOTHING TO WORRY ABOUT.
UM...
DOKIN (BADUMP)
THE UNDYING THAT WAS WITH ME... DID HE NOT ESCAPE...?
COULD IT BE THAT YOU CAUGHT HIM...?
DOKIN
OH, NEITHER.

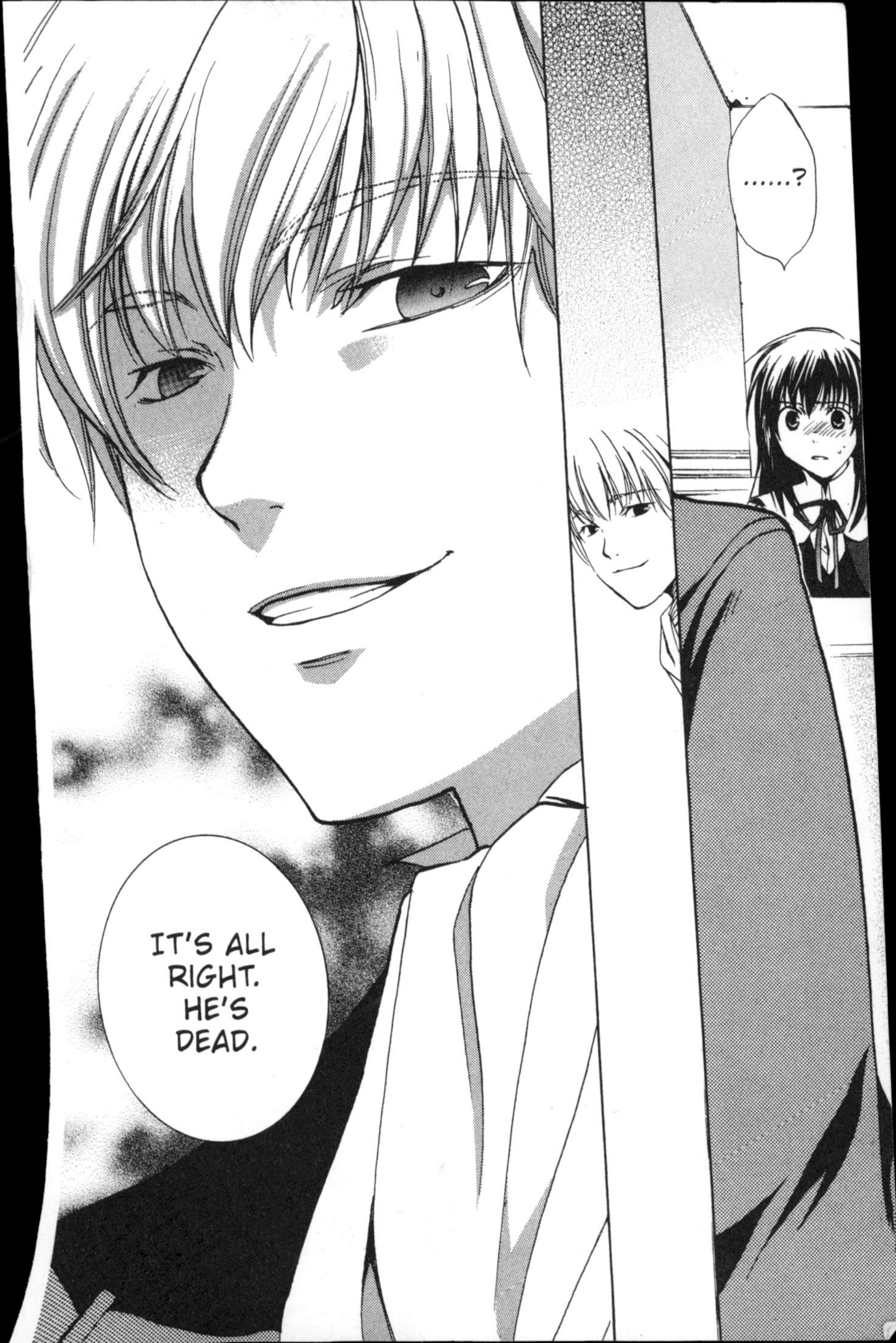
......?
IT'S ALL RIGHT. HE'S DEAD.

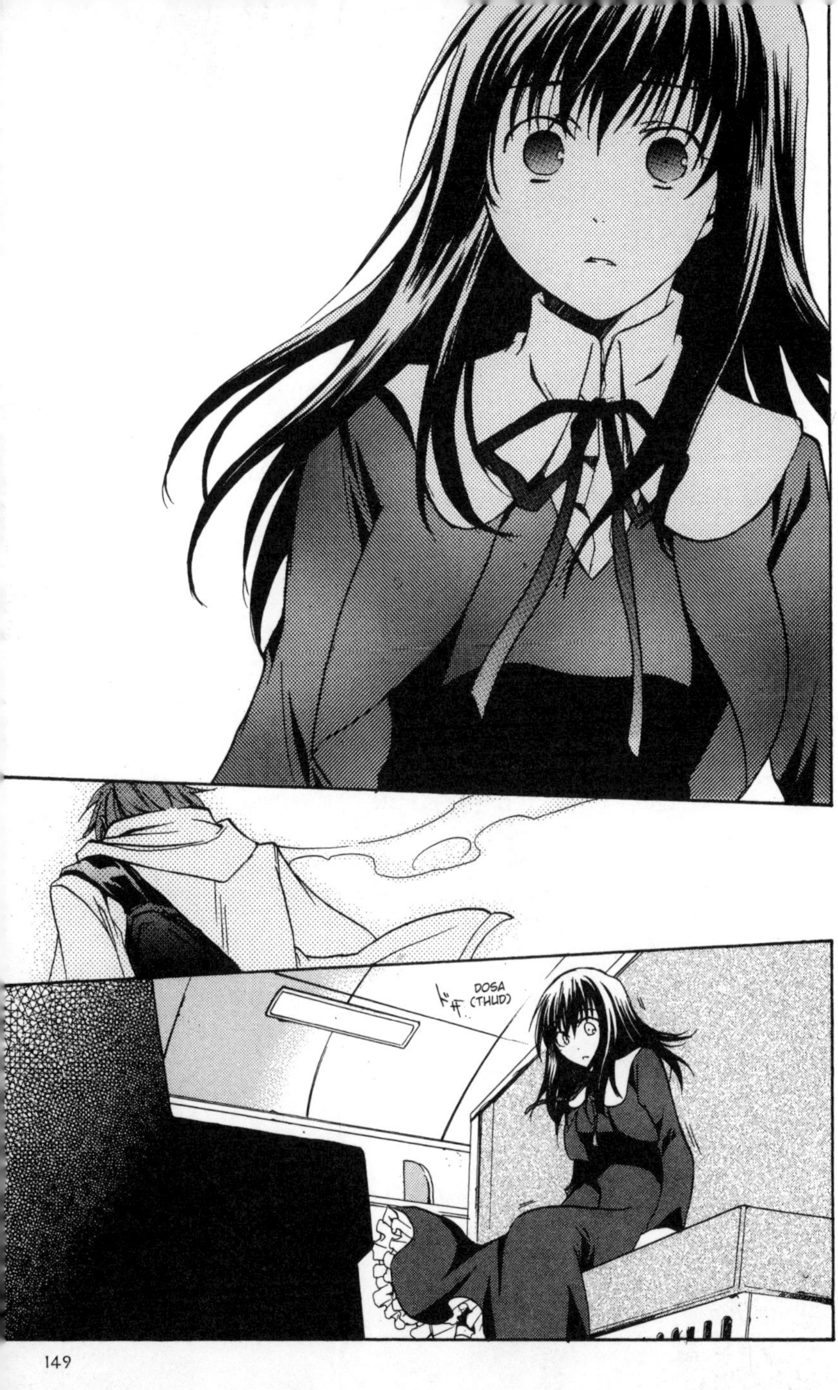
ドサ
DOSA (THUD)

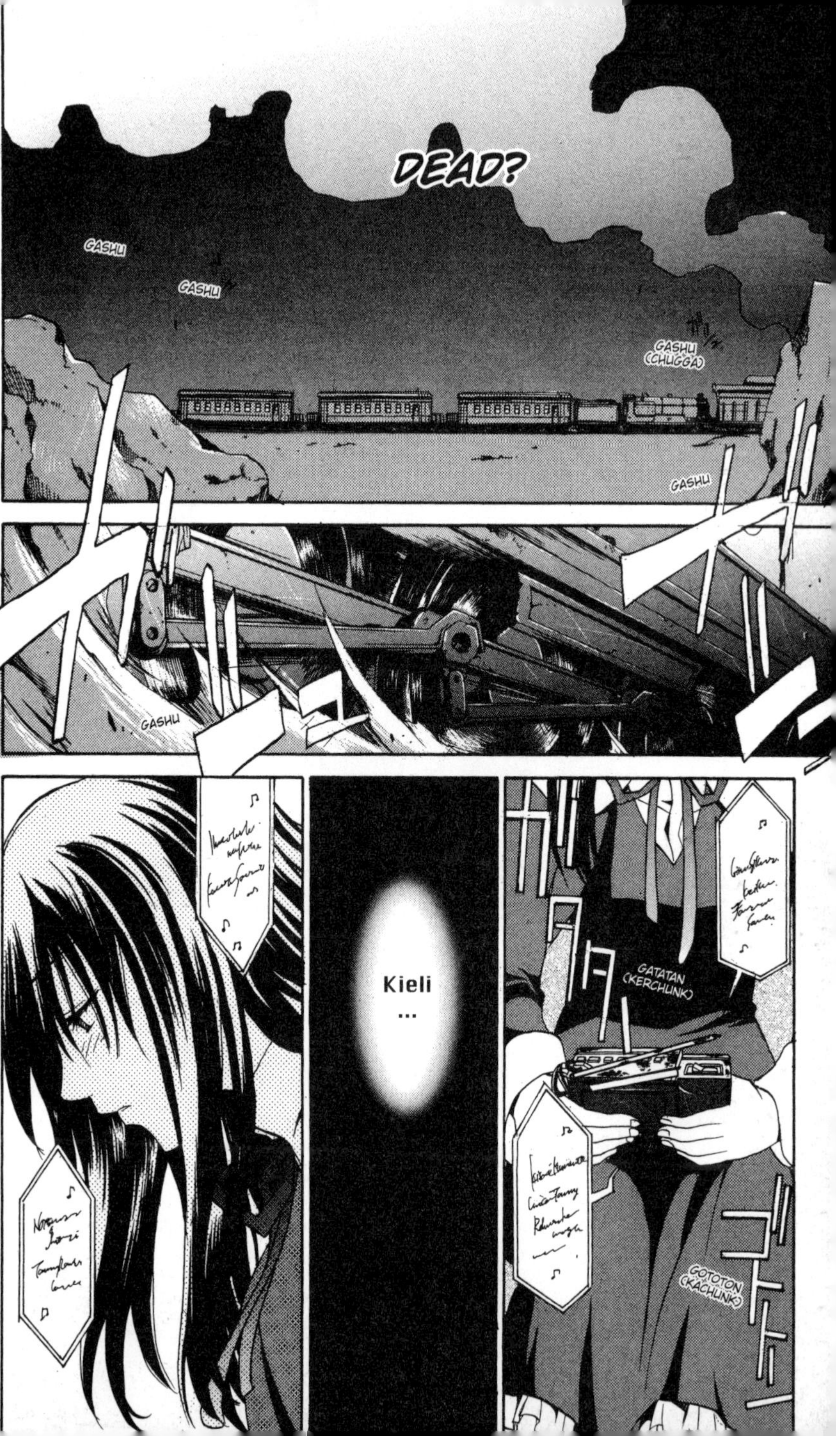
DEAD?
GASHU (CHUGGA)
GASHU
GASHU
GASHU
GASHU
GATATAN (KERCHUNK)
GOTOTON (KACHUNK)
Kieli ...

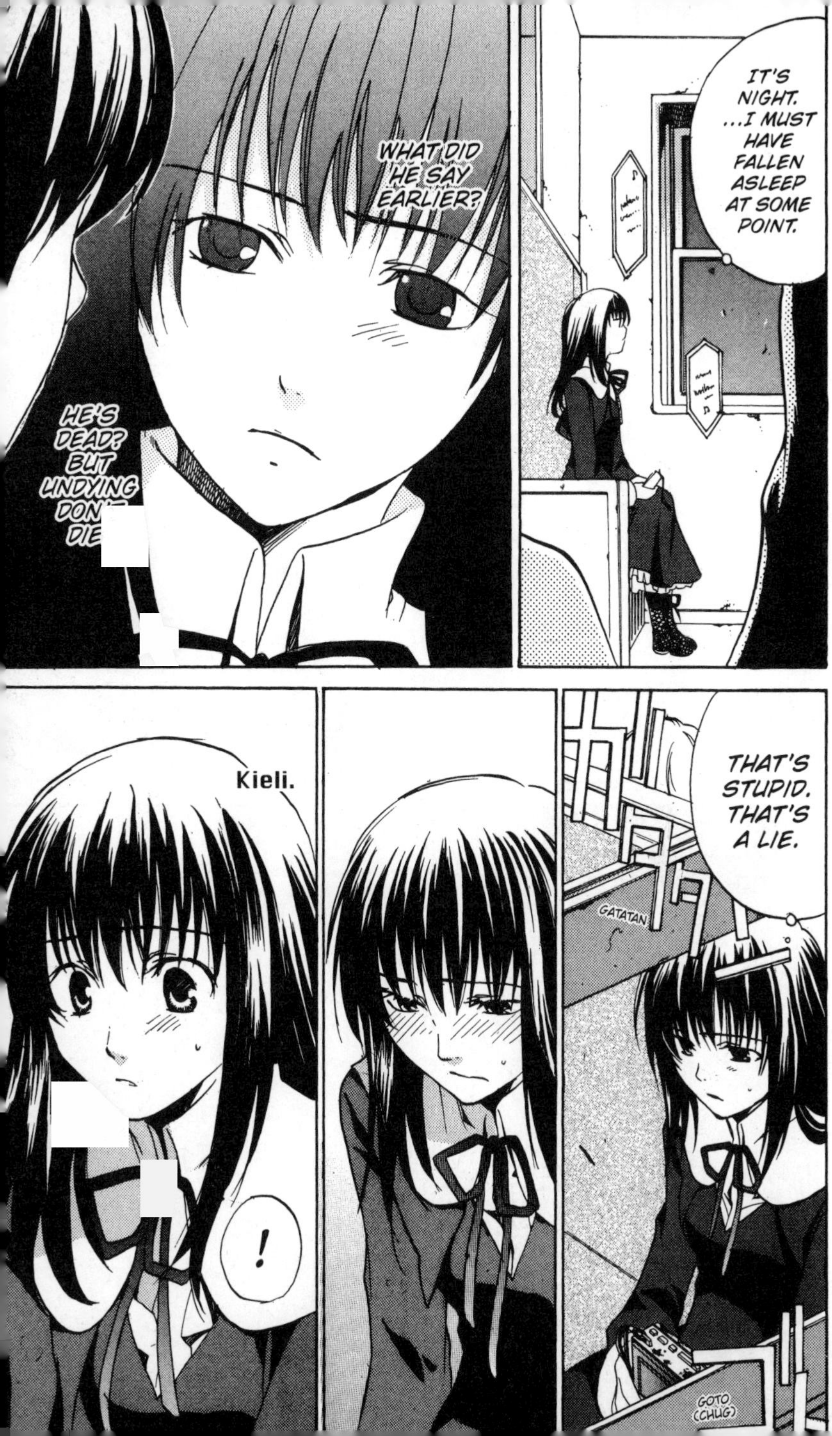
IT'S NIGHT. ...I MUST HAVE FALLEN ASLEEP AT SOME POINT.
WHAT DID HE SAY EARLIER?
HE'S DEAD? BUT UNDYING DON'
DIE
THAT'S STUPID. THAT'S A LIE.
GATATAN
GOTO (CHUG)
Kieli.
!

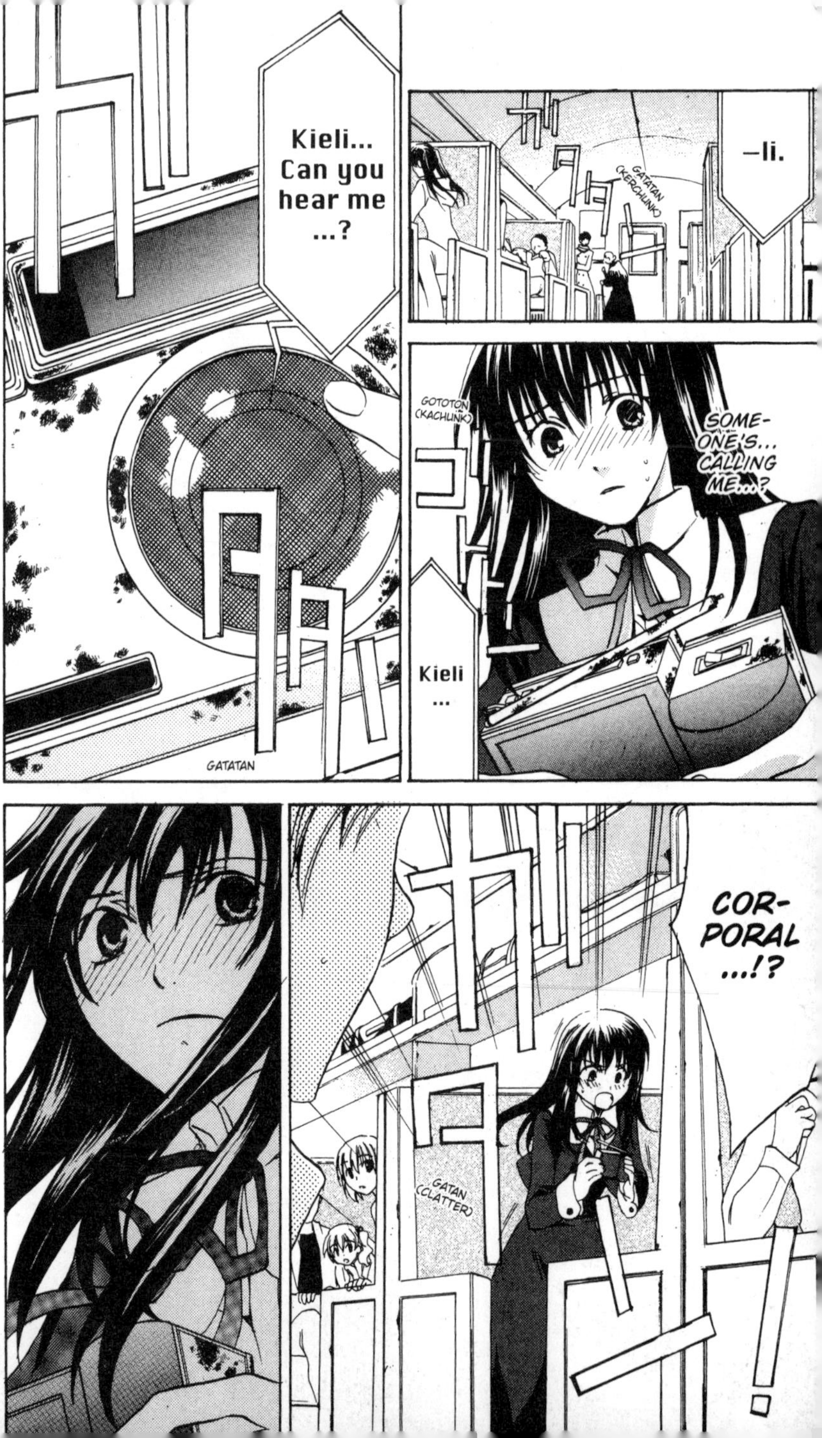
—li.
GATATAN (KERCHUNK)
GOTOTON (KACHUNK)
SOME-ONE'S... CALLING ME...?
Kieli ...
Kieli... Can you hear me ...?
GATATAN
CORPORAL ...!?
GATAN (CLATTER)

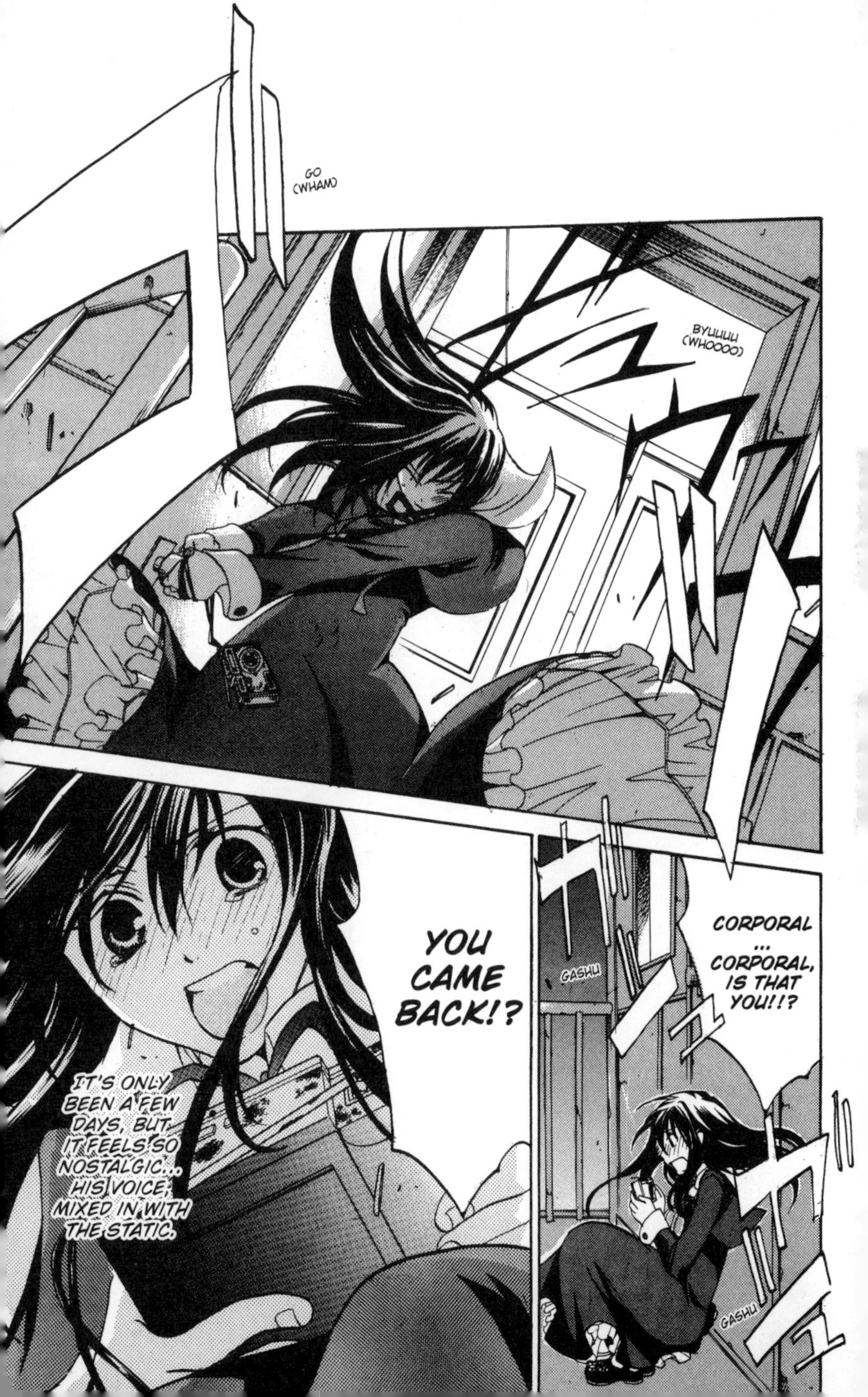
GO
(WHAM)
BYUUUU
(WHOOOO)
CORPORAL ... CORPORAL, IS THAT YOU!!?
GASHU
GASHU
YOU CAME BACK!?
IT'S ONLY BEEN A FEW DAYS, BUT IT FEELS SO NOSTALGIC... HIS VOICE, MIXED IN WITH THE STATIC.

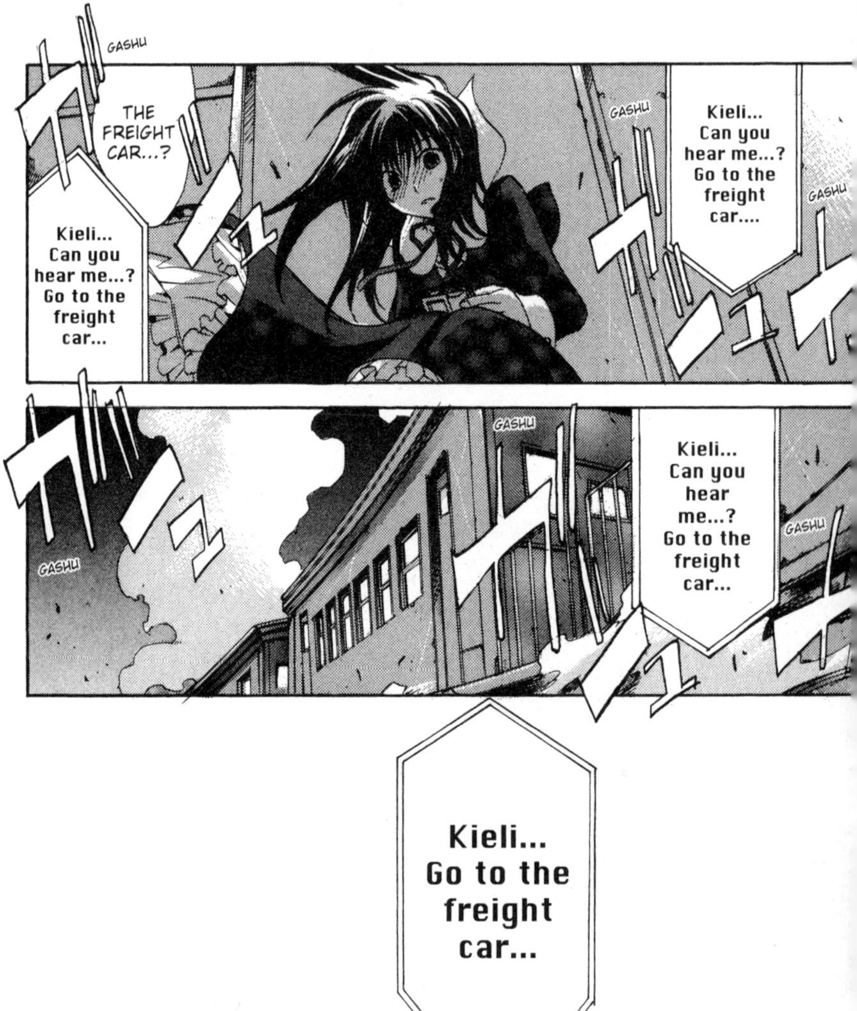
GASHU
Kieli... Can you hear me...? Go to the freight car....
GASHU
GASHU
THE FREIGHT CAR...?
Kieli... Can you hear me...? Go to the freight car...
GASHU
Kieli... Can you hear me...? Go to the freight car...
GASHU
GASHU
Kieli... Go to the freight car...

CHAPTER 6: HOW MANY MORE STEPS TO THE BEACON OF LIGHT? / FIN

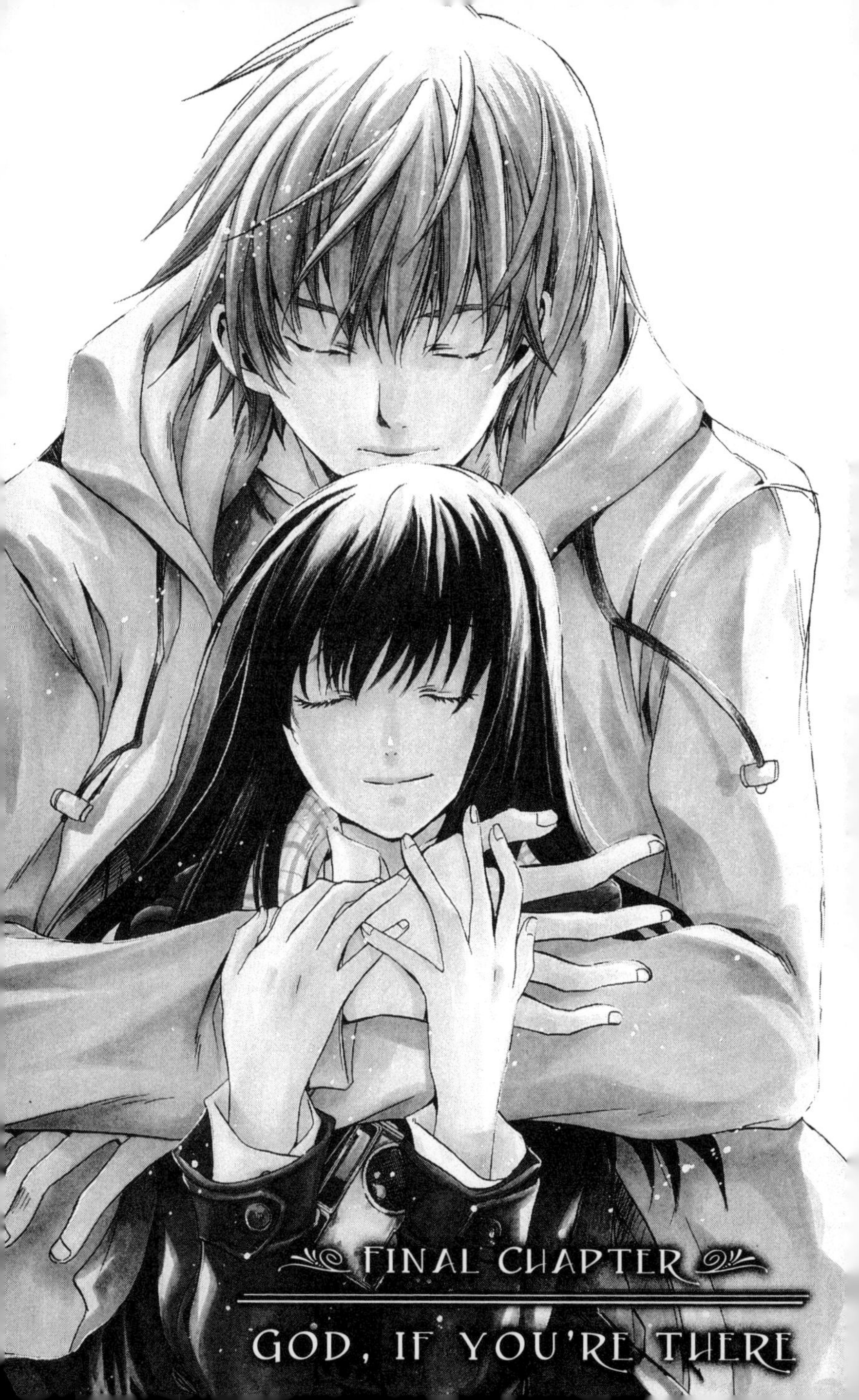

FINAL CHAPTER

GOD, IF YOU'RE THERE

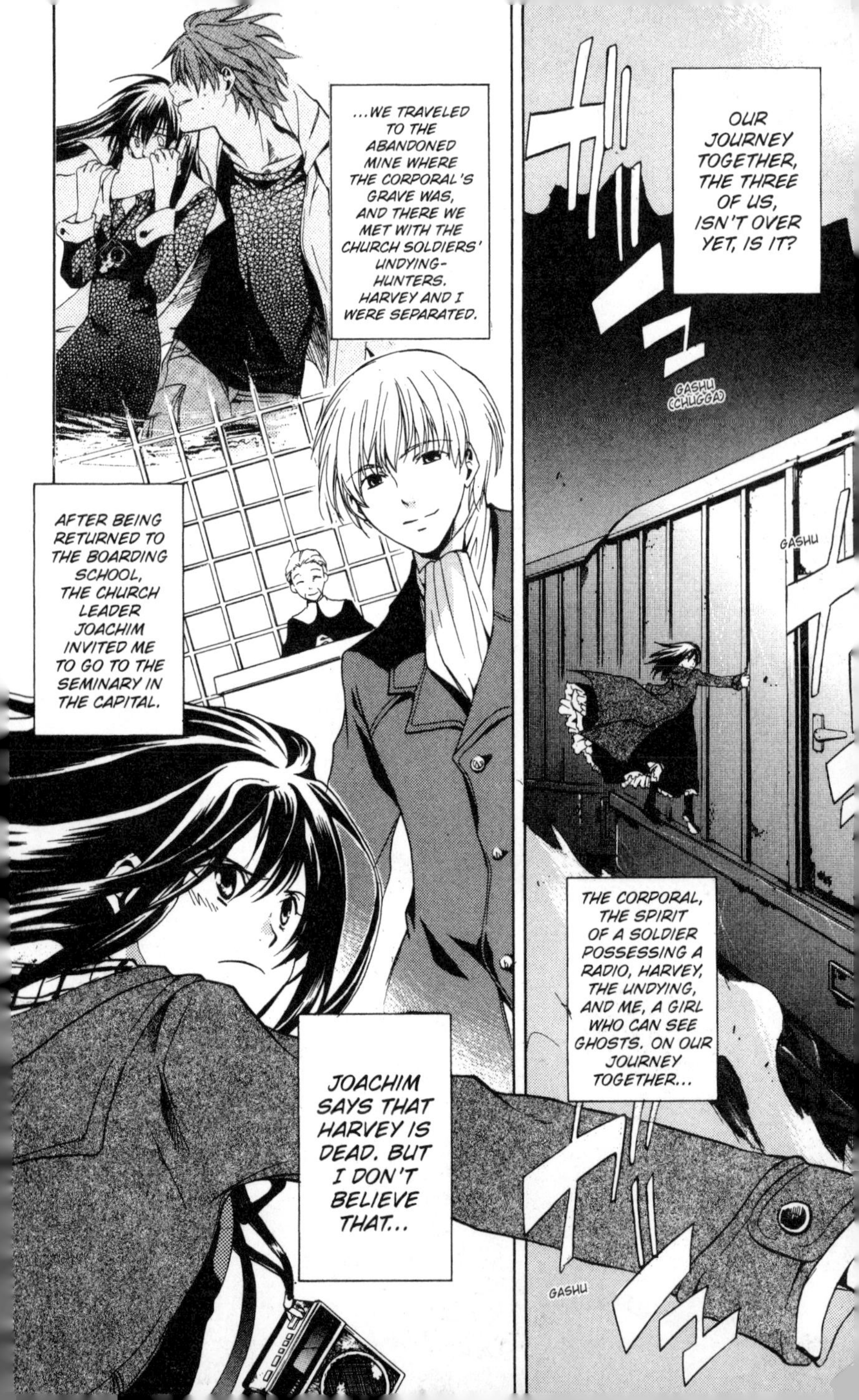
OUR JOURNEY TOGETHER, THE THREE OF US, ISN'T OVER YET, IS IT?
GASHU (CHUGGA)
GASHU
THE CORPORAL, THE SPIRIT OF A SOLDIER POSSESSING A RADIO, HARVEY, THE UNDYING, AND ME, A GIRL WHO CAN SEE GHOSTS. ON OUR JOURNEY TOGETHER...
GASHU
...WE TRAVELED TO THE ABANDONED MINE WHERE THE CORPORAL'S GRAVE WAS, AND THERE WE MET WITH THE CHURCH SOLDIERS' UNDYING-HUNTERS. HARVEY AND I WERE SEPARATED.
AFTER BEING RETURNED TO THE BOARDING SCHOOL, THE CHURCH LEADER JOACHIM INVITED ME TO GO TO THE SEMINARY IN THE CAPITAL.
JOACHIM SAYS THAT HARVEY IS DEAD. BUT I DON'T BELIEVE THAT...

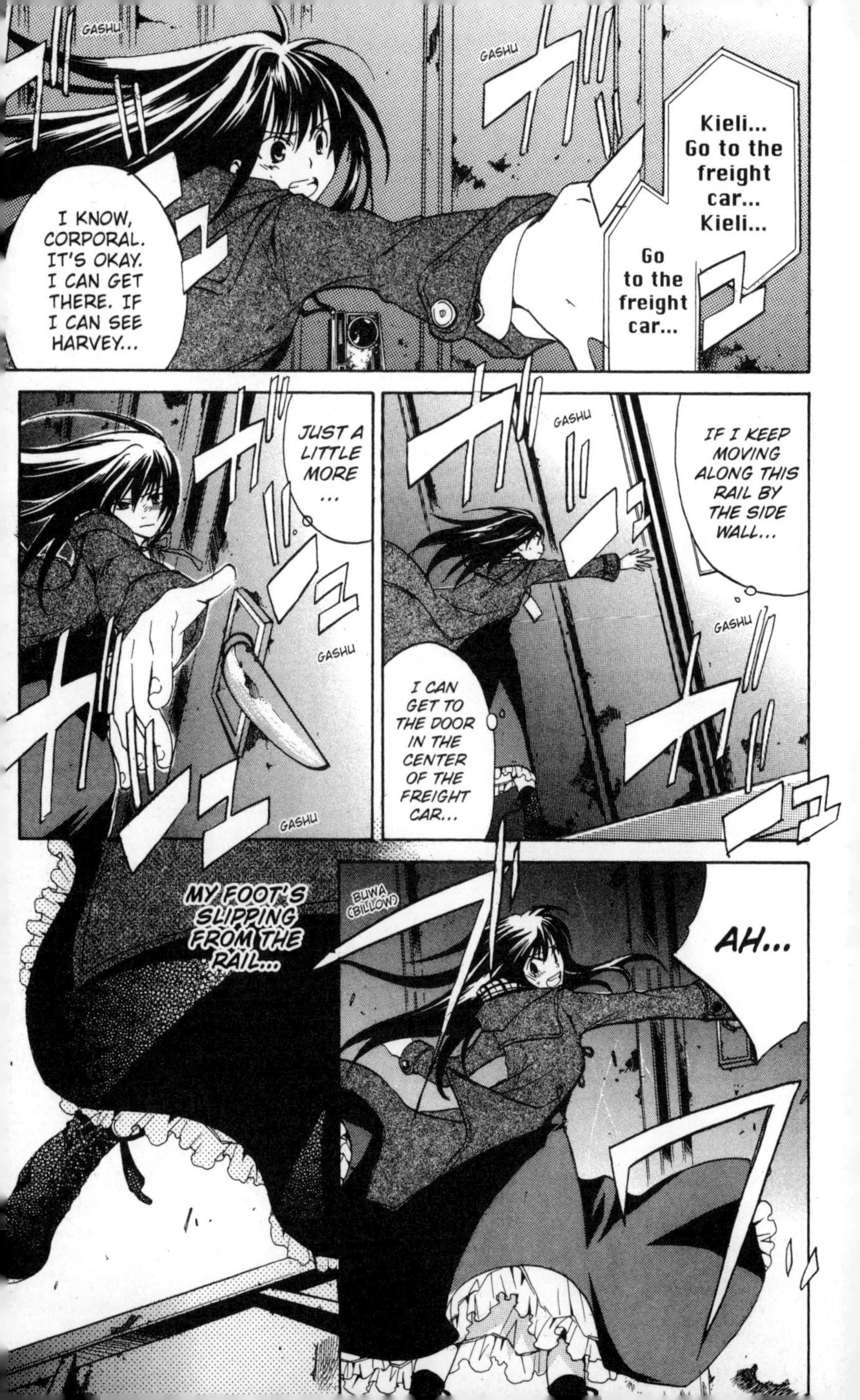
GASHU
GASHU
Kieli... Go to the freight car... Kieli...
Go to the freight car...
I KNOW, CORPORAL. IT'S OKAY. I CAN GET THERE. IF I CAN SEE HARVEY...
GASHU
IF I KEEP MOVING ALONG THIS RAIL BY THE SIDE WALL...
GASHU
I CAN GET TO THE DOOR IN THE CENTER OF THE FREIGHT CAR...
JUST A LITTLE MORE...
GASHU
GASHU
AH...
BUWA (BILLOW)
MY FOOT'S SLIPPING FROM THE RAIL...

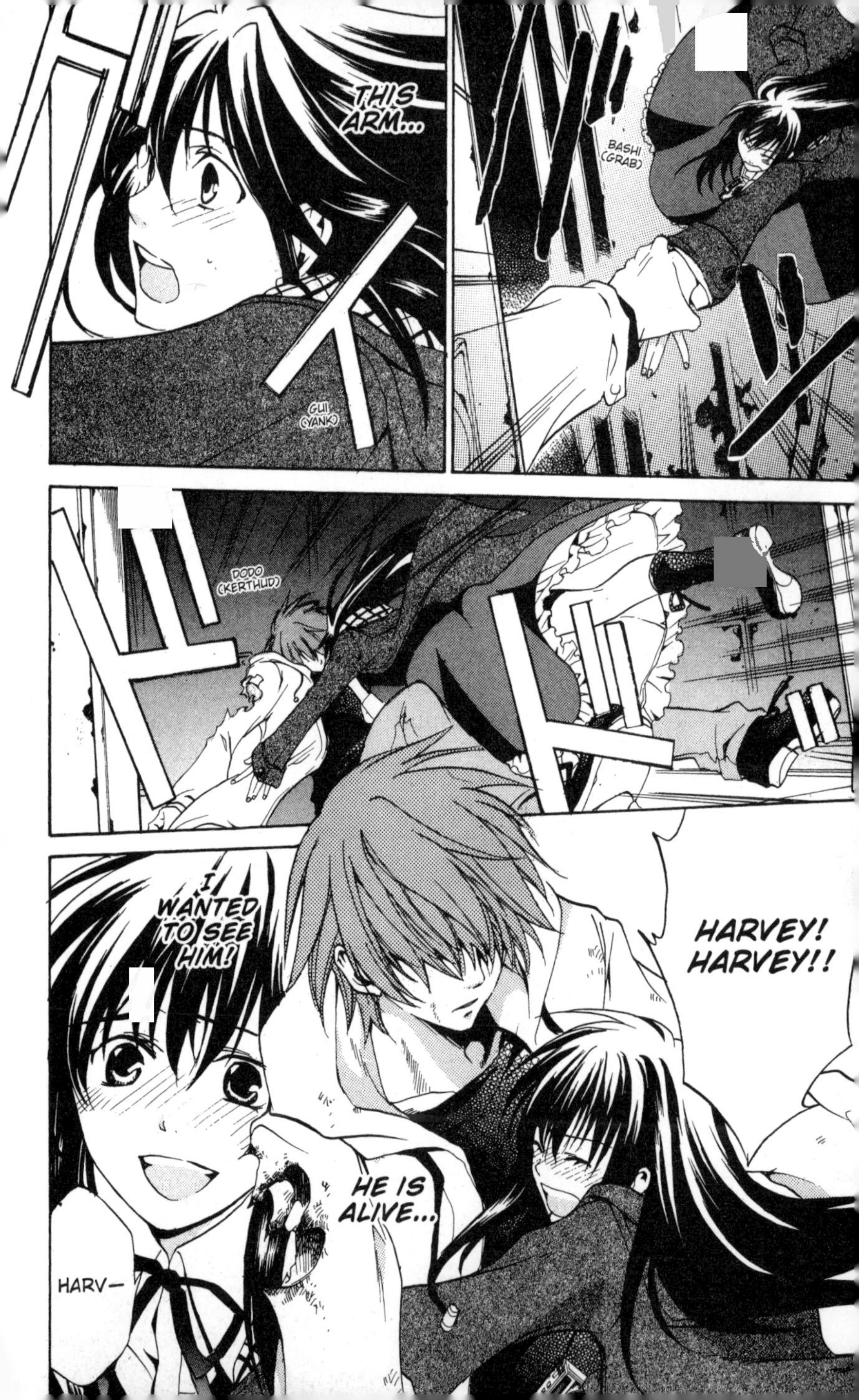
BASHI (GRAB)
THIS ARM...
GUI (YANK)
DODO (KERTHUD)
HARVEY! HARVEY!!
I WANTED TO SEE HIM!
HE IS ALIVE...
HARV—

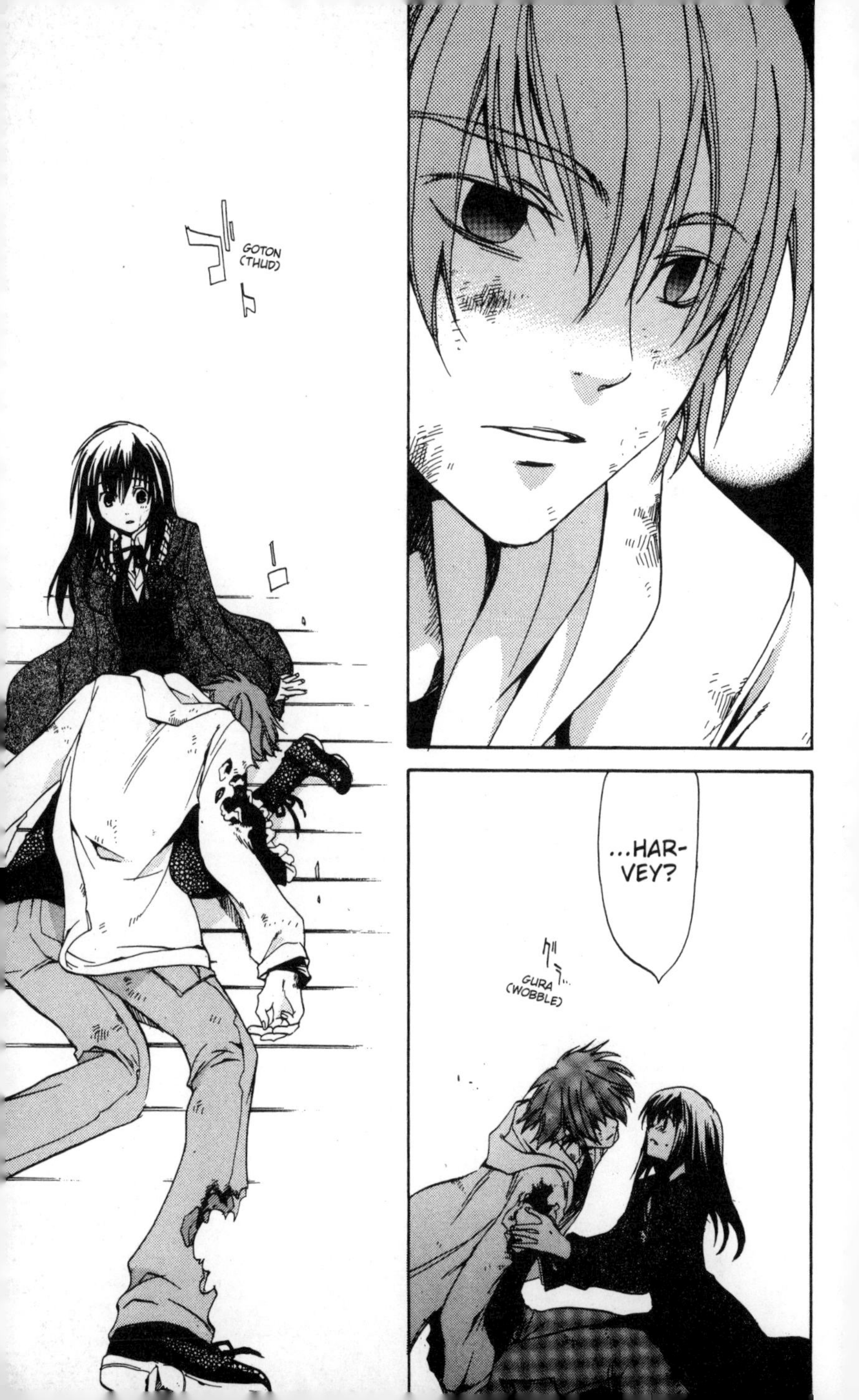
...HAR-VEY?
GURA (WOBBLE)
GOTON (THUD)

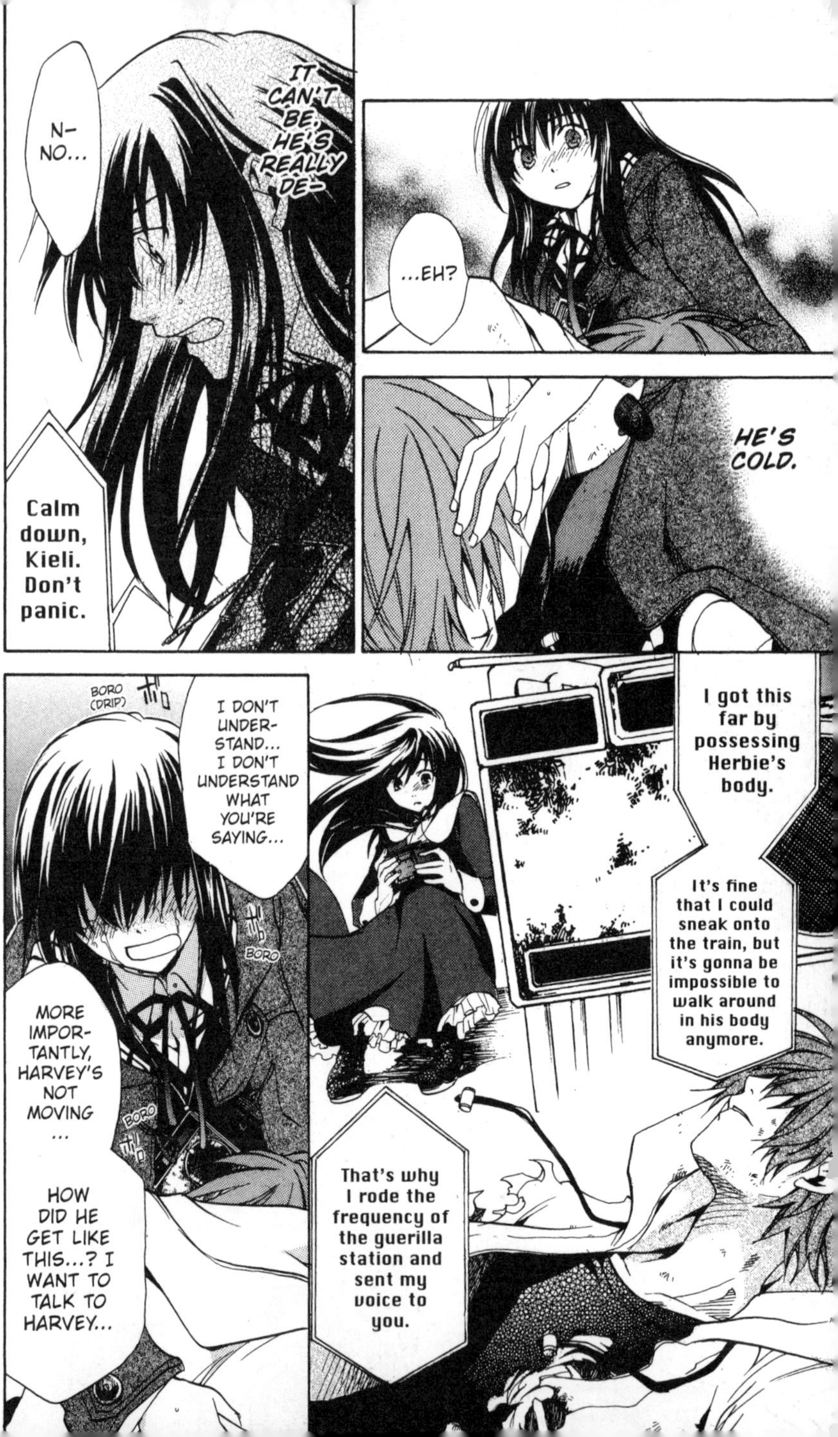
...EH?
HE'S COLD.
IT CAN'T BE, HE'S REALLY DE-
N-NO...
Calm down, Kieli. Don't panic.
I got this far by possessing Herbie's body.
It's fine that I could sneak onto the train, but it's gonna be impossible to walk around in his body anymore.
That's why I rode the frequency of the guerilla station and sent my voice to you.
I DON'T UNDER-STAND... I DON'T UNDERSTAND WHAT YOU'RE SAYING...
BORO (DRIP)
BORO
MORE IMPOR-TANTLY, HARVEY'S NOT MOVING...
BORO
HOW DID HE GET LIKE THIS...? I WANT TO TALK TO HARVEY...

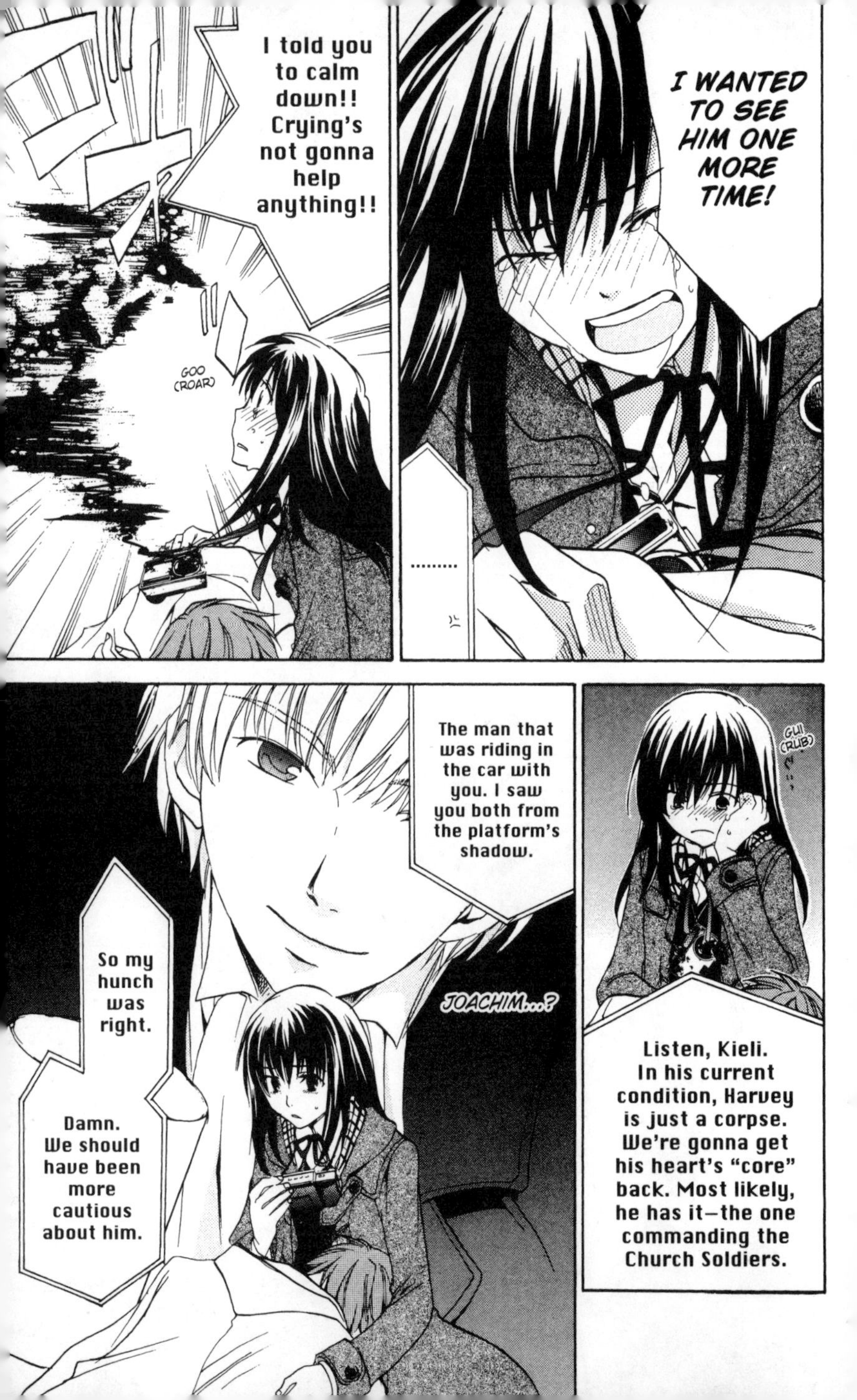
I WANTED TO SEE HIM ONE MORE TIME!
....
I told you to calm down!! Crying's not gonna help anything!!
GOO (ROAR)
GUI (RUB)
Listen, Kieli. In his current condition, Harvey is just a corpse. We're gonna get his heart's "core" back. Most likely, he has it—the one commanding the Church Soldiers.
The man that was riding in the car with you. I saw you both from the platform's shadow.
JOACHIM...?
So my hunch was right.
Damn. We should have been more cautious about him.

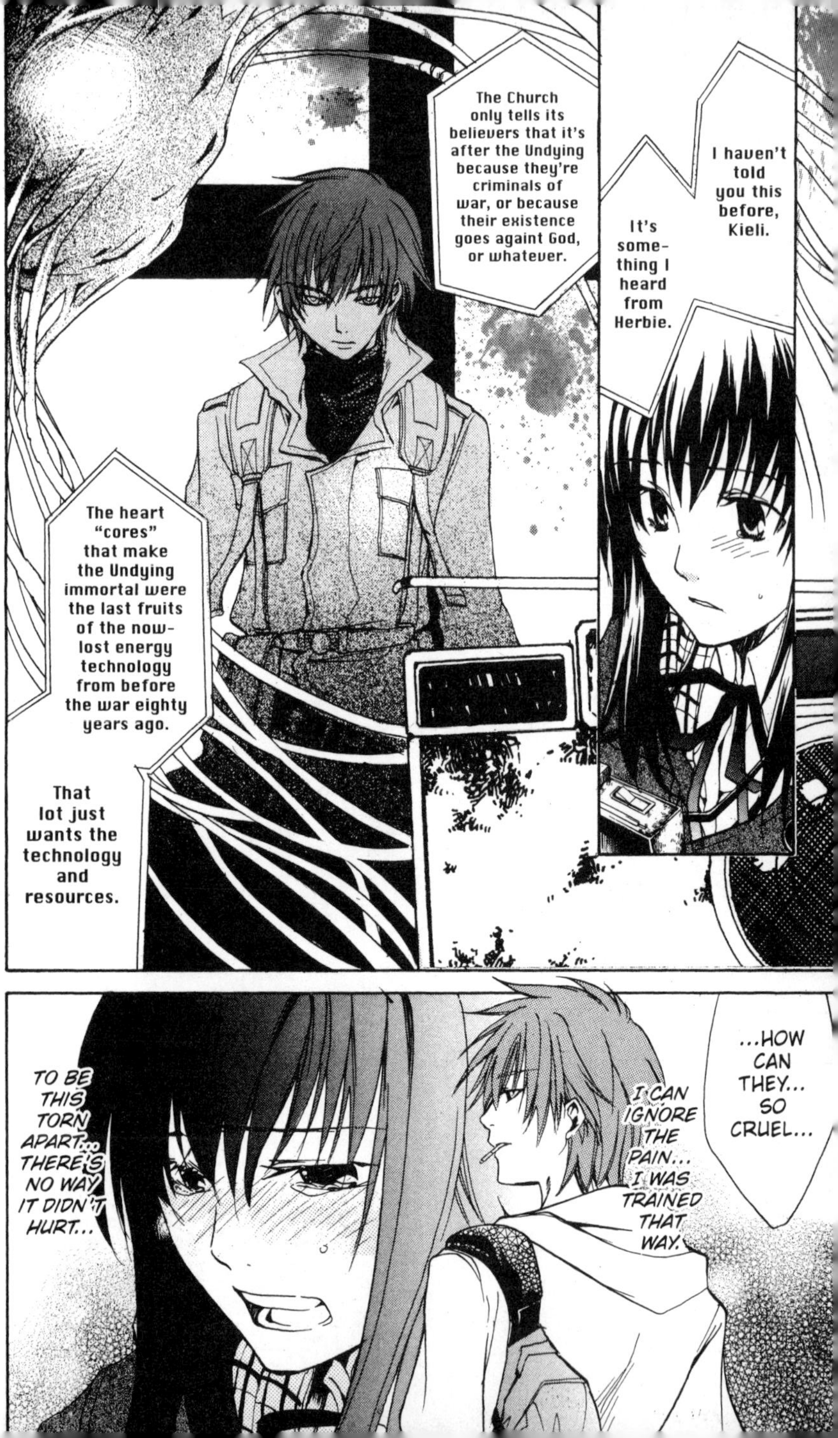
I haven't told you this before, Kieli.
It's something I heard from Herbie.
The Church only tells its believers that it's after the Undying because they're criminals of war, or because their existence goes againt God, or whatever.
The heart "cores" that make the Undying immortal were the last fruits of the now-lost energy technology from before the war eighty years ago.
That lot just wants the technology and resources.
...HOW CAN THEY... SO CRUEL...
I CAN IGNORE THE PAIN... I WAS TRAINED THAT WAY.
TO BE THIS TORN APART... THERE'S NO WAY IT DIDN'T HURT...

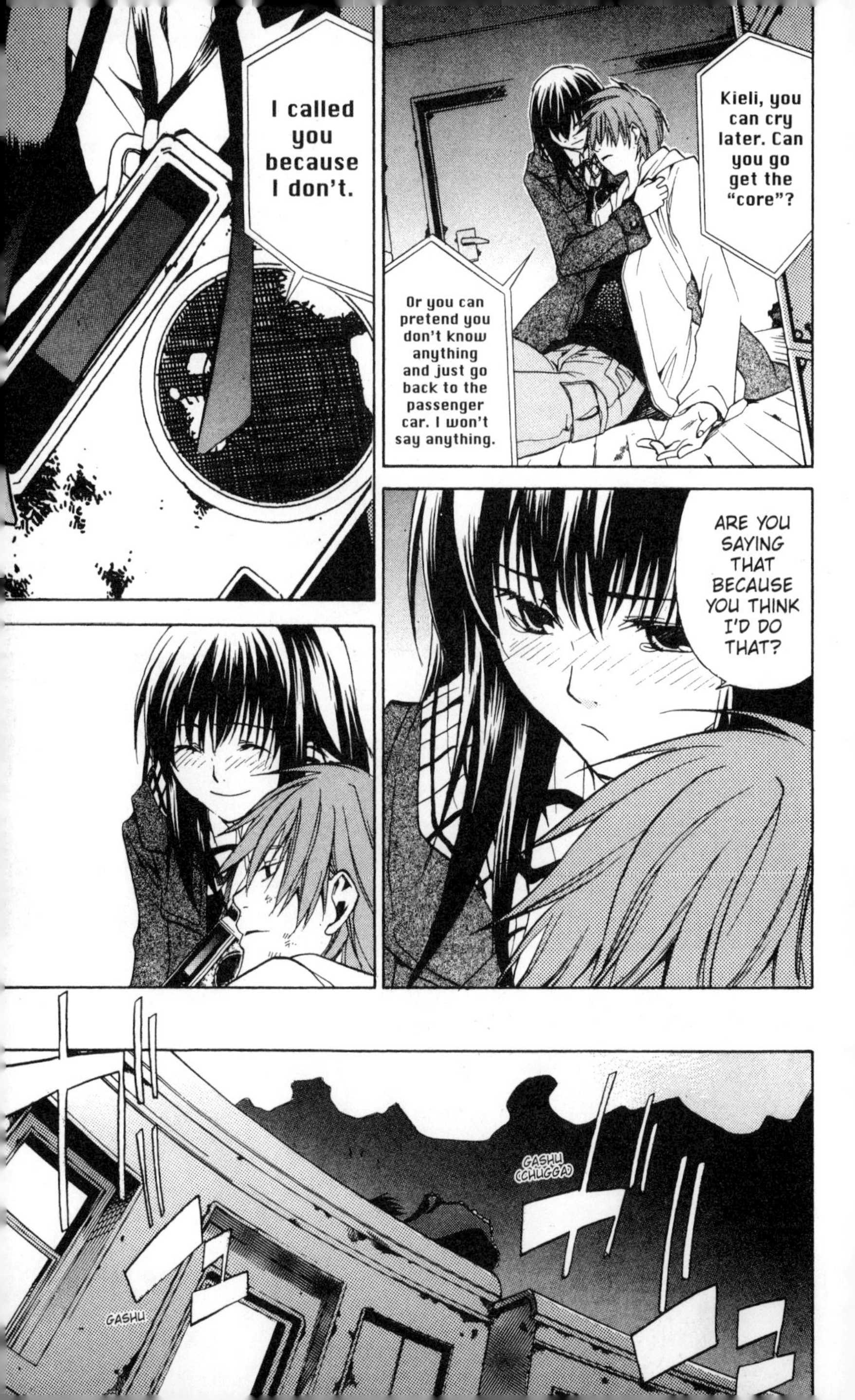
Kieli, you can cry later. Can you go get the "core"?
Or you can pretend you don't know anything and just go back to the passenger car. I won't say anything.
I called you because I don't.
ARE YOU SAYING THAT BECAUSE YOU THINK I'D DO THAT?
GASHU (CHUGGA)
GASHU

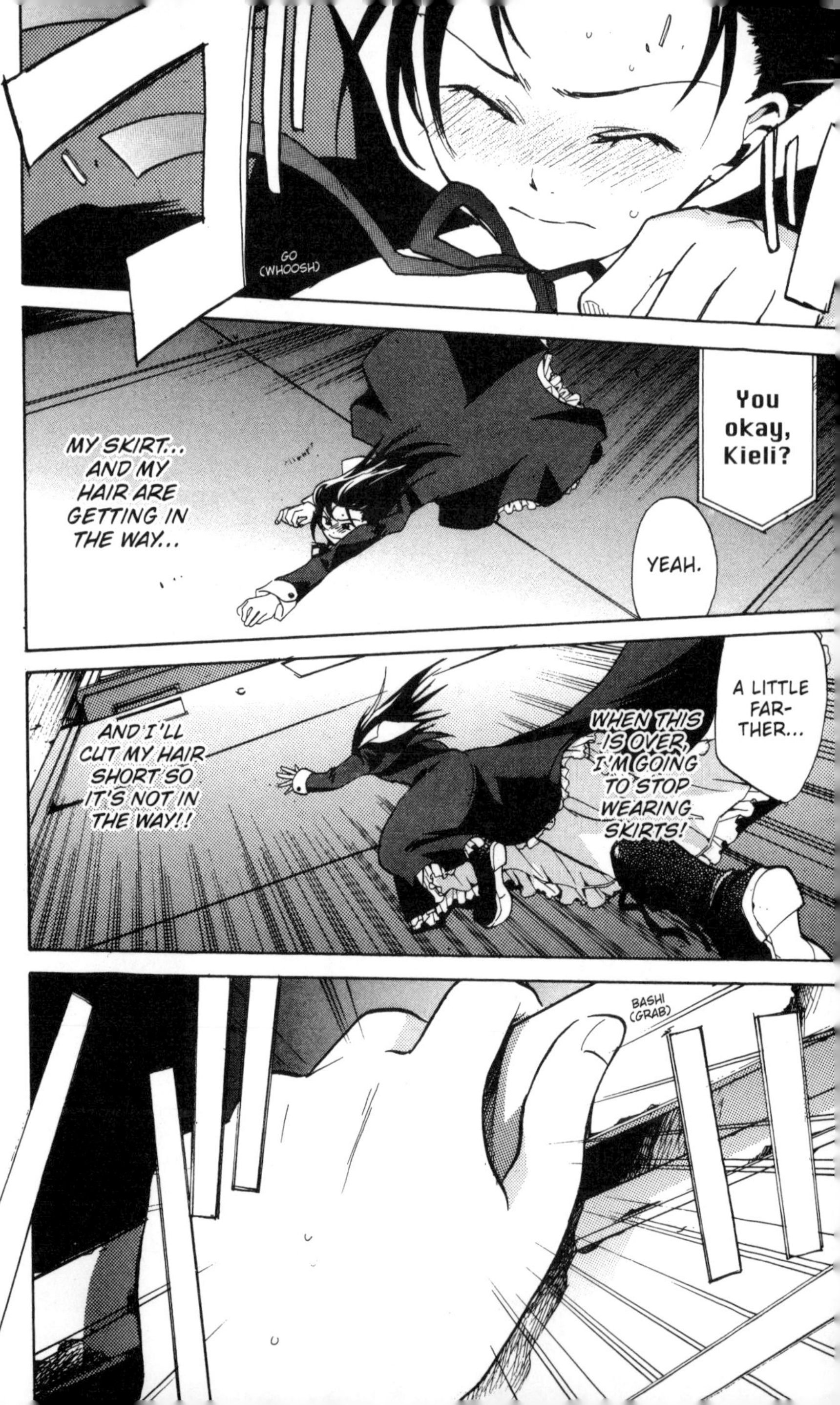
GO (WHOOSH)
You okay, Kieli?
YEAH.
MY SKIRT... AND MY HAIR ARE GETTING IN THE WAY...
...
A LITTLE FAR-THER...
WHEN THIS IS OVER, I'M GOING TO STOP WEARING SKIRTS!
AND I'LL CUT MY HAIR SHORT SO IT'S NOT IN THE WAY!!
BASHI (GRAB)

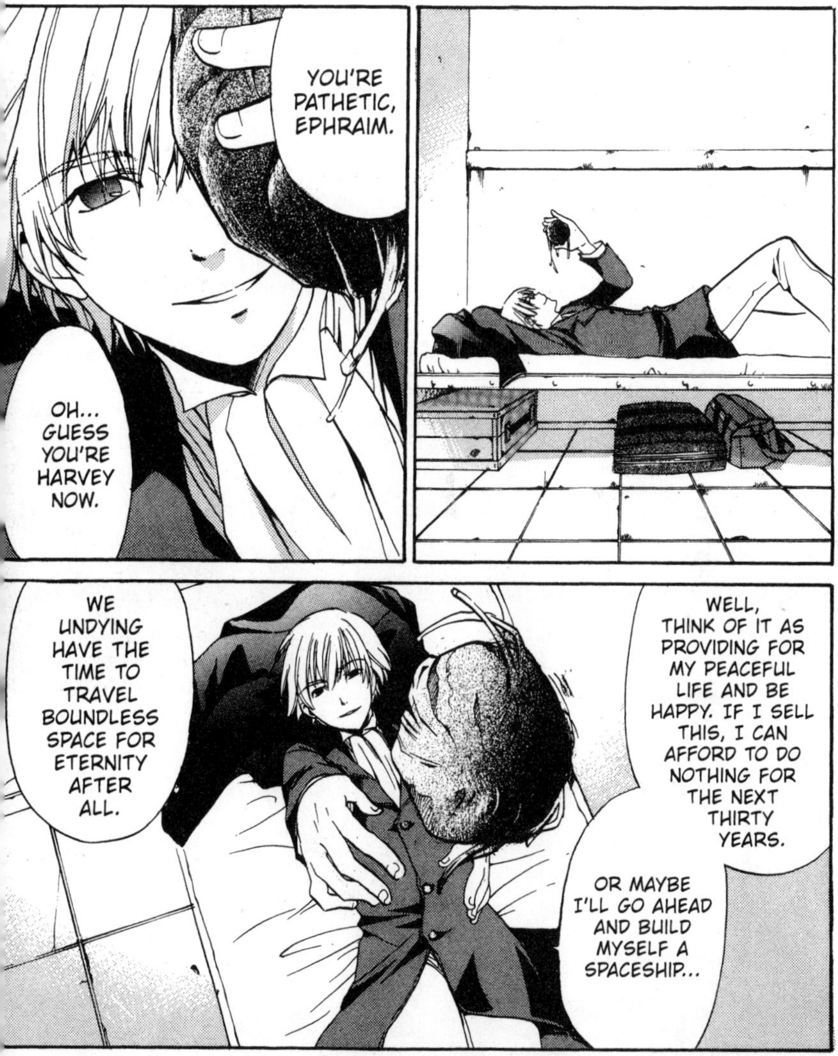
YOU'RE PATHETIC, EPHRAIM.
OH... GUESS YOU'RE HARVEY NOW.
WELL, THINK OF IT AS PROVIDING FOR MY PEACEFUL LIFE AND BE HAPPY. IF I SELL THIS, I CAN AFFORD TO DO NOTHING FOR THE NEXT THIRTY YEARS.
OR MAYBE I'LL GO AHEAD AND BUILD MYSELF A SPACESHIP...
WE UNDYING HAVE THE TIME TO TRAVEL BOUNDLESS SPACE FOR ETERNITY AFTER ALL.

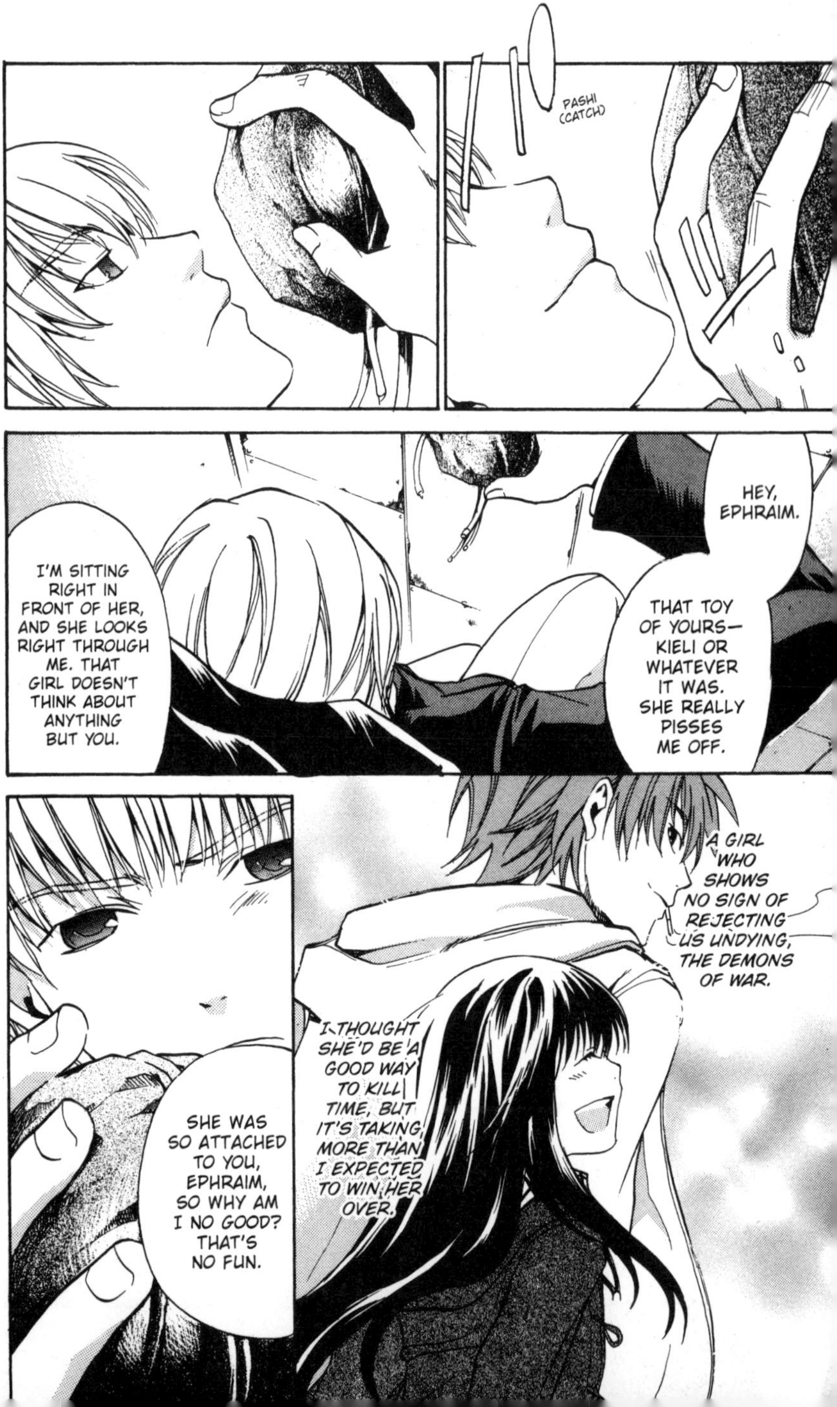
PASHI (CATCH)
HEY, EPHRAIM.
THAT TOY OF YOURS— KIELI OR WHATEVER IT WAS. SHE REALLY PISSES ME OFF.
I'M SITTING RIGHT IN FRONT OF HER, AND SHE LOOKS RIGHT THROUGH ME. THAT GIRL DOESN'T THINK ABOUT ANYTHING BUT YOU.
A GIRL WHO SHOWS NO SIGN OF REJECTING US UNDYING, THE DEMONS OF WAR.
I THOUGHT SHE'D BE A GOOD WAY TO KILL TIME, BUT IT'S TAKING MORE THAN I EXPECTED TO WIN HER OVER.
SHE WAS SO ATTACHED TO YOU, EPHRAIM, SO WHY AM I NO GOOD? THAT'S NO FUN.

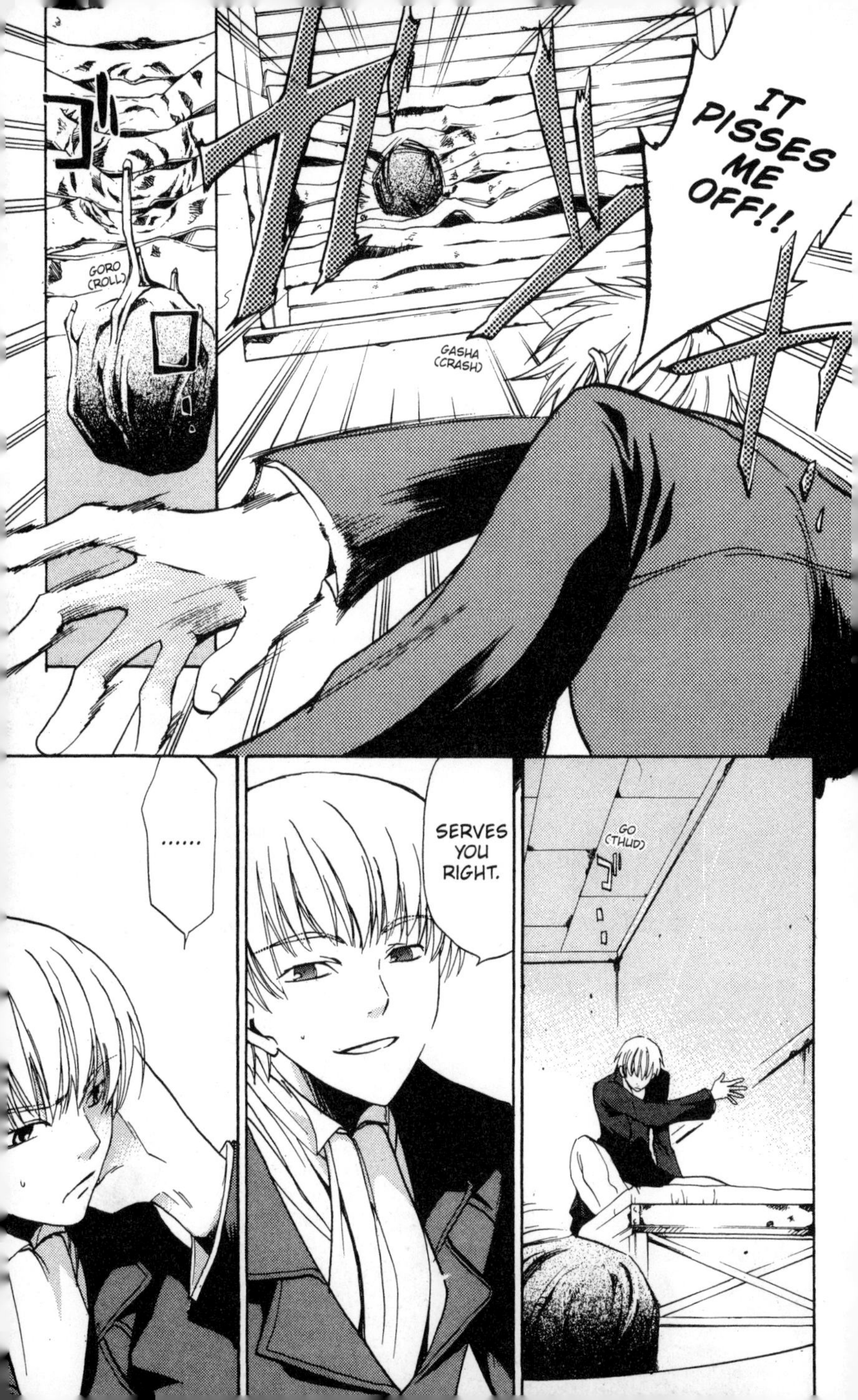
IT PISSES ME OFF!!
GASHA (CRASH)
GORO (ROLL)
GO (THUD)
SERVES YOU RIGHT.
......

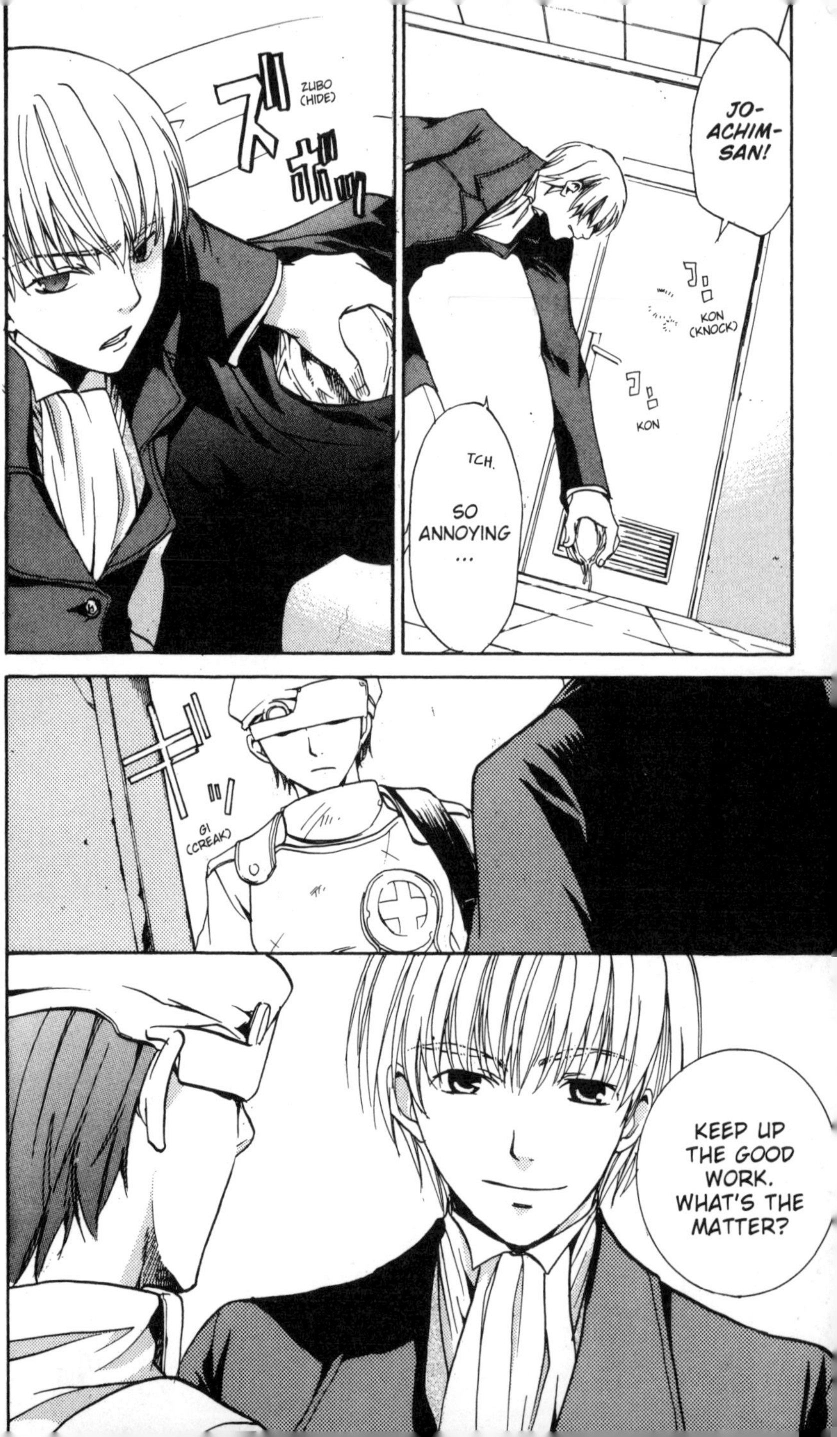

JO-ACHIM-SAN!
KON (KNOCK)
KON
TCH.
SO ANNOYING ...
ZUBO (HIDE)
GI (CREAK)
KEEP UP THE GOOD WORK. WHAT'S THE MATTER?

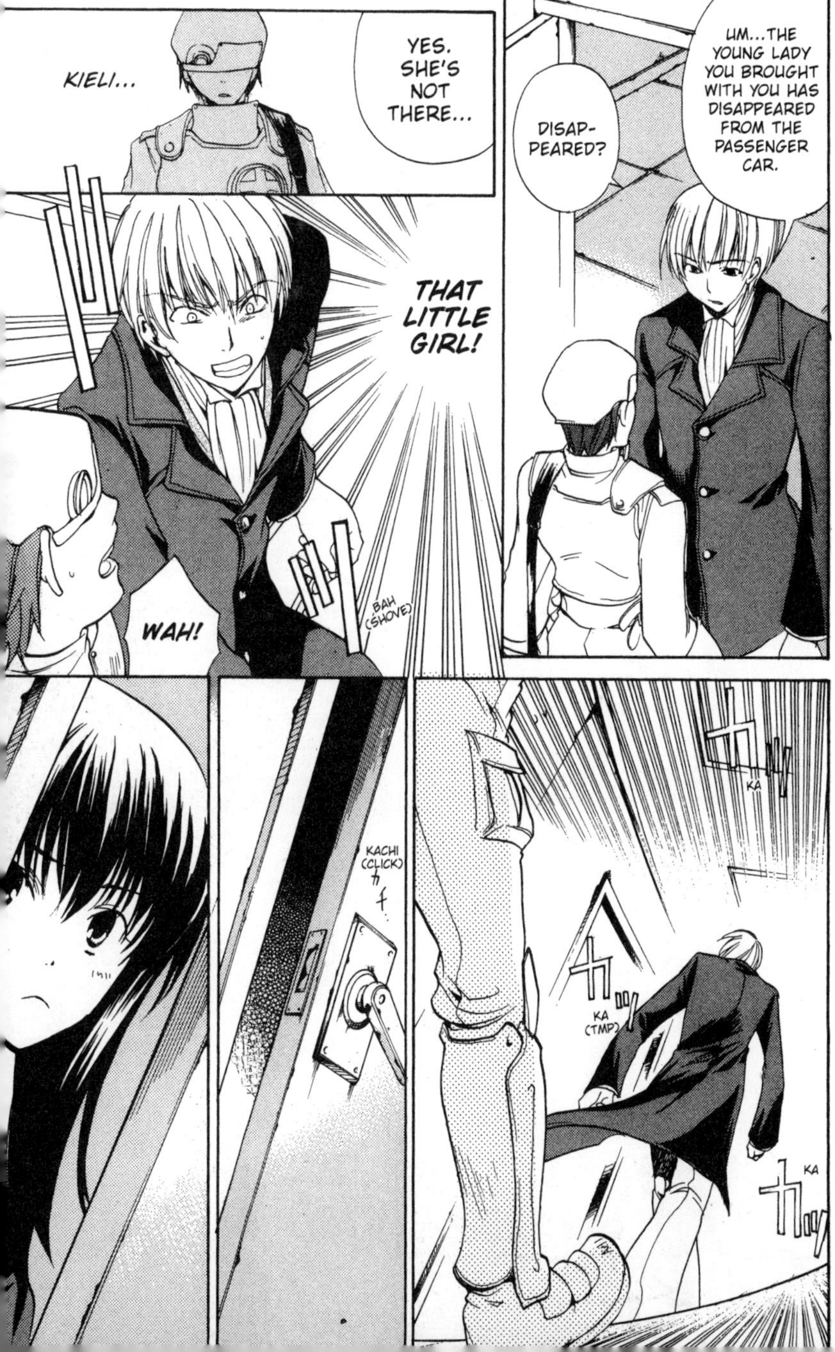
UM...THE YOUNG LADY YOU BROUGHT WITH YOU HAS DISAPPEARED FROM THE PASSENGER CAR.
DISAPPEARED?
YES. SHE'S NOT THERE...
KIELI...
THAT LITTLE GIRL!
BAH (SHOVE)
WAH!
KA
KA (TMP)
KA
KACHI (CLICK)

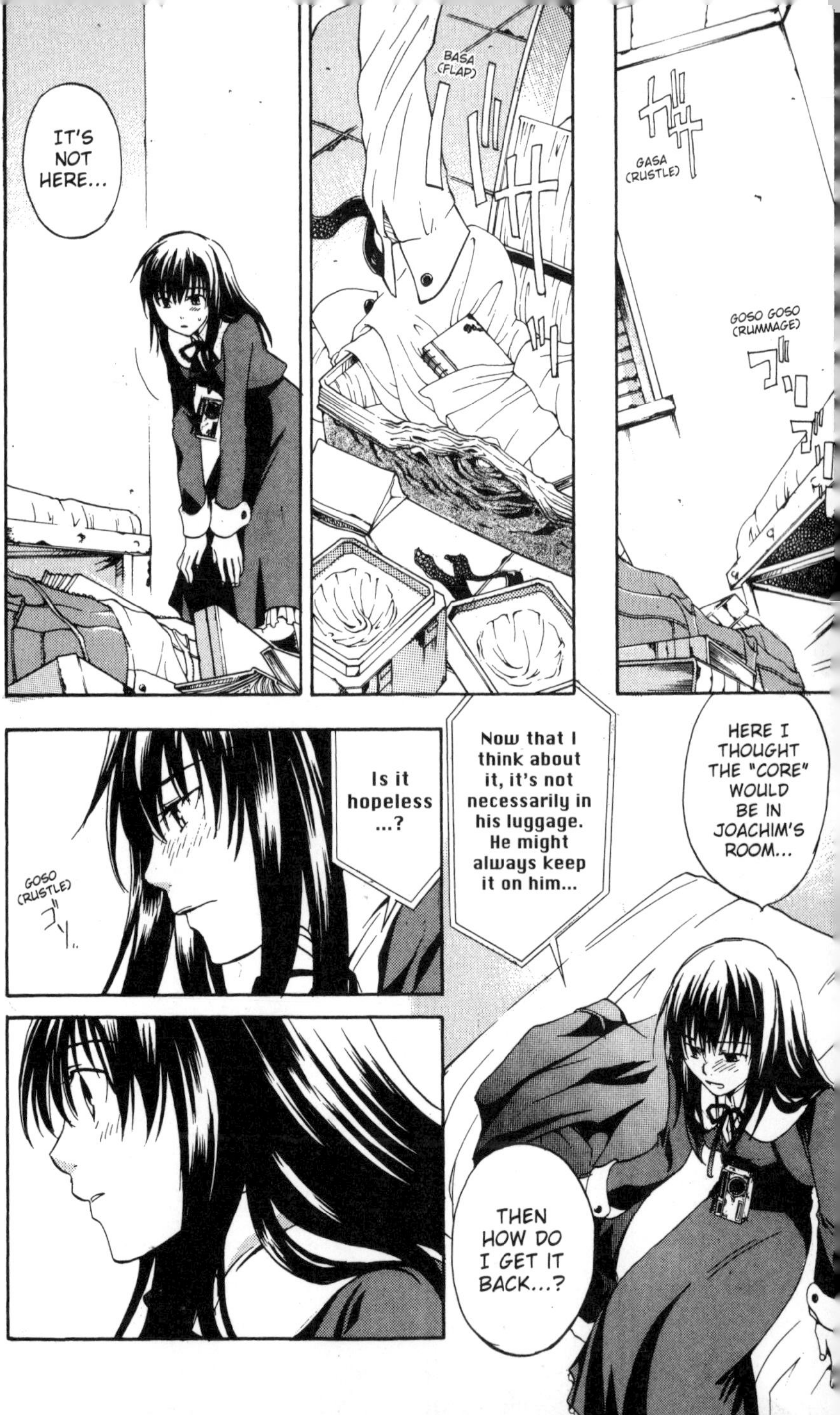
GASA (RUSTLE)
GOSO GOSO (RUMMAGE)
BASA (FLAP)
IT'S NOT HERE...
HERE I THOUGHT THE "CORE" WOULD BE IN JOACHIM'S ROOM...
Now that I think about it, it's not necessarily in his luggage. He might always keep it on him...
THEN HOW DO I GET IT BACK...?
Is it hopeless ...?
GOSO (RUSTLE)

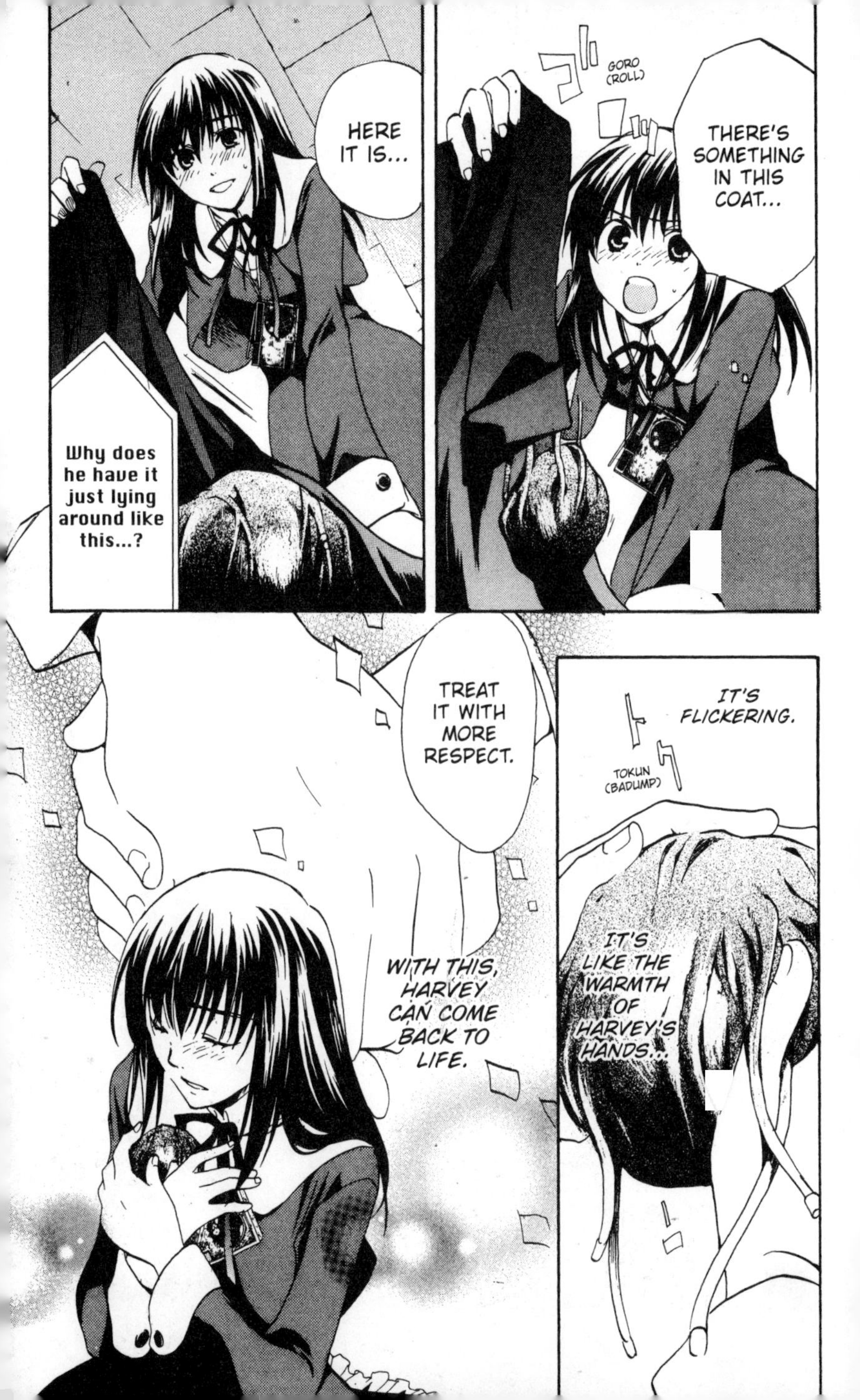
GORO (ROLL)
THERE'S SOMETHING IN THIS COAT...
HERE IT IS...
Why does he have it just lying around like this...?
IT'S FLICKERING.
TOKUN (BADUMP)
IT'S LIKE THE WARMTH OF HARVEY'S HANDS...
TREAT IT WITH MORE RESPECT.
WITH THIS, HARVEY CAN COME BACK TO LIFE.

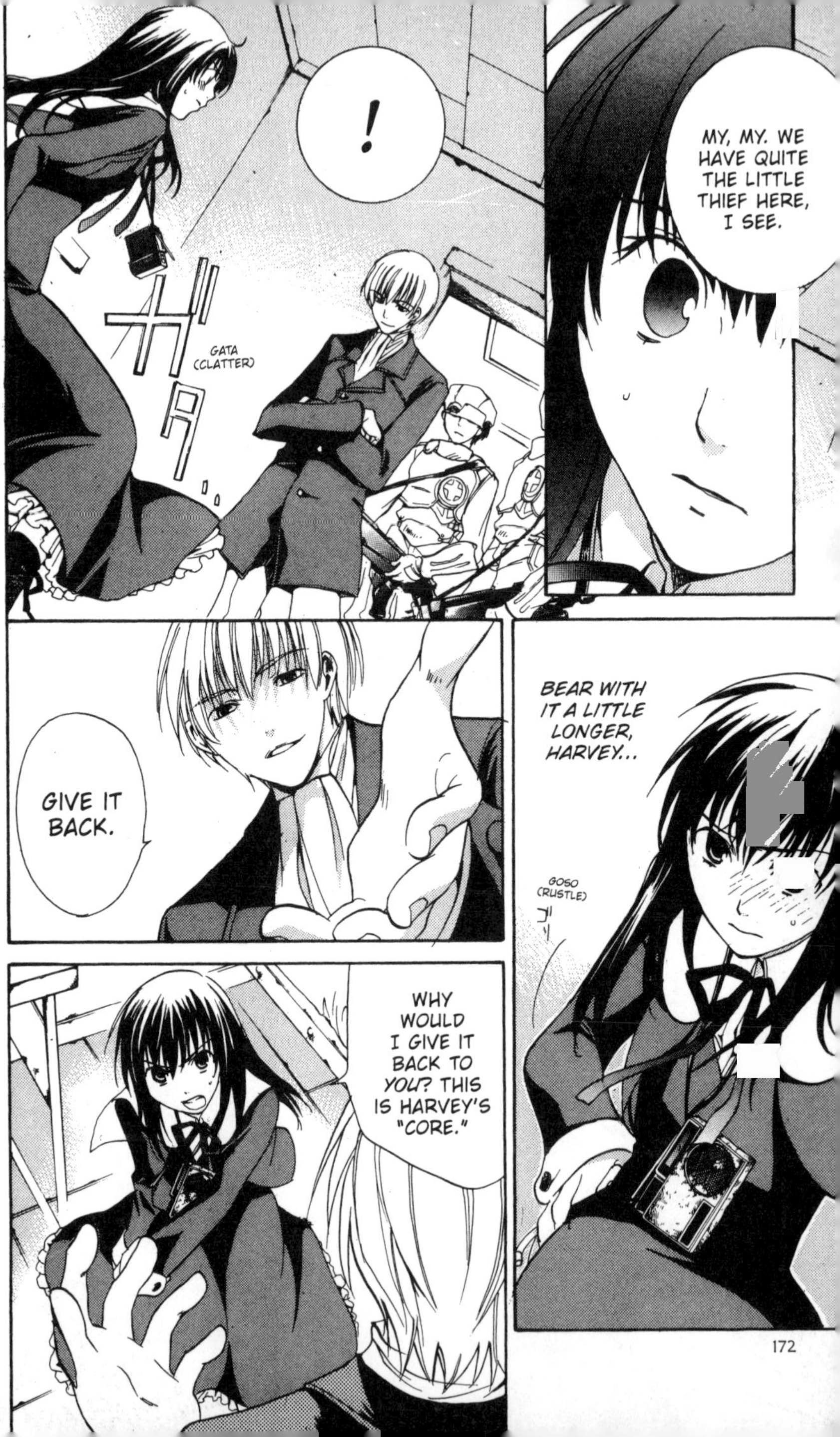
MY, MY. WE HAVE QUITE THE LITTLE THIEF HERE, I SEE.
!
GATA (CLATTER)
BEAR WITH IT A LITTLE LONGER, HARVEY...
GOSO (RUSTLE)
GIVE IT BACK.
WHY WOULD I GIVE IT BACK TO *YOU*? THIS IS HARVEY'S "CORE."

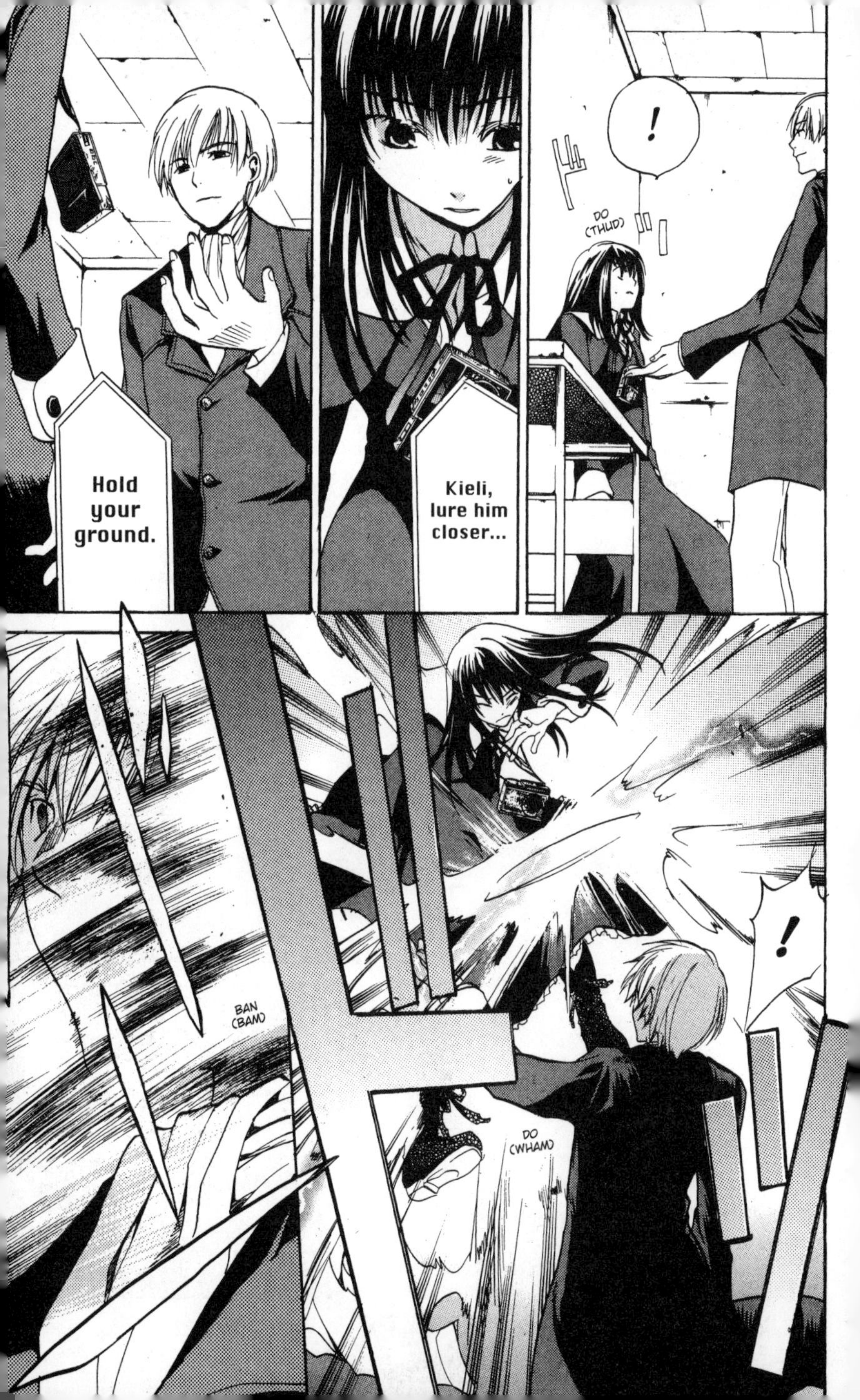
!
DO
(THUD)
Kieli, lure him closer...
Hold your ground.
!
DO
(WHAM)
BAN
(BAM)

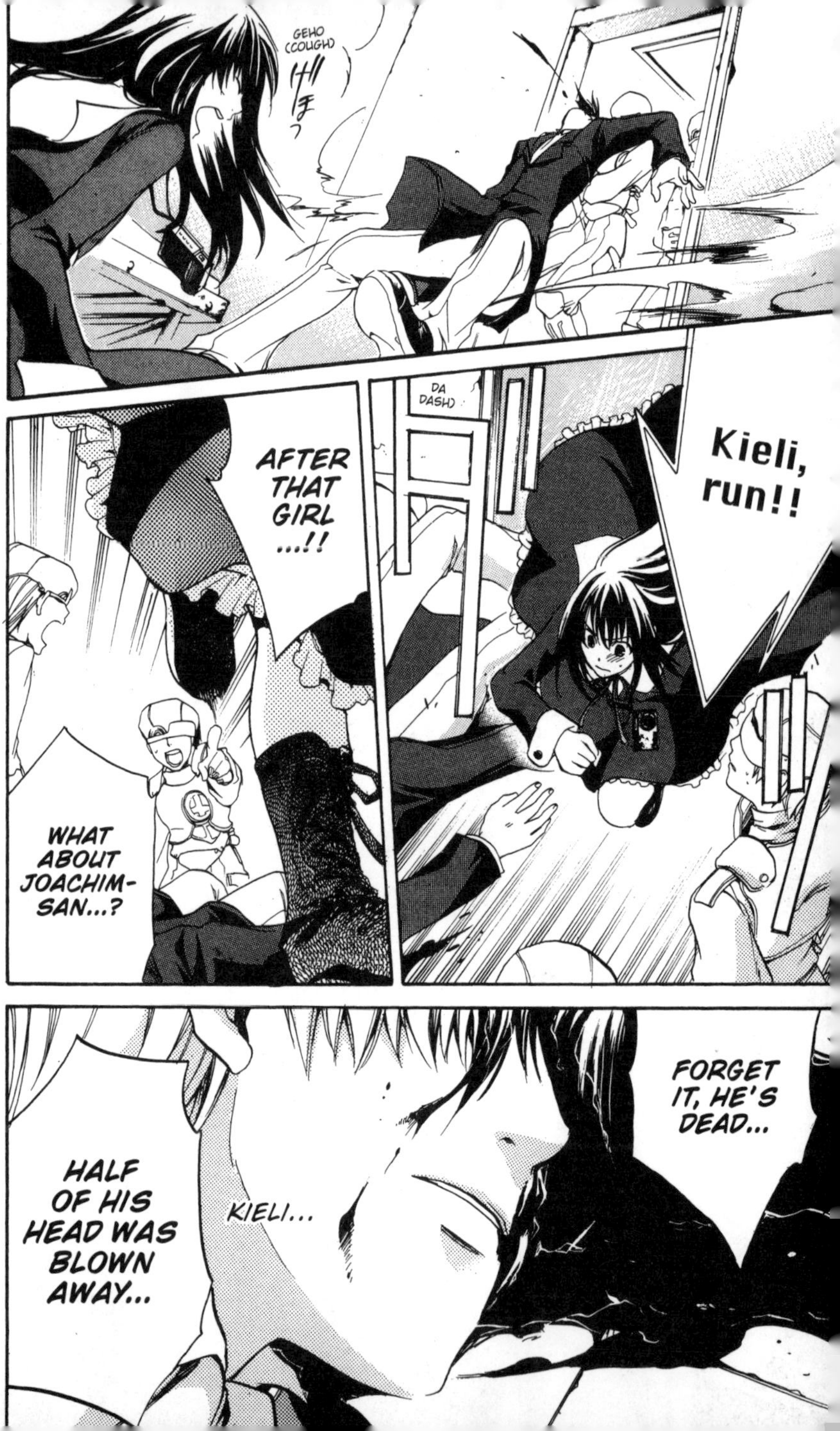
GEHO (COUGH)
げほっ
Kieli, run!!
DA DASH)
AFTER THAT GIRL ...!!
WHAT ABOUT JOACHIM-SAN...?
FORGET IT, HE'S DEAD...
HALF OF HIS HEAD WAS BLOWN AWAY...
KIELI...

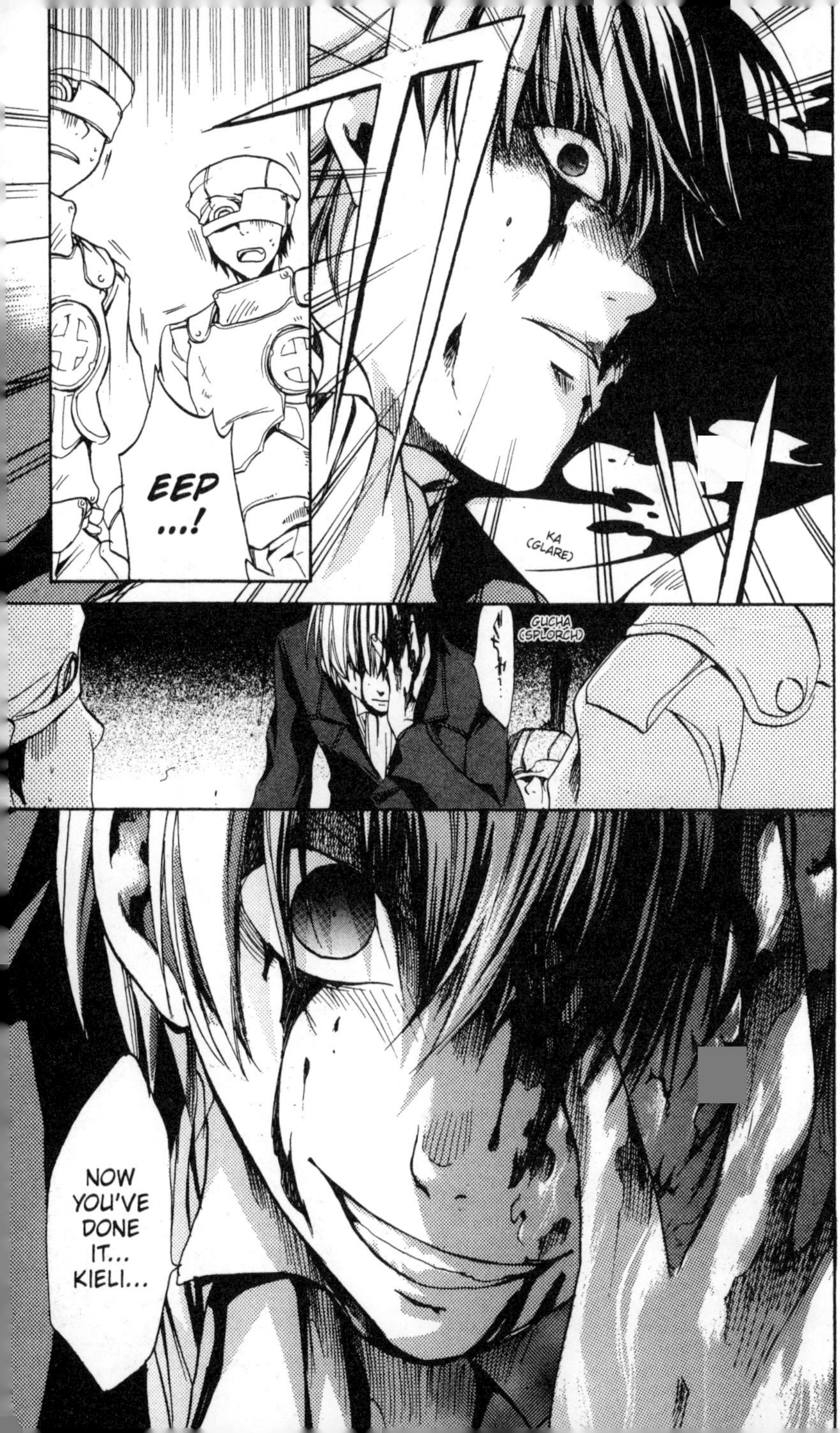
KA
(GLARE)
EEP ...!
GUCHA
(SPLORCH)
NOW YOU'VE DONE IT... KIELI...

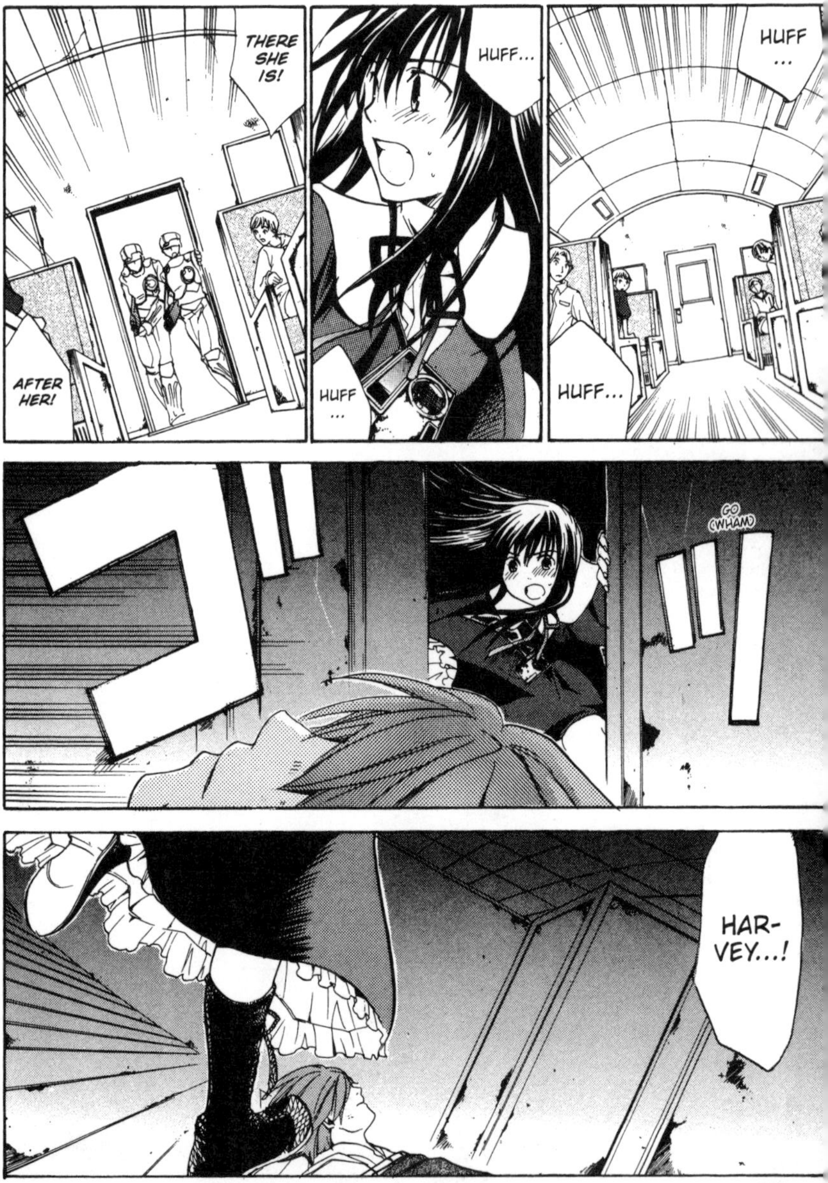
HUFF ...
HUFF...
HUFF...
HUFF ...
THERE SHE IS!
AFTER HER!
GO (WHAM)
HAR- VEY...!

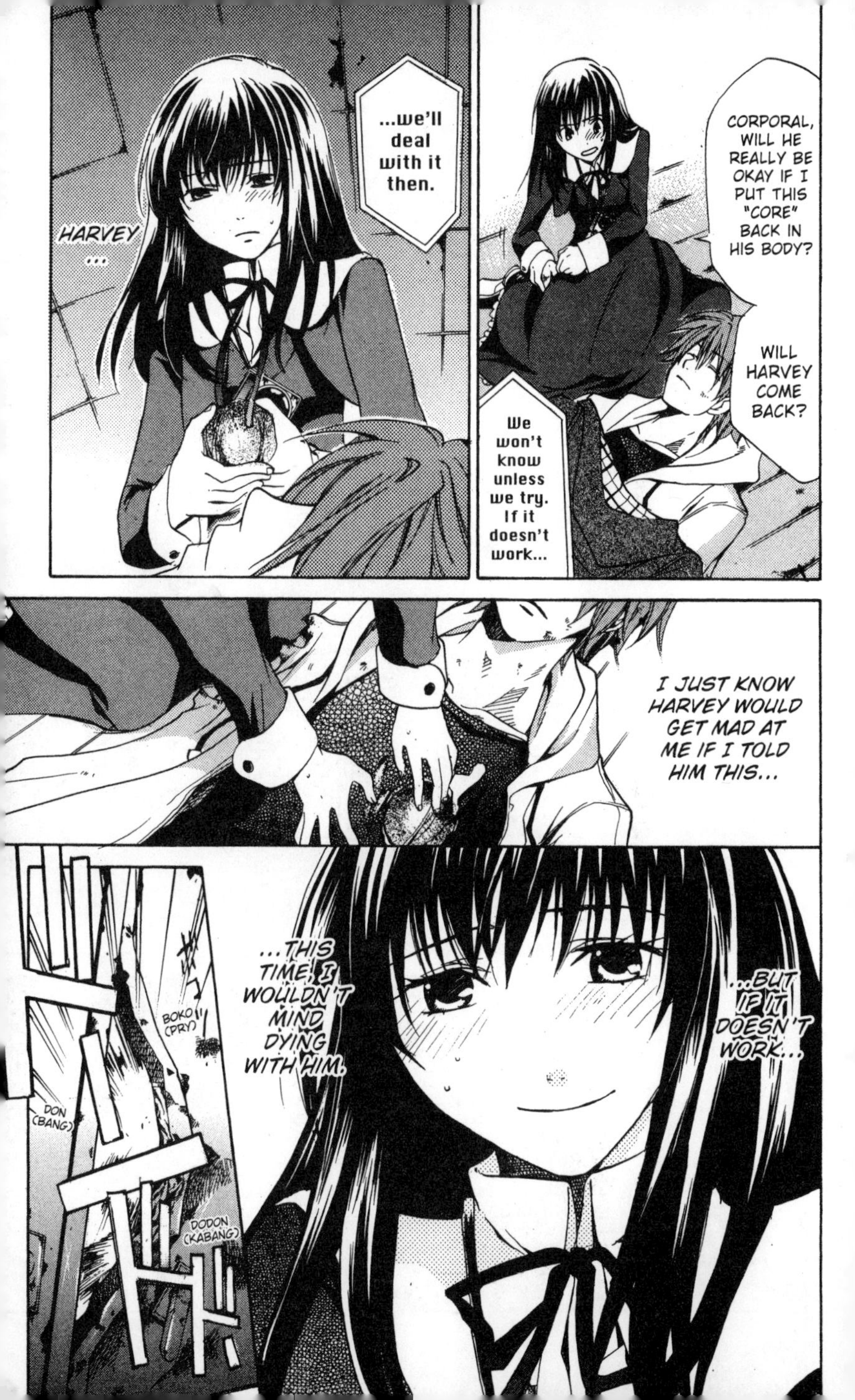
CORPORAL, WILL HE REALLY BE OKAY IF I PUT THIS "CORE" BACK IN HIS BODY?
WILL HARVEY COME BACK?
We won't know unless we try. If it doesn't work...
...we'll deal with it then.
HARVEY ...
I JUST KNOW HARVEY WOULD GET MAD AT ME IF I TOLD HIM THIS...
...BUT IF IT DOESN'T WORK...
...THIS TIME, I WOULDN'T MIND DYING WITH HIM.
BOKO (PRY)
DON (BANG)
DODON (KABANG)

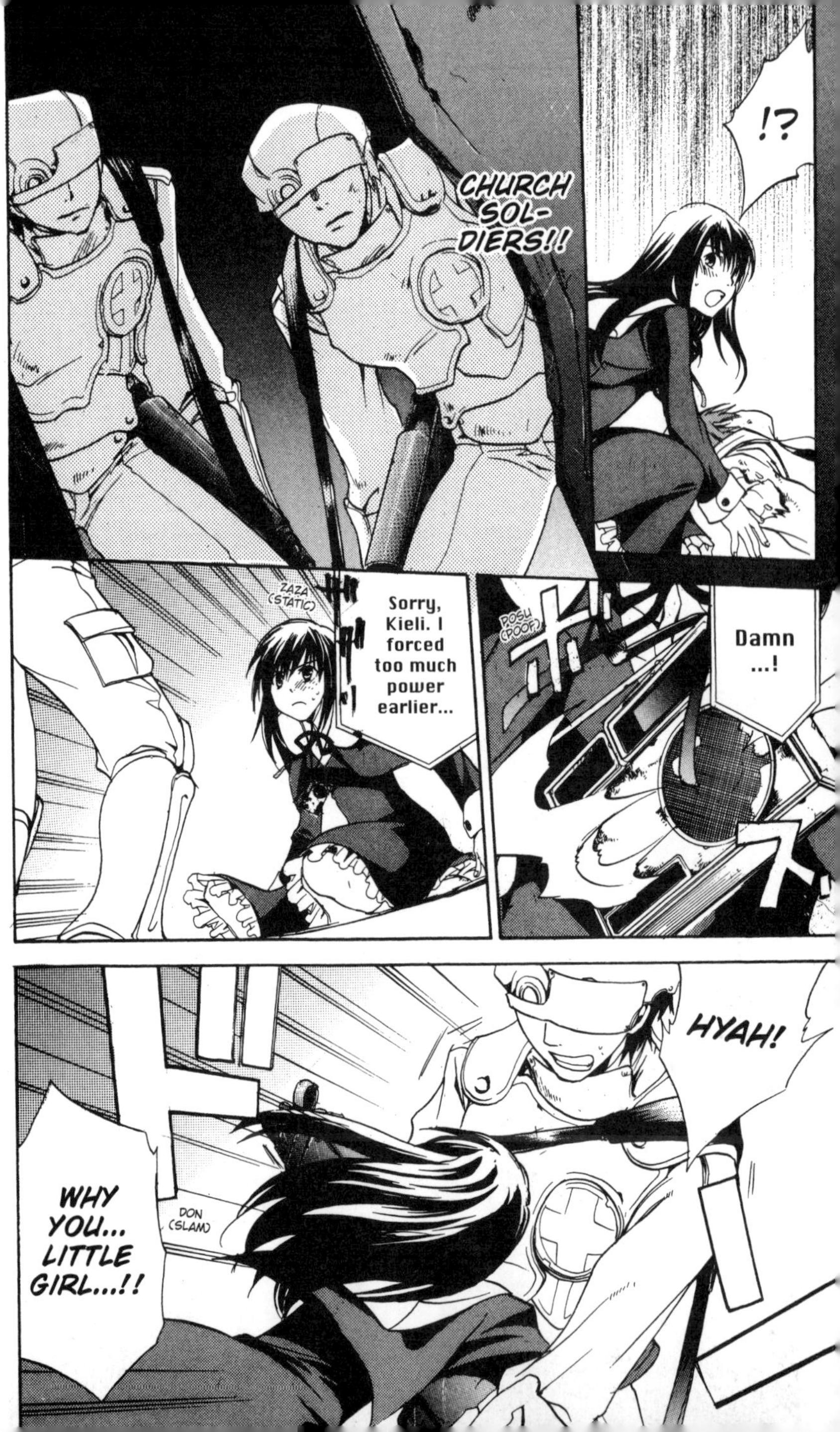
!?
CHURCH SOL-DIERS!!
Damn ...!
POSU (POOF)
ZAZA (STATIC)
Sorry, Kieli. I forced too much power earlier...
HYAH!
DON (SLAM)
WHY YOU... LITTLE GIRL...!!

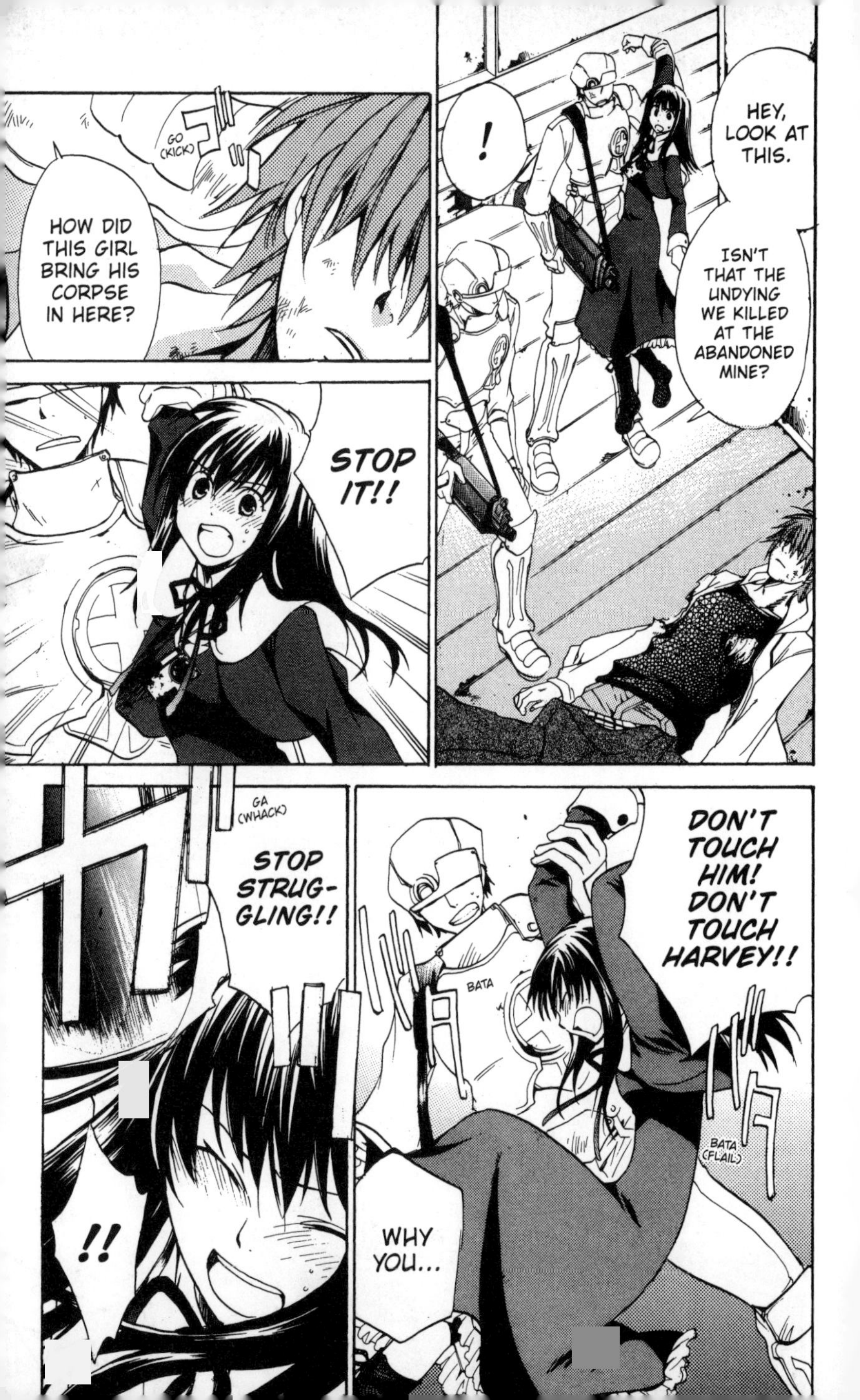
HEY, LOOK AT THIS.
!
ISN'T THAT THE UNDYING WE KILLED AT THE ABANDONED MINE?
GO (KICK)
HOW DID THIS GIRL BRING HIS CORPSE IN HERE?
STOP IT!!
DON'T TOUCH HIM! DON'T TOUCH HARVEY!!
BATA
BATA (FLAIL)
WHY YOU...
GA (WHACK)
STOP STRUG-GLING!!
!!

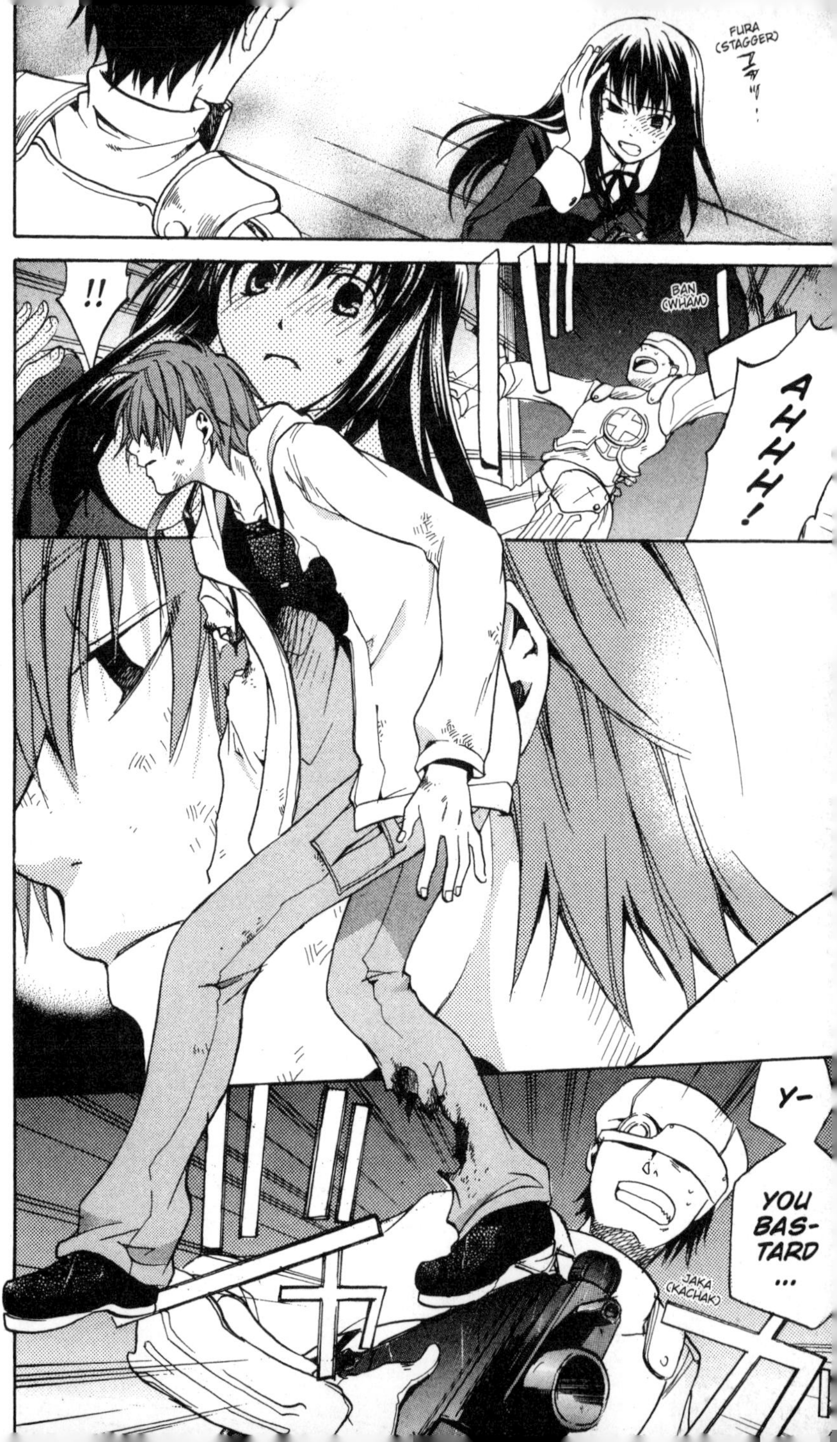
FURA (STAGGER)
!!
BAN (WHAM)
AHHHH!
Y-
YOU BAS-TARD ...
JAKA (KACHAK)

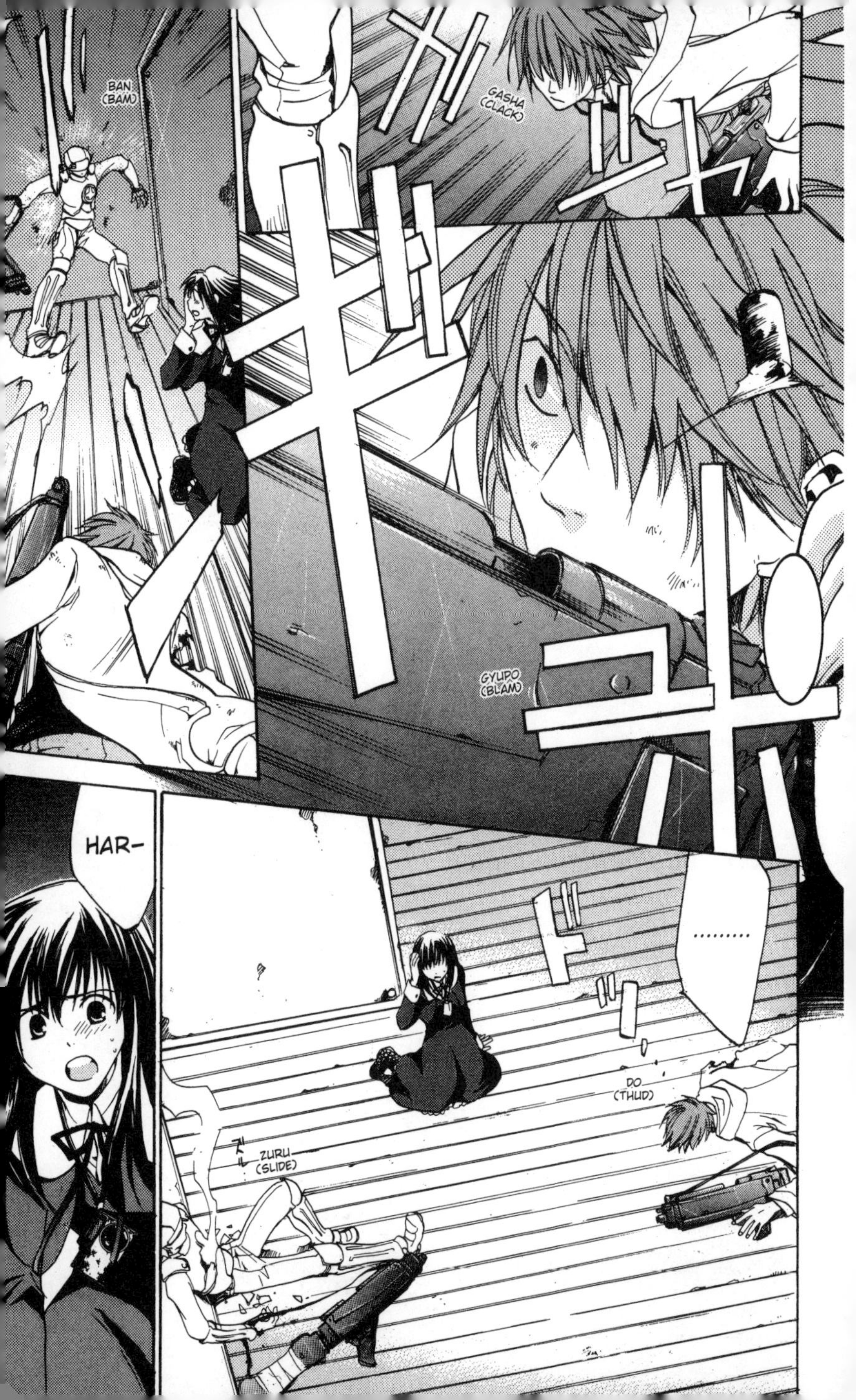
GASHA
(CLACK)
GYUPO
(BLAM)
BAN
(BAM)
....
DO
(THUD)
ZURU
(SLIDE)
HAR-

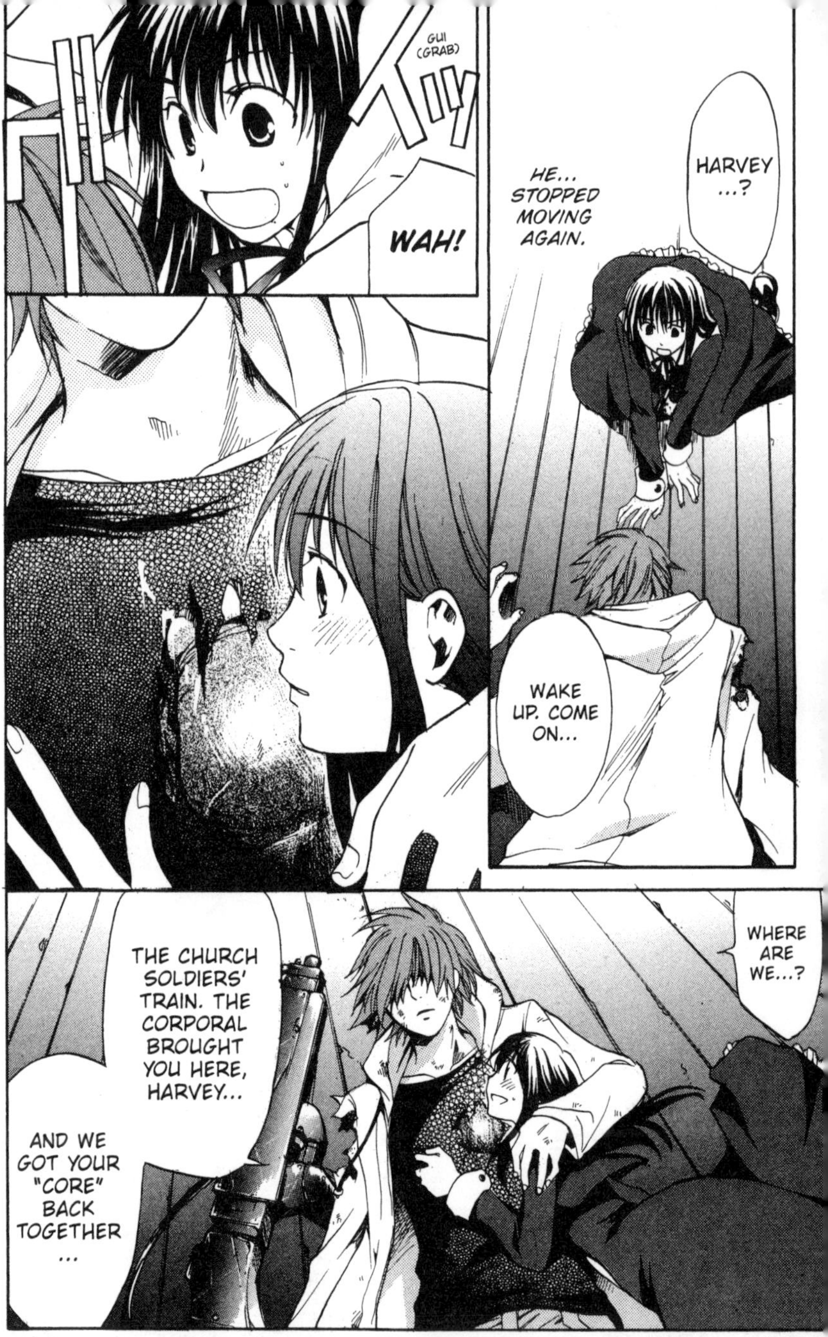
HARVEY ...?
HE... STOPPED MOVING AGAIN.
WAKE UP. COME ON...
GUI (GRAB)
WAH!
WHERE ARE WE...?
THE CHURCH SOLDIERS' TRAIN. THE CORPORAL BROUGHT YOU HERE, HARVEY...
AND WE GOT YOUR "CORE" BACK TOGETHER ...

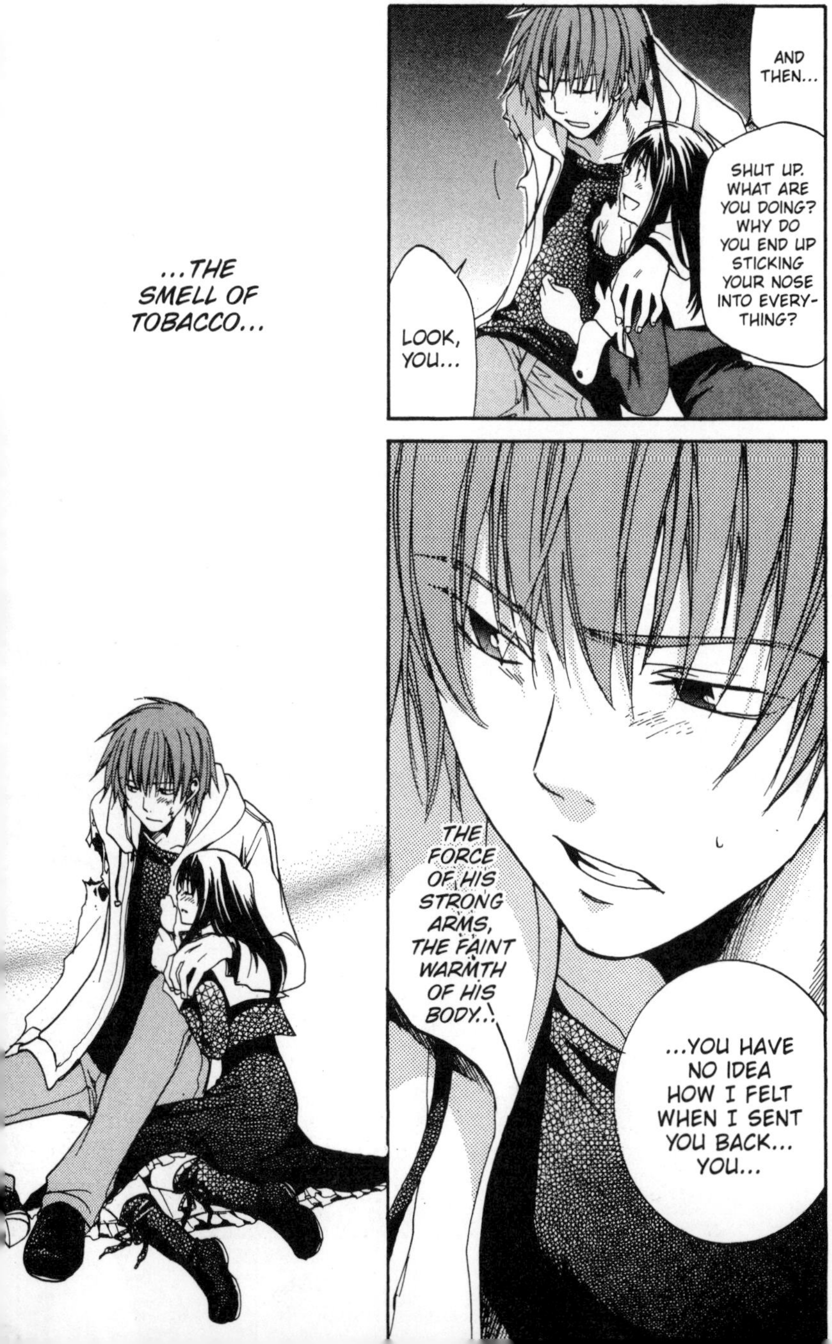
AND THEN...
SHUT UP. WHAT ARE YOU DOING? WHY DO YOU END UP STICKING YOUR NOSE INTO EVERYTHING?
LOOK, YOU...
...YOU HAVE NO IDEA HOW I FELT WHEN I SENT YOU BACK... YOU...
THE FORCE OF HIS STRONG ARMS, THE FAINT WARMTH OF HIS BODY...
...THE SMELL OF TOBACCO...

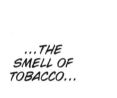

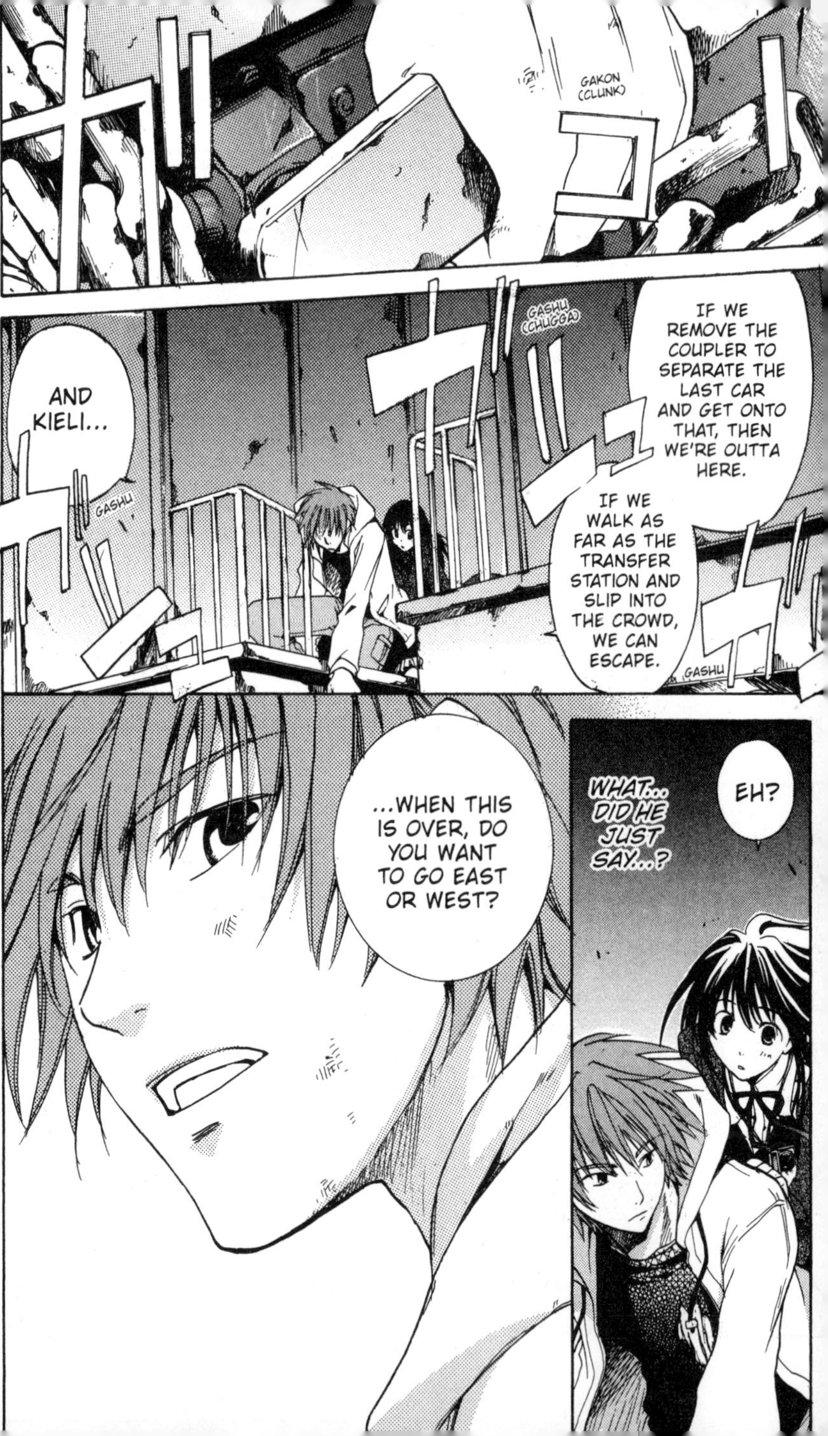
GAKON (CLUNK)
IF WE REMOVE THE COUPLER TO SEPARATE THE LAST CAR AND GET ONTO THAT, THEN WE'RE OUTTA HERE.
GASHU (CHUGGA)
IF WE WALK AS FAR AS THE TRANSFER STATION AND SLIP INTO THE CROWD, WE CAN ESCAPE.
GASHU
AND KIELI...
GASHU
EH?
WHAT... DID HE JUST SAY...?
...WHEN THIS IS OVER, DO YOU WANT TO GO EAST OR WEST?

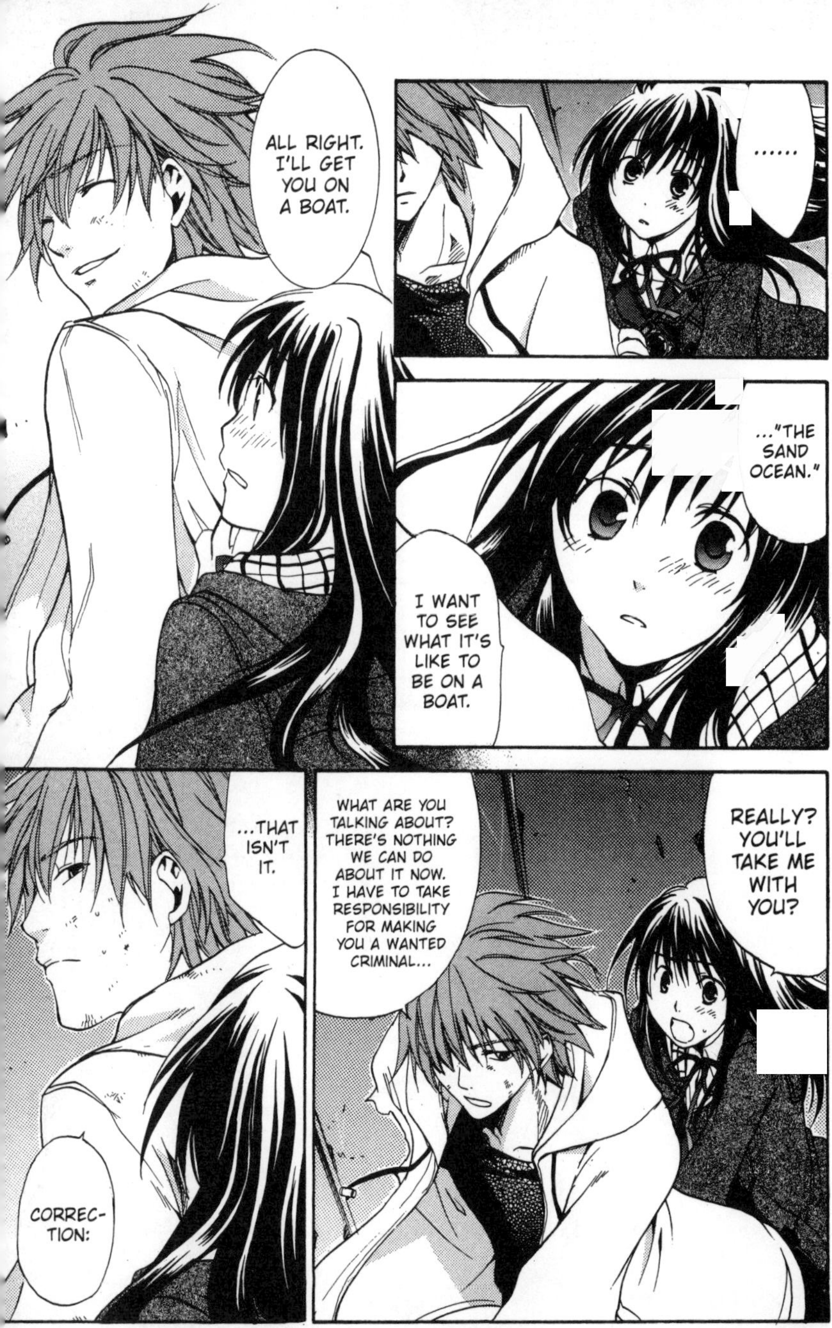
......
..."THE SAND OCEAN."
I WANT TO SEE WHAT IT'S LIKE TO BE ON A BOAT.
ALL RIGHT. I'LL GET YOU ON A BOAT.
REALLY? YOU'LL TAKE ME WITH YOU?
WHAT ARE YOU TALKING ABOUT? THERE'S NOTHING WE CAN DO ABOUT IT NOW. I HAVE TO TAKE RESPONSIBILITY FOR MAKING YOU A WANTED CRIMINAL...
...THAT ISN'T IT.
CORREC-TION:

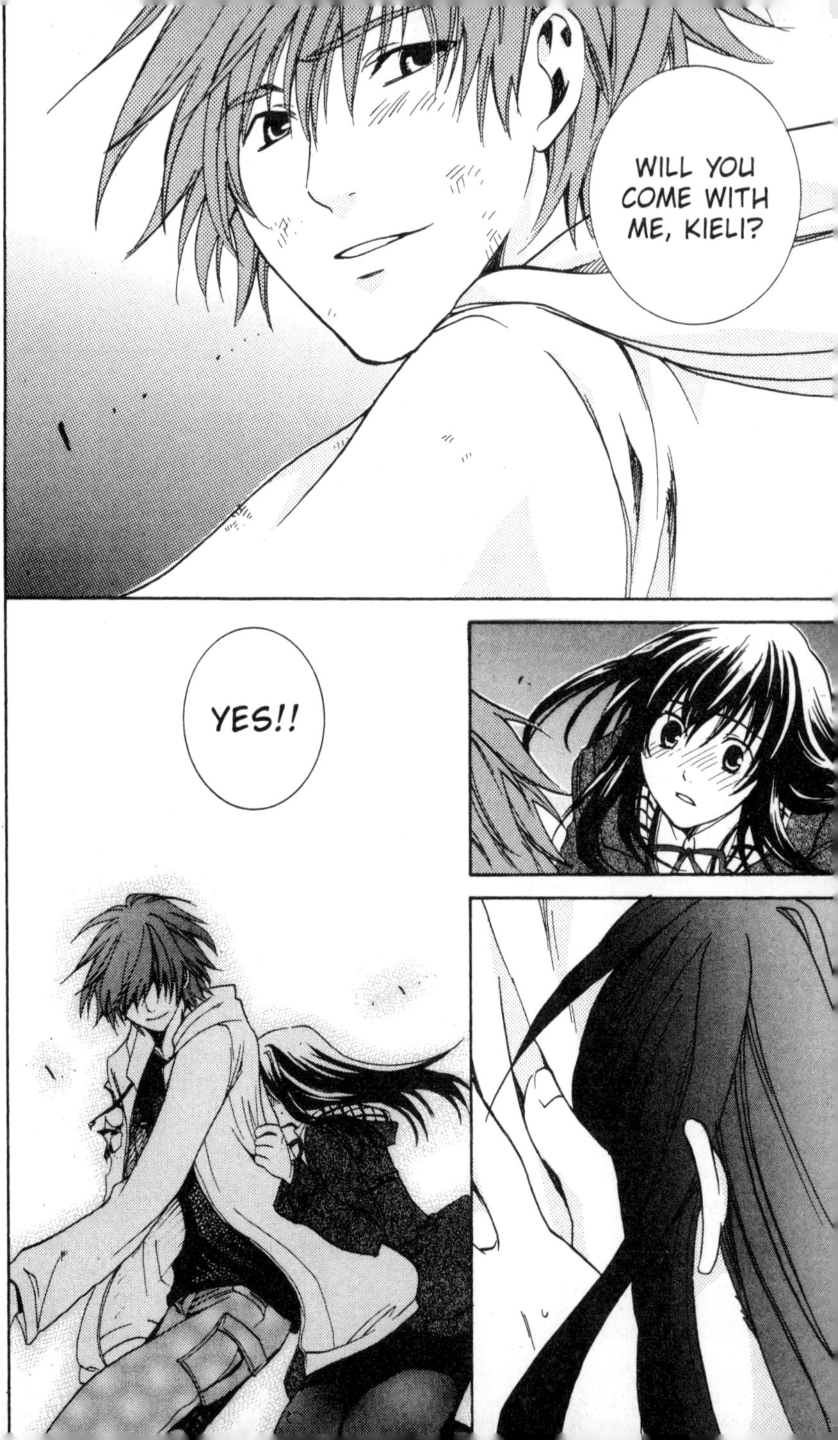
WILL YOU COME WITH ME, KIELI?
YES!!

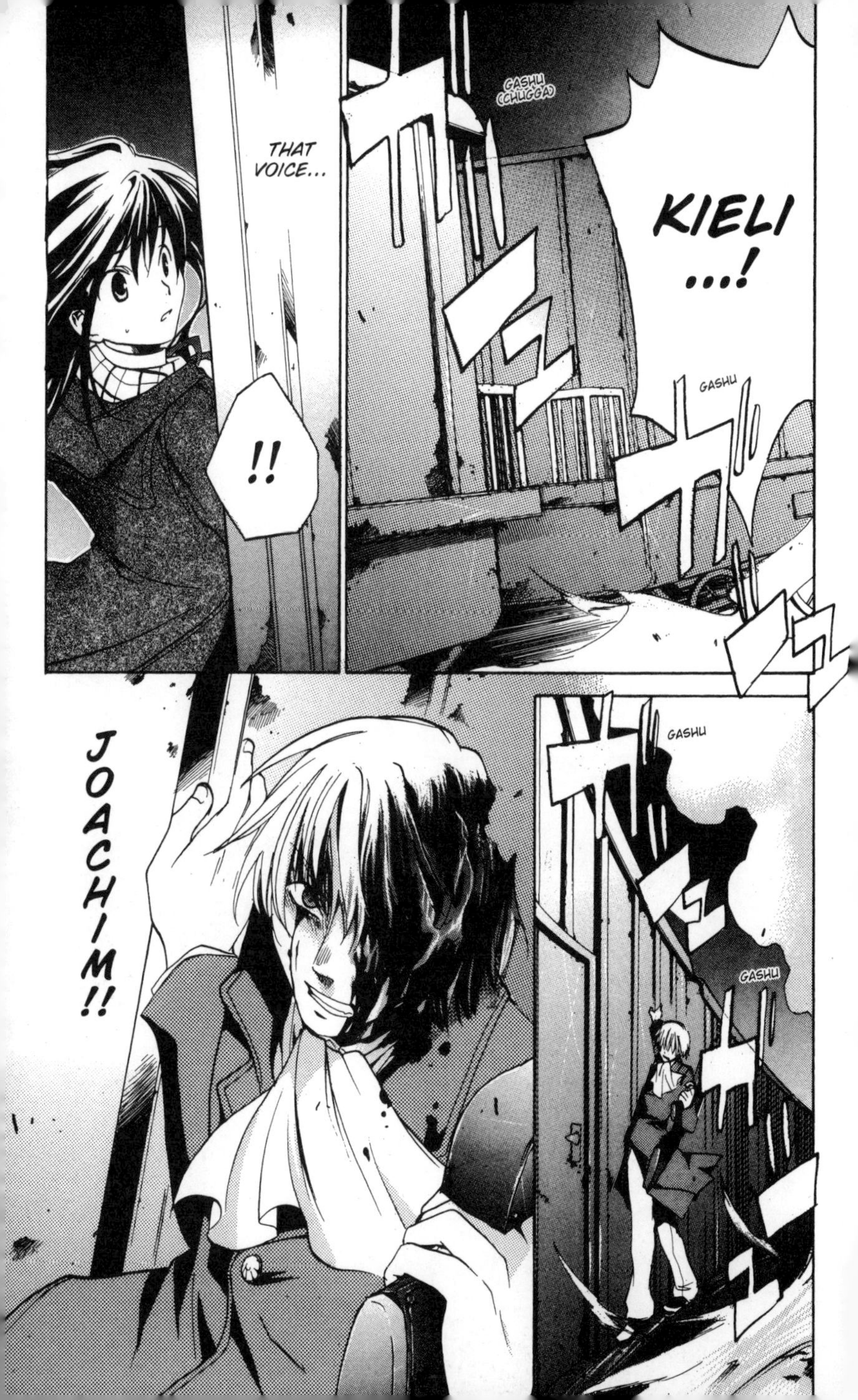
GASHU (CHUGGA)
KIELI ...!
GASHU
THAT VOICE...
!!
GASHU
GASHU
JOACHIM!!

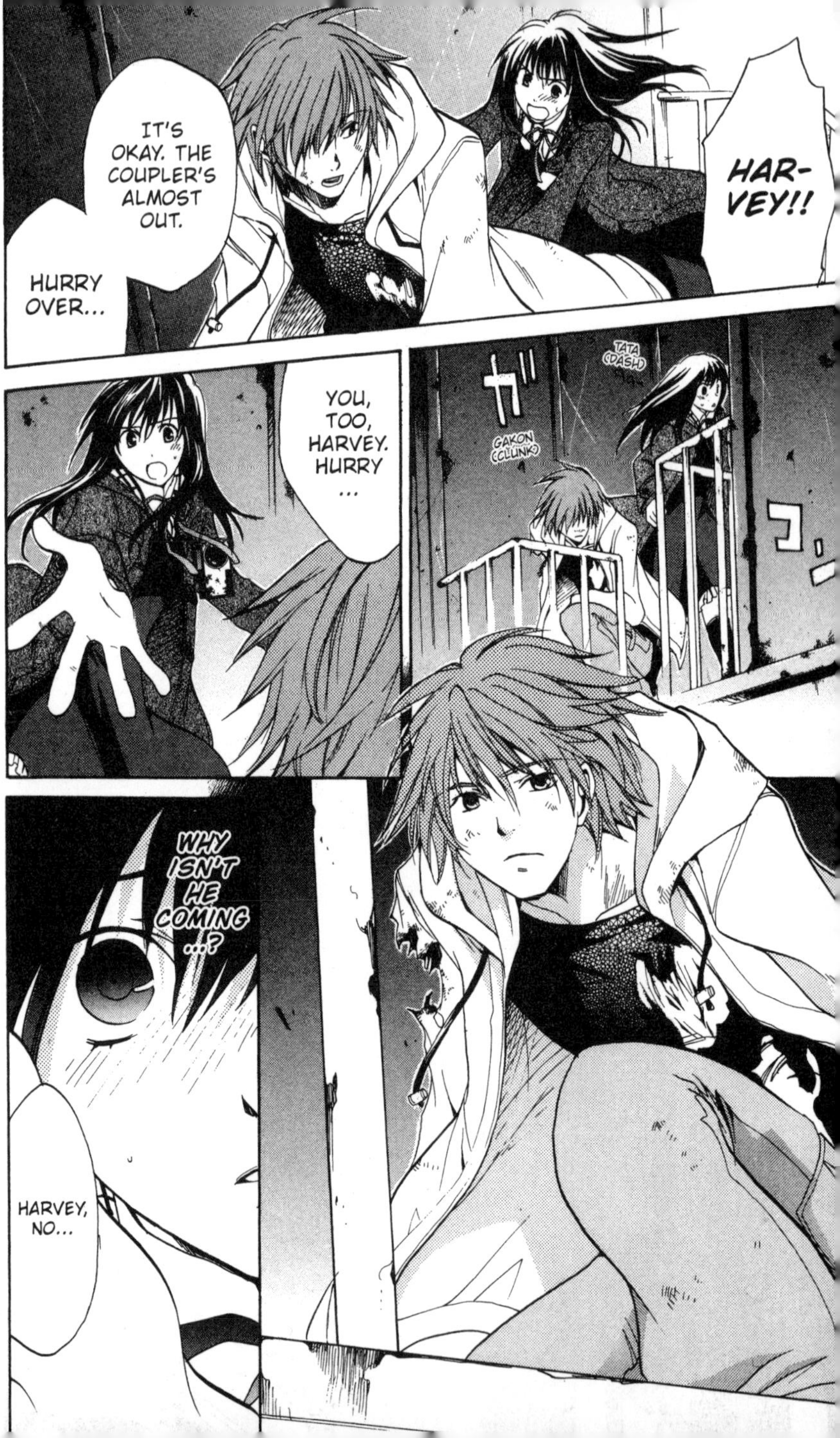
HAR-VEY!!
IT'S OKAY. THE COUPLER'S ALMOST OUT.
HURRY OVER...
TATA (DASH)
GAKON (CLUNK)
YOU, TOO, HARVEY. HURRY ...
WHY ISN'T HE COMING ...?
HARVEY, NO...

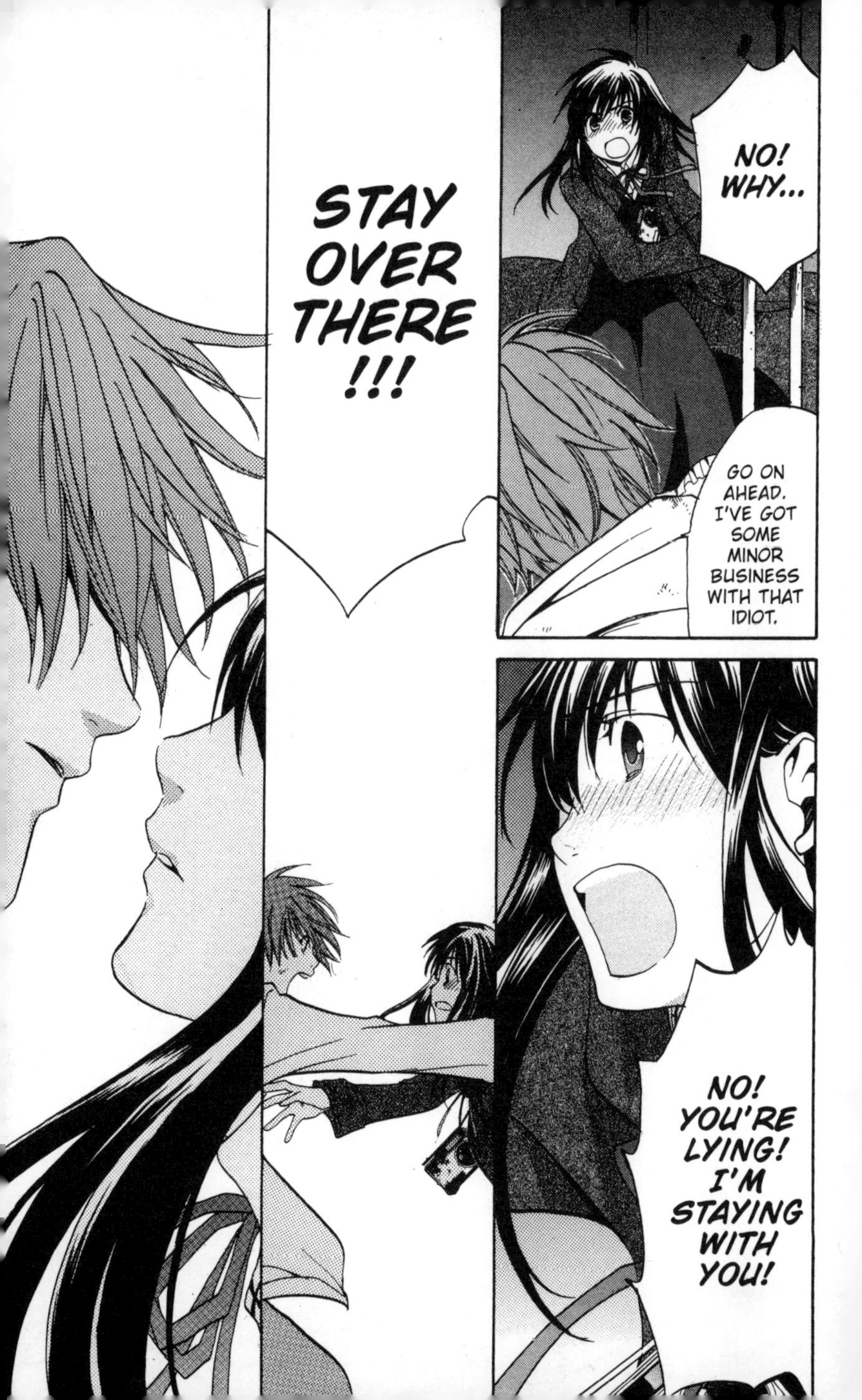
NO! WHY...
GO ON AHEAD. I'VE GOT SOME MINOR BUSINESS WITH THAT IDIOT.
NO! YOU'RE LYING! I'M STAYING WITH YOU!
STAY OVER THERE!!!

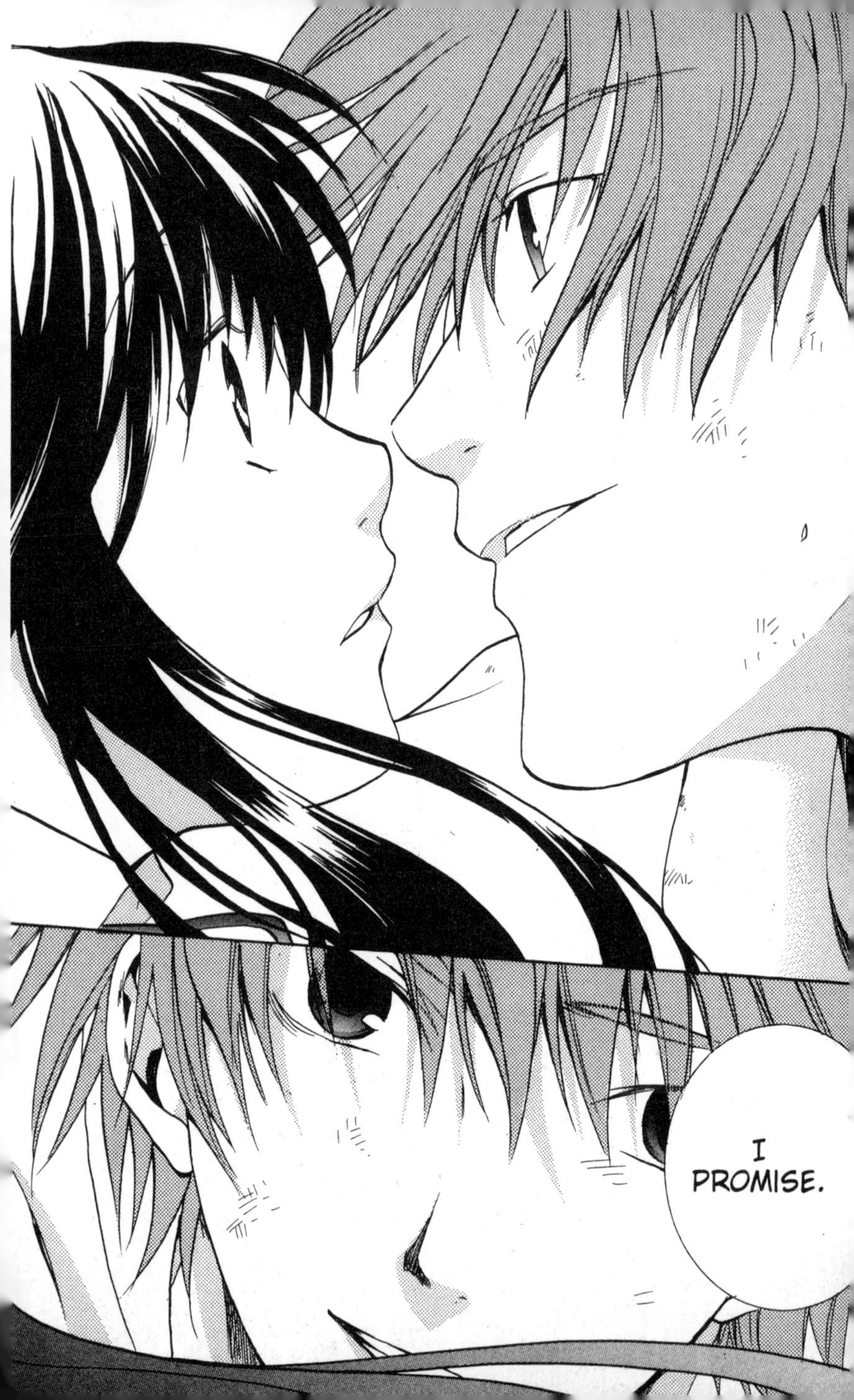
I PROMISE.

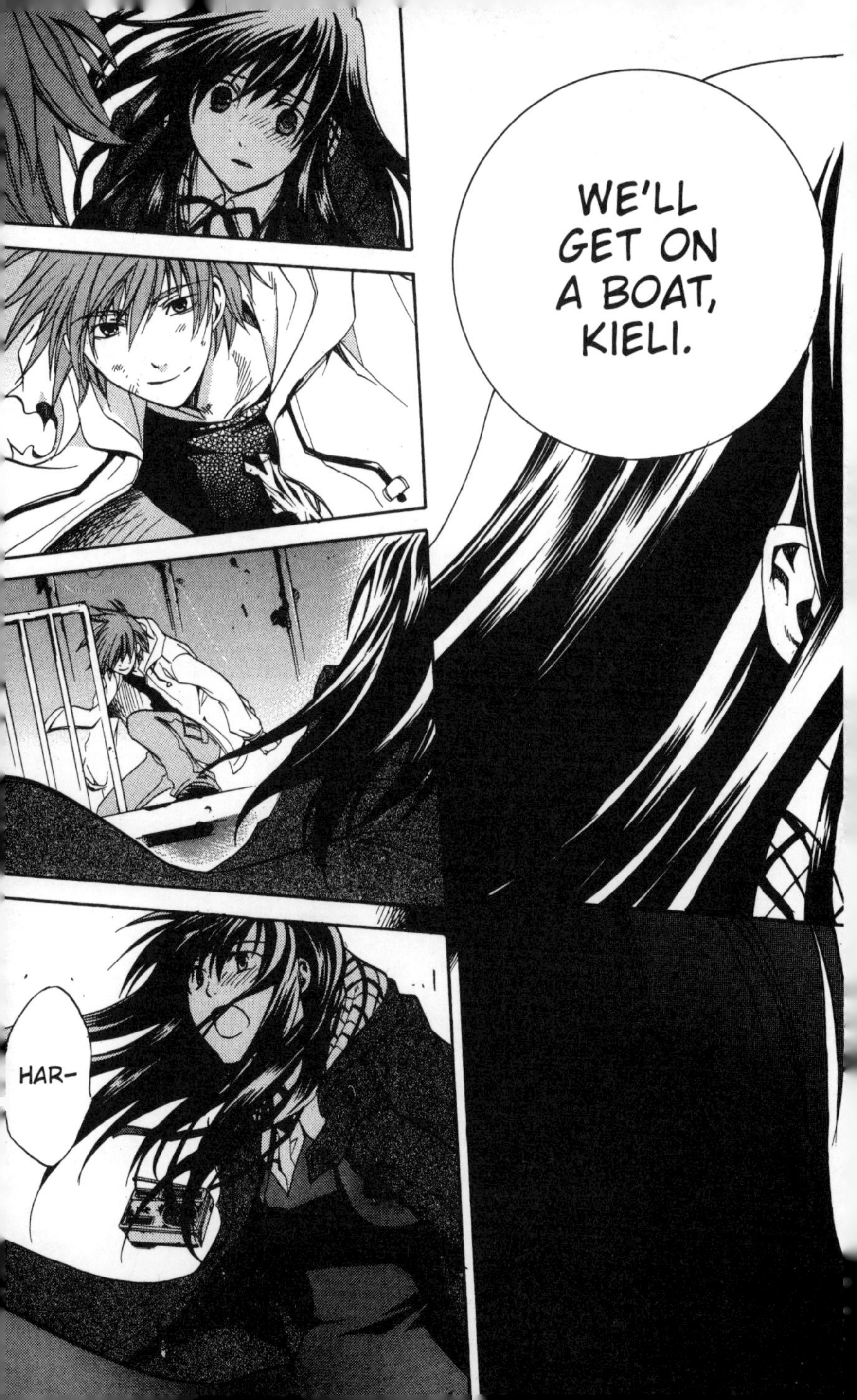
WE'LL GET ON A BOAT, KIELI.
..!
HAR-

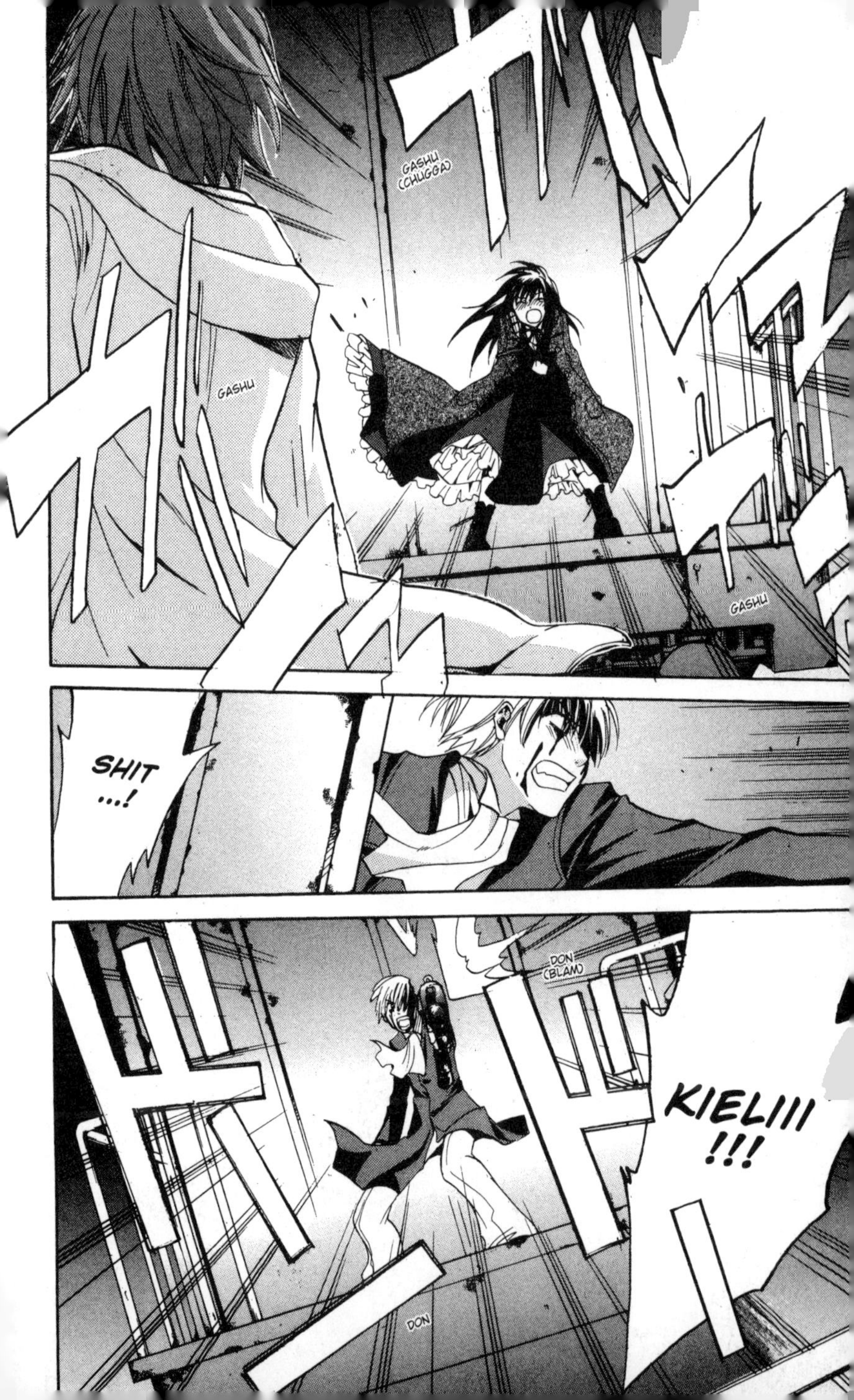
GASHU (CHUGGA)
GASHU
GASHU
SHIT ...!
DON (BLAM)
KIELIII !!!
DON

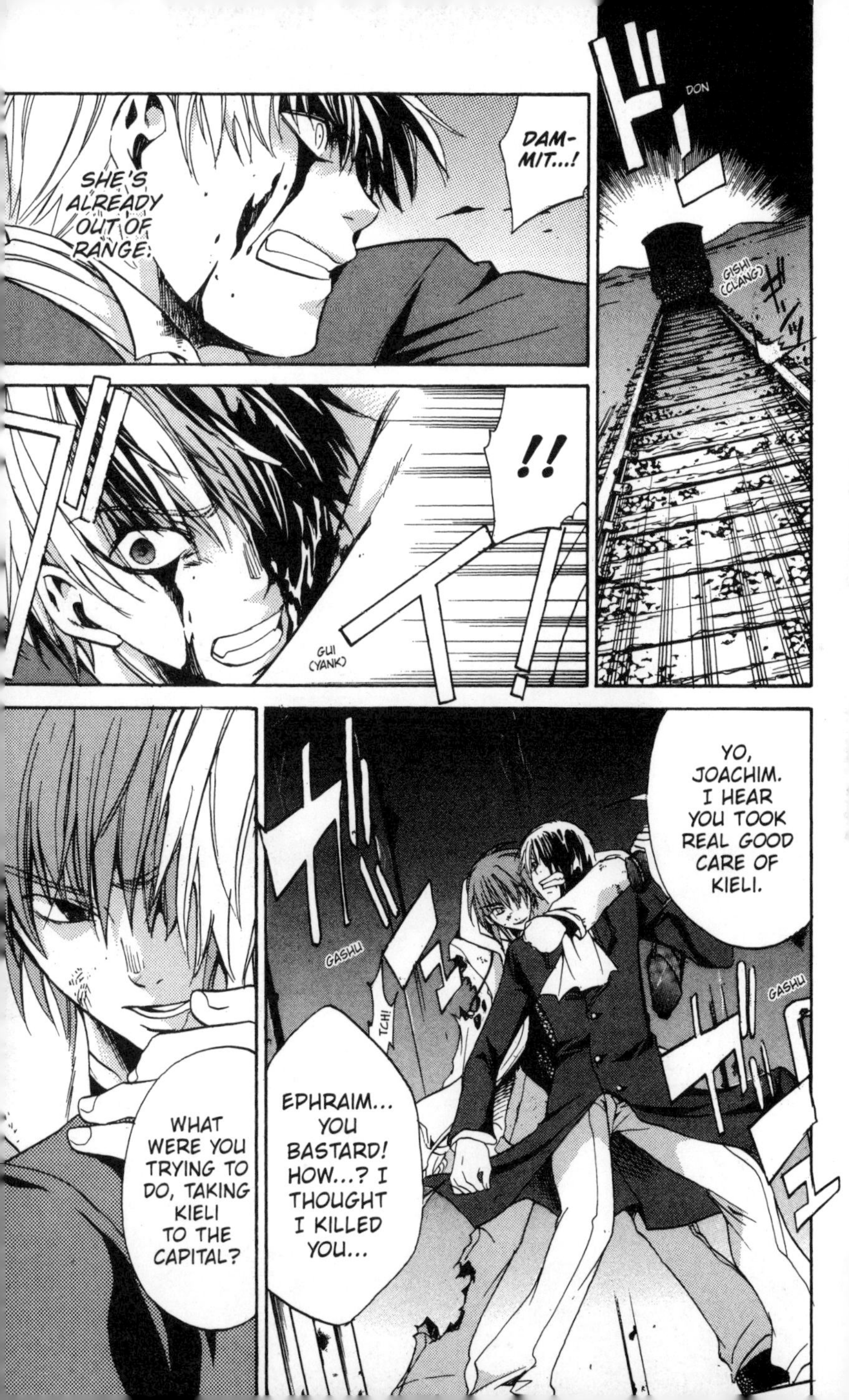
DON
GISHI (CLANG)
DAM-MIT...!
SHE'S ALREADY OUT OF RANGE.
!!
GUI (YANK)
YO, JOACHIM. I HEAR YOU TOOK REAL GOOD CARE OF KIELI.
GASHU
GASHU
TCH!
EPHRAIM... YOU BASTARD! HOW...? I THOUGHT I KILLED YOU...
WHAT WERE YOU TRYING TO DO, TAKING KIELI TO THE CAPITAL?

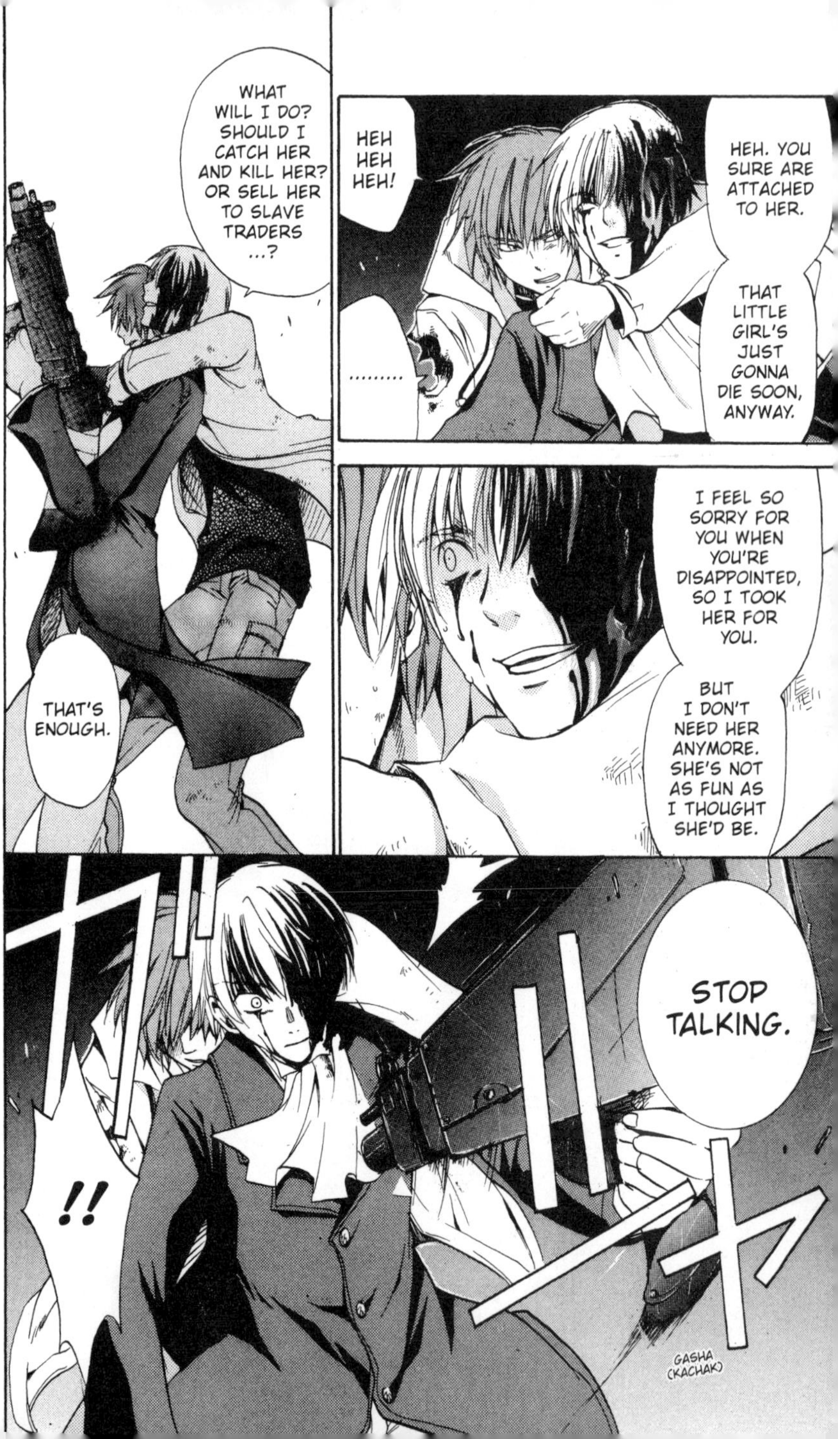

HEH. YOU SURE ARE ATTACHED TO HER.
THAT LITTLE GIRL'S JUST GONNA DIE SOON, ANYWAY.
HEH HEH HEH!
....
I FEEL SO SORRY FOR YOU WHEN YOU'RE DISAPPOINTED, SO I TOOK HER FOR YOU.
BUT I DON'T NEED HER ANYMORE. SHE'S NOT AS FUN AS I THOUGHT SHE'D BE.
WHAT WILL I DO? SHOULD I CATCH HER AND KILL HER? OR SELL HER TO SLAVE TRADERS ...?
THAT'S ENOUGH.
STOP TALKING.
!!
GASHA (KACHAK)

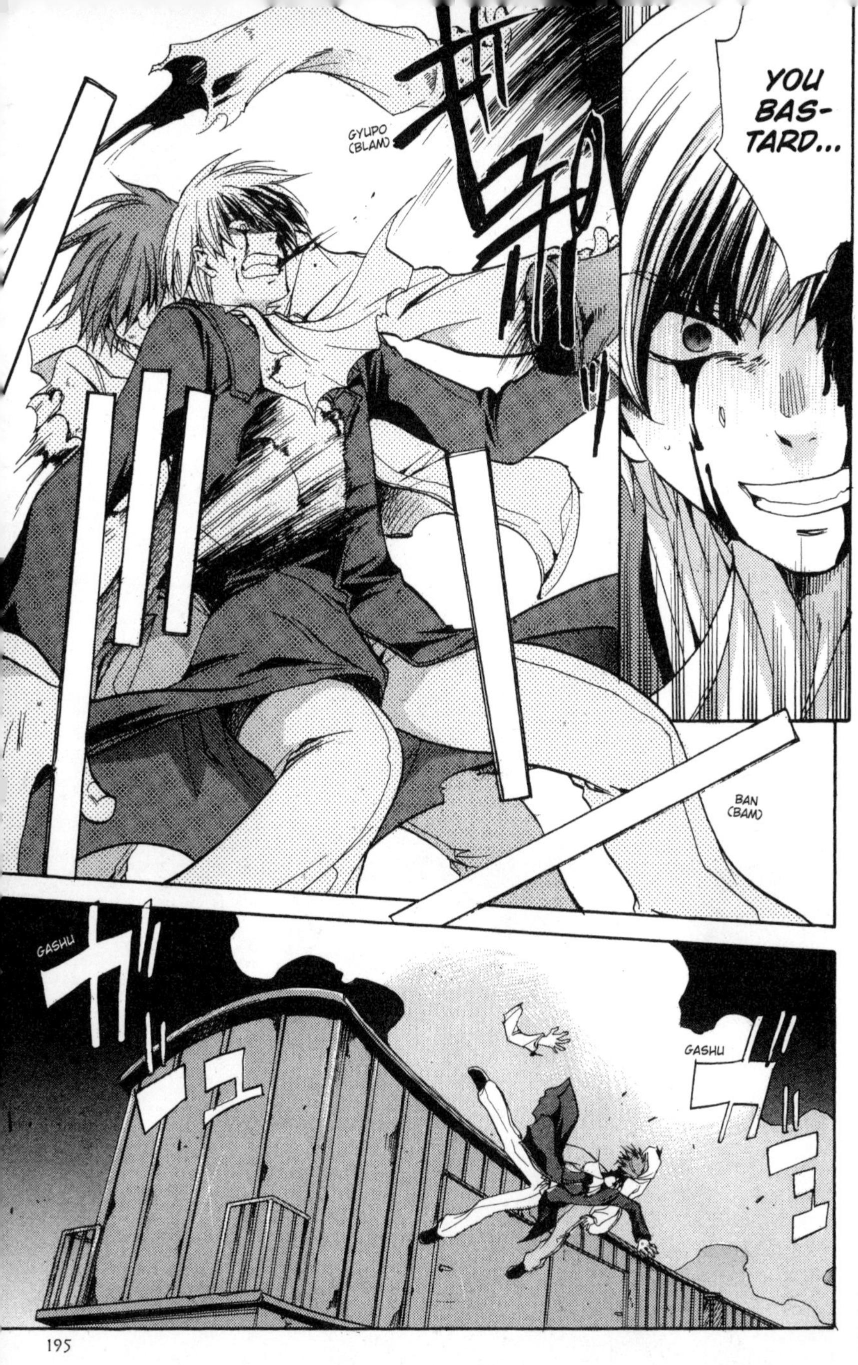
YOU BASTARD...
GYUPO (BLAM)
BAN (BAM)
GASHU
GASHU

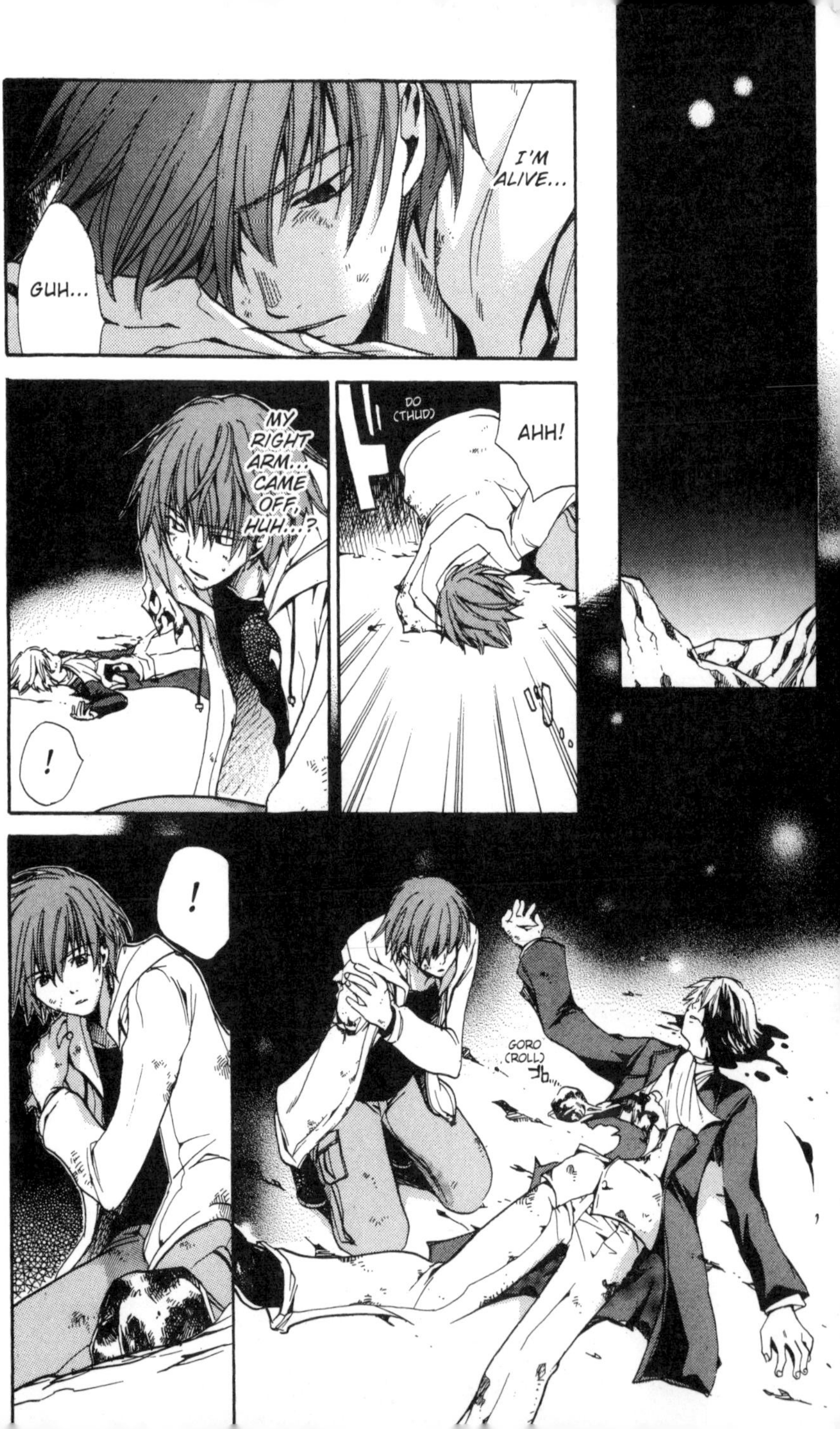
I'M ALIVE...
GUH...
DO (THUD)
AHH!
MY RIGHT ARM... CAME OFF, HUH...?
!
GORO (ROLL)
ゴロ...
!

JOACHIM'S "CORE," HUH...? THE CARBONIZATION GUN TURNED THE SURFACE INTO CHARCOAL...

BASHI (GRAB)

!?

BORO (CRUMBLE)

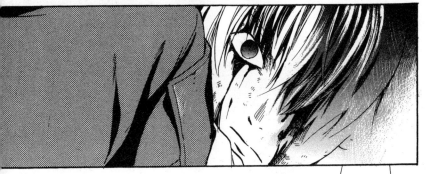

THE IDIOT...

IS HE DEAD...?

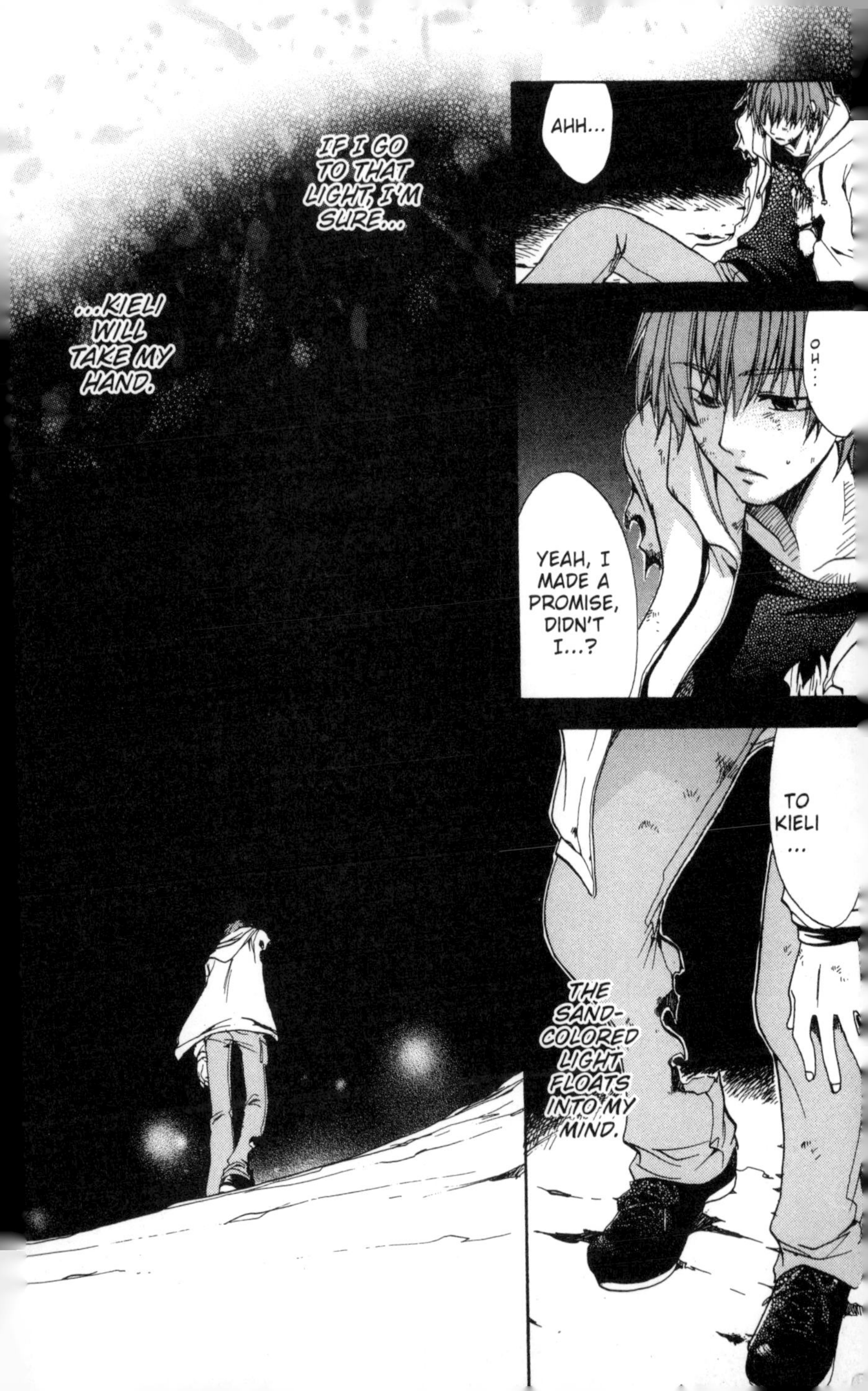
AHH...
OH...
YEAH, I MADE A PROMISE, DIDN'T I...?
TO KIELI ...
THE SAND-COLORED LIGHT FLOATS INTO MY MIND.
IF I GO TO THAT LIGHT, I'M SURE...
...KIELI WILL TAKE MY HAND.

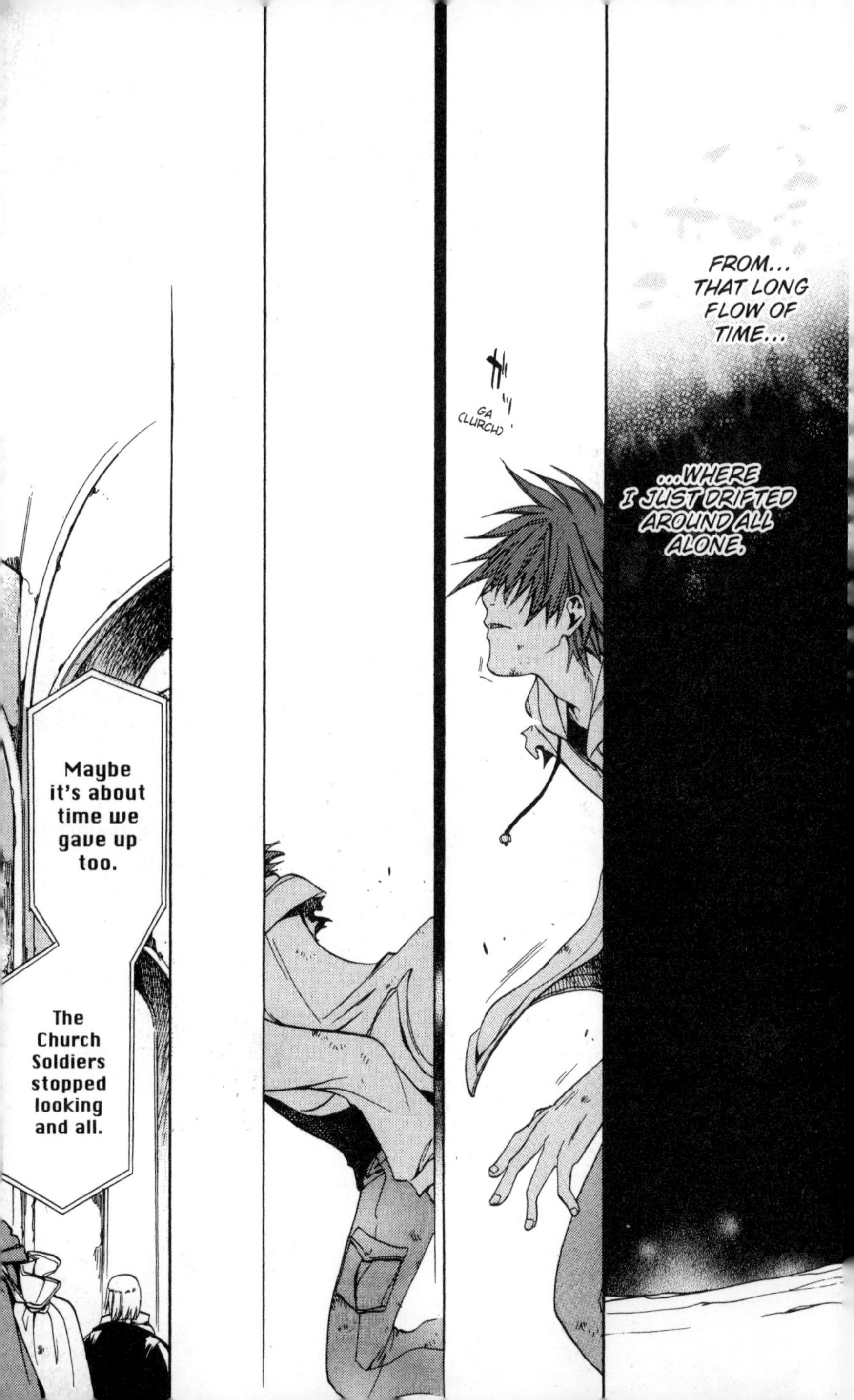
FROM... THAT LONG FLOW OF TIME...
...WHERE I JUST DRIFTED AROUND ALL ALONE.
GA (CLURCH)
Maybe it's about time we gave up too.
The Church Soldiers stopped looking and all.

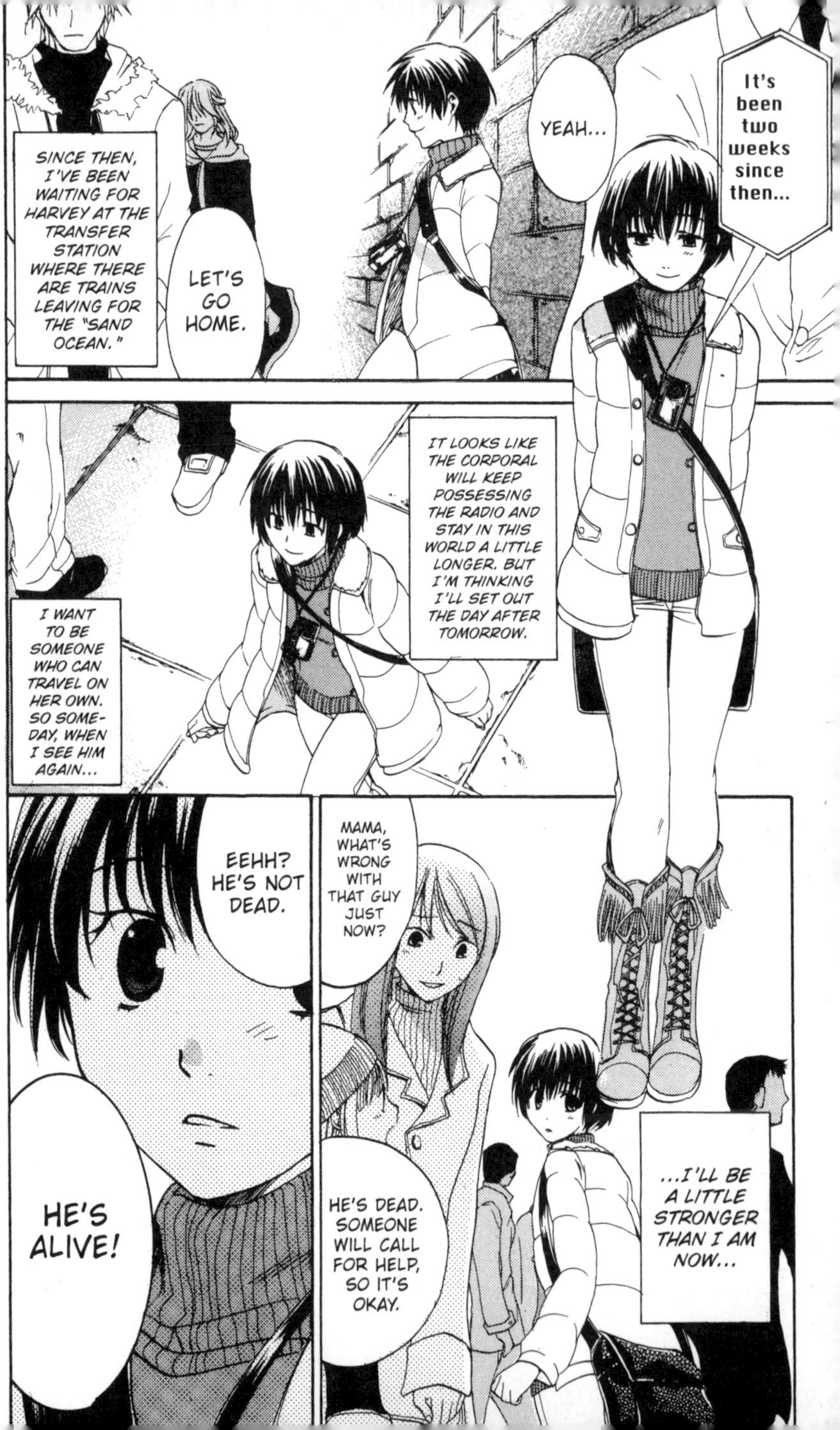
It's been two weeks since then...
YEAH...
LET'S GO HOME.
SINCE THEN, I'VE BEEN WAITING FOR HARVEY AT THE TRANSFER STATION WHERE THERE ARE TRAINS LEAVING FOR THE "SAND OCEAN."
IT LOOKS LIKE THE CORPORAL WILL KEEP POSSESSING THE RADIO AND STAY IN THIS WORLD A LITTLE LONGER. BUT I'M THINKING I'LL SET OUT THE DAY AFTER TOMORROW.
I WANT TO BE SOMEONE WHO CAN TRAVEL ON HER OWN. SO SOME-DAY, WHEN I SEE HIM AGAIN...
...I'LL BE A LITTLE STRONGER THAN I AM NOW...
MAMA, WHAT'S WRONG WITH THAT GUY JUST NOW?
HE'S DEAD. SOMEONE WILL CALL FOR HELP, SO IT'S OKAY.
EEHH? HE'S NOT DEAD.
HE'S ALIVE!

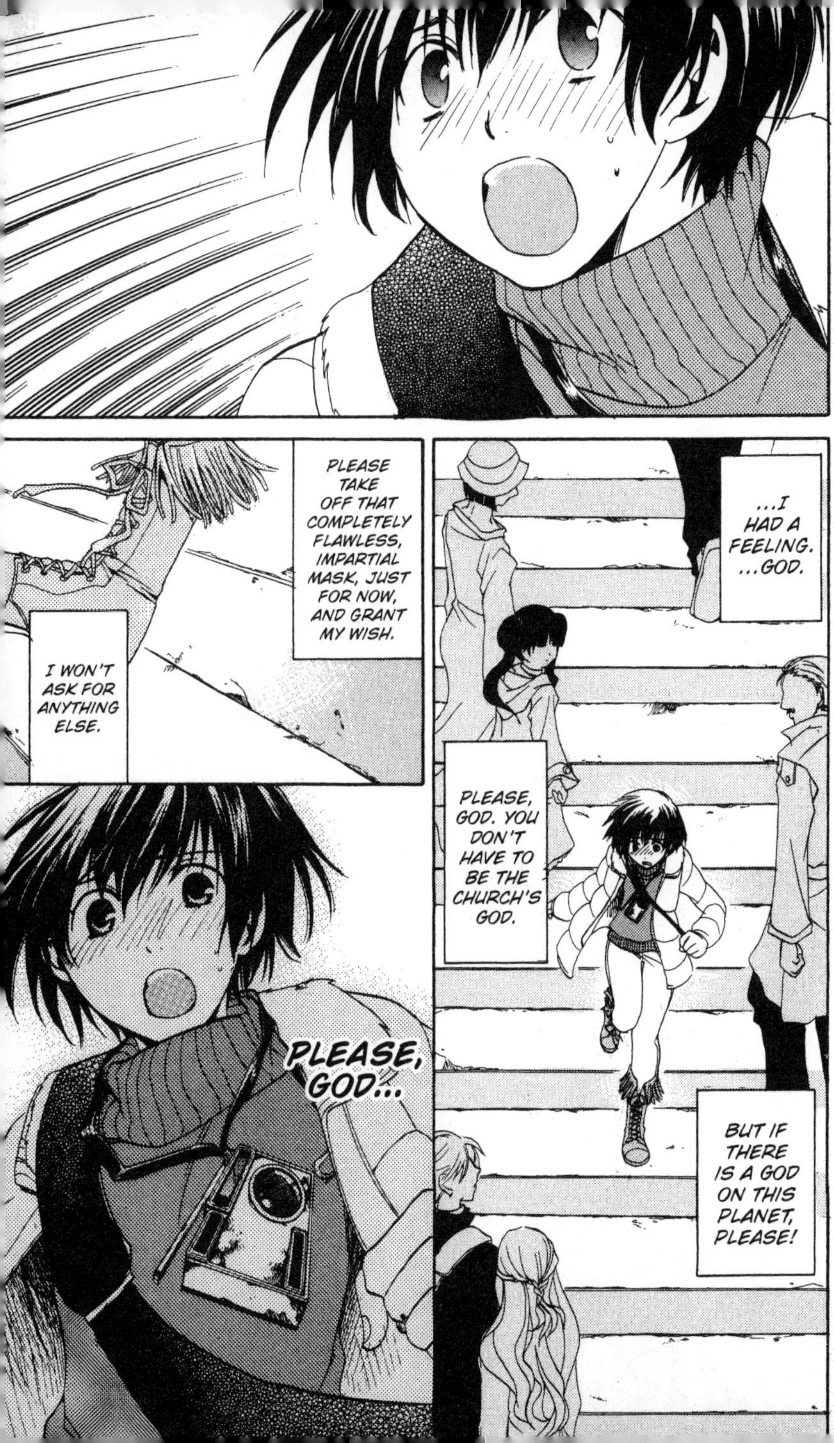
...I HAD A FEELING. ...GOD.
PLEASE, GOD. YOU DON'T HAVE TO BE THE CHURCH'S GOD.
BUT IF THERE IS A GOD ON THIS PLANET, PLEASE!
PLEASE TAKE OFF THAT COMPLETELY FLAWLESS, IMPARTIAL MASK, JUST FOR NOW, AND GRANT MY WISH.
I WON'T ASK FOR ANYTHING ELSE.
PLEASE, GOD...

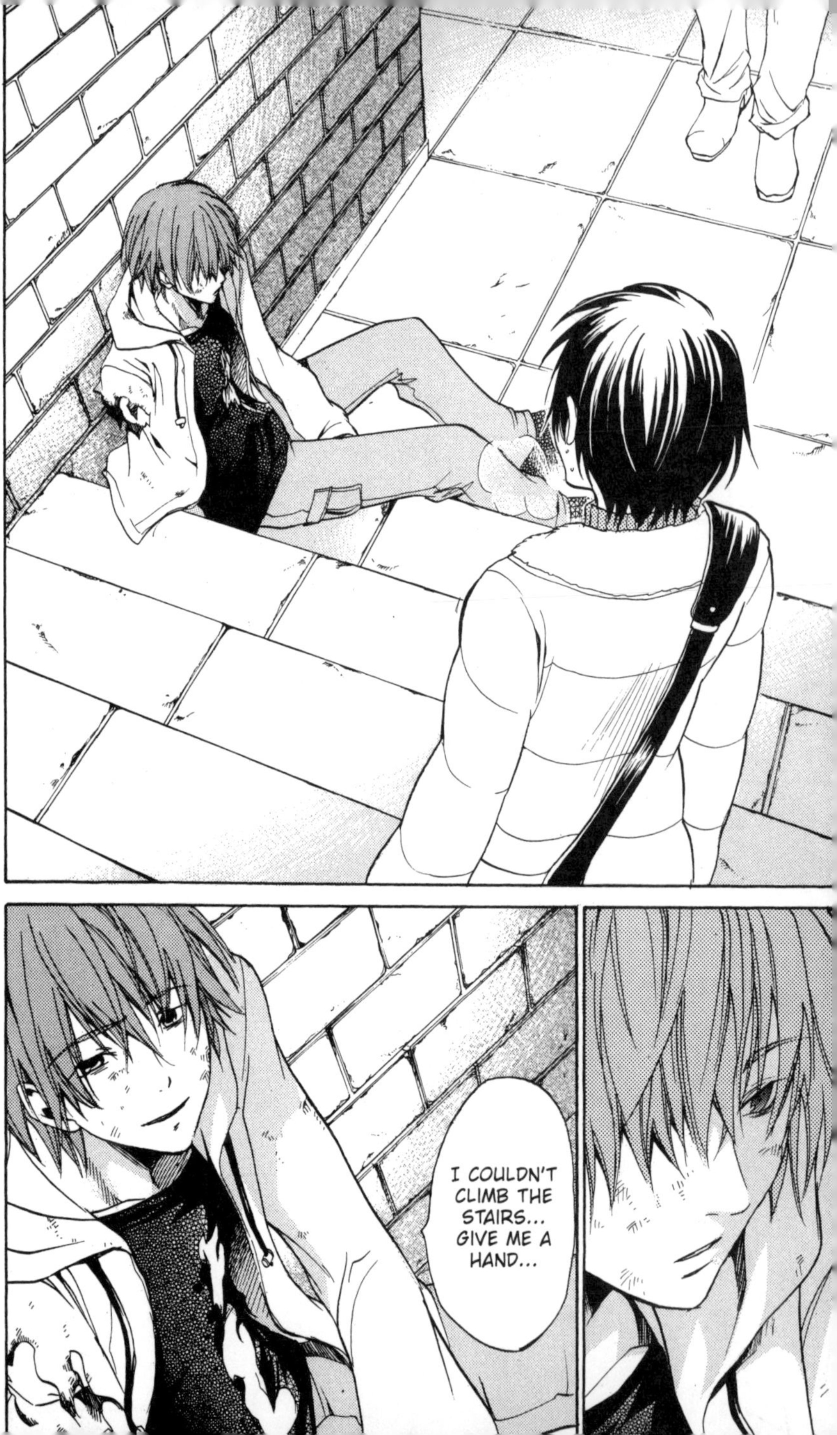
I COULDN'T CLIMB THE STAIRS... GIVE ME A HAND...

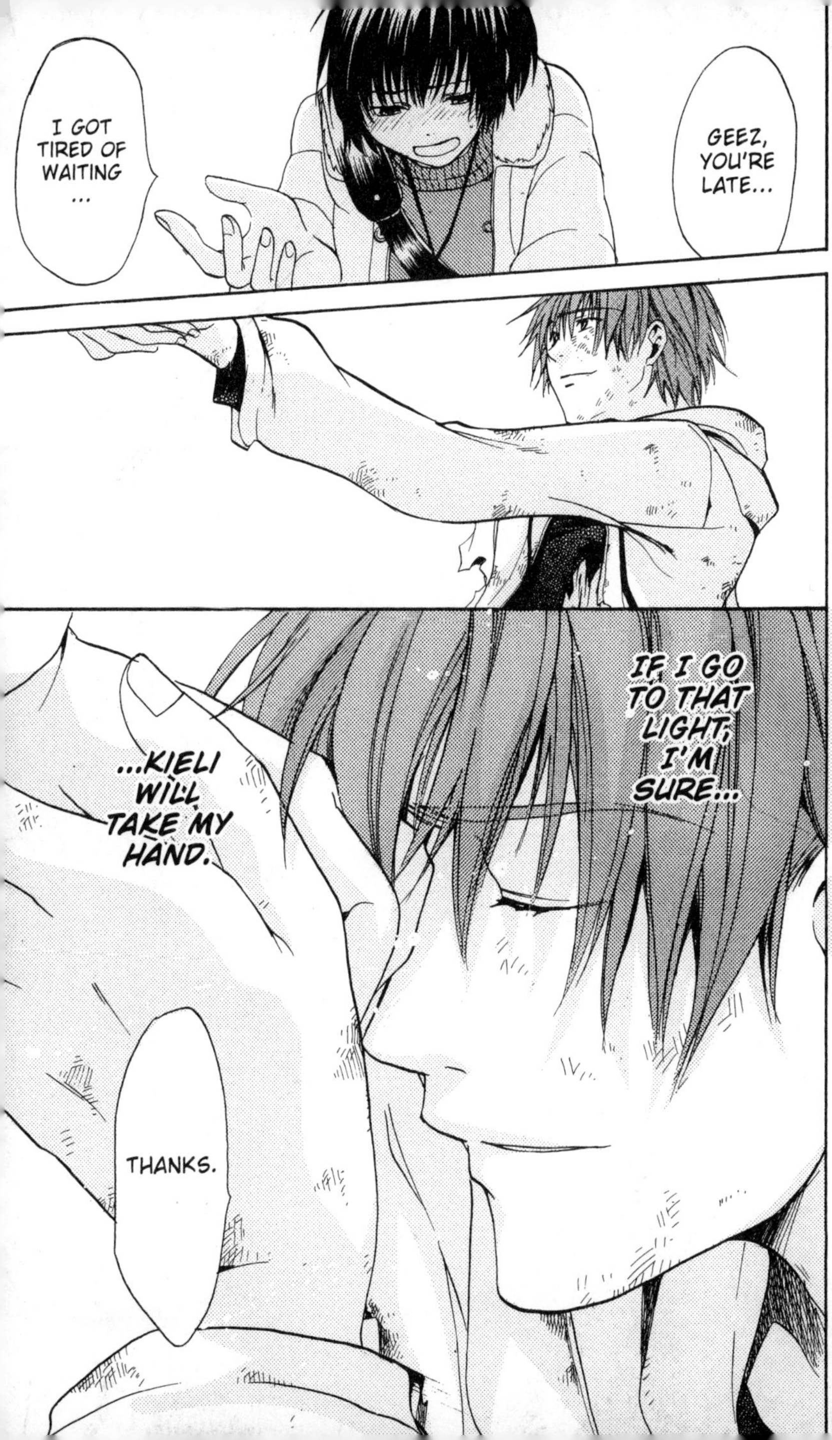
GEEZ, YOU'RE LATE...
I GOT TIRED OF WAITING ...
IF I GO TO THAT LIGHT, I'M SURE...
...KIELI WILL TAKE MY HAND.
THANKS.

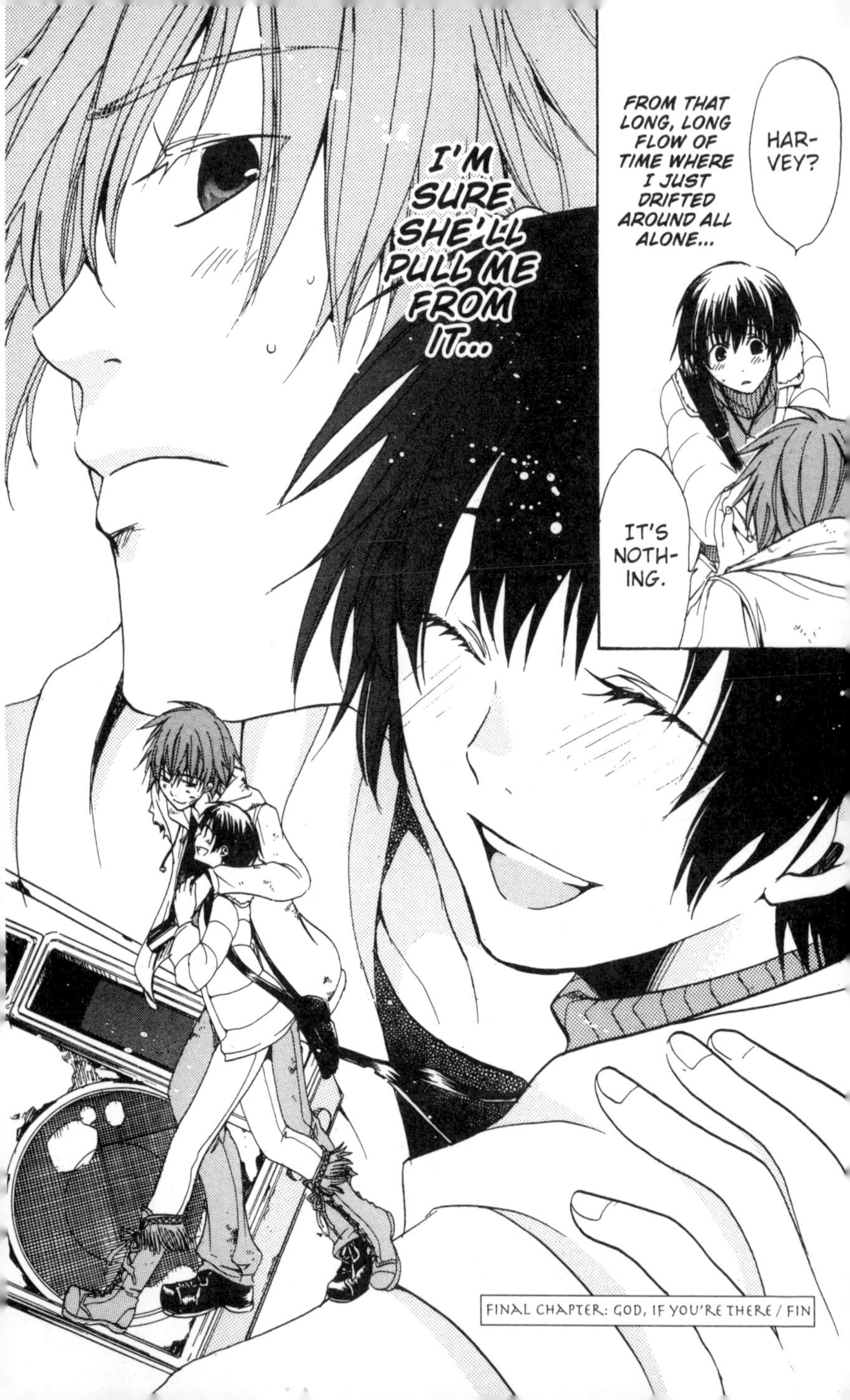

HAR-VEY?
FROM THAT LONG, LONG FLOW OF TIME WHERE I JUST DRIFTED AROUND ALL ALONE...
IT'S NOTH-ING.
I'M SURE SHE'LL PULL ME FROM IT...
FINAL CHAPTER: GOD, IF YOU'RE THERE / FIN

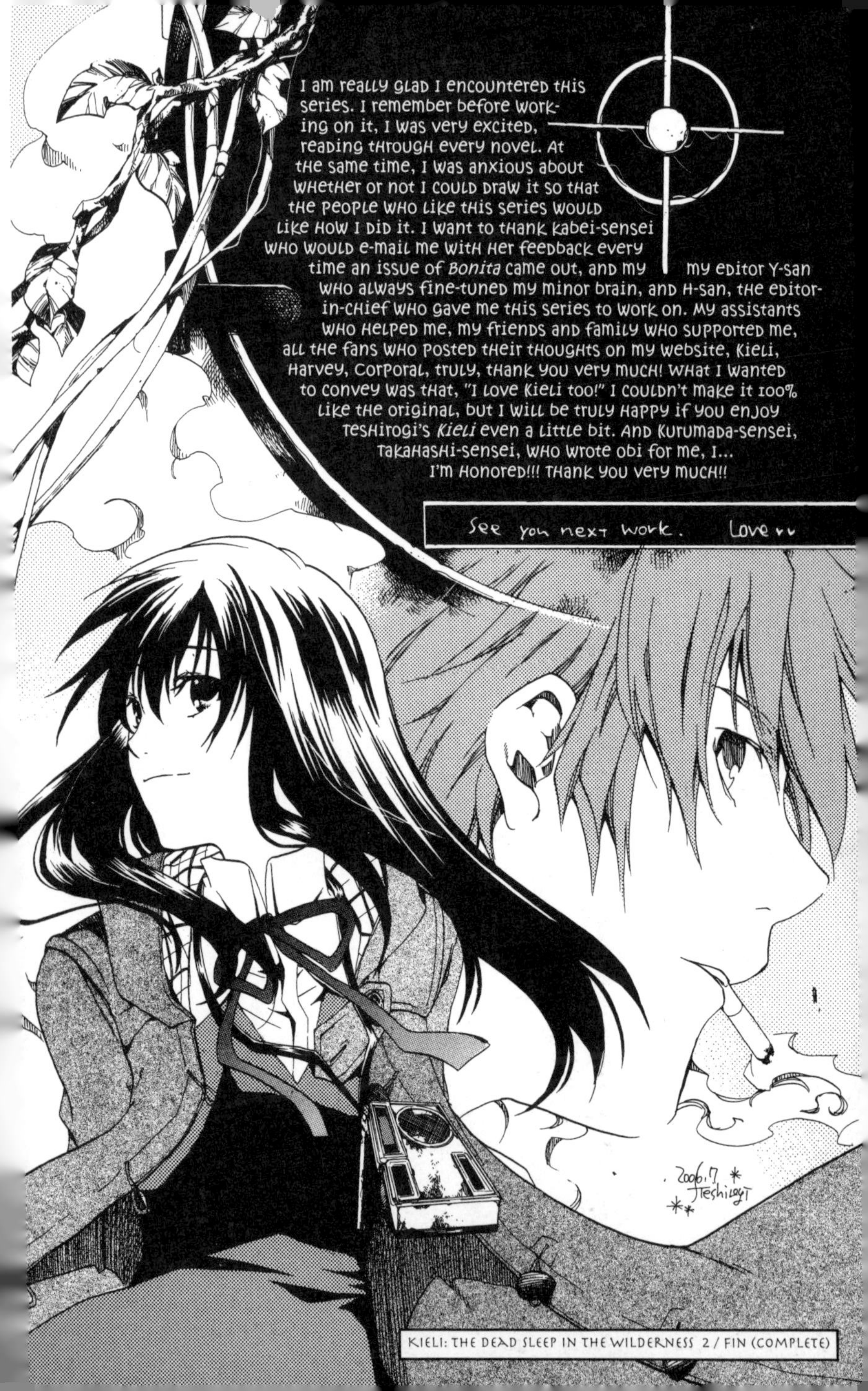
I am really glad I encountered this series. I remember before working on it, I was very excited, reading through every novel. At the same time, I was anxious about whether or not I could draw it so that the people who like this series would like how I did it. I want to thank Kabei-sensei who would e-mail me with her feedback every time an issue of *Bonita* came out, and my editor Y-san who always fine-tuned my minor brain, and H-san, the editor-in-chief who gave me this series to work on. My assistants who helped me, my friends and family who supported me, all the fans who posted their thoughts on my website, Kieli, Harvey, Corporal, truly, thank you very much! What I wanted to convey was that, "I love Kieli too!" I couldn't make it 100% like the original, but I will be truly happy if you enjoy Teshirogi's *Kieli* even a little bit. And Kurumada-sensei, Takahashi-sensei, who wrote obi for me, I... I'm honored!!! Thank you very much!!
See you next work. Love
2006.7 Teshirogi
KIELI: THE DEAD SLEEP IN THE WILDERNESS 2 / FIN (COMPLETE)

KIELI ②

YUKAKO KABEI
SHIORI TESHIROGI

Translation: Alethea Nibley and Athena Nibley

Lettering: Alexis Eckerman

KIELI: SHISHATACHI WA KOYA NI NEMURU, Vol. 2 ©YUKAKO KABEI/
ASCII MEDIAWORKS, ©2006 SHIORI TESHIROGI. All rights reserved. First
published in Japan in 2006 by Akita Publishing Co., Ltd., Tokyo. English
translation rights arranged with Akita Publishing Co., Ltd. through Tuttle-
Mori Agency, Inc., Tokyo.

English translation © 2008 by Hachette Book Group, Inc.

Yen Press
Hachette Book Group
237 Park Avenue, New York, NY 10017

Visit our Web sites at www.HachetteBookGroup.com and
www.YenPress.com.

Yen Press is an imprint of Hachette Book Group, Inc. The Yen Press name
and logo are trademarks of Hachette Book Group, Inc.

First Yen Press Edition: October 2008

ISBN-13: 978-0-7595-2852-9

10 9 8 7 6 5 4 3 2

BVG

Printed in the United States of America

Prologue

Why isn't God here?

On this planet, there is a Church, but there is no God. Kieli realized this fact when she was four or five years old, and she always thought it strange for a world to have such a prominent church even though it seemed so obvious there was no God. When she was seven, she finally hit on a very satisfactory answer to her dilemma.

"Grandmother, after I heard the sermon today, I finally figured it out." In her excitement, Kieli would sometimes skip or twirl around as she announced her brilliant discovery of the day to her grandmother on their way home from their church service.

That day, the chief priest had given a sermon on the Church's history. Apparently, the ship carrying the "Eleven Saints and Five Families" landed on this godless planet and built up a church hundreds of years ago, but that ship left its distant mother planet hundreds of years before that, and now no one remembers the name of that place. The very patient Saints traversed the universe for many generations before arriving here.

"God wasn't very patient, was He? I think their destination was *so* far away, He got tired and went home before He got here. I wonder why the important people in the Church can't figure it out. It's so simple! Do they think that God will stay with them forever?"

"Kieli," her grandmother said quietly, walking beside her. She would call Kieli's name simply like this whenever Kieli did something she shouldn't. She would never yell or lecture.

Without changing her expression or her gaze, she would just say, "Kieli," in a sad, quiet voice.

Kieli had promised that she would never, ever talk about God not being around when she was outside of the house. If she talked like that, "the Church's soldiers would gouge her heart out." The idea that the Church's soldiers would gouge out the hearts of bad children who didn't keep God's teachings was a cliché adults used to make their children behave. Apparently it came from the legend that the demon soldiers who killed so many people in the War long, long ago were defeated when the Church soldiers tore out their hearts.

"I'm sorry, Grandmother. I won't say it anymore." Dejected, Kieli shut her mouth, stopped skipping, and faced forward. But what Kieli was sorry about was that she had gotten carried away and broken her promise; that childish threat never scared her a bit.

There was a reserved kind of bustle on the streets as worshippers walked home on Sunday morning. They all wore hats of myriad shapes to worship in and bundled themselves up in dark-colored overcoats. The Colonization Days holiday was approaching once again, and the air was beginning to carry the scent of winter. To Kieli, the smell of winter was the smell of the smog spewed out by fossil fuels. An exhaust pipe stuck out of the roof of every building that lined either side of the street and sent thick grey smoke into the sky.

Kieli turned around again and walked backward for a little while. Pushing back the brim of her hat and looking up, she could see the grand and imposing domed roof of the cathedral standing in the center of the town, peeking out between the other buildings.

It was then that, behind her — in front of everyone else who, unlike Kieli, was not facing backward — there rose a sudden commotion. Just as she was making out jeers and screams in

3

the distance, before she knew it, they had migrated and were now very close by. The instant she turned around in surprise to see what it was, a man pushed aside a passerby that had been walking ahead of Kieli and jumped out right in front of her.

"Wah!"

Kieli instinctively drew herself back, and then…

Fwa-boom!

If she'd been forced to describe the sound of such an explosion, she'd have said it was like the heavy atmosphere being tightly compressed and released all at once. The sound roared through the morning street.

Before her eyes, Kieli saw the man's chest burst open. Through the gaping, round hole, she could see men covered from head to toe in strange white armor. Wisps of smoke rose from the barrels of several guns aimed her way. She heard a woman gasp somewhere, but Kieli just stood there, unable to remember to breathe let alone scream. After a bit, she finally staggered backward and fell on her rear on the paved street. As if in response, the man fell to his knees, then collapsed at Kieli's feet. His neck was bent at an unnatural angle, and his face was turned toward her. His unfocused gaze rested on the air, nowhere in particular, in front of Kieli.

Sensing someone running toward her, Kieli regained her senses and the crowd's stirring came back to her, as if she'd just remembered how to hear following a temporary loss.

"Kieli, are you hurt?" Her grandmother knelt beside Kieli and embraced her. Her aged, wizened hands trembled slightly. Kieli took her hand and answered in a somewhat monotone voice that she was fine.

Amidst intermingling whispers of both fear and awe, the crowd moved aside, and metallic footsteps echoed as the armored men marched through their center. Kieli, still sitting, watched them, and as a corner of her mind thought,

"Oh, they're coming this way," she returned her gaze to the fallen man.

Something had rolled out from what was now a cavity in the man's chest.

It was a black stone, about the size of an adult fist. It wasn't unlike a strange machine component. A few torn, narrow tubes that looked both like cables and blood vessels hung from it, and a thick liquid that resembled used oil twined around it. Inside the stone, a dull, amber-colored light blinked rhythmically, rhythmically, like a heartbeat.

She unconsciously reached out for it, but another hand snatched it up first. It was a grim, armored hand, wearing a white gauntlet made of special metal fiber. When she looked up, a soldier was mumbling something inside his mask. *We have just executed a wicked man. There is nothing to worry about. You didn't see anything.* She thought they said something like that, but none of it stayed in Kieli's mind.

After that, nothing she did would help her remember the face of the man who died there. Only the mysterious black stone and his open, empty eyes remained, burned forever onto her retinas.

Chapter 1: Roommate

Miss Hanni was a teacher, almost thirty years old, who wore her hair tied back in a bun and angular, rimless glasses. Aside from her tendency to be melodramatic and love of pop quizzes, she was a virtuous and devout believer. But to Kieli, "devout believer" was not a compliment.

"My goodness, Kieli! Honestly, whatever is the matter with you?"

Honestly, whatever is the matter with you? My Lord. Oh, what are we to do with you? For a while now, Miss Hanni had been lamenting the state of affairs with repetitions from her limited collection of phrases such as those, looking up at the ceiling with exaggerated gestures, and taking off her glasses to dab at her eyes with her handkerchief.

"Not only are you late, but dressed the way you are. Don't tell me you didn't know about today's service."

"I'm sorry, Miss Hanni," Kieli apologized, checking her desire to say, "I didn't know, Miss Hanni." She wanted to avoid giving lame excuses and having a pointless argument with her teacher. After all, it would look bad to say it was because no one had told her (even if that was the actual reason).

A few of her classmates snickered from the three rows behind Miss Hanni. They all wore their beautifully embroidered, white choir uniforms; Kieli alone was dressed in the normal black bolero with its big collar. Even the plain, black uniform had its own kind of dignity when everyone was wearing it, but right now, Kieli looked like a witch-in-training, wearing a cheap robe, who'd been thrown into a chorus of angels.

6

The parish's chief priest would be giving a congratulatory address on the first day of the Colonization Days holiday, so the service was not being held at the school's auditorium but rather in the cathedral in the center of town. Kieli and the other ninth-graders at the boarding school would be singing the hymns, so they were to wear their white choir uniforms and meet in time for rehearsal. The announcement was made at the student assembly last week, but Kieli was in detention doing a report and thus absent. The school dorms were double rooms, so normally it wouldn't have been a problem for one of the roommates to miss an assembly. Unfortunately, Kieli didn't have a roommate, and neither her classmates nor neighbors were kind enough to tell her. She was used to it, and she didn't feel like crying to her teacher over every little incident.

"Well, there's nothing we can do about it now. As long you're sorry, we'll let it go this time. Don't let it happen again." Maybe she'd made the right choice in opting not to make excuses, because Miss Hanni left it at that and let Kieli off the hook surprisingly easily.

"Now don't dawdle. Get in line. The service is starting. Go to the back where you'll stand out as little as possible."

"Yes, ma'am." Kieli gave a quick bow as she passed by her teacher and took her place in the very back row of the choir that was made up of all her classmates in their white uniforms. To her right, the freckle-faced, frizzy-haired Zillah let out a short laugh through her upturned nose. No doubt she was one of the girls who'd laughed earlier.

Blonde-haired Becca suddenly appeared at her left. She glanced at Kieli, raised the skirt of her own black uniform, and winked as if to say, "It happened to me, too."

Kieli blinked at her for a second, then looked at Becca and let out a small, wry grin. It wasn't as if Becca wearing the black

7

uniform would help Kieli at all, but it cheered her up a little. Sensing Zillah's dubious glare from her right, she suppressed her smile, erased the expression from her face, and turned forward.

The choir stood on raised platforms against the wall, so even from the back row, she could look out over the inside of the majestic central cathedral. A high, arched ceiling capped the white concrete walls. She'd heard that the impressive stained glass covering the walls to the right and left and the electric lights designed to look like candles were gifts from the Church in the capital. In the front, the black-robed priests were in neat lines on both sides of the pulpit, and behind them, the general congregation packed tightly into the pews. The diversely shaped hats of the parishioners wove together in an artless, uneven wave in contrast to the uniformity of the priests.

It baffled Kieli as much as ever that so many people would gather in reverence of a mother planet whose name they couldn't even remember and a God whose name they'd long since forgotten, but she didn't speak thoughtlessly of those things the way she used to. As far as Kieli knew, she was the only person who'd realized that there was no God in this church, and the Church's prestige continued, unwavering, to this day.

The rustling noise of the worshippers' whispers that had filled the space suddenly fell silent. The white-robed chief priest appeared from behind a curtain and proceeded to the pulpit at a leisurely pace.

Kieli hid her grimace at the reverent sighs that escaped the silent congregation here and there. She'd seen the chief priest many times since she was small, but she couldn't reconcile what was so holy about him that would elicit such appreciation of him from people. He was an aging man with thinning hair, and his stout build gave him a kind of dignity. Anyone

passing him on the street, though, probably wouldn't think of him as anything more than a man getting on in years with a decent amount of wealth.

For one thing, if he had any kind of sacred, divine insight, how could he fail to notice *that*? There was no better evidence that the Church possessed no holy powers than *that* weaving in and out of the chapel during prayers as if it owned the place.

Shifting her gaze, Kieli could see the image of a man with a rope around his neck, floating in the air above the chief priest's head. Swollen blood vessels colored his face a dark red as he peered with great interest at the manuscript from which the chief priest was reading.

The hanged ghost lifted his face as if he'd felt her gaze. His eyes met Kieli's, and his red, blood-swollen lips twisted in a crescent-shaped grin.

Kieli glared expressionlessly back at the hanged ghost and refocused her attention on the chief priest. Even his oh-so-wonderful sermon that spoke so grandly of death and rebirth didn't leave any deep impressions; it just sounded phony to Kieli's ears.

Kieli.

She heard a voice calling her name.

Kieli, it's starting.

"Eh?"

When she came to herself, Kieli looked in the direction of the voice and saw Becca's blue eyes, like the glass eyes of a doll, winking at her from the end of the choir row. At the edge of her field of vision, Miss Hanni's rimless glasses glared angrily at her as if to say, "Am I still going to have to talk to you before you're satisfied?"

The next thing she knew, the organ's accompaniment had started and the choir began singing "The Song of Our First Blessings." Kieli panicked and started dragging the lyrics from

9

her memory, practically lip-synching along with the alto chorus, and looked over at Becca standing next to her.

Becca stood as straight as she could, looking directly ahead, and her beautiful voice happily sang the soprano part. Kieli's row wasn't singing the soprano part, and Becca's lyrics were a little off, but no one but Kieli would pay it any mind.

After the service ended, it would be the Colonization Days holiday that her whole class looked forward to so much.

To Kieli, it would just be another boring, melancholy ten days.

• • •

At any rate, Becca was in a good mood today. Apparently she was going to see the sights in Westerbury during the holidays. Her parents and younger brother had gone on ahead and were waiting for her to meet up with them.

She was saying something about Westerbury being a city that had developed cable networking and audio-visual technology, and when the sun went down, screens on building walls projected sparkling colors that shifted dizzyingly along the streets as far as the eye could see. Something about a wondrous ice cream inlaid with pieces of stars being all the rage. Something about some experiential theater that just opened and how she was going to see a show there with her family at the end of her stay.

Kieli mostly ignored Becca as she bragged about her sightseeing plans in the unfamiliar city, interjecting the occasional "Hmm" or "Wow." She couldn't imagine what someone would experience at an experiential theater or how it would be experienced so Kieli had no idea if it was really worth all the excitement. The ice cream trend was the one thing that held some slight interest for her, but Becca veered away from

that subject the second she brought it up.

"You can expect a souvenir, Kieli."

While Kieli was using all the imagination she had to picture what ice cream inlaid with pieces of stars would look like, Becca stopped boasting for a minute and turned to face her, her coat twirling as she moved.

"What would you like?"

"I don't need anything," Kieli refused vaguely.

Becca pouted, "Aww, you could ask for *some*thing." Her sleeves fluttered in the wind as she turned and resumed her jaunty walk down the street.

Becca was a pretty girl. Today, instead of the school-designated travel clothes, she wore a brilliant red coat and carried, as expected, not the school-designated bag, but a brown Boston bag. As for Kieli, over her usual uniform she wore the school-designated black duffle coat, and the unfriendly bag (which most students preferred not to use because of its resemblance to a mail-sack) hung diagonally across her shoulder. Becca's supple, blonde hair fell in waves down to her waist and looked stunning against her red coat. Kieli's hair was black and catlike and just hung artlessly down her back. Becca was tall and attractive. On the other hand, if her class were to line up according to height, Kieli would be a little ahead of the center.

If someone on the street were to catch sight of Becca and Kieli walking together, there is no doubt they would think Kieli was exceedingly plain next to the girl as lovely as a fashion doll.

But apparently Kieli was the only one thinking of such trivial things. The passersby paid no special attention to the two girls and quickly walked on by, turning up the collars of their coats.

It was the first afternoon of the Colonization Days holiday, and people hunched over as they walked along the streets of

Easterbury, all bundled up for winter. Still, there was a sense of merriment in the air. Those who could take long holidays would be traveling with their families, and those who couldn't most likely planned to go home early to spend a leisurely evening.

The Colonization Days came every year as the seasons readied themselves to step through winter's door.

This planet had greeted hundreds of winters since the Saints' ship made its autumnal landing. The story was that, thanks to the abundant fuel resources they mined from the planet's strata, the planet used to be highly advanced. But before long, a war broke out over those resources, and the long war itself ate up almost all of them. That happened long before Kieli was born.

All anyone could mine on the planet now were the dregs of inefficient fossil fuels. Bundles of exhaust pipes projected from the roofs of all the houses, coughing up thick, yellowish-grey smoke as if to paint a sky already the same color.

The train station's clock tower came into view at the end of the main street, sandwiched between buildings to the right and left. People holding large bags were sucked under the vaulted roof; they were most likely going to spend the holidays in a different town. The station building had been remodeled just a few years ago when it adopted a new railroad line, and a magnificent domed roof matching the design of the central cathedral rose toward the sky. To Kieli, it was needlessly magnificent, and she felt she would still be more comfortable with the old abandoned station building on the other side of town with its simple and unfriendly concrete walls.

She went around the rotary, casually gazing at the three-wheeled taxis (these, too, used fossil fuels with frighteningly bad gas mileage and carried cylindrical fuel tanks resembling unexploded bombs on their roofs) waiting for wealthy

passengers in front of the station. When the entrance to the station drew near, a man's silhouette unexpectedly caught her attention. He was sitting on a bench toward the front, his head hanging down.

Kieli stopped walking for a second.

"Is something wrong? I'm leaving, you know." Becca looked curiously back at her from a few steps ahead.

"Yeah. . . . He's dead. . ." Kieli murmured shortly before she began walking again.

At this time of year, if anyone bothered to look, they could find the frozen corpse of at least one homeless wanderer somewhere in town every morning. They were generally elderly people, but the dead body on the bench still looked fairly young. He might be a seminary student. Seminarians from the university in the capital came on study pilgrimages for their priesthood exams, after all.

But then, a seminarian on a study pilgrimage would never die in the street, and considering his casual attire consisting of a nylon half-coat and rough workpants along with his rusty, copper-colored hair, she couldn't really say he was a proper seminarian. Regardless, the girls at her boarding school recognized all men about his age as seminarians, so, for lack of any better ideas, Kieli decided to think of him as a seminary student.

The seminary student had expired where he sat, his back leaning heavily into the bench and his head drooping. He must not have had any unfinished business, because she couldn't see his spirit around anywhere. Kieli had mixed feelings when she caught herself confirming that so casually. Most people wouldn't see a dead body and start looking for its ghost.

"Ugh, Kieli!" Becca urged.

Kieli picked up her pace and passed in front of the bench. She would inform a station attendant later. Then they would

contact the priests in charge of body disposal who would come clean it up.

Kieli was only a few steps past the bench when she stopped again. Out of the corner of her eye, she felt like she saw the corpse move. She thought it was her imagination. *I mean, there's no doubt about it. He's dead.*

She turned her head back stiffly and stared at the body on the bench.

Contrary to Kieli's expectations (though there's something wrong about *expecting* somebody to be dead), the seminary student on the bench slowly raised his eyelids. He twisted his neck as he took in his surroundings, a groggy look on his face. Finally, he stood and turned toward a now very rigid Kieli.

Eyes the same copper color as his hair met hers.

"Eek!"

Kieli let out an involuntary twitch of a scream. Immediately afterward, she started yelling that a corpse had moved in a voice that rang throughout the entire rotary in front of the station. The seminarian slipped off the bench, then, recovering from his daze, rushed to cover Kieli's mouth.

"I'm really very sorry, Harvey, sir. She's just a little weird."

Becca had no right to call her weird. Forced to stand next to Becca as she smoothed things over, acting as if she was the mature one, Kieli stared sullenly at the tips of her shoes. When Becca admonished, "Come on, Kieli, say you're sorry," she had no choice but to bow her head and say, "I'm very sorry." Her head still down, she turned up her eyes to glance at the seminary student.

Thrusting one hand in his coat pocket and ruffling his hair with the other, the seminary student spit out, "Well, it's fine now," with a sigh. First, a girl screamed at him in front of the station, then the station attendants came running, treated him like a suspected criminal, and nearly had him arrested.

So, having suffered enough calamities for the day, his face still bore quite a scowl for somebody saying, "It's fine."

Becca had introduced herself as Rebecca, the full name she used only when she had some ulterior motive, and had introduced Kieli as her roommate, almost as an afterthought. In exchange, they learned that the seminarian was named Harvey.

Seminarians were candidates to be leaders in the capital, and to the girls at the boarding school, getting to know one was a kind of status symbol. A group of trainees once came from the university at the capital to participate in a worship service in Easterbury, and Kieli's classmates ignored the service to whisper things like, "That tall one, second from the right! He's gorgeous!" They even had a popularity vote. It goes without saying that they had to endure a lengthy lecture from Miss Hanni that afternoon in homeroom and that the whole class had to write essays reflecting on what they'd done. (Kieli, who hadn't participated in the uproar, suffered quite the by-blow.)

So of course Becca was in high spirits over this fortunate encounter and one-sidedly lamented the fact that she had to leave Easterbury in exaggerated tones.

"Will you be in Easterbury until the Colonization Days are over? It would be nice if we could talk again after I get back."

"Oh, I'm leaving tomorrow. Going the opposite direction of Westerbury," the seminarian said without the slightest hesitation, easily crushing Becca's hopes. As other people bustled across the platform, Becca stood stock-still. "I see." She hung her head in disappointment, and her actions reeked of those of the heroine of a romance novel who'd resolved to leave her lover behind to go to the city. Kieli got a bit uncomfortable standing there and let her eyes wander.

As travelers heading toward Westerbury pushed their large bags onto the passenger car and boarded the train, they

looked annoyed at Kieli, who blocked their way in front of the car talking to her companions. Busily making the rumbling, exhaust-spouting noises of fossil-fuel power, the train announced its departure.

"Will you be boarding?" a railroad worker in a conductor's uniform asked in a somewhat irritated tone, leaning half his body out of the last car.

The seminary student answered with a "No," adding a "Take care," and the conductor turned next to Kieli. "And you, miss? Will you be boarding?" When Kieli shook her head, the conductor nodded and rang the bell to announce their departure.

"Hey! Wait, wait! *I'm* boarding," Becca cried in dismay. She lifted her Boston bag in both hands and hurried on to the passenger car steps. As the departure bell rang across the platform sounding much like an alarm clock, she turned reluctantly back to bid farewell to Kieli and the seminarian. "See you, Kieli. You'll be okay without me, right?"

Kieli's answer of "I'll be fine" was drowned out by the sound of the bell and the tumult on the platform. It didn't even reach her own ears, so instead of repeating herself, Kieli simply nodded. Becca nodded back in understanding and turned next to face the seminary student. "Harvey, I pray we'll meet again."

The seminarian said a few words in response, but Kieli couldn't catch them. Apparently Becca did hear them, however. Kieli didn't know what he said to her, but her beautiful face lost its expression abruptly as it looked down at them from aboard the train.

The bell suddenly stopped ringing. A strange moment of silence reigned over the platform, and then the train slowly started to slide away.

Even after the train started moving, Becca remained there, floating in the place where she had first gone up the steps. The walls of the cars that ran by passed smoothly through

Becca's body one after another, like an illusion.

To be more accurate, it was Becca's body that was like an illusion.

Her best red coat and her Boston bag, her plans to meet with her parents and brother, the new theater, the ice cream, the souvenir she was thinking of getting for Kieli — everything about Becca's travel plans was nothing more than a game of pretend that she'd made up for her own amusement. Becca's body for wearing coats and her hands for carrying luggage were actually already at the bottom of her grave, and Becca had eternally lost the ability to spend holidays with her family and stuff her cheeks with ice cream.

The conductor stared dubiously from his post in the last car at Kieli and the seminary student standing there until, finally, he too passed through Becca's body.

"You're stupid," Becca said, her expression still blank. "I just wanted to pretend I was going on a trip. It's not like you're really a seminarian, either, stupid!" The abusive words she spat from her comely lips could only be considered a parting insult, and Becca floated down from where the train had been, then suddenly ran toward them. Kieli drew back automatically, but right before Becca crashed into her nose, her image vanished, and her formless presence blew through the ticket barrier with a gust of air.

All that was left on the platform were Kieli, the seminarian, the moderate chatter of those who'd seen people off, and their footsteps as they headed home.

"I never once said I was a seminarian…" the seminary student (or not, apparently) muttered to himself in annoyance. Then he noticed Kieli gazing at him as she stood beside him and glanced sideways at her.

Kieli looked up at her tall companion and asked, "What did you say to Becca?"

"All I did was ask how long I had to play along with this travesty," the man answered with an exasperated sigh, picking up his own luggage that he'd left at his side (it may have been luggage, but it was very light for a traveler — just one backpack that wasn't very big and, for some reason, a small, old radio).

"I don't like to meddle in other people's affairs too much, but… It's better not to bother with guys like that — just ignore them. If you don't, they get carried away and never leave you alone."

"You should have told me that before this spring."

At Kieli's response, the man sneered, "Don't talk nonsense," and started walking away, joining the thin stream of people leaving the station. Kieli trotted after him, her shoulder bag bouncing against her lower back.

"You're not surprised about Becca."

"To my mind, you're more of a surprise. You have a strong spiritual sense?"

Kieli nodded, "But my grandmother told me not to let too many people know. She's dead now, though."

"Yeah. It's less trouble that way."

"Hey, can you see other dead people? How do you know so much?" She naturally became more talkative than usual as she tried to keep up with the man's athletic pace. This was the first time she'd met anyone other than herself who could see that world, and based on what her grandmother said, there weren't that many of them, so she must have felt something like a kinship.

He, on the other hand, stopped momentarily and let out a sigh of very obvious annoyance. "…Hey. Well, I can't say I don't know how you feel. So I'm sorry, but I have no intention of getting mixed up with a spirit-sensitive little girl. Now go home, do your sixth-grade homework, and have a nice holiday. Good-bye," he declared without a shred of the

sincerity expected of one who "knows how she feels." Kieli had stopped in spite of herself; he left her there and resumed his long stride. Without looking back once, he disappeared through the station's gaping, square exit into the white outside.

"Ah…" This brought her high spirits to a surprisingly sudden and crashing demise, and Kieli stood there, alone under the station's domed ceiling.

After standing in a daze for a while, she slowly began seething with anger. *He didn't have to say it like that. He really is nothing like a seminary student. Seminary students are friendlier and more gentlemanly.*

And who is he calling a sixth grader? I know I have the build of a sixth grader, but still. Kieli'd heard rumors that after they measured her height last spring, Miss Hanni doubted whether or not she was really fourteen years old and checked her citizenship form. If that was true, it would be extremely rude, and even if it wasn't true, it would be rude for a rumor like that to be going around as if it was.

Kieli gradually lost track of what she was angry about, and, feeling downhearted, she set off toward home.

Becca didn't come back (she was often quick to take offense and disappear, but she would usually be grinning close behind Kieli again in no time) as Kieli walked back to the boarding school alone, and Kieli realized that she hadn't walked around town completely alone like this since Becca's spirit started haunting her last spring. In the corner of her mind, she thought about how unexpectedly lonely and boring it was not to hear Becca's voice chattering away next to her.

THE DEAD SLEEP IN THE WILDERNESS

A novel by
YUKAKO KABEI

AVAILABLE SUMMER 2009

Flip the book over and start reading from the
second to last page for a sneak preview!